I0583006

Built for Trouble

Built for Love, Volume 2

Chelle Pimblott

Published by Chelle Pimblott, 2019.

This is a work of fiction. Similarities to real people, places, or events are entirely coincidental.

BUILT FOR TROUBLE

First edition. August 31, 2019.

Copyright © 2019 Chelle Pimblott.

Written by Chelle Pimblott.

Thank you to my 'Book Bitches'. You know who you are, and you mean the world to me xx

Thank you to my editor extraordinaire. Without our brainstorming sessions and many, many discussions this book wouldn't be what they are xx

Thank you to my proofreader who worked her tail off to get the last proofread done in what I think was record time xx

I want to dedicate this book to my high school friend, Kristy Lee. You put up a massive fight, but cancer sucks babe. I will forever use you as inspiration to live my life and to work hard at making this writing dream become a reality.

Love you always beautiful xx

Chapter One

KATY

There's an old saying that the boy who pulls your pigtails is the one that likes you, a lot. Joe French was that little boy, but I always kicked that little boy in the nuts. He made my best friend's life hell when we were at high school and still to this day I don't understand why. What the hell could he possibly have against one of the sweetest people I know? I don't think I'll ever know, because I've asked him to explain, and he refuses. What did Kami ever do to Joe that could possibly annoy him so much that he's held a grudge for all these years?

All of that is why I should be anywhere but here doing this, but here I am doing it anyway. This guy, he's always had an attitude, and I've always been attracted to him. As a teenager, he was an arrogant douchebag, and I have to be honest, as an adult he's still arrogant, but there's still something about him that I can't resist.

He made Kami's life and mine in turn as her best friend horrible. So, how do I tell my best friend I've been sleeping with her teenage tormentor? That may sound a bit dramatic, but Kami can't understand why Joe has always had it in for her and he made up that terrible nickname, Kamo Kami, for her at school. He was always so nice to me and everyone else, but for some reason, he couldn't bring himself to be nice to Kami.

Yet here I am, saying yes to going out to dinner with him. We've been frequenting the same café for a few weeks, he tells me he's been coming here for months, multiple times a day and my favourite waitress confirms it, but I've been coming here several times a day for months too and we've never run into each other before now.

We spent a few weeks circling each other and then one day, while we were 'sharing' a table, so we didn't unnecessarily take up too much space, he asked me out to dinner. Without hesitation or second-guessing myself, I said yes.

Now, as I stand here, looking in the mirror to make sure I look nice for our date, I'm having second thoughts. What would Kami say if she knew? I doubt she'd be very happy with the situation, that I know. I don't want to hurt her feelings, but there's something there with Joe, should I not explore that because Kami hates him? We're all adults now, surely the two of them can sort this stupid shit out. Joe really has more to sort through than Kami, he's the one that started the feud. Even James doesn't know why and trust me, I've asked him multiple times as well.

I walk out of my room after one last check and smile in the full-length mirror on my wall and hear a couple of firm knocks on my front door. Joe's here and right on time. He's never lacked that air of confidence and punctuality, even when we were kids. Some people call it arrogance, I see it as a strength and determination, shining through.

I pick up my pace a little and take a deep breath to calm my nerves. I still can't quite believe I agreed to a date with Joe freaking French, the generally surly, semi-approachable guy. The fact is though, there's always been something about Joseph Harrison French that has *always* attracted me to him. I'm not really a bad boy loving kinda girl, but then, I don't believe that Joe *is* what most people consider to be a bad boy. He's a guy who doesn't necessarily wear his emotions on his sleeve, and while he can be quite direct, making him seem harsh, I don't think that's necessarily a bad thing. I like knowing where I stand with people.

After taking a shaky deep breath, I open the door and find myself staring at the man he is today. Standing there, looking as handsome as he always has, but in dark jeans that fit his body like they were made for it, and a chocolate brown button-up shirt that brings out the brown flecks in his beautiful hazel eyes. My mouth has gone dry as a desert and I've lost the ability to speak. Instead, I look him up and down, drinking him in. He's always been an attractive man and sexy as fuck, but dressed in casual clothes, leaning up against my doorframe, looking at me like I'm dessert and he wants to skip the main course. Holy Shit!

"Are you ready to head to dinner Katy?" Joe's deep voice vibrates through my body, fuelling my lust-filled thoughts even more.

I clear my throat and reply, "Ummm yes, do you want to come in for a minute while I grab my bag and phone?"

I step back to allow him entrance to my house, he slowly moves his body off the doorframe to stroll passed me. I catch a whiff of his cologne and a masculine scent that is all Joe. I'm wishing that I'd walk away from the doorway and he'd let himself in because he smells divine. Edible, lickable and decidedly fuckable and suddenly I don't feel like going out to eat. What I *want* to do is stay home, jump his bones and fuck him until he can't walk. I'm not going to do that, but fuck do I want to.

"Is someone else joining us tonight Katy or are you going to come me inside?" Joe asks, with a sexy smirk. "Are you sure you're feeling OK babe? We could just stay here and entertain ourselves." That smirk of his grows and there's an extra spark in his eyes like he knows exactly what I'm thinking. Cocky bastard thinks he knows me so well now does he? Why the hell do I find his cocky attitude so god damn attractive?

"No, smartarse I'm not waiting for anyone else, I was just thinking about what I need to grab." I say, "But I can go find myself another date and leave your cocky arse here alone and waiting for *me* if you'd like?" I say, my voice is snarkier than I meant it to be. He just drags that attitude right out of me, and I can't help but wonder if that's going to make the sex between us explosive or whether our attitudes will make this whole thing implode before we get that far.

"Do you *want* to go find another date Katy?" he asks me, looking me dead in the eyes, making me feel like he's looking right into my soul and seeing my answer before I can speak. "If that's what you want, we can leave things here and forget that we tried." That's what I *should* do but I definitely want this date with Joe.

"Is that what you want Joseph? Are you regretting asking me out and hoping I'll pull the plug on this ill-advised date?" I'm hoping he says that's not what he wants, that he wants this date as much as I do.

"No, Kathryn. If I didn't want to go out on a date with you, I wouldn't have asked you in the first place, but if you're having seconds thoughts, we can cancel."

I can't help the shiver that runs down my spine at the use of my full name. No-one calls me that anymore, even my parents have finally given in to my requests and call me Katy. Then my mind catches up with what he just said. I want this fucking date and I'm going to have it, god damn it.

Shaking my head no I say, "If I wanted to go out with another guy, I wouldn't have said yes to you now would I, Joseph?" again, he brings out the snarky bitch in me and I don't know why.

"In that case, do you want to grab your phone and your bag? We have a reservation that I'd like to keep."

I'll give you a god damn reservation I think in my head, as I grab my phone and bag. Yeah, I still did what he asked, but if he didn't stop being a douche I wouldn't be able to bite my tongue for much longer.

He follows me back out the door and watches as I lock up behind us. "You know, I've locked up my house when I leave it without your watchful presence, ohhhhh I dunno, at least a billion times in my life Joseph."

"I have no doubt of your, *talents*, Kathryn, but what kind of man would I be if I didn't make sure you weren't safe, including all of your possessions?" Jesus, how can he make a word like talents sound so fucking sexy, I mean seriously? Maybe it's just been too long since I got laid and now that I've got a man around I'm ready and willing. Who am I kidding, I've been ready for Joseph French for years. If he hadn't been such an arsehole to Kami for so long I would have done something about my need for him a long damned time ago.

"I can see your brain ticking over Katy, what are you thinking about?" We're walking towards his car, he's got his hand resting on my lower back, directing me to where he's parked. Little does he know, I already know what kind of car he drives, and I can walk to it without him guiding me. "Reconsidering our date again already?"

When we reach the car, he takes a step away from me to open the passenger door for me. I hesitate before sliding into the seat and say, "No Joe. Actually, I was thinking I wish we'd done this years ago and then realised that's not what I wish, and I'm glad we're doing this now. As adults." I see the shock register on his face and then I slide my arse onto the plush leather seat of his car. When the door doesn't close behind me I look up to find him just standing there, hand still on the door, just looking at me. I clear my throat and he closes my door, walks around to the driver's door and drops his tight butt into his seat, starts the car and pulls away from the curb. He doesn't say a word, and I watch him as the concentrates on manoeuvring the car through the busy streets.

We can talk at dinner. The silence isn't uncomfortable, so I just enjoy the ride.

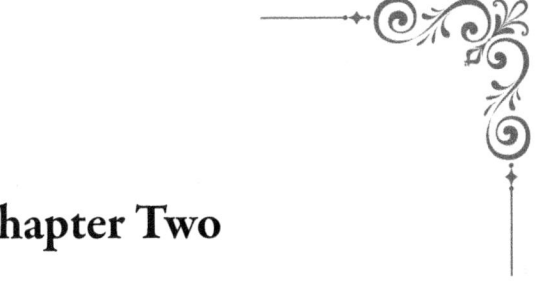

Chapter Two

JOE

I can't believe Katy agreed to go out to dinner with me. If I'm being honest, I've always had a thing for Katy Ellis, but she's always with Kami Parker and I can't stand that girl. I guess she's a woman now, either way, she just rubs me the wrong way. Not to mention the history she's not even aware that we share. The fact that she's oblivious grinds my gears as well, how can she *not* realise?

Then, there's James. He's been my best friend for as long as I can remember, so long in fact that he's more like a brother to me and he's got a pretty unhealthy obsession with Miss Parker. I've tried my best over the years to steer him away from her, even as early as our high school years, and yet, he still watches her with fascination any time we happen to cross her path.

But, back to Katy Ellis.

We ran into each other at the café near my work. Now I go to this café multiple times a day and how I've managed to not run into Katy before now, I have no fucking idea. Trust me, I would have remembered the sexy woman she's grown into. She works nearby and frequents the café too, but somehow we've never run into each other before now, and I'm not about to let this opportunity slip through my fingers. Not only is she close by, but she's not attached to Miss Kami Parker, therefore, I can approach her.

Slowly but surely, I've been working my way up to asking her out. At first, we'd just acknowledged each other with a quick nod of the head, then a smile, then we moved on to actually *saying* hello to each other, and now, for the past few weeks, we've actually sat at the same table enjoying our coffee or lunch – together.

One small leap at a time. With each step making me a happy man.

It's at one such moment of us sharing a table that I decide to just grab the chance and ask her out to dinner. Much to my surprise, she didn't flat out turn me down, but actually said yes. I didn't think she'd have to think too hard before saying no, but it was the opposite. Maybe I should have given her more time to consider her answer, but I wanted the date, so I set a time, location and date without giving her the opportunity to change her beautiful mind.

After all, I *did* make her best friend's life in school pretty hard, for what appeared to the rest of the planet, no reason. I had reasons, I've just never shared them with anyone else, not even James.

The night of our date, I'm actually nervous as hell. I was worried she wasn't going to be home when I went to pick her up, or that she'd say she changed her mind and just couldn't go out with a douchebag like me.

None of those things happened when she opened her door to me though, and I was struck dumb by just how gorgeous she was. I mean, obviously I was aware of her beauty, I've been attracted to her for years, but I was just so taken when she opened that door to me. Then she hit me with her sassy attitude, and it was all I could do to *not* drag her to her bedroom and strip her out of that dress she's wearing. The dress itself doesn't reveal a damned thing, most people would say it's quite modest, but it follows every curve of her luscious body, and it's taking everything in me not to pick her up, throw her down on her bed and bury my face between her legs.

Instead, I wait for her to invite me into her home and tease her about our date. I wonder for a second if I've pushed her too far when she hesitates before answering my question about her reconsidering our date. I was pretty certain she wanted to go out with me, but her pause causes my heart to stutter for a few seconds. If only she knew how long I've wanted this date with her. Would she take advantage of how willing I would be to give her anything she's ever wanted if she knew how much I'd be willing to give her?

I doubt it. That's not Katy.

When we reach my car, she shocks me by admitting how much she's wanted this date, and how long she's waited for it. She's stunned me silent, very rare in my world, and the car is filled with only the sound of the DJ's voice on the radio. It's not an uncomfortable silence though and I guess we're both working through our own thoughts about the evening ahead.

I pull the car into the parking lot of the restaurant, it's not the best one in town, in fact, I've taken us just outside of town and I wonder if Katy realises why I did it, but it's certainly not the worse place either. I didn't want to overwhelm her on our first date, I'm hoping there will be many, many more for me to pull out all the stops on, but this time, I want to just enjoy the woman that will be sitting across the table from me.

"I hope you like Italian food? I've never met a person who can't find something to eat in an Italian restaurant, so I took a chance." I say, with a smile. I'm rewarded with a bright smile when she looks at me.

"I've never met an Italian I haven't wanted to eat something off." She says with a smile and then blushes as she realises what she just said. "Menu. I meant an Italian *menu*, that I haven't wanted to eat off. You know not an Italian man or person." She stumbles over her words and it's the first time I've ever seen Katy Ellis rattled in any way, and it makes me laugh.

"I knew what you meant Katy, well I hoped I did, anyway. Thanks for clarifying it for me though, I certainly enjoyed your explanation." With another low chuckle I move to get out of the car, and I swear I hear her mumble, "geeez Katy, calm ya farm it's Joe why are you so nervous?"

Her little pep talk means she's still sitting in the car when I walk around the front and open her door for her. She looks up at me shocked when I open it and hold my hand out for her, and I have to admit, it hurts a little that she thinks I can't be a gentleman. I'm taking that as a challenge, and I'll prove to her I'm not the arsehole I've shown myself to be with her best friend. Katy definitely pushes different buttons that Kami does.

I bring my mind back to the woman in front of me and gently help Katy out of the car, close the door behind her and rest my hand on her lower back, guiding her into the restaurant. I felt the sharp intake of breath when I rested my hand on her back, it's nice to know I'm not the only one affected tonight.

I've been here a few times, not on dates but for business, and the hostess recognises me. "Good evening Mr French, please follow me." Then she leads us to our table, but not before I feel Katy stiffen beside me. I know what she's thinking, and I also know I have to chase her thoughts away.

"Thank you, Erin, it's nice to be here with a beautiful woman instead of the grumpy businessmen I'm usually here with," I say with a smile as I take my own seat, after settling Katy into hers.

Erin laughs and says, "I have no doubt, Mr French." She looks towards Katy and asks, "Can I get you something to drink before you order Miss?"

"Can I have a glass of Moscato please, Erin is it?" Katy says it with a charming smile, that isn't quite sincere.

"Yes, that's right. I'll just go get your drink order and you can have a look at the menu." Erin says with a smile and walks over to the bar. When I see who she's meeting over there, I can't help but smile myself.

"She didn't take your drink order."

"She didn't need to, I always get a scotch on the rocks when I'm here," I reply

"Of course. You're here so often you're on a first name basis with the waitress and she knows what you drink." Katy says, with a scowl on her face.

"Yes, I'm here on business very often and Erin is normally here, as is her right being the owner and all. I'm also on a first name basis with her fiancé, the co-owner of this very fine establishment." I look at Katy and wait until she's looking back at me, "They're also clients Katy, so yes I'm on a first name basis with them, and I like to bring prospective clients and colleagues here because it's delicious and I like supporting my clients when I can."

Before Katy can reply, Erin and Rohan walk over to the table and place our drinks down in front of us. I stand up to shake Rohan's hand and place a small kiss on Erin's cheek. "Good evening you two, I thought tonight was your night off?" I ask.

"Ahhh this is why he bought a woman in tonight because he thought we wouldn't be here to give him a hard time about it," Rohan laughs. "Too bad hey man?" He laughs at me then extends his hand to Katy, "Hi I'm Rohan and this is my fiancé Erin, it's nice to meet you ....?"

"Katy. It's nice to meet you too Rohan, Erin." Katy smiles, this time it's genuine and I chuckle to myself. Rohan gives me a look, one that says, 'I see why you're trying to hide this one', even though I'm not. I'd much rather be shouting it from the rooftops that we're together, but I'm being cautious. There could be a lot of fallout if this thing between us doesn't work out, therefore caution first. That and I want to keep Katy to myself for a while, I want us to work this thing out before we let anyone else into the equation.

"Sorry, Erin didn't really give me time to make any introductions earlier. Katy Ellis, this is Erin Brandis and Rohan Broadhurst, they own the restaurant, as you know." I say, looking into Katy's eyes, making sure she understands exactly what I mean. There is only her.

"I've been wanting to come here but I haven't had the chance." Katy smiles, "That and I couldn't actually get a reservation. It would appear that I've got a contact now." She smiles at me, taking my breath away.

Erin laughs, "We were booked out for a while, but it's easier to get in now. Just ask for me and I'll get you a table, Katy. Although you're right, you've got connections now." She winks at Katy and says, "Come on babe, Joe's right, it is our night off and we're getting out of here before we're dragged into something." She looks back at both of us and says, "Enjoy your night, I hope we see you again soon Katy."

"Enjoy your night off," Katy says with a cheeky smile.

Erin laughs and replies, "Oh we plan on it, don't you worry about that."

Chapter Three

<u>KATY</u>

D amn, I feel like such an idiot.

Barely even into our first date and I'm acting like a complete jealous idiot. I'm not even sure where the jealousy came from, that's not my normal behaviour. We've all got pasts, it's not like I don't have one of my own let's be honest here, but just the thought that Joe might have slept with Erin made me angry. I don't understand where this anger is coming from, I've known Joe for years, I've never cared who he spoke to before.

"Is everything OK Katy?" Joe asks, and I have no clue how to answer him. Do I admit I'm an idiot or do I make a run for it?

"Yes, yes everything's fine Joe, why do you ask?" There we go, I managed to deflect it back onto Joe.

"You're looking a little green around the edges, Katy." He doesn't laugh at me, not out loud anyway, but I can see the sparkle in his eye and the twitch of his lips, he's fighting the urge to smile.

"How was I supposed to know she was your client? How was I supposed to know that you don't sleep with your *clients*?" I ask, but I'm pretty sure I know the answers to both of those questions, and by the dark look Joe's giving me now, I know the answer before he speaks.

"OK, Katy let's get a few things straight right now. I don't sleep with my clients, ever. Erin and Rohan are my friends, as well as clients, and last, but by no means least, I bought *you* here for dinner, not Erin or anyone else. If I *wanted* to be here with someone else, I would be. I'm here with you and only you. If you think for one minute that I would take you to dinner at a place where I knew for a fact that we would run into an ex or whatever you were thinking Erin was, then you don't know me at all."

He's right and I feel like a bitch, but that doesn't make me any less annoyed. "How the hell would I know any of that Joseph? We've hardly seen each other since high school and we barely knew each other even back then." I take a deep shuddering breath, mainly because he was an arsehole to my best friend all through high school. Who knew I would get this worked up over a simple conversation? "Also, I admit to feeling a little jealous, OK? I didn't like the thought of having a previous conquest shoved in my face, but you know what I didn't know? Any of those of things you just told me? Do you know any of those things about *me?*"

"You were jealous?" he asks. I should have known that's what he'd hear out of everything I just said. The boost to his ego that means I was jealous another woman might look at him.

"Does your fragile ego really need that kind of boost, Joe?" I shake my head, clearing my thoughts. "Maybe this really was a bad idea." I place my napkin on the table and make to stand, Joe goes to speak but I hold up my hand to stop him. "No Joe, we both knew this wouldn't work from the beginning, there's too much other stuff going on."

"Please stay Katy. I'm sorry." He reaches out and holds my hand, not tight enough that I couldn't get away if I wanted to, but tight enough to stop me from moving. "Please give this a chance Katy. You're right we've got a lot of history, but none of it means we know anything about each other, especially not now as adults. I want to get to know *you* Kathryn Ellis, who you are now." A second of hesitation is all it takes, and he pulls gently on my hand, which causes me to go slightly off-balance, it's just enough that I sit back down in my chair. "Let's get to know each other?"

He asks it as a question, not a statement, and I feel myself give in. I nod and say, "OK Joe." I look up into his eyes, "On one condition. I'll stay if you explain to me why you hate Kami so much." I see the panic in his eyes, he's not going to tell me shit about why he hates Kami, but I don't move. I won't until he says something to me.

It feels like a long time before he takes a deep breath and starts to speak. He looks down at his hand, the one that I didn't realise was still holding onto my own, and then looks back up, right into my eyes and says, "I don't hate Kami Parker."

"I don't believe you Joe, and I don't think anyone we went to school with would either."

"It's not Kami herself that I hate OK? I don't even know her, I didn't at school and I sure as hell don't now. I don't really have any plans on getting to know her either, if that's a deal-breaker then I guess I understand. I know you two were always close, and I wouldn't ask you to choose between us."

"You wouldn't ask Joe? I wouldn't give you the chance to ask. She's like a sister to me Joe, and nothing can come between us, especially not a man. All I want to know is why?" I ask again because he never really gave me an answer.

"Like I said, it's not Kami herself that I hate. It's her family." He's dropped my hand and is sitting back in his chair, looking like I imagine he does when he's at work. Formidable.

He's left the ball in my court and I guess I have to decide whether or not that's a good enough explanation. "One dinner Joe," I reply, and he nods. We both take a large drink and relax back into our chairs. A few minutes later the waitress comes over and takes our meal orders. We both order another drink as well, we're going to need it.

I excuse myself to go to the bathroom, I need a few minutes to collect my thoughts. If I'm going to make this dinner work, I have to have my brain functioning at its best which means, no more alcohol.

I hear my phone chime and notice a text message, so I open the app to see it's from Kami. What wonderful timing she has, seriously.

Kami: *Where are you? I've been trying to call you*

That's when I notice the couple of missed calls I've had in the last five minutes. Shit.

Me: *I'm out to dinner. Is everything OK?*

Kami: *ohhh crap on a cracker, are you on a date?*

Shit. I can tell her the truth without telling her everything. Right?

Me: *yes actually I am

Kami: *what's his name? what's he like?

Me: *it's our first date now fuck off and let me get back to it

Kami: *no need to be so crass.. you're not sitting at the table messaging me are you?

Me: *no, now fuck off

Kami: *potty mouth*

I love that girl, but damn she's a prude. For obvious reasons I don't know what she's like in the bedroom, we've never been together in a sexual kind of way, but I can't help imagine that she's actually a freak between the sheets. Swearing though, I've never heard her say anything bad. Shit is the worst thing I think I've heard her say, I wonder if she'd swear if she knew who my date was tonight. That brings a smile to my face as I walk out of the ladies and back to the table.

As I sit down, I look over to Joe who is looking at me curiously. I raise an eyebrow at him in question and he says, "Are the toilets here amusing to you or did something happen while you were gone?"

"The bathrooms are exactly that, bathrooms, no amusement there just business as usual," I say, but I can't help grinning thinking about what Kami would say if she knew who was sitting opposite me right now.

"Yet something is still funny." Joe states.

"I was thinking about something someone said earlier and it made me smile, that's all," I say. Am I lying? Meh, I'd call it stretching the truth.

Before Joe can ask more questions, our dinner arrives, and we start eating in silence. It's an easy silence, comfortable really, we're both just enjoying our meals. I have to say it's absolutely delicious.

Chapter Four

JOE

I can't read this woman at all. One minute she's annoyed with me because I can't tell her why I dislike her friend so much and the next, she's smiling like a fool on her way back from the bathroom.

Maybe she only said yes to this date with me to work out why I've been such an arsehole all these years to her friend. The laughter could be because she's lulled me into a false sense of security before she takes me down for all the shitty things I've done in the past.

Before I can ask her any questions, our dinner arrives. We eat in companionable silence. It's not uncomfortable in any way, we're just enjoying the meals put down in front of us. As comfortable as it is, I still want to know if she's enjoying her meal, so I ask, "How's your pasta?"

The moan that slips through her lips before she answers me has my cock standing to attention. What I wouldn't give to make her moan like that in the bedroom, with her laying underneath me while I make her. "Delicious. The best burnt butter gnocchi I've ever had in my life." When she opens her eyes to look at me, I'm just staring at her, my own fork halfway between my mouth and my plate.

The waiter comes over to ask if everything is OK, and it's all I can do to answer him. "Yes, absolutely delicious," I say, and he nods and starts to walk away. "Excuse me. Could we get two serves of tiramisu to take away please?"

"Of course, I'll get them packed up and bought out when you've finished eating sir."

"Thank you," I say, without taking my eyes off Katy.

"Taking dessert home? That's a bit presumptuous isn't it Joe?"

"I don't think you want me to do what I have planned with dessert in a public place, Kathryn."

I watch as her eyes become a darker shade of chocolate brown than usual. She's just as turned on at the thought of what I could do to her as I am.

"I'm not sleeping with you on the first date Joseph." She says in a husky voice that is full of need.

"Nobody said anything about sleeping Kathryn." She lifts up her drink and takes a decent mouthful out of it. "Now eat up, you're going to need the fuel." I take great joy in the fact that she doesn't say another word but finishes her meal without looking away from my face. It's like she's daring me to keep my promise. I have every intention of keeping my word, there will be no sleeping tonight.

"You might want to finish your meal too Joseph, you're going to need your strength to keep up with those threats you just made."

"Promises honey. They. Were. Promises. Ones I have every intention of keeping."

Katy doesn't get the chance to respond because the waiter returns with our desserts and asks if there is anything else he can get for us. I ask for the bill he says that it's been covered. Erin and Rohan, I'll be having words with them as both their accountant and their friend for giving out complimentary meals.

I thank the waiter, rise from my chair and help Katy out of hers. I've got dessert in my hand, I reach out for Katy's hand and thread our fingers together. I hear her intake of breath at our touch and I know, without a doubt that she feels this simmering tension as well.

I lead her out to my car, open the door and help her in, then I place the bag with the desserts on the backseat. I walk around the car, get in the driver's seat, and start the car and start to move out of the carpark.

"I could have held them you know?" I look over towards her, I have no idea what she's talking about. "The dessert. I could have held them here you know, you didn't need to put them in the backseat. I wouldn't have eaten any before you got them home."

"I'm not taking them home Katy. Well, not to *my* house anyway." I glance her way, just long enough to see her confusion. "I thought we could have dessert at your place if that's OK with you?"

A small smile spreads across her face, "Yeah, that's OK with me."

We don't speak on the drive back to Katy's. I don't know whether it's nerves, excitement, anticipation or a combination of all of them. When I come to a stop in the driveway, I don't turn off the car. I sit there with the car idling, giving Katy time to think this through because I want her to *want* this.

Katy makes a move to get out of the car but stops when she notices that I haven't moved and the car's still running. "It's OK if you've changed your mind, Joe, you don't have to come in."

"I haven't changed my mind, Katy, I want to make sure that you haven't changed *your* mind honey'. I don't want you to feel like I'm forcing myself on you, and if I go in there," I point to her front door, "I don't know if I can hold back. I want to give you the chance to pull out and take it slow now before we go any further." She can't possibly know how much I want to walk into her house and taste every damn inch of her skin. I don't mean sex, I mean tasting every part of her, don't get me wrong my cock is hard and protesting very loudly about my offer to put on any kind of brakes for the night.

Lost in my own thoughts, I don't see Katy move until she's almost on top of me. With her hand resting on my knee, she leans over my lap and turns off the engine. She moves back slightly, her hand still on my knee, her other hand reaches up to touch my cheek. "Joe, thank you, but I haven't changed my mind."

"Katy.." I start.

"Please come inside with me Joe?" I nod my answer, fearing that my voice won't hold up to speaking. She sits back in her seat and reaches over to open her door and I immediately feel the loss of her touch. My body craves it. Craves her, all of her. Katy leans her head back in the door and says, "Are you *coming* Joe?" a cheeky smirk on her face and I realise she's said exactly what she meant to.

Without another word, I take the keys from the ignition, and I'm at her front door. Taking her keys from her fingers, I unlock the door and wave her inside. I throw her keys onto the small table she's got at the entrance, the door is closed, and I've got Katy backed up against it within seconds. "Are you sure you want this Katy?" I look into her eyes, trying to read her.

"Joe, I want you. Please." Her voice is like silk running over my body. Husky with need and her eyes darkened with lust. "Damn it, Joe, don't ask me again or I swear to god I will throw you out and give myself an orgasm."

"Over my dead fucking body." If anyone's giving this woman an orgasm tonight, it's me.

I pin her up against the door, I reach my hand behind her and make sure I've locked the fucking thing. I don't want anyone interrupting my plans for us. Boy, do I have plans for us. I hear a thump and realise Katy's dropped her handbag on the floor by her feet and then her hands are wrapped around the back of my neck, tugging on my hair, making me growl. I run my hands down her thighs to the edge of the skirt of her dress until I find naked skin. Then I run my hands back up her thighs and hold a bare cheek in each of my hands. This time the moan that fills the air is Katy's.

In her heels, we're almost the same height and I've never been happier because it allows her to wrap a leg around my hip, pressing the heat of her pussy against the front of my pants, causing my cock to twitch. I press harder into her body, letting her feel the proof of what she does to me. I don't want there to be a single doubt in her mind that this is what I want.

My hands massage her cheeks and my fingertips manage to push past the thin lace covering them to the wet heat of her pussy. Katy's hands roam all over my body, pushing my jacket off my shoulders, and I have to remove my hands from her luscious body for a second to shake it the rest of the way. She untucks my shirt from my pants and starts undoing the buttons before my jacket hits the floor next to her bag. The feeling of her hands on my skin makes me shudder, but when she teases and plays with my nipples, I can't hold back my groan. I shake the shirt off my body, and it joins everything else on the floor.

"Does this dress of yours have a zip or buttons or can I just pull it off your body honey'?" I growl in her ear, as my hands wander all over her back trying to find how I can get her out of the damned thing.

"Mmmm." Is all I get out of her as she continues teasing my nipples and kissing along my jawline.

Kissing up her neck I ask in a husky whisper in her ear," Katy, tell me how to get this thing off or I'm just going to rip it off you."

"Mmmm," she moans again, then she seems to shake her head for a second and says, "Zip. At. The. Side." She hisses out between breaths and kisses.

I don't know who designed this damned thing, but it wasn't with an idea of getting anyone out of it in a fucking hurry that's for sure. My hands run up and down her sides, trying to find the zipper so that I can put my hands , my mouth and whatever else I can get on this woman. The dress needs to go, now.

"Katy," I groan against her neck, "Babe, I need to put you down for a second."

"Mmmm." Is her only response. She looks delectable, with her head leaning back against the door, making her neck stretch out and all I want to do is lick it and nibble on it.

Instead, I let her leg fall off my hip and place her foot on the floor, my hand gripping her hip. My other hand pulls down the zipper of her dress letting it fall to her waist. I let out what can only be described as an animalistic growl, a vocal declaration of the desire that's coursing through my body.

"Joe." Katy's voice is soft, husky and full of her own desire.

"Yes, Katy?" I reply. "What do you need babe?"

"You, I need you, Joe. God, I need you everywhere Joe."

"Everywhere? How do I get everywhere baby?"

"I don't know, I just know what I need." Her hands are running through my hair, over my shoulders, grasping my neck and running her nails up and down my back. It's like she can't get enough of me and I sure as fuck know I can't get enough of her.

"I know baby, I feel the same way. I'm trying to get us there but this dress.."

Katy places her hands on my chest and gently pushes me away from her. I feel the loss of her touch immediately when she takes her hands away to step out of her dress. It looked amazing on her beautiful body, but I like it even better as it pools at her feet on the floor. She uses one foot to push it to the side with my clothes and then hooks a finger in the waist of my pants to pull me closer. "Now, where were we?" I don't get a chance to answer, because she plants her lips on mine and kisses me like she'll never get another chance, and I lose every thought in my brain.

She tastes better than I could have ever imagined. I doubt that I can give her up.

Chapter Five

KATY

I've been looking for this kind of connection my entire adult life. Who would have thought that I'd find it with Joe French? Then again, I've always known there was something about Joe that others didn't see, underneath all the gruffness is a man that is gentle and loving. I want all of him, I want to know every part of him. Right now I don't care what anyone else would think about it either.

I drop my dress and push it out the way to join Joe's clothes. I want to feel him everywhere. I start to unbuckle his belt and pants, at the same time his hands are making a mess of my hair and his lips are kissing up and down my neck, to my collarbone, then back up again. I can't hold back the moan that slips out of my lips. He feels so damned good.

His pants hit the floor and I hear a ringing I assume is the buckle hitting the floor, as he toes off his shoes and pushes them to side with everything else. The ringing continues and my brain is in too much of haze to register what the noise really is.

Instead, I pull his lips back to mine and kiss him like I'll never get the chance again in my lifetime. My hands are tangled in his hair and my legs are wrapped around his hips. He pushes my back against the door and pushes one knee up so that my butt can rest there, but now his hands are free to roam my body. I don't know how he's managing to touch me everywhere, he only has two hands, but it feels like they're everywhere at once and I can't get enough of him.

Then that noise starts again, and I can't ignore it this time. "What's that noise?" I ask in a whisper against Joe's lips.

"I think it's your phone." He replies. I should check that, but I don't want to let Joe go, I don't want to stop, even though we should. I mean this is moving damned fast, we've only had one date.

My mind knows it's too fast, but my body can't stop. Won't stop, pushing against Joe and pushing him for more. There's a beeping noise and then my phone starts ringing again. I sigh against Joe's lips and say, "Just let me look at it to see who it is and if I can send them a message to shut them up I will, OK?"

He nods and lets my legs gently slide down his body until my feet touch the floor. His hands are still resting on my hips and he places a light kiss to my lips. I wrap my arms around his waist, resting my cheek against his chest and I don't want to move, but then my fucking phone starts again. I reach down to rummage through our clothes to find my bag and I hear Joe groan, loudly, behind me. "I'm sorry it won't take me a second to work out who it is ..." I look up to find a pained expression on his face, his boxer briefs at his ankles, and his cock in his hand, stroking himself and his eyes are almost closed.

"You bent over right in front of me babe, I was already hard and ready to fuck you, what did you expect me to do?"

I close my mouth and nod. I have no words, it's the sexiest thing I think I've ever seen. That I can make a guy want me that badly, that he can't help but, well fuck his own hand, is amazing to me. It takes everything in me to tear my eyes away from Joe to look down at my phone. Before I can do anything with it, the bastard thing starts ringing again, I swear to god there better be a damned fucking good reason for whoever is calling my phone like this. I answer it without even looking at the screen, and that's my first mistake.

"Kathryn *why* couldn't you answer me the first time I rang. *What* are you doing that is more important than answering a call from me?" I close my eyes and sigh, that's a mood killer if ever there was one.

I look up to Joe's face and say, "Hello mother. Sorry, I didn't answer you the first time you called, I was a little... preoccupied." I say and Joe laughs.

"Is that a man I hear in the background Kathryn?" she shrieks in my ear, so loud that I actually pull the phone away from my ear, making Joe laugh more.

"Yes mother it is, no I'm not telling you where I am or whom I'm with and before you ask, no you don't know him." I get in before she even has the chance to ask me, but Joe stops laughing and starts putting his clothes back on. I touch his shoulder and shake my head no, but to my frustration he continues putting his clothes back on.

"Kathryn what have I told you about being in the company of strange men?"

"Mother, he isn't strange, well OK maybe slightly, but he's well-known to *me* and that's all that matters. You don't get a say in the people I keep company with, male or female." I can't believe she chose this moment to call.

"Kathryn, I'm just trying to protect you, that's all ..." I don't let her finish.

"No mother, you're trying to protect *you* and *your* image, it has nothing at all to do with me. If there's nothing important you wish to talk to me about, I was in the middle of something very important."

"I'm your mother and when I call to speak to you it's always important. You know your sister doesn't behave like this when I call her." Anna Ellis huffs in my ear. Nothing like being compared to the 'perfect sibling' to end all thoughts of being horny.

"Look, mother I'm not my sister and I'm busy, so if there's nothing urgent I'm going to say goodbye now." Nothing pisses me off more than my mother comparing me to my perfect sister, except dealing with my mother. I don't like Joe seeing me in this situation either, the woman makes me crazy, and I sure as hell don't want him to leave. The woman starts to speak again, but I cut her off saying, "No mother, it's late, I'm busy, I'll call you in the morning. Goodnight."

I hang up the phone, put it on silent and look towards Joe. He's almost completely dressed now, with the exception of his shoes and I'm not very happy.

"Excuse me, but can I grab my shoes please?" Joe asks. I realise then that I'm between him, his shoes, and his escape out of my house.

"Why?" I ask him. I want to know why he's suddenly ready to leave me standing here in my underwear and heels.

"Why? Because I want to put my shoes on and they're behind you."

"No. Why do you need them? Why am I standing here in my underwear and heels while you're dressed and ready to run out the door like nothing was happening a couple of minutes ago?" I take a shuddering breath, but don't give him the chance to answer yet. "I mean I know talking to mother on the phone was a bit of buzz kill, but it was only for a few minutes and I'm more than sure we can get back to where we were before she called. I silenced the phone, so even if she tried to call back, we won't hear her now." I sound desperate. I *am* desperate. He has me so wound up and ready for him and he's finding it so damned easy to walk away from me tonight.

"It's not that we were interrupted or who you were talking to Katy. It's what you said to them that means I need to leave. We're not going to work, you know it, and I know it, we were just kidding ourselves that anything could happen between us." Joe takes a deep breath, while closing his eyes and shaking his head, like he's trying to clear it. "I'm sorry Katy, but I have to go, and to do that I need my shoes. Please." He looks at me finally and his face is full of regret.

Well I'm not going to be anyone's regret and I'm glad we didn't go any further. I never thought I'd be grateful to get a phone call from my mother, ever. I step around him and grab a large cardigan I have resting over the back of the couch and wrap myself up in it. Shielding myself from him, from the pain and shame.

"I'm sorry Katy, this isn't how I wanted tonight to end." He steps towards his shoes and slides his feet in them. "In fact, all I wanted was to take you out to dinner and get to know you."

"Well then you shouldn't have come inside my house Joe. You should have walked away just like you'd planned and then none of it would have happened and you wouldn't be regretting being here with me." I step out of my heels and walk past him to open the door, so he can leave.

"I don't regret being with you tonight Kathryn."

Wrapping my cardigan around my body tighter as I say, "You should leave now Joseph."

"I'm sorry Katy..."

"Yeah, I know you're sorry. Goodnight Joseph."

"Goodnight Katy." He says and then he's walking out my front door, closing it quietly behind him as he goes.

I pick up my shoes with the intent of putting them away, only to throw them at the closed door in frustration. I can always trust that my mother will ruin my day. She seems to have perfect timing, knowing exactly when my life appears to be going my way, the way I want it to and then bang! She arrives either in person or via a phone call and everything seems to just float away on a gentle breeze.

This time I'm more than annoyed, I'm pissed the fuck off. I'm not sure what just happened except that answering that phone call was the absolute wrong thing to do. Not only did I have to endure that ridiculous conversation with her, but Joe left me high and dry. Well, OK not dry because I'm so horny that a light breeze would give me a chill right now. Not that I plan on doing anything with it, I wanted Joe and if I can't have him then. Wait a fucking second. I can ease the ache between legs without Joseph French.

Leaving my shoes and dress in a crumpled mess at the front door, I stomp to my bedroom, strip out of my clothes, dumping them on the floor. I rummage through my beside drawer and find just what I need.

"Hallelujah." I yell out to the empty room. No audience here, just me, myself and my trusty rabbit. I jump on my bed and make myself comfortable. I turn on the vibrator, I'm excited to get this show on the road. Who needs Joe French? Only there's nothing. So, I switch it off and then back on again. Still nothing. I shake it a bit to jiggle the batteries about. Still, nothing. God damn it! Just my luck. I open my bedside drawer, shift things around. No spare batteries in there.

I leave the bedroom and head for the kitchen. I look in every drawer. No batteries. I head to the spare room that I use as my office. I open all the drawers in my desk and cupboard. Nothing. Not a damned battery in sight. Motherf.... I run out to the hall table and start to rummage through everything that opens and shuts in it, but I still come up empty handed.

Frustrated doesn't even come close to explaining how I feel right now.

It's been so long since I've had a man in my bed, that my rabbit vibrator and a few other toys, and I have become my very good friends. They're handy, they don't talk back, and they don't walk out the fucking door leaving me high and dry either. Well, he left me high on adrenaline and with drenched underwear.

Now I'm horny with a ready pussy and I've got no batteries in the damn house. I've screwed myself over and not in a good way.

I know there are more ways to than one to get myself off, obviously, but after Joe leaving me wanting and now even my vibrator can't get it up, I can't be bothered anymore. I walk over to the kitchen bench where I've got a shopping list written out ready for a trip to the supermarket tomorrow and add, 'BATTERIES', in capital letters.

All of a sudden a loud laugh escapes me. I can't help it, it's loud and I know it must sound crazy. Maybe I've gone insane? I don't know, but I can suddenly see the humour in the nights events. Especially as I realise I'm standing in my kitchen, naked after walking around the entire house looking for batteries, not finding them and then writing a note to buy some.

I'm laughing so hard there are tears rolling down my cheeks and I'm gasping for breath. I force myself to stop laughing, catch my breath and shake my head. I wander back into my bedroom and put my rabbit away. No point keeping it out, nothing's happening with it now.

I'm not sure what happened tonight, or why it went as pear shaped as it did. What I do know is, that this seems to just be the way my life is running at the moment. Doesn't seem to matter what I try to do, with whom or where, it all goes belly up somehow.

I need a good night's sleep and maybe, just putting it out there, maybe things will look better in the morning. Or I could sleep until early afternoon and not worry about the morning hours at all?

I pull back the covers, get into bed, turn off the lamp and snuggle down to get comfortable. As I lie there on my back staring at the ceiling, I can't help thinking about Joe. He was into it, into *me* as much I was into him, so why did he get dressed so quickly and leave without explanation? He's the one who told me to answer the phone and then get rid of whoever was on the other end. Another opportunity with a man thwarted by my seemingly always knowing mother. She always seems to know when I have a man around.

I guess it's for the best though. It's not like Joe and I could have gone any further than one night anyway. He hates my best friend and she hates him. I already feel like I betrayed Kami by sharing a table at a café with him. I feel even worse after having dinner with him. Best to just let him leave for good.

If only I could get him off my mind and stop wishing he was here, kissing me again. I tell myself to go to sleep, before I start getting all hot and bothered again. If only that had been explained to my dreaming mind as well.

Dream me is having fun imagining where tonight *could* have gone before it was ended so abruptly. I wake up hot and bothered, cursing Joe French all over again.

Chapter Six

It took everything in me to leave Katy tonight. I know my friends, James included if he knew, would call me an idiot for walking out. I've called myself an idiot the whole drive home, while I had a shower and even as I got into bed.

I had Kathryn Ellis right where I've always wanted her, right where I've wanted her since we got reacquainted months ago at the café. She was in her underwear and heels with her hand on my very hard, very willing cock.

I hadn't planned on things going that far tonight. I wanted to take her out to dinner, get to know her and show her the real me. Make her understand that I'm not always the arsehole that gives her best friend a hard time. Well, OK I *am* him, but I want her to see more than that in me. I always have.

Hearing her tell her mum that she wouldn't know me stung a little. Stung a lot actually, because I've known the Ellis family for years. I also know that Anna Ellis is a difficult woman to deal with and Katy has always clashed with her mother, but not even mentioning that I was nearby, that hurt.

Once she brushed off who she was with as unimportant, I couldn't bring myself to stay and I had even less desire to make love to her. I've spent my life being rejected not because of who I am, but because of who I'm not. I couldn't stay there and look in her beautiful eyes seeing anything but desire.

As I lie in bed, staring at the shadows being cast on the ceiling by the small amount of light getting in my curtains, I let my mind wander. I let it think about where we would have gone if that phone call had never happened. I close my eyes, letting it play out in my mind.

With Katy's legs wrapped around my hips, her back hard up against the door, I kiss her. Softly at first because I want to feel her lips, I want to know how they feel. I run my tongue along her bottom lip, then take a light nip, making her gasp. I take full advantage and push my tongue into her mouth, searching for her tongue. The sound that she makes, shit I want to bottle it. It makes my cock harder and I didn't think that was possible. I want this woman like I've never wanted anyone else before.

With my hands gripping her butt, massaging her cheeks not so gently, I run a finger along the seam of the scrap of lace covering her pussy and the globes of her arse. As she moans into my mouth, I pull back from the kiss just enough to speak and say, "Do you like that honey?"

"Mmmmm. More Joe. Please, more."

"More what Kathryn? Tell me, use your words babe." I say, my lips smiling lightly against hers.

"Urghhh Joe. Don't make me ask. Please just touch me?" she says with a frustrated sigh.

"That sounded a lot like you asking me for something honey." I say, and her thighs tighten around my waist, making me chuckle. "Can I do something for you, Kathryn?"

"Touch me Joe. Touch me everywhere. Anywhere. Please. Just. Touch. Me." she begs, and I can't resist her any longer.

"Open your eyes honey, let me see you and I'll touch you where you want me to." Her eyes snap open and stare into mine. I pull back a little more so that we can see each other better, then I slide a finger under the lace covering her and run it along her lips.

Katy tries to push her hips down so her pussy slides down on to my finger, but my other hand has a very firm grip on her butt and I'm not letting her get the relief she's seeking. I can see it in her eyes, she's going to kill me any minute and I love seeing that I've worked her up so much, that she needs me to touch her.

"More.." she starts to speak, but before she can finish her thought, I press my thumb onto her clit, just enough that she can feel it there and feel the promise of relief.

"Eyes open honey." I remind her, as they flutter close at my touch.

"Ohhh Joe." Her voice is barely a whisper. "Please."

The begging in her voice is my undoing. I push my finger inside her pussy and pump it in and out a few times, before curling it up as if beckoning her to 'come here', hitting that spot that I know will drive her crazy. As I hit that spot, I increase the pressure of my thumb on her clit and I can feel it. Her orgasm is building, her hips are moving against mine, her hands are wrapped up tightly in my hair, scratching at my scalp.

I stare into her eyes, "That's it honey come for me. Come all over my hand, now." She needs no more encouragement, her orgasm hits her, and she screams out my name. It's the sexiest thing I've ever heard, and I plan on hearing it over and over again.

After a minute she catches her breath, and she says, "Holy hell Joseph, that was ...."

What the fuck? Ahh hell, it's my alarm interrupting the best dreams I've had in living memory.

As if I need any proof of that, I'm awake with my cock in my hand and my very own orgasm spread across my stomach. I reach over to my side table to grab some tissues, only to find it empty. I close my eyes take a deep breath and head for the shower instead. Before I'm even awake properly, I stumble awkwardly across my room, trying not to make a mess on my floor. If anyone saw me now, they'd think I'd had a fucking stroke with the way I'm walking.

I turn on the water and step inside, closing the door behind me. I step under the water and scream, fuck it I forgot to turn on the cold water. This is how awake I am right now. After making the temperature warm instead of scorching, I run my hands through my hair to wet it. It's only as I reach for the shampoo that I realise what I've done. I hadn't touched anything yet with one hand because I needed to wash my come off it and that's what I just did, by rubbing it in my hair.

After washing and rinsing my hair three times, I wash the rest of me as well. Using a little extra soap and scrubbing action on my stomach. I step out, dry my hair and my body, then wrap the towel around my waist to walk into my kitchen to make my coffee. If the start of my day is anything to go by, I'm going to be needing every drop of coffee I can get.

"Good morning sunshine, aren't you in a delightful mood today?" I groan at the voice and remind myself to get his key off him. If I'm lucky enough to get another chance with Katy, and we end up here, I sure as fuck don't want him walking in on us. "Then again, you're this delightful at all times of the day."

"Fuck off James." I grumble. I am *not* in the mood for his shit this morning. Why the fuck is he here so early on a Sunday anyway?

"Did you forget about our date this morning handsome? I should be offended but I'm used to you forgetting about me." The idiot says with a dramatic sigh. After all the years I've known this guy, I still have days when I wonder how we've managed to remain friends.

"What date? What are you doing here so early?" I ground out while pouring coffee into a mug and taking a sip. Too hot god damn it. I turn to glare at the bastard sitting at my kitchen bench

"I am wounded Joey, wounded I tells ya." He screeches and I want to kick him in the balls right now, and not just for screeching.

"Stop being so dramatic *Jimmy* and tell me why you're actually here, because you and I both know we didn't have anything planned." How am I so sure about this, even though I'm still half asleep? I know this without a doubt because I had plans last night and there is no way in hell I would have made any this early with this tool after a date with Katy Ellis.

"Did that long shower not quite take the edge off your crankiness, Joey? All that spanking the monkey, whacking off, doing the five knuckle shuffle, pulling your pud under the warm water just didn't do it for ya huh?" I look at the bastard and his grin spreads across his face and his eyes are just begging me to deny it.

"Whatever dude. What. Do. You. Want?" I growl at him. Jesus, I need more coffee to deal with him this morning.

"So, you're not even going to deny that you were jerking off in there?" He jerks his thumb towards my bathroom. "You really *were* jerking off in there? Man, I was just joking, I figured you were soaking your weary old bones. You said you couldn't hang out with me last night because you had plans. I assumed they were with a woman, but if you were self-servicing in there just now then...?"

"Ohh for the love of god would you shut up." I drop my body onto a stool at the kitchen counter and look at him, "What I do or do not do in my house or my shower is none of your fucking business, but if you really must know, then yes I had a date. No it wasn't with anyone you know. No I'm not going to tell you her name. Yes, the date went well, no we didn't have sex, because I know you'll ask. We got, let's just say we got interrupted and I left."

He opens his mouth to speak but I hold up my hand to make him stop and continue, "Before you ask anything else, let me say that I enjoyed my shower and leave it at that, OK? Good."

There's silence for five seconds and then the bastard cracks up. He's not just laughing, he's got tears rolling down his face and he's clutching his stomach like he's in pain. I decide to sit there and wait him out, if I speak to him it'll just prolong his fit. I've learned over the years to just let him ride it out.

"Oh. My. God. I didn't think you'd really admit to getting off in the shower over last night's date." He says through deep breaths.

"I didn't you moron. I said I enjoyed my shower, I never once admitted to any 'self-servicing', as you so politely put it." I put my empty mug down on the bench and stand up. "Now, if you don't mind, seeing as though you don't seem to plan on telling me what the hell you're doing here, I'm going to go put some clothes on."

"Oh, don't get dressed on my account Joseph. I don't mind checking out all the hard work you've been putting in at the gym, I know it's all for me anyway."

"You're such a douchebag. If you're going to tell me what you're really doing here, then feel free to stay, but if you're just here to bust my balls this morning, then be gone before I get back out here. I don't have it in me today to deal with your bullshit James."

I leave the room without looking back. I don't care if he leaves or stays, I just need to have clothes on before we continue this line of conversation. He's my best friend, but he can be a real arsehole sometimes. It doesn't help that he knows just how to get under my skin. Guess that happens after decades of not just a friendship, but a brotherhood and relying on each other.

When I walk back out to the kitchen I find that the idiot is still here, quietly drinking another coffee. He might be quiet, but I can see him watching me over the rim of his coffee, just itching to ask me something, or give me more shit.

"Well you're a real peach this morning, even more so than usual." He takes a drink of his coffee. I don't speak, he didn't ask a question, but I know one is coming. "So, how did you fuck up last night then?" he asks, sounding interested, but with a smile on his face.

"Why do you assume that I screwed up somehow?" I ask. I'm curious, he isn't wrong after all.

"I assume because it's *you* Joe," he says waving his hand up and down in front of him, indicating me from head to toe. "You're not exactly the smoothest dude with the opposite sex, Joe."

He's still not wrong but it's still insulting and I'm still not in the mood for it. "Piss off James, cause you're just the smoothest cat in history aren't you? You can get any woman you want? Well, you haven't managed to get the one that you've wanted for years have you?" It's a low blow, especially when I know it's partly my fault that Kami won't give him the time of day.

"That was uncalled for Joseph. There's no need to get nasty dude." He says and moves like he's about to leave. I can't help but feel like an arsehole.

"You're right that was a dick move, even for me." He smiles, my confession stopping his exit almost immediately. It doesn't shut him up though. No all I've done is give him a reason to give me his opinion, whether I like it or not.

"I guess neither of us are very lucky when it comes to love hey?" he asks, the mood suddenly dark and moody. Too bloody dark and moody for two grown men.

"No-one said anything about love Jim. Remember our teenage promise?"

He laughs and replies, "Oh yeah, 'no woman shall ever come between us because love isn't for us. Brothers always." We fist bump like the douche bags that we were then and still are.

"Let's go get a beer." I say.

"It's still morning Joe. Let's go get some breakfast, that's what I came over for in the first place. Not all this sappy shit."

I know that he says that for my benefit. I know it's not just 'sappy shit' to him, he's in love and we both know it.

"Let's get out of here then. You're buying." I grab my keys and wallet as we walk out the door, making sure it's locked behind us.

Chapter Seven

KATY

I'm standing in my kitchen, leaning up against the bench drinking my morning coffee, scrolling through messages on my phone when its starts ringing. The vibration and the noise in the quiet scares the crap out of me and I jump. I can also admit I squeal a little in surprise. Then, I groan.

I answer the phone with, "Good morning Anna, what can I do for you at this early hour of the day?"

"I've told you a million times Kathryn, it's downright rude to address your mother with her first name. No matter how much of an adult you think you are, I have earned the title of mother. I carried you for nine months and then gave birth to you after hours of labour."

I can't stand to hear the same old complaints. I know it's my own fault, I enjoy winding her up and therefore, I have to cop the consequences, but I really should know that this is the kind of crap that's going to come out of her mouth. It does every time.

"You're right mother and I apologise. As your daughter I shall always call you mother and show you every respect." I say contritely.

"Well, there's no need for that kind of sarcasm this early in the morning young lady." She replies with a huff. This conversation isn't going wherever she planned it to. "Are you still coming to afternoon tea at the house today Kathryn?"

I roll my eyes as I reply, "Yes mother, I come to the house for afternoon every Sunday if I'm free. You know this." I'm glad she can't see me through the phone. I would be getting another lecture about behaving and respect. My eyes are almost rolling into the back of my head at her condescending tone, and she's lecturing *me* on respect!

"Well, that's my point Kathryn, you come if you're not busy. How am I supposed to know one week from the next if you're attending? It's not like you ever call me to let me know one way or another."

"I'm sorry mother. Next week I'll send you my work schedule and let my boss know that I have to be at the house for afternoon tea on Sundays. I'm sure he won't mind that one bit when we have to go out of town or work over the weekends."

"Again with the sarcasm and smart mouth young lady. I'm just saying I wish you'd let me know sooner so that I can cater for you or not. I know you think that one person doesn't make a difference, but it does to me." she says and this time, her tone sounds hurt.

Honestly, I don't think she's really hurt about me going or not going, or even with the fact that I don't let her know. It's got more to do with appearances. Believe me when I say, one person missing or joining in with afternoon tea, does not make a difference up at 'the house'. Mother isn't slaving over the stove and she isn't counting numbers either. It's all about who she's invited this week and who needs to be seen attending. Most of the time it's my father's business partners and people he wants to schmoooooooze. If it's a schmooze fest then all offspring need to be there to show support and show off perfect family values.

My dad doesn't care too much if my sister and I are there. He understands we have lives outside of 'the house' and we both have jobs. He also understands that I've worked hard to get to where I am and that I need to travel for my work. Something my mother doesn't understand because to her, a woman's place is at home, looking after her husband and the house. Kids are optional.

I've drifted off into my own thoughts and only realise I'm still on the phone with my mother when I hear her repeating my name over and over again, trying to get my attention.

"Kathryn. Kathryn. Are you listening to me?" she asks.

I decide to go with honesty, makes for a nice change every now and then. "I'm sorry mother, I kind of drifted off there. I was thinking about all the things I'm going to have to get done this morning so that I can make it to afternoon tea on time."

"I was kind of hoping you could meet me for breakfast this morning?" she asks quietly, and I have to say I'm surprised. She wants to see me twice in one day? I can't help but wonder what's going on. Then the bomb comes, "Your sister will be joining us, she's bringing a young man with her that she wants to bring to afternoon tea."

Ahhhhhh. There it is. My sister is her favourite, make no mistake about it, but she can be hard to handle. They're so alike that they clash, sometimes all it takes is a small spark to set them off. I'm the buffer, especially for this poor guy who will undoubtedly get stuck in the middle!

"Please Kathryn," She doesn't exactly whine, but my mother very rarely begs, anyone or for anything, and as I close my eyes she says, "I will excuse you from afternoon tea for the next month if you do this for me. Give me this morning and this afternoon, that's all I ask."

"Jesus Mother, what is wrong with this guy?" My eyes shoot open, she has to be desperate.

"She's in love with this one Kathryn."

"Olivia is always in 'love', mother." I say in exasperation, because while my mother isn't too happy about my single status, she's even less impressed with my little sister always claiming some dude as being the 'love of her life', every few weeks. Personally, I find it completely entertaining, if only because I get to see the vein on my mother's head pop right out and I didn't cause it.

"Yes, well, be that as it may, this one is the real deal. I really want you to meet us to see if she really is serious about this one. Please, Kathryn."

Again with the please? I close my eyes, take a big drink of my now cold coffee and say, "Sure Mother. Where and when?"

"Oh thank you Kathryn, and I mean it, no need to come to afternoon tea for the following month. I know how much you hate coming."

"I don't hate attending mother, I just get busy sometimes and can't make it." There's no point telling her any different though, the truth is, I don't like going to the damn things, but I won't admit it to her.

After I get all the details off her, the where, when and the promise to be there ten minutes early, I get myself in to some 'breakfast with Anna Ellis' appropriate clothes. Clean nice jeans, heeled boots and a nice blouse, with a light cardigan. Just in case.

When I walk into the café my sister is already sitting at a table. She looks up to the door expectantly when she hears it open and then close behind me. She doesn't look disappointed as such, I can just see that I'm not who she was hoping or expecting to see enter the café. I guess Mother didn't tell her I was coming.

"Good morning Olivia ...." I start to say in the cheeriest voice I can find this early in the morning.

"Don't you good morning me Kathryn." She frowns at me. This is going well already. "She called you and asked you to come, didn't she?" I could feign ignorance and ask who she's talking about, but the fact is, we both know.

"Yes she did. I assumed she would be here already though." I reply.

"Knowing Mother, she's sitting in her car somewhere watching to see if we show up first." She says with a snort that our mother definitely wouldn't approve of, but I find adorable, simply because I know our mother would hate it.

"You're probably right." I laugh. Then, as if we conjured her up, the door to the café opens and in walks our mother. If I didn't know better, I'd think she had the damned café bugged and knew what we'd just said. I turn from the door and look at my sister, and we can't help it, we crack up laughing.

Our mother, who hates loud outbursts, whether of anger or laughter, shushes us when she reaches our table but that does nothing except make us laugh louder. You'd think she'd know better by now, but loud laughter seems to be the biggest faux pas of all to my mother. It's like enjoying yourself just isn't allowed in polite circles. She sends a glare my way, because of course, I'm the older sister so therefore I should know better and set a good example.

"Shush girls please, you're drawing the attention of the other diners." I roll my eyes at her, but cough to calm my laughter anyway. For a woman that loves being the centre of attention, she only wants it on her terms.

"You're right mother, how dare we look like we might be enjoying life."

"That's not what I mean, and you know it Kathryn. You just don't have to enjoy life quite so enthusiastically." I can tell she wants to keep giving me a talking to, but Olivia has squealed quietly in excitement and moved to the side of our table.

I look over to see what's gotten her so excited and have to honestly say, I can see why she's excited. The man standing next to her is, tall, handsome, nicely built and well dressed. Completely the opposite of what Olivia normally brings to any family event.

"Mother, Katy, this is Thomas." She has her arm wrapped around his waist, the other hand is resting on his chest and she's wearing a huge smile on her face.

For his part, Thomas has his arm wrapped around her waist, pulling her in close to his side like he can't bear to be too far away from her. He leans down slightly to drop a light kiss to her forehead, and I swear I sigh along with my sister. He reaches out his free hand and I automatically reach mine out to shake it. "It's nice to finally meet you Katy, Liv has told me so much about you, I feel like I almost know you already." He stops talking and blushes, Jesus he actually blushes a little then says, "Sorry, that sounded kind of creepy didn't it? I didn't mean it that way."

"No, not creepy at all, I understood what you meant." I smile so that he knows I am truly OK with it. "I'm glad to finally meet you too, Thomas." I say, because even though I haven't heard his name before now, I can tell that he's good for my sister and he makes her happy.

He drops my hand and turn his attention to our mother, offering his hand to her as well, which she takes. Although, she looks like she's in a state of shock. "Mrs Ellis, I am very happy to finally meet you as well. I hope you don't mind, but I wanted to meet you before I came to your home. I asked Liv to set up a breakfast meeting when she asked me to come with her to your family afternoon tea today. I know how my mum would react if I turned up with an extra for a family function without telling her."

"That's a lovely thought, thank you Thomas." I don't think I've ever seen Anna Ellis so frazzled before in all my life, and let me say, I took that as a challenge every single day I was living under her roof. She didn't even say a word about him shortening Olivia's name either, I must learn his magical powers.

Olivia and Thomas sit down across from us at the table and discuss what they're going to order for breakfast. I turn to my mother and whisper, "Close your mouth mother, it's very unbecoming." Earning me a dirty look and a head shake.

"What do you want for your breakfast Kathryn?" I laugh quietly and get my usual, eggs benedict with a pot of tea.

Conversation is flowing easily, even as Anna questions the very sweet and unflappable Thomas, about everything from his parents and family, to his job and his plans for the future and *our* Olivia. He answers everything with an ease I haven't seen in forever from a guy of my sisters choosing.

As for my sister, she's glowing and I couldn't be happier for her, she's had her fair share of bad boys and idiots, it's about time she found a good one. I'm glad I came out for breakfast and find that I'm actually looking forward to afternoon tea today as well. Let me tell you, it's pretty rare I'm happy to attend one of these events.

I'm sitting there, enjoying my meal and the company and obviously the universe decides I'm enjoying myself a little too much because I hear my mother speak and then a deep voice from behind me answers her and I feel a hand rest on the back of my chair. I hope no one else at the table sees me flinch away from his touch.

"Good morning ladies and gent. What brings the beautiful Ellis ladies out so early this morning?" he asks. How can he be standing so close to me and appear to not be affected?

"Joseph French, it's been too long." Anna exclaims. Doesn't she know she's attracting stares now?

"You're right it has been Anna, but I've been pretty busy with getting the business up and running." He replies, not moving away from my chair. He leans down and gives Anna a light kiss on the cheek.

"We joined Olivia and her boyfriend, Thomas, here for breakfast." Anna finally answers his original question and then Olivia does the follow up introductions.

I'm left sitting there, quietly wishing that I could just disappear. Then I hear my mother invite Joe to afternoon tea and him accepting the invitation and I can't sit there quietly anymore.

"What? Why do *you* want to come to afternoon tea Joseph?" I ask. My mother sends me a dirty look, I've committed one of her largest sins, questioning a guest of their intentions, but I need to know why he wants to be there. Can't he just leave last night's humiliation as exactly that?

"I want to come because your mother invited me, and it's been a while since I attended one."

Anna obviously reads the look on my face perfectly, because she leans in and harshly whispers, "You will attend Kathryn, don't forget the promise you made to me this morning."

Holy crap on a cracker, to use a phrase Kami loves to use in such situations. If I don't attend today's afternoon tea, I can kiss my free weekends for the foreseeable future goodbye.

"Well, then I guess it will be nice to catch up with you later. Right now, I'm sorry mother, Olivia, but I have to get going. I have a few things to catch up on so I can make it later." I look over to Thomas, while trying to ignore the brush of Joe's hand down my side as I stand. "It's very nice to finally meet you Thomas, and I look forward to getting to know you better."

With all the pleasantries over and done with, I look at my mother and say, "I will see you later." Then I lean in and lightly kiss her cheek. With my daughter duties done, I turn to leave, until I feel a hand lightly grab my upper arm, and I turn slightly to look at him.

"I'll see you later today then Kathryn?" Joe says, but it's more like a question.

I smile widely and look at him, I shouldn't have looked into his eyes, they draw me in. I take a deep breath and reply, "I will be at my parents' house later today, so yes, if you join us then you'll see me later Joseph." He nods and lets my arm go. I can feel my sister staring into the back of my head, but I don't look back before saying a general goodbye to everyone and walk out the café door.

When I get to my car, I open the door, drop myself into the driver's seat and let out a huge sigh.

Joseph bloody French! Of all people to walk into that café today. The universe is surely trying to fuck me over.

I start the car, put it in drive and head for home and refuge. I've never wanted the peace of home more than right in this moment.

Chapter Eight

<u>JOE</u>

I couldn't believe my luck when I walked into the café this morning, after James ditched me to go check on something at one of his job sites and I saw all the Ellis women sitting at a table together having breakfast. When I noticed the guy sitting there, my first instinct was to ask what the hell he was doing there. Thankfully, I actually took a second to take in the situation and realised he was there with Olivia.

My second thought was, why the fuck would I be upset if he was there with Kathryn? It's not like we're together. We had one date and it did *not* end well. I've never felt the primal urge to destroy someone who has what is mine before. I shake my head and remind myself, Kathryn Ellis isn't *mine* to get all primal over.

"It will be good to see you at afternoon tea Joseph, I'm sure Frank will be glad to catch up with you as well. It's been too long young man."

I know Kathryn has issues with her mum, but I've never found Anna Ellis to be anything other than polite and kind. I'm not her son though, so I have no clue how she behaves behind closed doors. I'm the poster child for parents behaving one way in public and another in the privacy of their own home. I push those thoughts aside and smile at Anna.

"It will be great to catch up with Frank again. It's been too long Anna." I look over to Katy's sister and her boyfriend and smile, "I'll see you two again later at the house?" I ask, because I assume these two are a package deal these days.

I'm rewarded with a huge smile and Thomas replies for them both, "Yes, Joseph, you will."

"It's Joe." I say, "I guess I'll see you all later then." I give Anna another light kiss on the cheek, grab my coffee from the front counter and walk out the front door feeling better than I did when I walked in there.

I've got a date with Katy, even if she doesn't see it that way. That's enough to bring a smile to my face and make the rest of the day leading up to afternoon tea at the 'House of Ellis', which is what we all named Katy's parents' house when were kids.

I pull up to the house and take a deep breath. I can see Katy's car parked in the circular drive, and I can't help checking to see if she has an easy escape before I get out of my car. She's never made a secret how much she hates being here for these get togethers, but I also know she doesn't want to upset her parents.

I pocket my keys and walk to the front door, before I can knock it swings wide open and I'm greeted by the one person I really wanted to see this afternoon. I wasn't planning on seeing her so pissed off though, and I'm really hoping that she's not going to direct that my way.

"Why are you here Joe?" Guess I should have hoped harder.

"Your mother invited me and she's right, it's been a while." I reply, with what I hope is a charming smile on my face. Although I have been told that my smile isn't as charming as I think it is.

"I know, I was there Joseph. I want to know why you didn't make an excuse to *not* be here? We both know you don't need to be here" she says in a quiet kind of yell.

"How do you know I don't want to be here Kathryn?" She's pissing me off now and that's when I feel the need to use her full name. I like using it when she's about to scream out in pleasure too. Fuck! I can't think like that right now, if she sees an erection, I think she might just take me out.

"I know you don't want to be here, because I don't want to be here. No one wants to *be* here Joseph, least of all the younger set. We're all here out of obligation. So, again, my question to you, seeing as you have absolutely *no* obligation to be here today, is *why are you here Joseph?*"

"Honestly?" I ask, because she's right. I have no obligation to be here. If I had said I was too busy to come, Anna Ellis would have accepted that excuse and my parents wouldn't care either way.

"That would be nice, yes." She says, in a huff.

"I wanted to see you." It's simple and it's true.

"Are you serious?" she asks me, and I can understand why she needs to. I walked out on her the other night after all, not the other way round.

"Deadly. You asked me for honesty and that's what you got." I reply. "James made me realise that I stuffed up last night and I've been trying to work out how to see you again since I saw him this morning. Then, I saw you at the café and Anna invited me over this afternoon, and well, you know the rest. I couldn't resist."

"You told James about us?" she asks, in a much calmer, quieter voice.

"Is that all you got out of what I just said? That I outed us to my best friend?" It's my turn to get pissed off now.

"No. I just ...." she doesn't get the chance to finish her thought because Frank Ellis opens the door.

"What are you two kids doing out here? There's good food and alcohol aplenty inside." He says, laughing. "Ohhh come on laugh a little you two. You've always been too serious around each other, anyone would think you're in love. You need to have more fun, maybe even having that fun together would make it more fun. Who knows?" he says with a wink, holding the door open, waiting for us to enter the house.

I look at Katy and wave my hand to indicate that she should walk ahead of me. It's the gentlemanly thing to do, her dad is watching after all, and the bonus is, I get to watch her walk away. I look up as she walks passed her dad and into the house, only to see the grin on her dad's face turn to a scowl. I move to hold the door open so that he can enter the house first, but he says, "No, no son, it's my house, you go on in behind *my daughter*." Yeah, Frank Ellis knew exactly what I was doing. Checking out his daughter's behind, but I'm grateful he doesn't call me out on it, especially as his wife walks up to greet me.

"Good to see you again Joseph and so soon too." Anna says, while planting a light kiss on my cheek.

"It's nice to see you again too Anna." I say, and honestly, it is truly good to see them again. It's been a long time since I've attended one of their get togethers. I stopped coming when my parents stopped forcing me to go to their friends events. Had I known Katy still attended, I might have changed my mind. "Thank you for inviting me."

"You never need a formal invitation Joseph, you're always welcome." Frank adds and I hear a snort behind me. I know who made the noise even before Anna voices her disapproval.

"Really Kathryn, that's not a very ladylike noise." Anna tuts, but Frank just chuckles.

"Leave the girl alone Anna." He tells his wife.

"Come on inside, we can't stand at the entrance all afternoon." Anna says and leads the way into the party.

Frank walks beside her, Katy behind him and I fall in beside Katy. I rest my hand on her lower back, lean in closer, lower my voice and say, "I like the noises you make when you ..."

"Stop right there." She says in a low growl. Damned if I don't find it sexy as hell.

"What? Do you think your mother would call those noises you make ladylike?" she glares at me and I chuckle quietly. "Personally, I've never heard anything sexier in my life." I say and step away from the danger zone before she can hit me, either with a glare or her hands.

Suddenly I'm busy saying hello to all the people I haven't seen in months, if not years, at these shindigs. While I never lose sight of Katy, I don't really get another chance to talk to her all afternoon. So much for my plan to win her over and getting her to agree to another date with me.

I've said goodbye to the Ellis' and I'm talking to Olivia and Thomas, when I sense someone standing just behind me. Before she even touches me, I know who it is. "Liv, Thomas, you don't mind if I steal Joseph away do you? I've got something to show him in the study." Katy says with a smile to her sister and her new boyfriend. As I found out just now, they've only been together for a few weeks.

"I just bet you do Katy, feel free to steal him away. Thomas and I have to get going anyway. It was nice to see you again Joe, I get the feeling I'll be seeing you around more often."

"Nice to meet you both." Thomas says and before either one of us can say anything else, they've both headed for the door.

I turn to Katy and say, "Lead the way gorgeous."

"Shhhhh Joe, someone might hear you."

"What do I care Katy? You *are* beautiful, and anyone who can't see that is freaking blind." I say, keeping my manners in check and not swearing. We are after all still in her parents' home, they deserve some respect.

"I care Joe." She huffs at me. I'm struggling to understand why it means so much to her that no one knows about us. Not that there *is* an us right now.

We've reached the study before I even realise how far we've walked. When I step in through the door, Katy closes it quietly behind me.

"Why did you come here today Joe?" she asks, not looking me in the eye. I'm not used to Katy not being as bold as brass.

"Why can't you look me in the eyes Katy?" She looks up, meeting my eyes dead on, challenging me. "I already told you why I came today Katy. I wanted to see you and when Anna extended the invitation, while also mentioning you would be here, I decided it was the perfect opportunity."

"Perfect opportunity because you knew I wouldn't make a scene at one of my parents events. You *know* I always try to at least to behave at one of these things." She says, her voice full of exasperation.

"That was one of the reasons, yes." I can admit that I didn't want to cause a scene anywhere else either. "But the honest truth is, I wanted to see you again. I wanted to look at you, drink you in, touch you again. Most of all, I wanted to apologise." I sigh and draw in a deep breath. "I was an idiot last night Katy and I'm sorry."

I didn't realise how close we'd gotten while I was talking. It's like there's a magnet pulling us together and after all these years of ignoring that pull, the attraction I have to this woman, I can't hold back anymore. I reach out and drag my knuckles along her cheek and jawline. Her eyes close and she breathes out a long sigh. Could it be possible that she feels this pull too?

My other hand reaches around her waist and pulls her in closer to my body. I give her plenty of opportunity to pull away, but she doesn't. With her chin resting in the palm of my hand, her body nestled into mine, I slowly lean down to kiss her.

"What are you waiting for Joe?" she whispers, in this husky, sexy as fuck voice, and I can't hold back. I drop my lips to hers and take them like I'll never get another chance. Let's face it, it's a real possibility that this could be my last chance at these lips, and this woman.

I take possession of her mouth, her lips, her tongue as if they're mine for the taking. Our tongues tangle, and she's all I can taste. The only thing I saw her drinking was an iced water with lemon slices, and I can taste the faintest hint of lemon on her lips and tongue. I move back slightly, to take a quick breath and I'm ready for my lips to be on hers again, but she speaks.

"Why Joe?" she asks.

My muddled brain can't think, so I ask, "Why what Katy?"

"Why did you leave last night?"

Ahhh the million dollar question and she deserves an answer. I just don't have the brain power to string the necessary words together right now, but I know if I don't answer her, things will end much more abruptly than I want them too, and I'll no doubt end up in pain.

I look her square in the eyes and tell the truth, sort of. "I was annoyed that you wouldn't tell Anna that you were with me."

"Oh Joe." Katy lightly rests her forehead on my chest, takes a deep breath and continues speaking. "I'm not ashamed or embarrassed to be with you, Joe."

"Are you sure about that Katy'? Cause I get the distinct impression that you'd rather no one knew anything about us."

"I just need some time Joe, and I want to keep us to us for a while. So that we can enjoy it without other people getting involved."

"And by other people, you mean Kami." I say, resigned to the fact that her best friend is not going to like the idea of her dating me.

"Well, yes but no." she sighs. "I don't want it to matter Joe, but it does."

"I know." I understand. I really do, I don't want to, but I do. I don't want it to matter either, but I know it does.

"I'm sorry." She mumbles into my chest.

I place my finger under her chin and draw her eyes up to look into mine. "Don't be." I murmur and then slam my lips back onto hers. I kiss her until neither of us can breathe.

"Joe, what are we doing?" she asks, her voice breathless and sexy, her lips a breath away from mine.

"If you don't know that baby, then I'm not doing it right, now am I?"

She huffs out a small laughs and says, "You know what I mean Joe."

"We're kissing Katy." I say, and lightly kiss her lips. "With any luck kissing will lead to sucking, which could possibly lead to ..."

"Hello, Katy honey are you in there?" The door handle rattles and there's a couple of loud knocks on the door. "Has the door handle jammed again honey?" Frank Ellis sure does know how to spoil the mood.

"Ahhhh geeez Dad, way to ruin a really good moment." Katy mumbles into my chest, as I start chuckling. "Yeah Dad, I'm in here, but no the door isn't jammed. I, ummm, I locked it."

She pulls away from my body and while she's combing fingers through her hair and straightening out her clothes, I'm trying to think of anything that will make my dick relax.

Katy looks at me, then my crotch and I realise that my dick isn't going down before she opens that door, so I sit in the nearest chair and pick up the book sitting next to it.

The door opens and Katy says, "Hey Dad, come on in. I was just showing Joe some of my favourite books in your library."

"Hey Frank," I say with a nod in his general direction.

"Uhuh, sure you were sweetheart." He looks between us with a knowing smile spread across his face. "Your mother is looking for you, she thought you'd escaped without saying goodbye and she's not happy. I said I'd come looking for you."

"OK, well I'll come out and say goodbye now then." Katy says.

When Frank looks at me expectantly I cough and say, "I'll be right out Frank, I just need to use the bathroom first."

"Of course you do son." He laughs and steers Katy out of the room. She looks back at me and mouths, 'sorry', as she disappears. I want to be sorry, but I'm not. I'm not sorry her Dad thinks he knows what we were up to, but I *am* sorry we didn't get as far as I wanted to. *Again.*

I take myself to the nearest bathroom and pull myself together, only then do I trust myself to go find Katy's parents to say goodbye.

Chapter Nine

KATY

Oh. My. God! I can't believe my *father* almost caught us in the act, not that we were doing anything bad. Yet. I've never been so grateful for my brain thinking ahead and locking the door as we came into the room. Otherwise, god only knows what my father *could* have walked in on.

I follow my dad out of the room, leaving Joe behind to take care of his, *excitement*, let's say. I can't help the giggle that escapes me, and my dad turns to look at me. He's got a smile on his face and I'm not sure what he's smiling about. That could have quite easily been a very awkward situation for all of us. Before he can say anything though, my mum appears from nowhere.

"Where have you been Kathryn? You disappeared, even Olivia couldn't find you. Lucky you did Frank dear, where was she?"

"Oh, I forgot that I asked her to take Joe into my study to show him a couple of papers I've been reading through. They were in there, totally engrossed in what they were doing and didn't hear any of us calling for them." Dad to the rescue, I wonder if he knows how much I love and appreciate him? I'm going to have to send him a bottle of his favourite gin tomorrow.

"Sorry about that Anna, we got a little carried away. Reading those papers, very interesting stuff." Joe's deep voice says from behind me. I didn't even hear him walk up.

What's with these men not letting me get a word in? I get that they're trying to save me from explaining what was *really* going on to my mother, but still, geez. "Well, they weren't *that* exciting to be honest mother, but I was a little interested in seeing where they were heading."

My dad chuckles and says, "Well, I guess Joe should work a little harder in keeping your attention then, Katy." Anna sends him a weird look and he says, "You know, maybe he should be reading something a little lighter perhaps."

I'm not sure he saved himself from an inquisition from his wife later, but I sure do appreciate the heat he just took off me.

"You know dad, you might be right. It could be that Joe needs to work a little harder to keep me interested. My mind does tend to wander if the subject matter doesn't hold my interest."

"I think I had your *mind* just where I wanted it." Joe grumbles, and my dad chuckles again. How can he find almost catching his daughter in a compromising position so amusing?

"I don't know what you two were doing," my mother points between Joe and myself, "and I have even less idea of what you're up to Frank, but right now, I don't care. I need you," she looks to my dad, "to behave yourself for just a little bit longer."

"Yes ma'am, I can do that." My dad salutes his wife and I can't help laughing. I'm not sure what made these two get married, but my dad has always been the more light-hearted of the two of them. My mother takes life way too seriously most days.

"I'm sorry Anna, but I'm going to have to excuse myself and getting going. I've got a prior engagement that I can't miss." Joe says. He has somewhere else to be? Does he have a date?

"Oh, well thank you for coming Joseph." My mother says, because she never and I mean never, uses a shortened version of someone's name unless that's all she knows them as. "It was lovely to see you again. Don't be a stranger OK? The invitation to afternoon tea is a standing offer."

"Absolutely Joe, you're always welcome here." My dad grins and looks at me, "Isn't he Katy?"

I smile back, even though I feel like swatting my dad on the arm for his bluntness. I don't want my mother to pick up any kind of insinuations that something could be happening between myself and Joe. She'll like it too much and start pushing for it because in her eyes he's a perfect fit for our family, in every way. "Of course dad, this is your house after all, you can invite anyone you want."

"Well of course we can Kathryn." My mother says, looking at me like I've grown an extra head. Who knows, after what happened in the study, I just might have, because I can't think about anything except getting Joseph French alone again so that we can finish what we started.

"Are you OK Katy?" my dad asks.

I blink up at him and blush. I can't believe my dad just caught me in the middle of a sex fantasy about Joe! "Yeah, dad I'm fine. Why?" I ask too late.

"You look like you were thinking about something that was quite desirable." He looks slightly behind me, to Joe and says, "Have a great night Joseph. Be good to your *prior engagement* and make sure to treat them right. Understand?" he says. How mortifying.

Joe shakes my dad's offered hand and says, "Always sir. Never doubt it." My dad sends a nod Joe's way.

"Come on Anna let the kids go, Katy's been here long enough today. I'm sure she has other things she needs to get done before her working week begins too."

"Yes. Of course. You should go too Kathryn, I know you have other things you wish you were doing."

"That's not quite true mother, but yes, I do have things I need to get sorted." I think I hear my dad mutter, '*I bet you do*', but I'm not certain.

I lean in and give my mother a kiss on the cheek, then reach over and give my dad one too. He draws me into a tight hug and whispers in my ear, "He's a good guy under all the gruffness, but do your old man a favour and be careful still, OK?"

"I know and I promise Dad. I love you." I whisper in his ear.

Joe shakes my dad's hand again and lightly kisses my mother on the cheek, thanking her once again for having him. Which pleases my mother no end.

"I should go and find Olivia and Thomas so that I can say goodbye to them too." I say and start to move off.

"It's OK, darling, we'll tell them you left, and you'll catch up with them during the week. You don't want to go walking through the house to find them. You could be here for a while." My dad says, pushing me towards the front door. Anyone would think he's happy to get rid of me today.

"Can I walk you to your car Kathryn?" Joe asks me and I see my mother actually swoon over him. Pretty sure I heard her sigh with happiness too, not just because he's behaving like a gentleman, but he also used my full name in her presence. He just won my mother over with eight words. He'll never do anything wrong in her eyes now. Ever.

"That's such a kind offer Joseph," I smile at him and he smiles back at me. "But, I'm pretty sure I can find my own car in my parents driveway, thank you." My mother gasps in horror, and my dad lets out a loud laugh.

"You're right, how stupid of me to assume you'd need assistance Kathryn. Perhaps it's me who needs the assistance to my car? It *has* been a very long time since I've visited your parent's house."

"In that case, allow *me* to walk *you* to your car Joseph." I say, and the men laugh. My mother is still standing there with her hand on her chest and her jaw is swinging in the breeze.

As Joe and I reach the front door, I hear my father say, "Close your mouth dear."

"But she just ..."

"Yes dear, be proud that we've got a strong woman for a daughter." My dad cuts off his wife before she can finish speaking, as I close the door behind us.

I let out a laugh as Joe and I walk down the steps to my parents driveway. When I head towards my car, Joe reaches for my arm and lightly holds on to my wrist. "Hang on, where are you going? I thought you were going to walk me to my car?"

I look back at him, see his pleading, puppy dog eyes and laugh. I shrug out of his hold and say, "Joseph French you don't need my help to get to your car. You don't need my help for *anything*."

"Well now, you and I both know that's not true honey." He smiles and takes a step closer to me, and my car.

"Honey? Really?" Is he for real? We went out on one date and he left before we could take it further, and he's calling me honey? "Walk yourself to your car Joe."

"Can you *please* walk me to my car Kathryn?" I'm about to say no, when I look up at see *both* of my parents watching us out of a front window. Damn it, if I don't walk him to his car, my mother will give me grief for months about it.

"*Fine Joseph*." I growl at him. "But understand, I'm doing it because my parents are watching, and I don't want to disappoint either of them today."

"I completely understand, *honey*." He replies with the most ridiculously beautiful smile. How can he irritate and attract me all at the same time?

He follows right behind me. He's so close in fact, that I smack into his chest when I turn around to speak to him. Instinct brings my hands up to rest on his chest, and seconds later, while I'm feeling his pecs, I wish they hadn't moved of their own accord, because I can feel his heart beating, fast. My own heart isn't much slower.

"Katy." His voice is a whisper, a breathe over my cheeks. His hands are lightly gripping my upper arms, stopping me from falling after bumping into him. Luckily, his instincts didn't cause him to reach for my boobs. Just what a girl wants her parents to see while they think she's not watching.

Joe's lips are less than a breathe away from my own and he's looking deep into my eyes. Trying to read my mood, to see if I'd be receptive to him putting his lips on mine. "Joe." I say, my voice breathy, raspy. It sounds like nothing I've heard from myself before.

"Mmmmm." Is all he manages in reply, and I feel it vibrate against my lips.

"My parents are watching us through the front windows." I say, quietly. So quietly, I'm not even sure he heard me until he jumps back like touching me is burning him. "Guess now I know what our safe word is." I mumble.

Joe coughs and then laughs. Loudly. "What's so funny Joseph?" I ask, absolutely gobsmacked as to what could be so damned funny.

"What isn't funny? That you're parents are watching us like we're teenagers, or that you want a safe word?" he reaches for me again, but I step out of his reach. He won't be touching me while he thinks I'm so freaking hilarious. "We haven't even had sex yet, and you want a safe word?" his smile is spread across his face, his eyes glittering with amusement.

"Yeah, we haven't, and we're not likely to either." He goes to speak, but I hold up my hand and take another step away from him, just to make a point. "If I remember correctly Joseph, *you* walked away from *me* the other night."

"It was a stupid mistake Katy, and I'm sorry." He says, with a look of regret on his face.

"Thank you Joe." I say and walk past him to head towards my own car, but he reaches out to take hold of my arm again.

"Have dinner with me tonight Katy." He asks.

"I thought you had plans tonight Joe?" I ask without looking back at him. I don't want to know if he has plans with another woman.

"I was hoping they would be with you." He says quietly.

"Me?" I ask, turning around, surprised.

"Yes, you. Who else would I have made plans with?"

"Anyone else on the planet, I would have assumed, Joe. What kind of question is that?" Doesn't he know that after the other night, I wouldn't know what he's thinking? Men think women are hard to read, well I say they're just as stupid sometimes.

"Please Katy? Come to dinner with me?"

"When?"

"Now."

"Where?"

"Anywhere."

"Anywhere? Really Joe? Anywhere I want to go for dinner, you'll go?" I know a few things about adult Joe, and one of those is how much of a food snob the man is. I turn to look at him, because I want to see the look on his face when he makes his decision. Will he leave his eating decision making up to me, even for one meal?

"If you'll join me then yes, I'll eat anywhere tonight Kathryn Ellis," he says, but I see his Adams apple bob as he swallows nervously.

"You want to come to dinner, with me, anywhere I choose to go?"

Chapter Ten

JOE

I know everyone considers me a food snob and I guess to a degree, it's true. The fact is, I just know what I like and I'm OK paying for it. I can't say I like *cooking*, but I do like eating and I've never been shy of spending money on great food. Katy knows how I feel, and I know she's testing me right now, but if it means I get to spend some more time with her, then I will eat dinner wherever the hell she wants.

"Yes Katy. I will join you for dinner at any restaurant of your choice." I say, hoping that I can get that little detail passed her. Of course I don't.

"No-one said anything about a restaurant Joseph. You said you'd eat with me *anywhere* I wanted to, that includes a lot of places that aren't what *you'd* consider restaurants, my friend."

Friend? I don't want to be her *friend*, with benefits or not. That thought hits me with a jolt. I don't want to be her friend at all, I want to be her lover, her man, the one she comes to when she needs something, anything.

"Is that what we are Katy, friends?" I ask, and I hate how pathetic I sound, but I need to know.

"No. I don't know." She sighs deeply, "I have no freaking clue *what* we are Joe, but I'd like to think we're friends, at the very least." My heart plummets down to my feet. "Friends building up to something, but right now, I don't know what I'd call us Joe. Do you?"

I shake my head, not daring to speak. I don't think I can trust my voice or my mouth. If my voice works, I don't think I'll say the right thing. Nothing she's ready to hear yet anyway.

"Alright, I guess we agree then?" she says but doesn't sound too convinced either. I nod, so she continues. "You want to follow me, or would you rather drive?" I start to answer but she doesn't give me the chance. "Who am

I kidding? Follow me to my place? Then, I'll direct you to where we're going, OK?"

She doesn't wait for my answer, just walks to her car, gets in and pulls away. Leaving me to either get in my car and follow or not, the choice is mine.

I get in my car and meet her at her house. My decision was made before she walked away from me. I'll take any time I can get with her, even it means eating sub-standard food.

I sit in my idling car, waiting for her to lock up her car and get her stuff. Watching her walk, strut really, her way to my car knocks me for six. She's the sexiest woman I've ever met, and I can't believe I've got another chance with her. I make a promise to myself not to fuck it up.

When I look up she's standing at my door, waiting. For what I have no clue, so I lower my window and ask, "Are you going to get in the car tonight Katy, or are we walking somewhere?"

"You're parking your car in the garage and coming inside my house Joseph." She says.

"I am? I thought we were going out for dinner Katy?" I ask, completely confused.

"No, I asked if you would have dinner with me *anywhere,* Joseph, I never said where we might be going. Only that you were to follow me here." With that, she walks away from me and my car, towards the door in the garage that leads into the house. Stunning me for a second, then suddenly I'm moving. I park the car in the garage, hit the close button and I walk into the house closing the door behind me. I turn around and I'm a hairs breadth behind her, as she bends over to take her shoes off leaving them near the door.

I swear I'm back to the first night I was here, I'm pretty sure this view got me in trouble that night too.

It takes me a minute, but I realise Katy is talking to me. She's turned around to face me without me noticing, and she's talking to me. I spaced out staring at her rear end like a pimply faced teenager and she's been trying to have a conversation with me.

"Joe. Joseph." She says, her voice is full of exasperation. "Hello, is there anyone in there?" She asks, and the next thing I know, she's tapping her knuckles on my forehead.

"Cut it out," I say, while swatting her hand away. She doesn't bloody stop though, she keeps trying to get passed my hands to keep tapping at my forehead. "Stop it, NOW!" I growl out and manage to capture wrists.

Suddenly, the air is full of electricity. The vibe gone from mucking about to what I think most people would call, sexual tension. I look into Katy's eyes and watch them change from mischief, to shock and then they darken. With lust.

"Katy." I growl. There's no other word for it, I fucking growl out her name in a voice I don't recognise as my own. I'm so full of need. I want to kiss her. Taste her. Finish what we started a few days ago. No interruptions this time.

"Joe?" she asks, in an unsteady, husky, sexy as fuck voice.

"I'm going to kiss you now Katy, if you don't want me to, just say the word." I give her a second to decide, before I slam my lips down on to hers.

A sigh escapes Katy's lips and I take full advantage, slipping my tongue into her mouth and flicking it against hers. She moans and I push both of her wrists into my right hand and plunge my left into the hair at the base of her neck to pull her closer to me. I can't get enough of her now that I'm tasting her again. Her hips push against mine, her body trying to get as close to mine as it can. I walk her backwards, towards the wall behind her. It's not the same wall as the other night, so I'm hoping the results will be different.

I push her back hard up against the wall, her hands above her head, still trapped in my hand. I push my knee between hers and press up in between her thighs. I can feel the heat radiating from her pussy onto my leg.

"Joe." She says my name on a sigh and it's the sexiest thing I've ever heard. My cock jumps to attention at the sound, because he's taking it as an invitation. One where he gets to enter her body and relieve some tension. My cock doesn't rule my mind though, and I want to take it slow, well slower, and savour every little thing about this woman I have in my arms. Finally.

"What do you want Katy? What do you need honey?" I need her to speak to me. To tell me she needs this, needs me, as much as I need her. Damn do I need this woman, right now.

"Joe. Don't stop." She breaths out, against my lips. "For the love of all that is holy, don't fucking stop." Her eyes are closed, her head tossed back against the wall. Her breasts are stretching the fabric of her shirt and pushing the limits of the buttons holding it closed, her breathing deep and harsh.

"Katy, look at me." I say and wait for her to open her eyes. "I'm going to let go of your hands, but you're going to leave them where they are." She looks at me, her eyes searching mine to see if I mean it. I fucking mean it alright. She nods, slowly, agreeing to do what I ask. "Good girl."

Slowly, I let go of her wrists, making sure her hands don't move from the wall where I put them. I can see the muscles in her arms, pushing to make sure her hands don't move. I drag my knuckles down the side of her face, along her cheek, jawline, then her neck. Resting my thumb on her pulse, feeling it thrum with excitement. My other hand has moved up her side, over her ribs and along the side of her breast. I feel her breath shudder through her body, the anticipation of what I might do, where I might touch, causing electricity to spark off her.

I rest my hand on her collarbone for just a second, then pop open the first button of her blouse. Her breathing falters, stutters, then she sighs as I pop another button, and then another. I can see the lace at the top of her bra, and it causes my blood to pound in my ears. I can't hold back for another heartbeat. Quickly I pop the rest of the buttons, exposing the silky skin of her abdomen and breasts to me. I reach behind her, undoing the clasp of her bra, making it hang loosely over her luscious breasts. My mouth is salivating at the thought of wrapping my lips around her nipples.

I reach for her wrists and bring them down, but only long enough so that I can get her shirt and bra off her shoulders. I watch her clothing hit the floor, I'm close to her body, but I'm not touching her. She's on display for me against her wall, and she's never looked sexier than she does right now. My cock is straining against my pants, I run my hand over the front of my pants, trying to give myself a little bit of relief.

"Where's your phone Katy?" I ask. I see the confusion on her face and give her addled brain a few seconds to catch up.

"In my pocket." She says, thrusting a hip at me. I reach in there and pull out the phone. I turn it off then pull my phone out of my pocket and turn it off too, placing them both on the table next to the door.

"No distractions or interruptions tonight Katy Ellis." She smiles, a brilliant smile that lights up her face and lights up my heart. "Definitely no distractions tonight. You're mine tonight and I don't want your mind anywhere else."

I see her take a deep swallow. Do I make her nervous or is that anticipation.

"No distractions tonight Joe French, not one. Tonight I'm yours." My turn to take a deep breath and a gulping swallow. "And you're mine Joe, all mine."

Holy shit. Grateful that's she already removed her shoes, I pop the button on her pants, pull down the zip and strip her pants and underwear down and off her legs. Leaving her bare and standing in front of me.

"Please Joe, can I touch you? I need to feel you. I want to undress you too." How can any red-blooded man say no to that? I nod my permission, mainly because I don't think I can speak right now.

Katy takes half a step away from the wall, her fingers immediately working on the buttons of my shirt. The only noise in the whole house, is our heavy breathing. I swear she's taking longer to undo my shirt, than I did with hers. Either she's got an amazing amount of patience, or I'm lost in a fog of lust and time has slowed down.

When she finally pops the last button, she spreads the two edges apart and rests her hands on my chest. Skin on skin. She drags her nails over my pecs and up to my shoulders, causing little shudders in my body as she goes. Then my shirt is joining hers on the floor, and my pants are undone. She might have taken forever on my shirt, but my pants are on the floor before I know what's happening. I toe off my shoes, drag off my socks, and kick them along with my pants, to the side.

I'm left standing there in just my boxer briefs, the head of my cock just poking out the top of the band. I can see the glistening pre-cum slowly dribbling out. I don't know why she left me in my boxers, but I don't really care either.

I reach out for her and she steps in closer to me, wrapping her arms around my neck. I run my hands up and down her side, her hips and then I'm palming her butt. I hook one of her legs around my hip and keep kneading her butt cheeks.

I take her lips with mine again, tenderly this time, trying to show her just what this night means to me. Pulling her hips in close to mine, I push my hips into hers, letting her know what she's doing to me. She groans in my mouth and I squeeze her cheeks tightly. She takes advantage of my grip and makes a little jump, her hands holding tightly onto my head for leverage, and then she's in my arms. The heat of her pussy sitting right on top of my swollen cock.

"Bedroom. Now." She says between kisses and breaths.

"Which way, honey?" I ask. I never got further than the front door before. The entrance to her house not her pussy.

"Left. No. My. Left." She says.

"I can't see where I'm going." I say as she plants her lips on my neck and sucks. Holy shit, my knees buckle, my breathing falters and my cock throbs. Now I can see where I'm going, but I need my eyes to focus.

I knock into something and realise I've found the couch. Fuck the bedroom, the couch is going to have to do right now. I throw myself backwards down onto the cushions and wrap a hand in her hair, while the other pinches a nipple.

"Arghhhh. Joe I need you. I need you inside me. Now." Her teeth are grazing my neck and my shoulder, covering my entire body in goosebumps.

"I need a condom."

"Where?"

"In my jeans. Back pocket."

Katy is off my lap in a flash and I miss her warmth the minute she's gone, but I don't have to wait too long before she's back. She doesn't sit back in my lap though.

"Lift up." She demands and it takes my horny brain a few seconds to get her meaning, as she motions with her thumb for me to move. "Hips. UP, Joe."

I lift up my hips, giving her the help she needs to remove my boxers. Once they reach my knees, she lets them go, rips open the foil packet and rolls the condom onto my cock. Then, she's back in my lap, my face in her hands and my hands on her hips.

"I want you Joe, tell me you want me too." Her eyes pleading with mine to tell her what she needs to hear.

"I want you more than anything I've ever wanted in my life Kathryn Ellis." My eyes never leave hers and with those words barely spoken, she lowers her body onto my lap. My cock slowly sliding into the warmth of her pussy. She's so wet, so turned on, that there's no resistance at all. When she's full to the hilt, she sits there, just taking me all in and I wait. I wait for her to move, because I don't want to break the spell, even if it's killing me to hold back. I want, I *need* her to want this as much as I do.

She throws her head back, pushing her nipples into my face and starts moving slowly, giving herself pleasure. Giving *me* pleasure. I flick my tongue out, tasting her nipple and it's better than I could have imagined. My hands wrap around a breast each and knead them, while taking turns sucking them into my mouth, playing with them, nibbling, biting, licking. I can't get enough.

Katy's hands that were resting on my knees to balance her, are now scratching at my scalp. Pulling me in closer to her chest, smothering me in her breasts, but I don't care. Breathing verses boobs and boobs win every single time.

"Ohh Joe. Yes. Joe. Yes. Fuck. Ohhhh Joseph."

I don't like people, anyone calling me Joseph it feels patronising, but with Katy above me, riding my cock, giving us both pleasure, it sounds perfect.

"Katy. I'm. Close." I can feel the tingling starting in the base of my spine, the tightening in my balls and I know I won't be able to hold out for much longer. "Gonna need you to come baby."

"Ohhh Joe. Joe. Joe." She repeats my name like a chant. I feel her pussy tighten around me and then she screams out. "Joeeeeeeeeeeeee." And I'm right there with her.

"Oh fuck me, Katy." I empty my load into the condom.

I pull her lips down to mine and kiss her like there will never be another chance. When I bring us up for air, she rests her head on my shoulder and shudders.

"Oh my ... that was something else Joe." She mumbles into my shoulder.

"Yeah, I know." Is all I can say.

I'm not sure how long we sit there, catching our breaths, but eventually I start getting a little chilled, so I wrap her body around mine, and stand up. Vaguely remembering her telling me to go left to find her bedroom, I walk that way. When I reach the doorway, I look inside the room and find a big king size bed with a fluffy comforter and pillows on it. I pull back the covers and lay her down. When I move to stand up, Katy holds on tight.

"Don't go Joe. Please?" she asks, her eyes are closed, I don't think she can open them. "Stay with me. Stay the night, please?"

My heart swells, she wants me to stay, that has to mean something. Right?

"I just need to go to the bathroom for a minute baby, then I'll be right back, OK?"

"OK Joe." She says, sighing. I head to the bathroom, quickly take care of the condom, use the toilet and flush. When I get back to the bedroom, she's curled up on her side, looking like an angel. Looking for all the world, heavily asleep, I'm considering just leaving her to her sleep and leaving her a note. So, when she speaks, she scares the shit out of me, "Don't be a creeper and stand there watching me sleep Joseph, come get in this bed and spoon me like you've never spooned before."

How she knew I was standing there, I will never know, but I do what I'm told and pull back the covers to slide in behind her. Spooning her like I've never spooned before. One arm under her neck, reaching around to hold onto a boob, the other holding her hips and pulling her in close to my body. I can feel my body stirring with desire again at the closeness of our bodies.

"Sleep now Joe. Round two later." She sighs softly and then she's asleep. I lay for a while just enjoying the woman lying in my arms.

It's better than I ever imagined it could be.

Chapter Eleven

I've never felt so completely taken over by lust and then had that need so satisfied before. The need to have Joe inside me was overwhelming, but believe it or not, it wasn't part of my plan bringing him here tonight. I truly had planned on making him dinner.

Resting on Joe's chest, I can feel his heartbeat slowing down and it's steady beat is soothing. To my mind, and my soul. We lie there, naked on my couch together for I don't know how long, before I feel him stand up with me still wrapped around him. I shimmy to lower myself to the floor, "Stop moving, or we'll both be on the floor." Joe whispers in my ear. I hold on tight and let him carry me to the bedroom.

He lowers me to my bed and gently covers me up. I start to panic thinking he's going to leave me, I don't want him to go.

"Don't go Joe. Please?" I ask him without opening my eyes. I don't think I could open them if I wanted to. "Stay with me. Stay the night, please?"

"I just need to go to the bathroom for a minute baby, then I'll be right back, OK?"

I nod, and maybe hum my agreement, I'm not sure. I relax knowing that he doesn't plan on leaving me. I can hear him moving around in the bathroom and walk back into my room. When his footsteps stop, I say, "Don't be a creeper and stand there watching me sleep Joseph, come get in this bed and spoon me like you've never spooned before."

He pulls back the covers on his side, climbs in the bed and curls his body around mine. One arm slides in under my neck and holds on to a boob and the other one grips onto my hip and pulls me back into him. I can feel his cock stiffening behind me, but I can't do another round yet, and I tell him as much. He chuckles and tells me to go to sleep. I don't need to be told twice.

I wake up a few hours later needing to go to the toilet. As I become more aware of my surroundings, I feel trapped suddenly, then I realise that there's a man in my bed and he's got me wrapped up so tightly in his arms that I can't move. I *have* to move though, otherwise I'm going to make a mess in my bed and not of the good variety.

Gently I try to pull out of his arms, but when I move, he grips me tighter. I try to peel his arms off me, but his grip is like iron. I'm thinking about elbowing him in the stomach, since that's all I can reach, when he grumbles sleepily behind me, "I'm not letting you go Katy, you feel too good in my arms."

I don't know if he's awake, but his words make me melt inside. I don't want him to let go, but I *really* need to go pee now. "Joe." I say quietly, he doesn't respond. "Joseph." I say a louder and slap at his arm.

"Mmmm. Katy, if you want to hit me I'm all for it, but I need to be awake for kinky shit." I roll my eyes, I know he can't see me, but I do it anyway. Sighing, I push against his arms again.

"Come on Joe, I need to get up."

"Nope, it's too early to get up yet." He mumbles into my hair, making my skin on the back of my neck prickle.

"Jesus, Joe, I need to get up."

"You don't need to get up Katy, you don't start work before the suns up honey."

"You're right, I don't and it's only 3am, I'm telling you now though, if you don't let me up you're going to wish you had." My threat makes him laugh.

"Why? Are you going to hurt me Katy? You never know, maybe I'd enjoy that." I can feel the bastards smile spreading across the back of my neck.

"No, no pain for you yet Joe, but you might get wet."

"Ohhhh really? You wet for me again honey?"

"NO Joseph, I need to pee!" I'm yelling now and wiggling around trying to get up. My bladder is about burst and he's not loosening his grip at all.

"Ohhh kinky Katy. I didn't know you were into water sports Miss Ellis, but I'll try anything once." The last word comes out as an oomph, because I elbow him in the stomach. When he moves back to try to get out of my reach before I can land another elbow in him, I pull out of his arms and bolt for the bathroom.

I've never felt as wiped out after sex like I do after my night with Joe. Feeling relieved, I stand from the toilet and stretch my body out. It aches in all the right places that mean you had a great round of sex. I stroll back into my bedroom, expecting Joe to be sleeping soundly. I'm not even sure he was awake when I got up.

He's lying on his back, one arm behind his head, the other resting on his chest. The blankets are resting at his waist, showing off his hairy, muscular chest, which is rising and falling gently with every breath he takes. God, he's magnificent and I know exactly what those covers are hiding, and I can't wait to follow the happy trail to pleasure again. I won't wake him up though, that hardly seems fair. For all I know he doesn't get much sleep and I can't rob him of the sleep he's getting, I love my sleep.

"Don't stand there staring, get back into bed and bring yourself and your gorgeous body here."

I gasp. I thought he was asleep and him speaking scares the shit out of me. He hasn't moved a muscle, his eyes are still closed, the only things moving are his lips and they're now twitching with the beginnings of a smirk. Arsehole knows he scared me by speaking.

I crawl back into bed, get close to him and slap his chest, making him jump, but his eyes still don't open. "Thanks for the permission to get back into *my* bed Joseph."

"You're welcome." He chuckles, holding out his arm that was resting on his chest he says, "Now come here and let me go back to sleep, honey."

I sigh and wrap my body around his again. "Don't get used to this Joseph French." I mumble into his chest.

"To which bit Kathryn Ellis, sleeping with, cuddling or telling you what to do?"

"All of it Mr French. All. Of. It." I say in warning.

"I wouldn't dare Miss Ellis, I wouldn't dare." Then, I feel him relax and the steady beating of his heart lulls me back to sleep again.

When I wake again, the sun is streaming in through the window, because I didn't bother closing the curtains. Which is ridiculous, because I *always* close them, I hate the sun coming in at me, which is why they're blockout curtains. I stretch out and reach for my phone to check the time, only it's not on the bedside table like it normally is.

That's when I realise what I did last night and that my bed is empty this morning. I listen to see if I can hear the shower or any other movement in the house, but there's none. I can't believe he left me sleeping in bed without a goodbye. Joseph French is a lot of things, but I didn't think he was a jerk.

Yes, I know how much of a jerk he was to Kami, but this doesn't seem like him. Maybe he regrets last night, and this is his way of making a clean break. He got what he wanted and now he's gone. So be it. I'm a big girl, I can move on from this, it's not like I'm in love with the man or anything.

I sigh and get out of bed and head to the bathroom. I hop in the shower and turn it on hot, steaming up the entire room. Just the way I like it. Normally I'd have some music playing but my phone is out in the loungeroom and I couldn't be bothered going to get it. So I start to hum to myself which turns into me singing loudly like a lunatic. Oh well, who cares, it's not like there's anyone else in the house and the neighbours are too far away, they won't be able to hear me.

I'm belting out my own rendition of a PINK! song, when a deep voice cuts through my own, "That's a great set of lungs you've got there. I didn't realise you were holding a concert this morning. If I'd known, I wouldn't have left to go get us some breakfast."

I jump, covering up all the important parts, but almost landing on my naked butt in the process.

"Hell, Katy be careful in there, the floors slippery you know." He says, with real concern in his voice, not that I care too much, because it's his fault I almost took myself out in the shower.

"Are you for real Joseph?" I screech at him. "You walk in here, scare the crap out of me and then tell *me* to be careful. What the hell were *you* thinking?" I've managed to rinse off the last of the soap on my body, turn the shower off and step out to wrap a towel around myself. There's no way I'm having a morning after conversation with this man while I'm naked. Especially when he's fully clothed. "Forgive me for believing that I was *alone* in *my* own house."

'You were alone, but I just went out to get us some breakfast." He replies, like I should have just known that's what he was doing.

"Well, I didn't know that now did I? I was just having a peaceful shower, alone in my house, like I always do"

"You thought I'd left without a word didn't you?" he asks, sounding hurt.

"What was I supposed to think Joseph?" I ask, glaring at him. "I woke up and you were gone. No note, no hint of what you were doing, no idea what your plans were. Am I supposed to just guess at what you're doing?" I'm angry, so angry, but I'm not sure what exactly it is that I'm angry at. Is it that he left without telling me? I don't have a clue.

He walks cautiously towards me, like I'm a lion about to pounce on him and not in a good way either. "Katy, honey, I didn't want to wake you. You looked so peaceful sleeping, and I wanted to make breakfast for us, but let's face it honey, you've got nothing in the house to eat." He says with a hesitant smile.

"Well, I'm a single girl who likes to eat out or order in." I say, feeling defensive about his assessment of the state of my fridge.

"I'm not passing judgement honey, just stating a fact." He shrugs a shoulder. "I mean for a woman who loves her coffee so much, you don't even have decent coffee in the kitchen." He's right, I do love my coffee, but I don't have anything decent in the kitchen.

"I get my coffee on the way into work. They make it better than I ever could." I say, with less anger and more annoyance in my voice. I should be able to make my own decent coffee, I mean I know the difference between a good one and a bad one, but it's never been one of my talents.

"Which is why I went out and bought some, along with something to eat, seeing we missed dinner last night."

His mention of us missing dinner last night makes me blush as I remember *why* we miss it. We never did have that second round last night. While I've been remembering last night's efforts he's managed to get close enough to touch me.

He cradles my face in his hands, making me look straight into his eyes, he says, "Katy, I would never, and I mean never, ever leave you without telling you that I was leaving. I would wake you up with a kiss and tell you or leave you a note if I didn't want to wake you." He takes a breathe and continues. "Last night, Katy. Last night wasn't a one night stand for me, but even if it was, I wouldn't have just walked out. That's horrendous behaviour. Last night, was the beginning. I want more nights and mornings like this. Well you know, not with you angry with me but waking up next to you, with you in my arms."

I'm stuck for words, I'm never stuck for words.

"Well, you *were* gone Joe and there *wasn't* a note or a message, so in fact you *did* do it." I shrug out of his hold. I know I'm being a bitch, but he hurt me, then scared the living daylights out of me and now he's being sweet. Or he's explaining it to me like he thinks I'm an idiot. "I'm not an idiot Joe. I know what guys want and you got it, you don't need to be nice or sweet just because we've known each other forever. Feel free to make your escape."

Now I'm just being a nasty bitch. I guess I'm testing him, and protecting myself, trying to see if he's going to stick it out, soothe my feelings and feed me.

"I'm sorry Katy. I honestly thought I would be quick enough to get breakfast and be back before you woke up. You were dead asleep, and I thought I had time." With that, he walks out into the other room, while I go to my room and close the door.

I sit down on the edge of my bed, wiping away the few tears that run down my cheeks. Well, that's that. I guess I pushed him too far and let's face it, I was protecting my own heart. It would be very easy for me to fall deeply for Joe French. He's always been that easy for me, which is one of the reasons I kept my distance from him.

I reach over to the bedside table for my phone, when I remember it's not there, just as my fingers touch something there. It's my phone. Joe must have bought it in for me, he didn't even turn it on, giving me the courtesy of him not seeing anything on it.

Turning it on so that I can check the time, I realise I screwed up. It wasn't Joe that ruined this. This time, it was me. I screwed up.

Another tear runs down my face, but I swipe it away and take a few deep breaths. I did this and I can live with it. I have to get moving if I'm going to get to work on time. I open my underwear drawer and grab the first pair I find. Time to pull up my big girl knickers and move the hell on. I've got work to get to and a life to live. With some kick arse underwear on under my work clothes, I walk out to my kitchen to find my bag and everything I need for work.

What I also find in my kitchen is Joseph French, sitting at my table with breakfast set out on plates and waiting for me so we can eat. He waited for me.

Chapter Twelve

JOE

I realised my mistake as soon as she turned around to see me standing in her bathroom. The fear of someone else being in her space, turned to absolute anger. Anger that was directed firmly at me.

I honestly didn't think that she would wake up before I got back, and if she did, then she'd somehow know that I hadn't left her. Making last night a one night stand. Hell, I stayed, and held her all damned night, did she really think I was that kind of guy.

James has a bad reputation, not totally undeserved, but he's always been upfront with the women he sleeps with. Me, I've never been a one night stand kind of guy. Have I had them? Sure, but everyone knew what the score was, and I've never left a woman while she was sleeping. I've never even thought about sneaking out and making an easy escape. To know that Katy thinks I could do *that* to *her* of all people cuts me like a knife.

I let Katy walk away, escaping into her room to get herself together, but even then, I never thought to leave. I bought us breakfast and I want to enjoy it. With her. I guess other guys might have taken his share and left. Taken the hint that she didn't want him around, but I'm not most guys. I also don't want to leave with Katy thinking that I had walked out on her, in any way.

Instead, I move around her kitchen, searching for plates, bowls, mugs and everything else I needed to dish up our breakfast. Then I sit there, waiting for her to emerge. She has to eventually, it's Monday morning after all, so she has to leave for work eventually. I hope so anyway, I don't really know her work schedule. Yet.

I'm sitting at the table, reading through some emails on my phone. Breakfast is laid out in front of me. Luckily I didn't get anything that had to be eaten hot. Although the coffee probably isn't going to be at its best anymore.

"Good morning honey, are you hungry?" I ask, taking a few seconds to look up from my phone, when I hear her gasp. I heard her leave her room, and I was hoping like hell she'd walk out here and not right out the front door.

Katy stops mid step, her footing stutters for a second and then she rights herself. "What are you still doing here Joseph? I thought you'd left."

"Yeah, I get that, but I went out and bought us breakfast. I want to have breakfast with you, please Katy. I meant it as a nice gesture, something to let you know that I wasn't going anywhere. I see now how that backfired on me, but it doesn't make my intention wrong." I haven't moved, she hasn't moved. We're just looking at each other, not sure what our next moves are. "Please Katy. Indulge me, my ego is fragile, and I'll think you were just using me for great sex if you throw me out now." I go with humour, because I know she'll at least respond to that.

"Great sex! I don't think your ego is in any danger there Joe." She snorts and fights a smile. She's calling me Joe again and trying not to laugh, I think I'm on a roll.

"Awesome sex then?" I say, as a smirk spreads across my face. "You know I'm right."

"I never said any such thing Joe." She replies, folding her arms across her chest, pushing her breasts up in the process making my brain malfunction for a second.

"You didn't need to honey, I was there. Remember?" she picks up the tea towel that's close by and throws it at me. I don't even try to duck out of the way. "Come and have something to eat before you head out to work. I even bought you some decent coffee, although, I doubt it's still hot. Someone took too long performing a concert in the shower."

She sinks down in the chair opposite me at the table and drops her face into her hands, but not before I see the blush creep up her face. "How long were you standing there before you spoke?"

"Plenty long enough to know that PINK! has some competition on her hands if you ever decide to take on singing as your new profession." I say, trying not to laugh. To be honest, I loved listening to her sing, but I'm not sure she could make it on the world stage.

"Well, hasn't this been an embarrassing and revealing morning? Why can't I just be normal?" She mumbles into the croissant she's taken a bite out of.

"Normal is over-rated honey. I don't think there's any such thing, but I loved listening to you sing, and I'm quite partial to your normal."

"Yeah but *normal* isn't embarrassing, it's boring and normal damn it."

"Do you hear yourself? It's boring, predictable and horrible. I'd much rather know someone that is unique, fun and loving than what you describe as 'normal.'" I reach over and gently tug the hand that's covering her face away. "Don't hide from me, Katy, ever."

"You say that now, but this isn't even the worst I can do." She says, a scowl on her face.

"I'll have you at your worst, most embarrassing, as long as you never hide the real you from me, any day of the week."

"You're such a sweet talker Joseph French." She smiles at me and it's the most beautiful thing I've ever seen. I can only I hope that this isn't the last morning I get to see it.

"Just telling you how it is Kathryn Ellis." I say, then change the subject because now I'm feeling uncomfortable and slightly embarrassed. "So, what's on the work calendar for this week? Are you going to be busy, or can you squeeze me in for a lunch here and there. A dinner or two?" I ask, in a voice that I hope doesn't sound too desperate, but I want to see her again. As much as I possibly can, and I will fit in to her schedule to do it.

"Speaking of work, shouldn't you be at work by now?" she asks, a little too innocently. I get the feeling someone's been keeping tabs on me.

"Usually I am, yes. I messaged Jenny and said I had an important appointment to keep and to hold all my calls unless they were important. She's rescheduled any meetings I might have had this morning, but there wouldn't have been many. I hate having meetings before 10am unless I can help it."

"How is Jenny?" It's an innocent enough question, but I can see the other questions in her eyes.

"Jenny and her husband are doing great. They've got a daughter arriving in a couple of months, so I got her an assistant, so she didn't have to work so much."

"Well, isn't that sweet of you?" she says with a huge smile. Like she didn't know Jenny was pregnant with her first child or who her husband is. They both went to our high school, and they're just a couple of years younger than us.

"Well, yes and no. It serves two purposes. Jenny isn't run off her feet when she comes in to work every day and the assistant can take over for her while she's on maternity leave. Meaning I don't have to teach someone else how to do the job."

"You can be the hard-nosed businessman with others, but I know you're really just a marshmallow behind all that sexy gruffness." This woman knows me like no-one else does. Not even James would say that to my face, well not in the same way, anyway. If he finds anything about me sexy I might have to rethink our friendship.

"My gruffness isn't an act Miss Ellis. I am the surly businessman to perfection, but I'm really happy to know you find it sexy." I wink at her and take the last bite of my breakfast, chewing slowly. I knew the minute she realised what she'd said, but I wasn't going to let her get away with it. I'm carrying that little nugget around with me all day today while I'm being a gruff businessman.

"It's just a figure of speech. I find a lot of men sexy, not just you." Her cheeks flame red as a blush works up from her neck to her gorgeous face. I just sit there and smile back at her. "You know what I mean Joseph."

"I know exactly what you mean Kathryn and I will take that compliment and carry it with me while I work today. Thank you." I say as she huffs out a breathe at me, and I can't help but chuckle. "You know you're not too bad yourself. I've seen you in business mode and while I wouldn't call you 'sexy gruff', you're definitely sexy in business mode. Smiling when needed, tough when needed and everything in between. Almost makes me wish I'd snapped you up for myself. In the business sense."

"You haven't snapped me up personally yet either Mr French." She says, standing up from the table and starting to clean away the mess.

"Haven't I Miss Ellis? Well then, I guess I have some work to do then don't I? Luckily I have an amazing work ethic and attention to details. Hmmmm?" I say while cleaning up my share of the mess and then taking hers out of her hands as well. I bought it all in, the least I can do is take it all away. I put the rubbish in the bin and the dishes in the washer. "Anything else to go in here?" I look up at her and ask. She shakes her head.

"No, nothing. I'll leave it until tonight after I've had dinner and do a reasonably full load. Thanks for helping."

"Anytime Katy." I smile, but I don't touch her, not yet.

"OK, well unlike some, I can't reschedule my day so easily, so I have to get to work." She grabs her phone, checks that her bag has everything she needs in it and heads to the front door. I'm right behind her as I pocket my own phone, before she can open the door though, I reach out and gently spin her around to face me.

With one hand still holding on to her upper arm, I slide my other hand behind her neck, and spear my fingers into her hair. I see the realisation of what I'm about to do in her eyes and give her a few seconds to move away. When she doesn't, I lean down and gently lay my lips on hers. It's what I've wanted to do since I woke up but haven't had the chance. She gasps and I take the chance to slip my tongue into her mouth and play with hers. I step in closer to her, deepen the kiss slightly and hear her moan.

I step back, releasing her from my embrace and give us both some space to catch our breathe. I watch her chest heaving, breathing heavily, as her hand reaches up and touches her lips. Is she trying to rid herself of me or trying to make the memory last?

"Joe." She breathes out.

"I know, but if I don't move away now, we're both going to be late for work. Or end up not going at all and while I know I can get away with that, I know I shouldn't keep you from your job." I pull my keys out of my pocket and go to walk passed her to the garage door, but I can't resist one more taste of her before I leave her for the day. I brush my lips over hers again and moan myself. I open my eyes and look at her. "I have to leave before I'm no longer capable Katy. Can we have dinner again tonight, please?"

"We didn't have dinner last night Joe." She says with a smile.

"I know. Tonight I promise to feed you. My place? After work? Can you come by around 6.30pm?"

She nods her answer and then as if she suddenly finds her voice she says, "Yes. Yes Joe I'll come to your place at 6.30."

"You know where I am, right?" I haven't moved for years, I don't see the point.

"Yes." She smiles.

"Good. I'll see you tonight then?" I give her another light kiss and walk away before I'm tempted to drag her back to bed and make her mine. Again.

THE FRONT DESK RECEPTIONIST looks a little taken aback when I say good morning to her. Do I not say that every morning when I walk in when she's there? I'm pretty sure I do, because even though Katy says I'm a surly businessman, I'm never rude.

When I get to my office, Jenny looks up at me and says, "Good morning boss, I hope your morning meeting went well?"

"Good morning Jenny, my morning meeting went better than expected. How are you doing? Are you feeling OK?"

"Ahhh yes, I'm feeling great thanks Mr French. Thanks for asking." She says, almost hesitantly. I can't be that much of a grumpy bastard every day. Can I?

"Anything I need to look at right away Jenny, or can I get on with what's on the schedule from now?"

"We changed everything we could, so you should be good to go now with the new schedule I just emailed."

"Thanks Jenny."

"You're welcome sir." She smiles at me and find myself smiling back.

As I reach the door to I hear Nadine, the young girl training to replace Jenny while she's on leave whisper, "I think he got laid on the weekend Jen, what do you think?"

Then Jenny whispers back, "Shhhhh you can't talk about the boss like that." There's a pause and then Jenny whispers, "but I think you might be right." Then the ladies are giggling. I leave them to their gossip. I don't care what they think, the fact is I did get laid and it was best sex of my life.

I'm not going to broadcast it across town or the business, but I'm definitely a happy man.

Before I close my office door I say, "Nadine, can you bring me the report on the new client when you've stopped gossiping please?"

Both women have the decency to look embarrassed, but I can't help the chuckle I have when I turn around to walk to my desk. There's a knock on the open door before I even sit down in my chair. "Yes?" I look up to see Nadine standing in the doorway. "That was quick."

"Ohhh no sorry boss, I'll have that report for you in a second, I just wanted to check if you wanted a coffee first. Then I can bring them both in together."

"Yes, thanks. A coffee is exactly what I need right now."

She nods and moves away to get what I need. What I really need is to be wrapped around a naked Kathryn Ellis. I can't think about that otherwise I won't get any work done, so instead, I take the coffee and report and get down to work.

Chapter Thirteen

KATY

Joe's words and actions leave me standing at the doorway to my garage stunned. I shake my head and walk out the door, locking it behind me and getting into my car. I reverse out, following almost the exact path that Joe just went, only when I get out of the garage I hit the button on the remote to close the door. While I sit here waiting for the door to close, I come to grips with every damned emotion I felt this morning.

Loss. Tick. Anger. Tick. Happiness. Tick. Joy. Tick. Hunger. Tick. Lust. Ohhhh hell yes. I run through them all again on my drive in to work. This man is going to drive me insane.

I get into my office, take a seat at my desk and turn on my computer, just as my boss pops his head in the door. "Good morning Katy, how are you this morning? I hope I'm not interrupting you so early, but I have a meeting I'd like you to join in on, please."

I smile at him, "Now?"

"Yes, that is if you don't have anything you need to get done right away?" he asks.

"Nothing that can't wait for a half hour or so. Let me grab my notebook and a pen and I'll follow you in."

"Great. That's great." He says as I bundle up everything I'll need and follow him out my door and into a conference room. I'm not his secretary and generally, I don't take notes in meetings, but I feel like I need something to do this morning to keep my mind off Joe. Mr Wilks makes the necessary introductions and I take my seat at the table, setting out my notebook and pens. I pour myself a coffee from the jug in the middle of the table and then Mr Wilks starts the meeting. I don't have any more time to think about Joseph French and all the things I want to do to him tonight.

Not until lunch time anyway. Then my mind wanders to all the ways I'm going to make him pay for walking out on me this morning, then scaring the crap out of me as well.

I want to talk about it with someone but my go to person is Kami. I can't talk to Kami about Joe though, she'll never understand. I have a few friends here at work, but we never really get into the nitty gritty of men and our personal lives.

There's only one person I can talk to about this, but I'm not sure how I feel about asking her to listen.

Me: *Do you have time to have lunch today?*

Once I've sent the message I wait for a return one, but when it doesn't come right away, I put my phone on the desk and get back to work. I pull out the notes from this morning's meeting and start entering them into my computer, when my phone buzzes with an incoming text.

Olivia: *yeah sure where and when?*

Me: *the sushi bar near work, at 1pm?*

Olivia: *no worried, I'll meet you there.*

I sigh, not realising how relieved I am to have someone to talk to about, whatever it is, with Joe. My phone buzzes again with another message and I smile thinking Olivia is messaging me again, only my heart contracts when I see the name on the message. Kami Parker. She's asking me if we can catch up for lunch at the café near her bookshop. At least I don't have to lie to her, yet.

Katy: *sorry lovely, I'm having lunch with Liv.*

Kami: *of course you are ..where you going?*

Katy: *the sushi place near work*

Kami: *OK, I'll catch up with you girls next time, that stuff is gross*

I laugh, I know how much sushi makes her stomach churn, and no, that's *not* why I chose to go there to talk to my sister about Joe. I know that my sister *loves* sushi and she won't pass up an opportunity to eat some. Ever.

I guess the added bonus is, we're not likely to run into Kami in a sushi restaurant any time soon. So I guess that means that somewhere in the back of my mind, I'm meeting my sister there on purpose? Now I feel like the biggest bitch on the planet.

I get some more work done and my phone, thankfully stays quiet, until it's time to go meet Olivia. As I start to walk towards the front doors I hear my name called out, hoping it's not my boss wanting me to do something for him before I go to lunch, I stop and turn around. The smile I have on my face falters when I realise who it is calling my name.

"Katy Ellis, is that really you? Of course it is, I don't think you've changed a bit. Well, except grown up of course."

"Thank you James, I think." I look him up and down like I haven't noticed him around town in the years since we left high school. Of course I've noticed him, I've checked him out with my best friend, because she's had a crush on him for as long as I can remember. "You've done some pretty decent growing up yourself Mr Harvey."

He grins, and it's the devasting kind that makes women's underwear fly off their bodies, and yet, strangely enough, it does nothing for me. Can I see that he's handsome, and drop dead attractive? Hell yes I can, I'm not dead, but he certainly isn't getting any of my underwear off my body any time soon.

"Why thank ya ma'am." He says with what I assume is suppose sound like a Southern American drawl, a chuckle and a tip of his non-existent hat. He's such a dork I can't help but laugh at him. I can't really be laughing *at* him though when he's laughing at himself. He always did have an amazing sense of humour.

"Walk with me while we catch up? I have to meet my sister for lunch?" I ask him.

"Where are you headed to meet with little Miss Olivia?" he asks. I'm surprised he remembers my sister's name, it's not like we ever ran in the same circles.

"The sushi place just up the road." I nod in the right direction as we walk out onto the street.

"Sure, I'm walking that way to get to my truck, I would love to have the company of a beautiful woman while I do it." Oh yeah, this man is full of charm.

I shake my head at him, but I'm smiling while I do it. "So, how are you Harvey? What have you been up to the last, ohhh I dunno however many years?" I ask, even though I know he's made a go of his business, Harvey Carpentry, and done well.

"I have been keeping busy Miss Ellis, very busy indeed." He smiles, what I think is his winning smile, but I must be immune. I'm waiting for him to keep talking and when I don't respond, that's exactly what he keeps doing. "I started up my own carpentry business, which is doing well."

"Doing well? That's very modest, James." I say, smiling.

His grin widens and turns into a smirk, "So you *do* know what I've been up to Katy? Have you been stalking me?"

"Sprung, that's exactly what I've been doing. Walking around town keeping tabs on you and your business Harvey."

"I knew it! You've always had a thing for me haven't you Katy Ellis?" he smiles, and I can see the mischief in his eyes.

I bat my lashes and swoon at the man in front of me. "Oh James finally my secret is out. I don't have to live the lie anymore." My hand lands on his bicep, and what a bicep it is. I can't help but give it a light squeeze but then I pull my hand away, only to swat him. "You idiot. You're not my type James and I have a suspicion I'm not yours either." In fact, I know I'm right but I'm not going to tell him who I think his type is.

"You're right there Katy, but that doesn't mean we can't have some fun as friends, right?"

"You're right." I stretch up on my toes and place a kiss on his cheek. "Thanks for walking with me James, enjoy the rest of your day."

James leans down and kisses me on the cheek, "Enjoy your lunch Katy. Tell Miss Olivia it's unladylike to stand there with her mouth open, Anna would be horrified." He laughs and walks away to his truck.

I shake my head and turn around to walk into the restaurant only to find my sister standing there, with her jaw almost hitting the floor. I wasn't expecting her to be here on time, but I certainly wasn't expecting her to be early.

"Close your mouth Liv you'll start collecting flies soon." I laugh and walk passed her to grab us a table.

"Was that James freaking Harvey you were kissing out on the footpath? For everyone to see?" she asks me, in disbelief.

"Hello Liv, I'm happy to see you and so glad you could join me for lunch at such short notice." I say, my voice full of sarcasm.

"Yes, yes. Hello Kat, I'm more than happy to be here." She waves her hand in front of her like she's shooing away a fly. "Was that James freaking Harvey kissing you out there?"

"Yes that was James Harvey I was *talking* to out there. He was near my office and saw me when I was walking out to meet you. His truck was parked up here, so we walked together. The kiss on the cheek was a friendly kiss, and nothing more." Damn, it's not like I stuck my tongue down his throat in public or anything. Trust my little sister to have witnessed a talk with a handsome man and then take it all out of proportion.

"James freaking Harvey *kissed you in public.*" Liv squeals in such a horrible noise, I'm almost expecting our mother to jump out from nowhere to admonish her.

"Well that was a horrible noise Liv. Can you stop it, please? There's nothing going on with James and myself, there never has been and there never will be."

"Are you sure about that sis, cause you two looked pretty cosy. Touching, laughing and kissing each other." She gives me a sly smile, like she thinks she's on to something.

"I'm very sure Liv. It was two old friends catching up in the few minutes it took to walk from my office to here. Now can we order some lunch please?" I look down to my menu to direct our attention that way and it works. My sister is easily lead, it's both her best and worst trait.

"Whatever you reckon sis." She smiles at me like she knows a secret.

"It's the truth Liv, nothing ever has or ever will happen between James Harvey and me." I assure her. "He's not my type. I like them a little grumpier and more clean cut."

"Like Joe French hey?" she says, laughing at her own joke. When I don't answer her, she stops laughing at looks at me. "Really? Joe?"

"Really." I say. I don't know what else to say to her. It's the truth and I need to talk to *someone* about it.

"You and Joe?" she asks, and I nod. "Has something already happened or are you saying you've got a thing for him?"

I can't speak. I can't answer her. My voice just won't work, and I don't even know what I'd say to her if it *was* working.

"Oh my god! It happened at mum and dads didn't it? We were all looking for you and no one knew where you'd disappeared to and then dad found you with Joe." Liv stops talking for a second and then I see the realisation hit her. "Ohhh shit, DAD found you and Joe together didn't he? That explains that look on his face, all that amusement and mother's complete confusion." She just sits there, staring at me, the coffee she ordered before I got here, forgotten.

We're both silent and unmoving until the waitress brings over our lunch, then we're startled into conversation again.

"So, tell me what happened Katy? I didn't even know you liked Joe in anyway, never lone in a sexual kind of way."

She says sexual like it's a dirty word, and I guess to a degree it is, but in relation to Joe, it's not. Well OK, it *is* dirty but, I won't be sharing *that* with my *little* sister.

"Well then, I guess you don't know your big sister too well then do you Olivia, cause I've always liked Joe French, it's just complicated." I've managed to skip right over her question about what happened at mum and dads, go me.

"You're right, it is complicated. How did Kami take the news?" she asks. When I give her a puzzled looks she's says, "When you told her you were dating her enemy?"

I can't look her in the eyes when I admit, "I haven't told her Liv. I don't know how to."

"At least that explains why I was invited out for lunch then."

"That's not the only reason Liv, I wanted to catch up."

"Yeah, I'm sure you did Kat, but you know what? Never mind, we're here now let's enjoy some sushi and catch up."

That's what we do for the next forty minutes, until my phone beeps, letting me know it's time to go back to work.

"Thanks for meeting me for lunch Liv, I enjoyed it." I say, and I really mean it. I feel bad that we don't do it more often and vow to make more of an effort to do so.

"I enjoyed it too Kat. Maybe we could do it more often? Specially if we come to sushi, I know you can't get Kami to go with you to eat it." Then suddenly it's like a light goes off in her head and she realises why we came to sushi and not a café. No chance in running into Miss Parker here.

"You're the only one I know that I can get to eat sushi, even the other girls in the office turn their noses up at it. I felt like sushi and talking to my little sis. No ulterior motives, I promise."

"Ohhhhh OK, but let's be honest sis, you needed to talk about Joe and don't think for a second I'm letting you off from telling me what happened at the house on Sunday either. I can hear it from you, or I can hear it from dad. Your choice." She smiles and then we say our goodbyes. We both have to get back to work, but not before making a promise to have dinner with her and Thomas one night soon. She even invited Joe as well and gets a dig in by saying, that's if we can find our way out of the bedroom.

I laugh and hug my sister goodbye.

I sit down at my desk, start up the computer and grab a coffee. Yes another coffee, it keeps me going during the day. I start reading my emails when a message vibrates my phone, I look down and see Joe's name.

Joe: *Can I bring dinner to you tonight?*

Me: *There's an offer a girl can't resist*

Joe: *That was certainly the aim ... you do mean me* coming *over, right?*

Me: *Yes Joseph* that *was the offer a girl couldn't resist, ever. I thought I was coming to your house though?*

Joe: *I changed my mind. See you at 6.30?*

Me: *If I'm not out of here and home by then, I think I'll just die here.*

Joe: *Don't do that honey, I'd miss you*

Me: *See you at 6.30 Joe*

Joe: *See you then Kathryn*

A shudder makes its way through my body. What is it about him using my full name that makes my whole body want to wrap itself around his? Anyone else calls me anything other than Katy and I get pissed off, but not Joe. No, he calls me Kathryn and I get all hot and bothered.

"Miss Ellis, how are those reports coming along today? Will I get them in my inbox today?" my boss asks as he walks passed my desk.

"They're coming along perfectly Mr Wilks, you'll have them before I leave today." I say with a smile.

"Perfect. Thank you Miss Ellis." He smiles and continues on his way.

I take one last look at my phone to see if Joe sent me another message, and when I see he hasn't, I put my phone away and get to work. I get the reports done for Mr Wilks and leave the office just after 5.

Plenty of time to get home, clean up, have a shower and be ready for Joe.

Chapter Fourteen

I've become one of those guys that James and I always laugh at. I want to see Katy again, even though I just saw her last night and this morning. I want to spend as much time with her that she'll let me, and I don't care who knows it to be honest. Not that I'm able to tell anyone yet but give me enough time and we'll be shouting it from the rooftops.

With my dinner plans settled and knowing I get to see Katy again tonight, I settle back into getting some work done.

The intercom buzzes, I don't even know how much later and Jenny's voice crackles through the speaker. "Mr French, Mr Harvey is here to see you."

"Send him in please Jenny."

James strolls in and closes the door behind him, then takes a seat in a chair across from me at my desk.

"Do you really make Jenny call you Mr French? Jesus Joe, we all know each other from high school man." He shakes his head in disgust.

"I don't make Jenny do anything, except her job. I've asked her several times to stop calling me Mr French, but she says I'm running a business and it's more professional for her to call me Mr French." I roll my eyes at him. "The only times she calls me Joe is if we're out of the office and not doing anything regarding work. It drives me fucking insane."

"Your employee showing you respect, yeah that's annoying as fuck man." He laughs loudly, too damned loudly.

"Shut up idiot." I growl at him. I was in a good mood before he got here. "What did you want anyway?" I ask, hoping that I can get him out of my office, so I can get away from here a little earlier than usual.

"I was in the neighbourhood and was wondering if you wanted to come to the bar for dinner with me?"

"Why were you in my neighbourhood? Shouldn't you be on the other side of town finishing a job?" I ask, avoiding answering his question for as long as I can so that I can think of an answer. I know the bastard won't take a simple no, so I'm going to have to come up with something he *will* accept.

"I didn't know you cared so much Joe. Keeping tabs on me, knowing where I'm supposed to be. It's a little bit creepy when you think about it you know. I mean I know we're friends and all, almost brothers, but that's a little too much Joseph." He's got a shit eating grin on his face and if we weren't in my office, I'd be smacking it right off him.

"Seeing that you're keeping tabs on me, I guess you already know who I ran into before I came here then?" he asks.

"Do I look like I want to play guessing games with you today James?" I ask, irritated.

"Come on, I want to see if you can guess." James says, his enthusiasm is annoying as fuck. "Fine you grumpy bastard, I'll tell you. You know you suck the fun out of shit some days." he sighs dramatically.

"I'm not interested." I say over him, because I'm not. Well, not until I hear Katy's name anyway.

"Katy Ellis. Can you believe it? Of all the people in town to run into. I haven't seen her since, well I've seen her since we all left school, but not for ages." I let him keep talking, I'm too stunned, almost nervous to answer. "Damn but she's grown into a beautiful woman. She's still a spitfire too, I do love having a sparring of words with her, always have. Didn't you have a thing for her back in school?" he asks, finally taking a breath.

"Yeah. I've always liked Kathryn, she's always been pretty feisty that's for sure." Not a lie, but not the truth either. "What's she up to these days?" I ask in what I hope is an indifferent voice. I can't help wondering if she mentioned that she's seen me at all.

"Working hard like the rest of us as far as I know. She was meeting Olivia, her sister for lunch." He says. "You know, I didn't notice a ring on her finger, maybe you should look her up. You know, take a chance and ask her out?" He suggests. If only he knew.

I pick up my phone as if to dial her right now. "Uhuh, sure James I'll get right on to that. Did you happen to get her number for me?" I ask sarcastically, as I look up from my phone.

"No, I didn't, sorry man." He looks at me apologetically. "I was just giving you shit man, I didn't think you'd take me seriously." I know he was just giving me shit but he still annoyed me. "So, about dinner, what do you say? Get out of here early and join me?"

"Sorry James, I can't." I look down at my work, trying to show him I'm busy. "I've got loads of work to get done today."

"You know you have to eat, right? Man cannot survive on air and coffee alone." I nod, agreeing with him. "I already checked with Jenny and she said you already planned on leaving on time tonight. So what's really going on Joseph?"

Of course Jenny told him what my plans were. She doesn't understand that he can't know who I'm getting out of here to see. I didn't tell Jenny either so that she couldn't spill the beans to anyone by accident. Now, I'm glad that I didn't tell her.

"I have a date, OK James?" I say, looking him in the eyes and hoping that he sees the truth there and shuts the hell up.

"A date? Why didn't you just say so? Who's the lucky girl?" That's one question I can't look him in the eyes to answer, so I look back down at my work, pretending to see numbers that are actually just a blur.

"No one you know James." Trying not to sound as annoyed as I feel.

"No one I know, or no one you want to tell me about?" He's suddenly looking at me all humour gone from his face and curiosity replacing it. "If you're ashamed about being with her, you probably shouldn't be going out with her Joe."

"Fuck you James." I throw my pen at him, but he ducks it pretty easily. "I'm not ashamed of being seen with her, I just want to see where it goes before I go shooting my mouth off." Normally we tell each other about who we're going out with and how serious it is, but I can't this time and he knows something's changed.

"OK then. I guess I'll go grab some dinner by myself then and see if I can't get myself a date." He says with an easy smile. I got out of that a lot easier than I was expecting to.

"We can catch up tomorrow or later in the week if you want?" I suggest, trying to keep the peace. I'd rather be wrapped up in Katy every night, but if it keeps James happy and off our backs, then I'm happy to do it.

"Yeah sure. Let me know when you're free Joe, and I'll see if I can fit you in to my busy schedule." I look at him to check how serious he is, only to see a stupid grin on his face.

"I'll let you know when my schedule can fit you in, James." There's a minute of silence and then we're both laughing. Through our laughter I hear the crackle of the intercom Jenny insists on using, then her voice comes out of the speaker, "Ahhh Mr French, is everything OK in there?" Her question makes us laugh harder and before long, the both of us are struggling to catch our breath. Just as we start to calm down, my office door opens and Jenny walks in looking confused.

"Are you two OK?" she asks.

"Yes Jenny, we're fine. We were just laughing." I say with a chuckle.

"I know you don't hear the grumpy bastard laugh very often in the office Jenny, but surely it's not too foreign a sound around here?" James, being the smart arse he is, asks her.

"Well, no Mr Harvey ..." she starts.

"James." He says.

"I'm sorry?" Jenny replies.

"Call me James, Jenny. I'm not your boss, I don't work here, and we've known each other for years. It makes me uncomfortable when you call me Mr Harvey, Jenny. That's my father and I'd really rather not be reminded of him on any given day. I'm sure you can understand that?" James says, and the fun just got sucked out of the room.

"I'm sorry James, I didn't mean anything by it, honestly. It's just that, because I've known Mr French, Joe, for so long, I feel like I need to keep some professionalism while we're at work. I don't want to seem too familiar with him. That would make *me* feel awkward, but I understand why you would feel awkward when I call you Mr Harvey. Not just because of your father but because of our past, but you know, *James,* that being said, it's not like we were ever friends at school. I'm a few years younger than you and we didn't have any friends in common."

"You're right but we all knew each other Jenny, it's only a couple of years difference after all." James replies. "Either way, I would still rather you stuck to calling me James. Grumpy might like to make you toe the line, but I'm happy to do without all the formality, if you don't mind?"

"Well, I can do that, but keep in mind, you are still a client for Mr French, and I will treat you as such."

"I'm his friend first and foremost Jenny but thank you."

"Are you two done now? Can we *all* get back to business please?" I ask in frustration. I have work to get finished so that I can get out of and go see Katy.

"Sorry, Joseph, I forgot you had a reason to get out of here earlier than usual." James says with a glint in his eyes. He said it to see if Jenny knows anything about my plans.

"Yes, that's right Mr French, you have that dinner meeting this evening and if you plan on getting to it, then we should leave you alone." Jenny looks at me with a smile on her face, she knows she's just helped me out.

Can I say, that I'm going to miss Jenny while she's on maternity leave? She never skips a beat and she's always got my back. I see the light dim slightly in my best friends eyes and have to hold in my chuckle. I know he was hoping that either Jenny didn't know about my date or that she would spill some, if not all, of the details. Little does he know she has perfected the art of saying not much at all even when she says plenty. She has more tact and poise than anyone I have ever met.

Apparently my admiration for the woman is written all over my face, and because my best friend knows me so well, he just has to take a chance to give me grief.

"You know she's married, right Joe? She's having the man's baby, you need to keep your hands off her."

"Get out of here James, some of us have work to do." I say, back to being the brusque bastard everyone is used to.

"I think you would know Mr French better than that Mr Harvey, honestly." Jenny admonishes James and I smile behind her back and flip him the bird. It's like being back in high school, only Jenny's the teacher telling us off.

"Great, now I'm back to Mr Harvey." James grumbles and this time I do laugh quietly, but Jenny's walking him out the door of my office and I'm not sure she heard me.

"Well, you of all people should know that he wouldn't do such a thing. Not to mention, you're the one that doesn't want to be associated with a certain reputation that you can't help. I would think you'd know better." She scolds. She's gonna make an awesome mother, without a doubt.

"You're right. I'm sorry Jenny." She gives him a stern look and he looks back at me through the open office door. "Sorry Joe. I know you'd never do that. Have fun tonight, we'll catch up soon."

I nod and wave at him because I don't think I could speak if I tried. Seeing James Harvey look so contrite as an adult, is fucking hilarious.

At least it is until Jenny sends that look my way as well. "Don't you laugh, get back to work so that we can *all* get out of here earlier tonight. I'm tired."

"Bye Harvey." I give my friend a nod and a quick wave.

"See ya French." I hear as I sit back down at my desk and hear the front door close behind him.

"What is it about men that makes them think they have to call each other by their last names?" Jenny mumbles and I'm pretty sure she doesn't want an answer, so I bury myself in work instead.

I bury myself so deeply in my work that I almost jump out of my skin when Nadine speaks to me and I realise she's standing in front of my desk, not in the doorway like usual.

"Mr French." She coughs and then repeats, "Mr French. It's time to close up for the day. Did you need me to do anything else for you before I leave?"

"Oh shit. What's the time Nadine?"

It's just after 5pm Mr French." She says, looking at me with concern. "Are you OK? Is there anything I can do for you?"

"No. I just didn't realise the time. You can go home now Nadine. I can close up, I'm heading out now as well anyway."

"OK, well if you're sure. Goodnight Mr French." I return Nadine's smile as I grab my crap so I can get out of here too. I want to go home and change out of my suit before I head over to Katy's.

I move fast when I get home. I have a quick shower, change into a pair of jeans and clean shirt. Then I grab my keys and wallet and leave again. I don't see more of my house than my room, bathroom and entrance, before I'm back out the front door and in my car again.

I go passed Katy's favourite sushi place and grab some dinner. Then I head over to her house. I know I'm going to be a bit early, but I can't sit around waiting for the time to tick over.

I want to see Katy.

When she opens the door, I can tell she's recently had a shower herself. Her skin is pink and still a little damp. She looks edible. Lickable.

She's looking me up and down with heat flaring in her eyes. I'm glad to see it's not just me who is excited about meeting up tonight. Then she sees what I'm holding in my hand and throws her head back, laughing. I step into the house and close the door before saying, "What's so funny Miss Ellis? Do I amuse you?"

I'm trying to look annoyed, pissed even, but I can't help laughing at the complete joy on her face.

I dump the bag holding our dinner on the kitchen bench. I didn't even realise we'd managed to walk so far into the house. Then I cage her in between my arms leaning on the bench on either side of her hips.

Katy stops laughing and looks at me. There's so much heat and desire in her eyes, that I can't be bothered trying to find out what the hell was so funny. I drop my head down and plant my lips on hers instead, causing both of us to moan. Loudly.

I stop kissing Katy, my lips resting on hers, I say, "Hi. I've been thinking about kissing you all fucking day Katy. It was a long day at work honey."

"You saw me less than 12 hours ago Joe, it can't have been that stressful."

I can feel her lips curl into smile against mine, and I open my eyes to look in hers. To see if she's teasing me or not.

"I missed you today too Joe." She touches her lips lightly to mine and I have to use every inch of self-control in me to leave it at that.

"Then what's so funny Katy?" I ask, taking a step away from her. We need to eat something, tonight she's going to need sustenance for what I've got planned.

"Umm. I had lunch with Olivia today."

"OK. How is she?" I ask, still confused.

"Yeah, she's really good. She really enjoyed her sushi today." She smiles at me.

"Well, that's good. I suppose." I say. Then it hits me. "Now I'm getting ready to dish you up sushi for dinner. After you had sushi for lunch with your sister."

"Yup." She says and wraps her arms around my waist from behind me. "Lucky I love sushi, hmmmm?"

"I'm an idiot. I should have checked before I grabbed something to eat. I just know you love sushi and you don't get it often because, well you don't." I grab her hands and loosen them so that I can turn to face her. "I'm sorry, I can order something else."

"Don't you dare Joseph French." She says, then pecks me on the cheek. "I'll get some plates, you can start unpacking everything."

Chapter Fifteen

KATY

I know Joe feels bad because I've already had sushi today, but I can't ignore the happy feeling inside of me. It's proof that he listens to me when we have those small conversations about everything and nothing. It also means he's taken note of what I said my favourite food was and *then,* made the effort to bring it over for dinner. Even though it might not have been something he necessarily wanted to eat, he knew that I would enjoy it.

Now, if that doesn't bring out all the warm and fuzzies in a girl I don't know what the hell will.

Joe comes across to most people, myself included most days, as this grumpy, gruff, arrogant kind of guy, but underneath it all, he's the most thoughtful man around. I can't help but wonder why some other woman hasn't managed to snap him up already. I shake the thought of out of my head. I know there have been women before me, but their loss, is my damned gain and I won't let them have any space in my head.

I turn around to face Joe at the kitchen bench and place plates down on the bench in front of him so he can divide up the food. I stand there watching him, and I know I'm grinning like a goofball, but I can't help it. He's made me stupid happy tonight.

"Are you sure you're OK with eating sushi again today Katy?" he asks, his frown wrinkling the skin between his eyebrows. He looks so adorable but if I know anything about Joseph French, he doesn't want to be called, *adorable.*

"Yes Joe. I'm more than happy to be eating sushi for the second time today." I stand up on my tip toes and reach over to kiss him lightly on the cheek. "Thank you for bringing dinner over tonight and thank you for bringing my favourite thing to eat."

He looks at me with an innocent look and says, "You mean me? Well, I had to come over with the food Katy, I told you I was bringing it."

It takes me half a second to get his meaning, and I slap his arm and laugh. "Well, if you play your cards right you never know, I might just be eating you later."

I grab my plate full of sushi and saunter, yeah I swing my hips like I mean it, over to the couch and then wiggle my butt a little before I sit on it.

"Shit. You're killing me woman." Joe mumbles behind me, still standing at the bench, looking for all the world like he's forgotten all about his dinner. Then he coughs, picks up his plate and joins me on the couch.

"I'm sorry, did you say something Joe?" I ask, sweetly.

"Nope not a damn thing honey. Not one thing." He can't look at me though and I take a quick glance down at his lap and realise he's feeling a bit uncomfortable and stifle a laugh. "So, what are we watching tonight?" He asks.

"Well, I was thinking," I wait as he takes a bite and starts eating, then I finish my thought. "That perhaps we could watch some porn tonight. What do you think?"

He chokes on his mouthful of food, stands up and heads towards the kitchen. Coughing and spluttering away for a few minutes. He looks up to find me grinning from ear to ear. "Are you OK Joe?"

"Are you *trying* to kill me Kathryn? Honestly?" he coughs again and has a drink of water, before continuing. "Do I feel like watching porn with you? Are you for real?"

"Well, yeah I am." I say with what I hope is a serious face.

"And you decided to ask me while we were eating? When I had a mouthful ... don't speak Kathryn ... of food."

"Would you watch porn with me though Joe?"

"One day? Hell yes, but not right now, no. Not tonight and most certainly not when we're fucking eating."

"OK."

"OK." He walks back over to the couch and sits down next to me, not looking directly at me. "OK. That's all you're going to say after that? OK."

"Yeah. I just wanted to make sure you would be OK with it. One day." Without another word, I turn on the TV and start scanning to see what movies are on tonight. Joe hasn't moved. He hasn't grabbed his plate, or a drink and he's barely even watching what I'm doing. Maybe I've shocked him, pissed him off? "Are you OK Joe?" I ask without looking at him.

He clears his throat before answering. "Yes Kathryn. I'm fine. You just surprised me, that's all."

"Why? Because women aren't supposed to enjoy watching porn?"

"No, that's got nothing to do with anything. It was just, well it came out of nowhere and the question surprised me, that's all." He looks over at me and I can feel the desire radiating off him and it's making me hot. "If you ever want someone to watch porn with Katy, I'm your man. Without a fucking doubt."

"OK Joe. I'll keep that in mind." I look back at the TV and say, "So, how about we watch an action flick? Something where shit gets blown up every which way it can." I suggest, because if we watch anything that could be slightly hot, we'll never see the closing credits.

As it turns out, blowing shit up is pretty hot and we don't get to see the end of the movie anyway, because our clothes are on one minute, then gone the next and I'm straddling Joe's hips on the couch. My naked pussy hovering above his hard cock.

Joe's hands are twisted in my hair, his eyes are closed, and he pulls my forehead down to his so they're just touching. My hands are massaging his pecs, upper arms and shoulders. I can feel the tension in his muscles, and I want to relieve that for him.

"What are you doing to me Katy?" he asks in a whisper.

"I'm about to fuck you Joe." I reply, my voice husky with desire.

"That's not what I mean Katy. Damn it, you're just ..."

"Shhhhhh." I place my fingers over his lips. I don't let him finish, I can't. I'm not ready to hear what he has to say and I'm not ready to say what he wants to hear back. "Just make love to me Joe."

He reaches down and somehow manages to find and grab his jeans, finding a condom in his pocket. I take the foil package from his fingers, and before he can drop his jeans back on the floor, I have the foil opened and the condom rolled on his cock. I raise myself up until I feel the head of his cock at my pussy lips and then slowly, so slowly it just about kills me, I lower myself down to sit in his lap, his cock deep inside my body. I take a few seconds to adjust and just enjoy the feeling of being filled up by the man underneath me. I've never felt anything like it before, the connection I have with this man is something you only read about in romance novels.

Joe's hands are tangled in my hair and he's pulled my head down so that I'm looking deep into his eyes. They're telling me everything I won't let him say out loud. I see his lips twitch, I can tell he wants to speak, so I kiss him instead. A kiss I hope tells him everything I'm feeling, without me actually speaking the words, while I slowly move my body up and down his hard cock. My lips attack his, unrelenting in their need and my tongue fights his. I ride his cock faster and faster, searching for my orgasm.

Joe tears his lips from mine and trails kisses from my jaw down my throat, to my collarbone, landing on my breasts. I groan as he draws a nipple into his mouth and sucks, then bites it, making my hips move even faster. Then his mouth swaps to the other nipple, he's untangled his hands from my hair, and one is pinching the nipple his mouth just played with, and his other hand reaches between us, finding my clit. My senses are in overload, and my movements become erratic and faster. Before I know it we're both calling out each other's names as we orgasm.

We collapse together on the couch and I pull the blanket I keep there, down over us. A feeling of bliss and contentment washes over me. I'm happier than I can remember being for a hell of a long time.

I start to drift off to sleep, when I feel myself being lifted up into the air and my body jumps, shocked by the sudden movement. "Shhhhh honey, I'm just taking us both to bed. It'll be much more comfortable in there." I relax in his arms and let him carry me to my room. He gently puts me on the bed, pulls the covers back and climbs in behind me. "Night honey. Sleep well."

"See you in the morning Joe." I say on sigh, catching myself *before* I tell him I love him. It's *way* too soon for that. I'll scare the poor man way.

I swear I hear him whisper, right behind my ear, "Please don't leave me Katy, I won't survive." but I tell myself I'm hearing things as I drift off.

WE SPEND THE NEXT FEW months in the routine of having dinner together whenever we can, which happens to be most nights. We rarely go out, usually we just end up at one or the others house. I don't know whether Joe does this on purpose, because he knows that I want to keep us on the quiet, but I can't bring myself to ask him.

We stay with each other those nights too, and we've both managed to have a collection of things at both houses to make life easier in the mornings. Shampoo's, soaps, deodorants, toothbrushes, all those kinds of things. Joe even bought me my own large coffee mug to use at his place.

When we can't see each other, we message all day and night long, until neither of us can keep our eyes open. There may or may not have even been a few phone sex sessions in there as well. What can I say, the man makes me hot when he speaks to me and one thing leads to another, and then we're both coming. I've gotten used to having him in my bed, in my space, in my life and when he's not there, I feel restless.

It's for that reason, not wanting to hide away anymore, that I message my best friend and set up a night out for dinner and drinks. I need to tell her what's been going on so that she can deal it. She *has* to deal with it, because I'm pretty sure I've fallen head over heels in love with Joseph French. She can't be annoyed with me for that, can she?

Me: *Dinner this week hun?*

Kami: *Absolutely. Whenever you're free, you know I can work my schedule to yours*

Me: *Friday night?*

Kami: *Sounds good to me hun. I'm free.*

With that sorted, I settle back down on my couch and watch some stupid TV.

Little did I know, that when I got to Kami's to see where she was, because she was late for dinner, which she never is, that I would find her tangled up in bed with Joe's best friend and her old crush from high school, James Harvey.

I cancelled our night out when James walked out of her bedroom in only a pair of jeans and looking like a very satisfied man. She tried to insist that she could be ready to still come out with me, but I refused her offer. I also took the opportunity to threaten James with a kick to the balls if he didn't look after our girl. As I left, I told them not to do anything I wouldn't do. I watched as Kami blushed and James chuckled.

While I'm over the moon happy for Kami, I'm a little bit shattered for myself. I'd planned on telling Kami about my relationship with Joe tonight, and now that's not going to happen. Am I a selfish bitch? You bet your arse I am. She gets to have her relationship with James out in the open and I'm still in the shadows. I know it's my own problem and I created it, but it's still frustrating.

When I make it back to my house, I'm so preoccupied with my thoughts, that I don't notice there's someone waiting for me on the front porch until he speaks, causing me to jump and squeak.

"You look like you're having some serious thoughts there Kathryn. I hope some of them include me and all the dirty things you want to do to me? Maybe even some of the dirty things you want me to do to you?"

"Holy shit Joe!" I say, my hand resting on my chest, over my rapidly beating heart. "You scared the shit out of me. How long have you been sitting there in the dark, waiting for me?"

"Long enough." He says, but he doesn't make a move to come closer to me or to join me inside.

"Did we have plans tonight?" I could have sworn he said he had a business meeting he had to go to tonight, or similar.

"No, we didn't have plans but mine finished early, and I wanted to see you, so I thought I'd come over."

"And when I wasn't here you decided to sit in a dark corner of my front porch and wait for me like a creeper?" I ask, with a bitchy attitude that even I can't explain.

"Did you have a date tonight Katy?" he asks, and I can hear the displeasure in his tone of voice. How dare he? We agreed to be exclusive, even if we aren't being overly open about our relationship, it's still very much a two person deal.

"And what if I did Joseph? What would you do about it, hmmm?" I ask, taunting him. I want to see how he'll react to the fact that I might have been with another man. I can tell you, I don't like the thought of him with another woman, or man for that matter if it's of a sexual nature.

"I'd go rip him apart for taking what's mine." He growls out.

"Yours? I'm not a possession Joe. I'm not *yours*, I'm *mine* and I'll do what I like, with whom I like, and you don't get a say in it." I turn back to my door and unlock it to let myself inside. I'd already managed to get the key in the lock before Joe scared the shit out me, so it doesn't take much of an effort to get inside. Before I can slam the door shut behind me, Joe is there, slamming it shut instead. I have no clue how he moved so fast, but he must have some superhuman speed in that body of his.

"You *are* mine, Kathryn Ellis. You want to know how I know that?" I don't get the chance to answer because he continues, not waiting for one. "I know you're mine because *I am yours*. Only yours." He growls.

Well fuck me. I've never liked the Neanderthal in a guy, I find them too possessive and I'm turned off almost immediately, but when Joe says I'm his because he's *mine*, I almost get giddy.

"I wasn't out on a date Joseph, you Neanderthal." I slap him on the upper arm, he won't feel a thing, but it makes me feel better. "I was supposed to go out for dinner with Kami but she," I look up at him and decide I'm not going to mention who she was with. "She was busy, so we had to reschedule."

"Then why did you make me think we you were with another man?" he asks, and I can see the vulnerability in his eyes.

"I didn't, you managed to jump to that conclusion all on your own, I didn't have to say a damned thing." I sigh and shake my head. I turn my back to him and walk through to the kitchen. I don't know if he follows me until I turn back around to pass him one of the bottles of water I took out of the fridge. "Why you would think I would do that to you, I don't know. Let's get one thing clear here though OK. This thing here," I wave my hand between us, "It's exclusive. We may not be public just yet like you want, but I don't do cheating or playing around. One man at a time is more than enough trouble for me, thanks very much." I thought it was the same for him, but now I'm not so sure.

"I thought we'd agreed to be exclusive Katy and then you walked up here looking all sexy and beautiful." He sighs. "You looked deep in thought and I …"

"You thought *what* Joe?" I ask, I need to hear him say it.

"I thought you were trying to decide which one of us you liked more." He says quietly and my heart about breaks for him. I'm not sure who broke him so badly that he thinks no one could want him, but I want to hunt them down and knock them out.

I walk over to where he's sitting at the kitchen bench, stand between his knees, place my hands on his cheeks and pull his face up to look in mine so that he can see that what I'm about to say is the truth.

"Joseph French, you are worth more than that and I would never, ever cheat on you and I would never go out with another man when you didn't know about it. Do you understand?" he nods his head, but I don't think he quite believes me.

Chapter Sixteen

JOE

I haven't even *thought* about being with anyone else since Katy and I started seeing each other, or whatever the hell this is. Even before we went out for dinner that first night at Erin's, I couldn't stop thinking about Kathryn fucking Ellis. She was in my dreams *and* my nightmares. The only trouble was, I'd wake up and realise she wasn't there at all.

Then when I saw her walking up to her front door tonight, the thought that she *could* have been out with another guy, well, it just about killed me to think about it. My heart did this funny thing where it felt like a brick inside my chest.

My hands reach out to touch her. I need to touch her, to feel grounded, as she stands between my knees. Her hands, lightly holding my cheeks, guide my lips until they're touching hers and she kisses me. It's the sweetest kiss I've ever had. How could I have ever doubted her?

"I need you Katy." I murmur against her lips.

"I need you too Joe." She whispers in reply. I stand up, take her hand in mine and I thread my fingers with hers, leading her to her bedroom. Neither of us saying a word, but I can feel it in the silence, the vibrations in the air. Things between us have changed tonight. There's still the unbridled need that has made us tear each other's clothes off in the past few months, but there's something more tender about tonight.

I sit down on the edge of the bed and pull Katy in close to me. My hands and eyes, roaming over her body, drinking her in. When my hands reach her front, I take my time undoing every button on her shirt. When I finally get the last button undone and the shirt parts, barely holding on to her shoulders, I run my hands up her stomach and massage her breasts. They're amazing, covered in pale pink lace and silk.

I knead and massage her breasts, watching her chest rise and fall with every deep breath she takes, making her breasts come closer and closer to my face with every breath. I'm mesmerised, until Katy's hands come up and rest on my shoulders, causing her shirt to fall down her back, to her bent elbows, trapping her arms. I run my teeth gently over each nipple and watch them pebble with arousal, causing me to groan.

"Arghh Joe. Please." She sighs.

"Please what honey?" I say, barely recognising my own voice, it's so deep and husky.

"More Joe. Please, more." Then she moans.

"More of this, Katy?" I ask, as I pull a nipple in to my mouth, as she throws her head back and lets out a loud yes, that sounds like a hiss, and her hands tighten on my shoulders, causing pain. I let out a loud groan of my own as her nails bite into my skin. I guess fair is fair, I am biting her skin.

My hands skim down her ribs, to her hips and then I'm undoing the button and zip on her pants, letting them slide down her legs. She takes a few steps away from me and kicks them off the rest of the way and starts to step out of her heels. "Leave them on honey. Please." She smiles and takes a step closer. "Stop. Turn around slowly for me. I want to see you, drink you all in honey."

Katy gives me an almost shy, but cheeky smile as she slowly turns around for me, and by the time she's come full circle, I'm about ready to explode like a teenage boy.

Pale pink lace and silk against her slightly tanned skin is making me damned uncomfortable. Dress pants are looser than jeans, and thank fuck for that, but I still don't have a lot of room to move in them. To give myself some breathing room, I undo the button and pull down the zip. I hear Katy's breathing hitch, and I look up to see what's wrong.

Instead of seeing panic or pain on her face, I see desire and heat. She's watching me as I pull my cock out of my boxer briefs, licking her lips. Her eyes dart to mine as she realises she's been caught watching me.

"Take it off Joe." She demands, her voice a low and raspy whisper, that I can barely hear.

"Take what off Katy?" I ask, wanting to hear her tell me what she wants. What she desires.

"All of it." She says without hesitating, but as I get to my feet, she stops me. "Shirt first Joseph." She demands and it's so fucking hot that she's willing to tell me what she wants.

I undo a few buttons and then rip it up over my head and throw it to the floor, waiting for my next instruction.

"Shoes and socks off." They're gone within seconds, and I wait for her next instruction. I don't have to wait long, thank fuck. "Stand up." I do as I'm told, but Katy still doesn't touch me, and I realise that she wants me to do this for her. "Take 'em off Joe."

"Pants and boxers?" I ask.

"Everything Joseph. I want you naked." Her wish is my command, and my pants and boxers join the rest of the pile of our clothes on the floor. We stand there, the two of us just taking each other in. Enjoying the view.

Then Katy's hands start to roam her body, she widens her stance and moans softly. My hand moves all on its own and I fist my hard cock, pumping up and down slowly, steadily.

"Arghhh Joe, that's so hot. Watching you fist your cock makes me so wet." She says, as her fingers disappear in behind lace and silk.

I can't take it any more I have to touch her. I take one step and we're almost touching, but I need her to come to me. "I need you Katy, come here, let me touch you."

"I am here Joe, you can touch me now."

I shake my head, "No honey, come to me." her eyes light up with understanding and she steps into my body, wrapping her arms around my neck and pulling my lips down to hers.

"Kiss me Joe." And that's what I do. I bury my hands in her hair and kiss her like she's my sole reason for living, right here in this moment she is.

Before I know it, she's taken her bra off, stepped out of the sexy underwear and heels, then she's pushing me back onto the bed. I wanted her to take what she wants, and she is. "Get comfortable Joe." She says, almost like a warning. So I push back up to the pillows and lie there, waiting for her to make her next move. I'm not disappointed when she does. My view is fucking spectacular as she crawls her way up from the bottom of the bed, over my legs and up my body, to hover her lips over mine. "Do you want to kiss me Joe?"

"Fuck yes." I answer, no hesitation at all.

"Oh well, we can't always get what we want now can we Joe?" she says with a smirk and moves away from my mouth. Instead she kisses along my jawline, bites along my neck until she reaches where my shoulder meets my neck and then she bites and sucks my skin. I moan and swear, "Arghhh fuck Katy, are you leaving a mark on me?"

"Hell yes I am Joseph, but it's OK, no one will see it, but we'll both know it's there baby. A secret between you and me." I close my eyes, attempting to control my body, my desire. "Open your eyes baby, I want you to see what I'm doing to you, not just feel it."

Who knew Katy Ellis would be so bossy and commanding in bed. Having a woman take control in the bedroom every now and then is as hot as fuck, and this woman in particular can take control of me in the bedroom any time she likes.

She makes her way down to my chest, kissing every inch of me and playing, biting my nipples until I'm not sure I can take anymore. "This is torture Katy." I whisper.

"Oh, I can stop if you like?" she starts to sit up, making to move away from me, but I reach out with my hands and pull her back to my body.

"A sweet torture but torture all the same Kathryn." Her name comes out as a sigh because before I can finish speaking, she's kissing my hip bones one at a time and my cock is twitching like he's got a cramp. When she runs her tongue along the slit at the top of my cock, I let a loud groan that I'm sure the neighbours down the fucking street can hear. I know what she thinks she's going to do tonight, but I can't take anymore, and with one quick move she's on her back, pinned to the bed.

"What the hell Joe? I was just getting to the good bit." She squeals.

"Yeah, I know but I can't wait any longer, I need to be inside you Katy."

"Oh," is all she says. I've found my jeans and retrieved a condom out of the pocket. Then I crawl back onto the bed, kneeling between her thighs, I roll the condom over my hard cock, with Katy watching my every move. When I line up our bodies so that I can push my cock in to her pussy, I stop and stare at her for a few seconds longer. I want to take it in, I want to remember exactly what she looks like in this moment. "What Joe? What's the matter?" she asks, running her hands up and down my arms.

"Nothing Katy. Nothing at all honey." I don't give her time to question me, or anything else, before I sink into her body. I pause for another second, letting both of us adjust, and then I slowly start moving in and out of her pussy.

Katy wraps her legs around my hips, taking me deeper into her body and rub against her clit. She matches my every move, her hands tangled in my hair, pulling my face down to hers.

"Jesus Katy." She moans in response. "Fuck me Katy." She moans louder, kissing all over my face, jawline and throat, wherever she can reach. I rest on my elbows, taking most of the weight off her body, and cradle her face in my hands. "Come for me Katy. I need you to come for me now honey."

I can feel her body start to shake and tremble, her pussy clenches around my cock and just as she starts to scream her release, I take her lips with mine and take her orgasm in to my body. As she starts the relax, my movements become faster, more erratic and then I shout my release.

I bury my face in the crook of her neck and place a million light kisses there, before I roll off her body and lie beside her.

"Wow Joe." Wow is right. I'm not even sure what that was, but I've never felt anything like it before. I don't know what to say, so instead of speaking, I get up and go to the bathroom to take care of the condom and when I come back, Katy's put on a t-shirt, and is under the covers.

I walk over to the bed and slide between the covers, but when I try to pull Katy into my body so I can hold her, she resists. Instead, she gets up and goes to the bathroom herself. Just when I start to wonder if she's actually coming back, she walks back into the bedroom and towards the bed. "I love watching you walk away honey, but I love it even more when you're walking towards me."

"Shut up Joseph. That was so corny. I expect much better of you." She says with a smile.

I shrug and smirk before answering, "My best friend taught me everything I know."

"James Harvey knows better than to use that kind of shit to pick women up. Not to mention he doesn't *need* to use pick-up lines, and you know it." She shakes her head, and crawls back into bed.

"Are you saying Harvey doesn't need pick-up lines, but I do Miss Ellis?" I don't know whether to be offended or not. She's right though, James sure doesn't need to use pick-up lines to get the ladies.

"I'm saying James doesn't need pick-up lines to get a woman to go out with him, corny and horrible, or not." She laughs.

"And me?" I ask, genuinely curious about her answer.

"And you what?" she knows what I'm asking, so I just look at her with a raised eyebrow, causing her to laugh and reply, "Well, you didn't need a pick-up line with me. You were just yourself, but I can't speak for the women of your past."

"I can't remember if I ever used pick-up lines, no one else has every complained though." Katy pulls a face at me and I pull her over to me so that I can kiss her. "I don't want to talk about people from our pasts." I say as I roll over to my back, put one hand behind my head, and stretch the other arm around Katy's shoulders and pull her in close to my side.

"I'm sure none of them complained Joe." She says in an overly cheery tone and I feel her body stiffen beside.

"They're in the past Katy, no one else is here. Just you and me." I say with my eyes closed. I can't keep them open.

"Hey, have you eaten?" Katy asks and goes to get out of my embrace and the bed.

"No, I haven't, but I'm not hungry right now either Katy." Just at that moment, my body decides to betray me, and my stomach lets out a loud growl. My eyes shoot open and Katy's laughing so hard she can't breathe. "Sure, I guess I could eat." I say. "Let me order something in."

"No, I can rustle us up some food from stuff in the kitchen. Why don't you stay here and relax, I'll be back in a minute with food." She wriggles out of my arms, still laughing quietly as she exits the room, leaving me with just my thoughts. The places my thoughts go aren't great. I should have worked out something to say to her after we had sex. It wasn't just sex, not for me, but I just couldn't find the right words to tell her how I feel. Not without saying the three words I don't think either of us are ready to say or hear.

I lie there, my eyes closed. I'm never this relaxed. Anywhere. Even in my own home, I'm always working or organising shit. Either for work or my father. Here, in Katy's home, after an amazing round of sex, even without that,

I feel comfortable. Relaxed and less edgy. I think I relaxed so much that I fell asleep, because the next thing I know, Katy's bringing food.

"Hey sleepy head, do you want to eat or sleep?" she asks, carrying in two plates of food.

I sit up and reach out to relieve her of them. It smells delicious and when I look at what she's managed to 'throw together', I realise I might have been asleep longer than I thought. "When did you have time to whip this up Katy?" I ask, absolutely amazed.

"Well Joe, I'd like to tell you that I'm a whiz in the kitchen and I just managed to pull it all together for you tonight," she says with a huge smile. "But the fact is, I had most of it already sitting in the fridge or cupboard."

"Do you mean to tell me you're feeding me leftovers?" I can't help asking, knowing that everyone who knows me thinks I'm a food snob, including Katy.

"Yes, I am Joe. You can eat it or not, I don't really care." She says with another laugh that makes my heartbeat faster and my chest constrict.

"I'll eat anything you offer me Kathryn." I tease.

"Anything Joseph?"

"Anything at all, Kathryn." I say, and I mean every damned word.

Chapter Seventeen

It takes me longer than I expect to pull dinner together with the leftovers I've got in my kitchen. When I've put enough together on the plate to resemble a decent meal, I walk back to my bedroom.

I freeze in the doorway, because seeing Joe asleep in my bed makes my heart skip a beat. He looks so peaceful and relaxed among my covers and pillows. He rarely looks like that when he's awake and I don't want to disturb him by waking him up. Taking that away from him feels almost cruel, but as if he can sense me standing there, or perhaps he can smell the food, his eyes open and he's reaching out to take the plates of food from me. Then he gestures with a nod of his head for me to sit next to him on the bed.

"When did you have the time to whip this all up Katy?" he asks, his voice husky from sleep.

Joe's a bit of a food snob, so I enjoy telling him I'm a whiz in the kitchen, especially when I have leftovers to pull together. He gasps in mock horror at my audacity to serve him up leftovers, but when I tell him it's his choice whether he eats or not, his answer of, 'he'll eat anything I offer him', sends a shiver down my spine and I have to concentrate on eating food. I don't want to get distracted with the physical attraction between us again just yet, so instead we eat and get to know each other a little better as adults. It's not like we haven't been getting to know each other over the past few months, but somehow, sitting here on my bed tonight, he just seems to be more open. More relaxed, and nothing seems to be off limits. We even manage to talk about Kami, he doesn't really say much, but it's a start. Bringing up Kami, brings up an entire batch of other questions too.

"Are we ever going to be able to tell people we're seeing each other Katy?" he asks me quietly, without looking at me.

"Yes." I say simply. I know how he feels, I think. I want to shout it from the rooftops. I'm in love with Joseph and I want the world to know about it. The only thing is, I think I need to tell Kami first.

"But?" he asks, still not looking at me. I hate that I'm making him feel insecure and slightly nervous waiting for my answer by the looks of it.

"No, there are no but's Joe. I just want to tell Kami first. I know that you don't care what other people think, least of all my best friend, but I do." I hold my hand up to stop him from talking. "We both know there's no love lost between you and Kami, but I think I owe it to my oldest friend to tell her I'm dating you first."

"What if she can't accept us?" He asks, this time he does look at me. Almost daring me to tell him that she matters to me more than he does.

"She'll learn to live with it then I guess." I shrug my shoulders and it's my turn not to look at him. Honestly, I don't know what the hell I'm going to do if she can't accept Joe and I being together, but I do know that I don't plan on giving up on us that easily. "I was going to tell her tonight, but when I got to her place she was busy. Something came up that she couldn't get out of and that's where I was coming home from tonight. Not a date. I hadn't been with another guy. Just give me some more time, please?"

"OK." He says.

"OK?" I ask shocked. "That's it, just, OK?"

"Yes." Fantastic, we're back to Joe giving me one word answers. I know he's frustrated, but I need to talk to Kami.

"I don't need, nor do I want, her approval Joe, but I do want her to find out from me and not someone else. That wouldn't be fair."

"OK. I understand."

"Do you? Really? Or are you just saying that to keep the peace?"

"Me, keep the peace? I don't do that Katy, you of all people should know that. If you want some more time, you've got it." I look up, directly into his eyes to see if he's just telling me what he thinks I want to hear. "Honestly, honey."

"I'll talk to her as soon as I can. I promise." He smiles at me and I can't breath for a second. "You know, we're not exactly a secret though right? I mean Olivia knows about us, which makes it a huge surprise that the whole town doesn't know as well. My parents suspect there's an us. Well, my dad suspects, my mother is hoping there's an us. It would almost be a dream come true for her. To have a man like you tame her unruly daughter."

"I don't want to tame you Katy, I like you just the way you are. I don't need, nor want you to change a thing."

"Aww you say the sweetest things Joe." I bump my shoulder in to his and laugh.

"Yeah, well don't tell anyone. I've got a reputation to uphold you know." He says grumpily.

"The town grump needs to keep up the appearance, I get it." I say, with a serious look on my face.

"I'm not the town grump." He looks at me thoughtfully and before I can answer him, to let him know I'm just teasing him, he says, "I am the town grumpy arsehole, aren't I?"

"I like you just the way you are Joseph French, you don't need to change a thing." I know I've repeated his words back to him, but they meant a lot to me and I'm hoping they can do the same for him.

"Awww you say the sweetest things Kathryn Ellis, as always." There he goes again, being all sweet and non-grumpy like. Before I can respond, he keeps speaking. "What are you doing next weekend? It's a long weekend and I was thinking of getting out of town and away from responsibilities for a few days. Maybe you'd be able to come with me?"

I sit there, on my bed, looking at him thinking. It takes me so long to think and he takes that as meaning I don't want to go with him.

"That's ok Katy, it was just a thought. I'd planned on getting out town that weekend anyway and I was just thinking that perhaps we could spend it together, but it doesn't matter."

"Joe, stop. I wasn't thinking about it because I didn't want to come with you, I was trying to think about my workload for the week and what we have going on. I think I can make it work. Let me check in with my boss on Monday and I'll let you know for sure, ok?"

The smile that spreads across his gorgeous face is enough motivation to convince my boss that I most certainly can manage to take four days off over the long weekend. Let's just hope I can convince him of that.

I'm still smiling from a great weekend with Joe, as I settle myself in at my desk on Monday morning. My friend Joy walks past and says, "Looks like someone had a good weekend. What's his name and do I know him?"

I laugh and say, "His name is Joe, I don't know if you know him and that's all you're getting out of me."

"You can't leave me hanging bitch." Joy says, but she's cut off by Mr Wilks.

"She can and she will Miss Vincent." He looks away from Joy, who is blushing furiously, and says to me, "Can I have a word please Miss Ellis?"

"Right away Mr Wilks." I reply, getting up from my desk, I grab my tablet so that I can take notes if need be. "See you later Joy." I whisper as I walk past her.

"Close the door please Miss Ellis." I do as Mr Wilks asks. I've told him to call me Katy, but he won't do it. I feel like he's talking to my mother, not me, when he calls me Miss Ellis.

I sit down in the chair that's facing his desk, tablet in hand, waiting for him to tell me what he needs.

"This coming weekend is a long weekend Miss Ellis and unfortunately that means we have a lot of extra work to get done before everyone has some time off." He takes a breath and continues, "I'll be needing you and the rest of the staff to work late every day this week to get it all done."

"Every night Mr Wilks?" I swallow. That won't leave much spare time to see Joe, and it means I won't get the chance to speak to him much either.

"Yes Miss Ellis. Unless of course you would rather be working this coming Friday and Monday while everyone else has four days off?"

"All four days off Mr Wilks?" I gasp. I don't think he's ever done it before.

"Yes, that right. Mrs Wilks has told me that it's a long weekend, and none of us will be working. You can thank her at the Christmas party." He says with a smile.

"I will remember to thank her next time I see her." I return his smile. Then he gets serious and I get a huge list of things that we all have to get done before Thursday night so that we can all have the time off.

I message Joe at lunch time and tell him I can't meet him for lunch, and I probably won't be able to have dinner with him either. When my phone starts ringing a few minutes later, I don't even need to check to see who it is.

"Good afternoon Mr French, how can I help this afternoon?" I ask.

"Why can't we have lunch or dinner today, Miss Ellis?" God, he sounds so sexy when he gets all businessman serious. I squirm a little in my office chair, then I remember I'm at work and should behave, but no-one noticed, they're all too busy getting shit done to get the weekend off.

"I won't be available to have lunch or dinner for the next few days, I'm afraid Mr French."

"I'm asking again, why not Kathryn? Please give me an answer this time." Ohhh Mr Bossypants is in the building.

"I'm going to be working my tail off here in the office for the next few days that's why Joseph." I take a deep breath. "If you want me to come away with you for four days, then you're going to have to go without having lunch and dinner with me for a few days."

"Really? You're going to come away with me Katy?"

"If you let me get my work done, then yes. Mr Wilks is shutting down the office for the long weekend, but that means we have to get some things done before we can take the time off. Therefore, sacrifices must be made."

"Lunch and dinner with me are your sacrifices?" he asks.

"Yes they are, all I'll be doing is working and going home to sleep." I reply. "It doesn't mean we can't be in contact it just means we won't see each other, and in the end, we get four days together."

"OK Katy, I can deal with that but have no fear, we'll be talking still honey." He replies in a low husky voice. "I ask just one thing. Can you do me a favour and message me to let me know you're home, please?"

"I can do that Joe." I've never had anyone other than my family and Kami ask me to let them know I'm OK.

His voice is still deep and husky when he says, "Talk to you later honey." I say goodbye, and then he's gone.

I spend the rest of the day working with Joy and some of the other people in the office to get as much work done as we can. We leave later than usual but not too late and when I get home, I strip down to my pyjama's, pour myself a glass of wine and message Joe to let him know I'm home.

Me: *Here's the text to let you know I'm home in one piece Mr French, as requested*

I hold my phone in one hand, my glass in the other, waiting for a return message. When one doesn't come, I put the phone down on the arm of the chair and let my head fall back to rest on the back of the chair, my eyes close, trying to relax before I head to bed. I'm not sure how long I sit there like that, but I finish off my drink, put the glass on the table because I'm too lazy to take it the few steps to the kitchen, and walk to my bedroom.

My bed is calling my name, but I need to go to the bathroom first. Just as I flush, my phone starts ringing, and my first thought is to not answer it. It's too late and I'm too tired to talk to anyone. When I reach for it on my pillow to silence it, I see who's calling and decide that maybe it's not too late after all.

"Isn't it a bit late at night to be calling me Joseph?" I ask, I'm going for an annoyed voice, but I think it just comes across as tired.

"I just wanted to hear your voice Katy." God I love listening to him say my name. Any version of it that he chooses to use, I don't care which one. "You sound tired honey. One long day shouldn't make you this tired." He says, his voice full of concern and my heart does a little dance in my chest.

"It was a full on day Joe. I barely got a break, but before you start, I wasn't the only one and what we did today, should make the next few days go better. Let's not forget, that a few days of tired means that we get to go away. Together. For a few days."

"I can't wait to have you all to myself Katy."

"Me either Joe, but tonight I need to sleep. I'm sorry we couldn't get together, but I'm falling asleep as we speak." I say as I get myself under the covers and sink into my pillow.

"Good night honey. I'll call you tomorrow, sleep well." He says, in a whisper in my ear.

"Good night Joe. I miss you." I whisper and then hang up without waiting for an answer. I put my phone on the bedside table and then I'm asleep.

WHEN MY ALARM SCREECHES at me the next morning, I wish I could turn it off and roll over, but if I want to go away, then I need to get my butt up and moving.

When I arrive at the office, I realise I'm the first one there. I've even beaten Mr Wilks this morning, as I open up for the first time in a very long time. Just as I'm about to lock the door behind me, Joy yells out, telling me to wait for a minute. Then it's just the two of us for about half an hour before everyone else starts trickling in the door. Then another day of mentally exhausting work gets going.

By the end of the day, we've all decided, that if we keep up the pace, we'll be able to have a five day weekend. Mr Wilks agrees to a half day on Thursday if we can get everything done by then, so we all start working that little but harder.

I don't get the chance to talk to Joe, I text him to tell him I'm going to be extra late tonight. I don't call him when I get home, just text that I'm home and to say good night, then I'm out for the count.

When I wake up the next morning, I find a few texts from Joe from the night before. There's also a couple from Kami checking in on me, so I answer those first.

After I've done that I tap a few buttons and wait.

"Good morning beautiful. I'm going to assume you fell asleep last night before you could reply?" Just hearing Joe's voice makes me want him. I must let out a groan because his voice is deep and full of want when he says, "If you keep making noises like that Kathryn, we're both going to be late for work and I'm going to get a speeding ticket."

"It's just nice to hear your voice Joe. Really nice." I say. I'm too tired to hold back, and I don't want to hold back from him anymore. I really need to have that conversation with Kami sooner, rather than later.

His voice has softened when he says, "It's nice to hear your voice too Katy. I miss it and you."

There goes my heart doing that little dance in my chest again. "I miss you too Joe." I sigh. "But I have to get to work. Just two more days and then we have a whole four together."

"I know. I'm looking forward to it Katy." We're silent for a minute, before Joe speaks again. "I have to get to work too, I've got an early meeting to get to. I'll see you soon beautiful."

"See you soon Joe." I sigh as I hang up the phone. It's only been a couple of days that I haven't seen him, and only a couple of months since we started seeing each other, but already I'm kind of addicted to him.

I grab my travel mug of coffee and head out to my car. When I get to the office, Joy is waiting at the door for me to arrive. "Why are you so early this morning?" I ask as I approach her.

"Couldn't sleep." She says with a smirk. "Well, OK I didn't get much sleep last night."

I put my hand up to stop her from telling me anymore, because if I know one thing about Joy, I know that without any prompting she will give me details on just how she spent last night. "I don't need the details thank you very much."

"Well, obviously you didn't get quite so lucky last night." She says with a frown. "Here we were all thinking that your happy mood was because you were getting lucky."

I hesitate as I open the door and look back at her. "What do you mean, 'we all'? Who all?" I ask, hoping she can't hear the panic in my voice.

"In the office. We were taking bets on how long this one would last before you found something you didn't like about him and moved him along." She says offhandedly.

"I don't do that." I reply in a very unusual high pitched voice. I don't do that, do I? I don't *think* I do that.

"Yeah, you do actually." When I go to speak, Joy raises her hand to stop me and says, "What about Dan? He was adorable and really liked you. You found him too clingy. Then there was Aaron, he was absolutely gorgeous, but you said he took too much time to get ready. Longer than any female you've ever met. Then there was Billy. He could have been an underwear model, but again he was too perfect and too into you. Again."

"Well no one likes a clingy partner." I say defensively.

"You're right, but these guys just wanted to spend time with you. I thought that maybe you'd found a guy who was just what you need, but apparently I was wrong."

Just as I'm about to defend myself again, Mr Wilks walks up and asks us why we are standing around chatting and not inside working already.

Instead of offering up an explanation, I unlock the office door and settle into work. Around lunchtime, Joy wanders over to apologise for offending me, but I let her know we're more than OK. Even though I've been thinking about what she said all morning and wondering if she's right. *Am* I too picky?

At the end of the day Mr Wilks asks a few people to come in for a couple of hours the following morning to finish a couple of things but gives the rest of us the extra day off.

"Thank you Mr Wilks." I say smiling as I walk passed him to go home.

"You've earned it Miss Ellis, enjoy your time off." He returns my smile and looks like he wants to say something else, but someone stops to ask him a question and he waves goodbye to me instead.

When I get home I send Kami a text, I have to know if I really did that to the guys I dated.

Me: *Do you think I'm too picky with the guys I date?*

Kami: *Where did that come from?*

Me: *It's just something Joy said to me today.*

Kami: *Are you picky? Yes. But hun that isn't necessarily a bad thing. No one wants a needy guy. Or one that takes longer than you to get himself ready.*

I groan as I read her reply.

Me: *So I am a picky bitch then?*

Kami: *No it's not being picky when you choose not to settle for the wrong guy. You know that, right?*

Me: *Are you happy Kami? Is James the right guy?*

I get out of my car, walk to my front door and let myself in. Kami still hasn't answered me, and I'm just about to call her, when I get a reply and I can't help laughing at it.

Kami: *James has always been the right guy, just the wrong time. Yes, I'm extremely happy.*

Before I can answer, another message comes through lightning quick.

Kami: *That was James replying, but he isn't wrong lol*

Kami: *Are you OK? I can be at your place in 5*

Me: *Yeah I'm good. Enjoy your man xx*

Before I jump in the shower, I send a quick text to Joe to let him know I'm home in one piece. I take my time under the warm, steamy water. I enjoy every second of being able to relax, trying to not think about what Joy and Kami both said about my decisions when it comes to guys.

When the water starts to cool, I turn it off and wrap a towel around my body and one around my hair. I walk out of the bathroom, heading towards the kitchen where I plan on pouring myself a glass of wine and checking out some take away menus, when there's a knock on the door.

I'm speaking as I open the door, expecting it to be Kami checking on me, "Oh hun, I told you I was fine and that you didn't need to come check on me." Only it's not my best friend standing on the other side of the door. It's Joe freaking French and he's looking at me like I'm a delicacy he could devour, and not regret it for a second.

"I don't know who the hun is you're referring to Kathryn, but I sure do hope you don't open your door to just anyone when you look like that." He almost growls at me.

"Well, I generally do open my door when its knocked on Joseph. I didn't realise it mattered too much how I was dressed when I did it though."

"You're pretty much naked Kathryn. Damp and wrapped up like a gift. I swear, if you were expecting someone else right now, I might have to kill them with my bare hands." Yeah, that time he was definitely growling.

"I thought you were Kami for a second, that's all. Not another guy or anything, and yes, before you ask, we have actually seen each other naked and in all other various states of dress and undress." I know I'm taunting him now, but I can't help it. I walk away from the open door, giving him the choice to follow me and close it behind him or to leave.

I hear the door close, and then he's pressed right up close behind me. "Can I unwrap my gift now Katy?" he growls into my ear and it sends a shiver down my spine.

"God yes." I breath out. "Don't wait another second."

Chapter Eighteen

When Katy opened the door to her house with only a couple of towels wrapped around her beautiful body, I almost swallowed my tongue.

I couldn't think for a full minute, while I took in the vision in front of me. Then I realised we were standing pretty much out in the open where anyone could see what I could, and I wanted to close the door on the world.

When she got sassy with me about her thinking I was Kami, it took a second for me to hear what she was saying. I finally registered that she was saying that her and Kami have seen each other in all kinds of states of undress, including naked, I was barely breathing again. Kami Parker may not be one of my favourite people, but thinking about two females, one of which I find extremely attractive, being naked around each other, is a definite turn on.

I shake my head as she walks away from me, leaving the door open and giving me the choice to walk away or inside. I'm inside, door locked and behind her in seconds. "Can I unwrap my gift now Katy?" I hear the growling desire in my voice.

Katy shivers slightly, from head to toe and says, "God yes." In a breathy voice. "Don't wait another second."

"Are you sure honey?" I ask, barely able to control myself.

"Don't hold back now Joseph." She says on a groan that hits me in the groin. My brain misfires and I can't think of any else, except the need to get my woman naked and coming. I press my body into hers. Her back to my front and reach around to her front to pull the towel from where she's got it knotted at her breasts. Katy rests her hands on mine, as I yank the towel from her body, moving back slightly to drop it the floor. I push her upper body over the back of the couch, her hands landing on the cushions below. The towel on her head unravelling in a pile, giving her a place to rest her head.

"Stay like that Katy and spread your legs." My voice is so thick with need, I can barely force my voice out of my throat. My voice isn't the only thing that's thick with need either, but my cock can stay where it is for now, that way I can control the temptation to fuck Katy a little longer. Not much, but long enough.

She spreads her legs and I groan, because from this angle I can see her pussy. Wet and waiting just for me. I fall to my knees, thinking about what I plan on doing to this pink pussy in front of me.

My hands run up the backs of Katy's calves, up her thighs and come to rest on her arse cheeks. Massaging, squeezing and gently coaxing them apart, so that I have a better view of her wet, pink pussy.

"Spread your feet wider Katy." I demand, quietly.

"Joe, I can't. I'll fall." She says, her voice barely a whisper.

I smack her left butt cheek lightly, she jumps and squeals, but that's followed very closely by a long moan. Her reaction causes my cock to jump and try to break out of my jeans.

"I won't let you fall honey, trust me."

Without a word, her feet side further apart on the wood floor and I watch, entranced, as her lips spread open, begging for my attention, and making my mouth water.

"That's it honey, spread them wide for me and I'll give you exactly what you want." I spread my hands over her cheeks and drag my thumbs down to spread her open even further for me, putting her on display.

I hear her suck in a breath and ask, "Everything OK there honey?"

"The cool air." She breathes.

"The cool what, Katy?"

"The cool air, its making me. Arghh." She moans and her whole body shakes with need.

"It's making you what Katy?" I ask, I love hearing her talk to me, telling me what her body is doing, feeling, when I touch her. Listening to how turned on she is, even though I can see the physical evidence, is a huge turn on. "I can see your clit getting harder while I look at it and your pussy is dripping wet. Are you sure you're ready for me honey?"

"God yes, Joe please."

"Please what, Katy?" I move so that I'm closer to her pussy, breathing on her, but not touching her. Yet.

"Touch me Joe. Just fucking touch me. Anyway, anyhow. I need you to touch me. Please?"

I'm on my knees between her feet, my shoulders supporting her thighs, I finally reach out my tongue to get a taste of her pussy. My tongue barely touching her clit makes her jump, but I've got hold of her hips, so she can't get away from me.

"Fuck Joe." Her voice is a hoarse whisper.

She pushes her body back into my face and I take full advantage of her movement by slipping my tongue between her pussy lips and dragging it up from the bottom all the way up to her clit, in one long swipe. I flick her clit with my tongue and pull back from her body. The room is filled with groaning, hers or mine? Who fucking cares? I've been wanting to taste her for days and now I'm here, with her pussy right in front of me.

I can't hold back, I push my tongue through her lips and into her pussy, fucking her with my tongue, using my hands to keep her open for me. Using my hands, I push her further up the back of the couch, planting her feet on my thighs, which has a double effect of helping to raise her body up and I don't need to be holding her hips to hold her up where I want her, freeing my hands.

I drag a hand down her arse cheek, running a finger down the cleft of her butt all the way down to her clit. My tongue hasn't stopped pumping in and out, and all around her pussy lips. Katy is above me, moaning and moving against my fingers and tongue. Her body starts to shake, and I slide one finger into her pussy, just in time to feel her clench and then, she's coming all over my face.

Katy collapses over the back of the couch, with a sigh. I'm up on my feet, dropping my pants to the floor and rolling a condom onto my cock in no time. I don't give her time to catch her breath, before I'm positioning the tip of my cock at her pussy lips, spreading them open so that I can be in her in her beautiful body.

"Oh Joe. I don't think I can." She whispers.

"Yes, you can honey. I need to be inside you." My words make her moan, and she stands almost upright, spreading her legs wide. When she looks over her shoulder at me and says, "Fuck me Joe." I can't hold back. I push my cock into her body and we both groan from the sensation. It's like the first time and yet so familiar. She feels like home, and I don't want to be with anyone else.

The thought jolts at my brain. I'm not the guy who thinks about forever, or happily ever after, but with Katy, *for* Katy, I could do forever.

"Fuck Katy." I growl in her ear. I need to bring it to the physical, I can't let my emotions run wild.

"Yes Joe. Yes. Yes. Yes." For a woman who said she can't do any more, she's so wet I'm gliding in and out of her pussy with ease and it feels amazing. Then I feel her clench around my cock and my brain is fried. No more thoughts, just a carnal need drives me on. Then Katy's having her second orgasm, screaming out my name and I follow right behind her, growling out her name.

The only sounds in the house after that is our heavy breathing. I'm not sure how long it takes for both of us to come back down to earth, but when we do, I turn Katy around, kiss her lips, scoop her up and carry her to bed. She wraps her arms around my neck, and it feels like heaven.

I gently place her on her bed, pull the covers over, kiss her lightly on the forehead and turn to go to the bathroom. I take care of the condom and when I walk back into the bedroom, I take a second to drink in the beautiful woman who has stolen my heart. I turn off all the lights, and crawl into bed behind her. Pulling her in to me. Katy wiggles her whole body until she's flush with mine, then sighs contentedly. I've never felt more relaxed, I think I hear Katy speak but before I know it, I've drifted off to sleep and I think I imagined it.

THE NEXT MORNING, I wake up to the sun coming through a small crack in the curtains and Katy's warm, delectable body still snuggled up close to mine. I look at the clock she keeps beside her bed and swear.

"Katy, honey. Don't you have be up for work?" I ask, quietly. Why I don't know seeing as how I'm trying to wake her up.

"Joe?" she asks, her voice all husky from sleep.

"Yeah honey, it's me. You're going to be late for work." I say, a little louder.

There's a husky growl and then quiet laughter from beside me, but no movement whatsoever. "I didn't get around to telling you, I have today off as well Joe. If you hadn't made me orgasm twice and turned me into a tired, limp noodle last night, I might have remembered to tell you that."

I swat her on the backside, and she squeaks but she still barely moves. "Well, in that case, I guess I'll go call Jenny and tell her that Nadine and her pregnant self, can have an extra paid day off as well."

"Wow, must be nice to be able to just decide that no-one has to work today." Katy murmurs into her pillow as I throw back the covers and go in search of my phone.

"That's the perks of being the boss, honey."

"Yeah, sure is, *honey*." She grumbles, into her pillow, again.

When I reach my pants and find my phone in the pocket, I see I've got a couple of messages and a missed called. All from Jenny. I check her messages and they all say exactly the same thing. She must have gotten her husband to send them.

Jenny: *I'm not feeling too well this morning boss, I hope there's nothing urgent you need me to do?*

When I listen to the voice message she left, she says that Nadine can do anything I need her to. I send Nadine a quick text to let her know she's having an extra paid day off and she replies instantly with a thanks bossman. Then, I call Jenny to make sure everything's alright.

"Hey boss, you didn't have to call me to check up on me you know." She might be about formality and boundaries at the office, but out of the office, I'm just the guy who went to the same high school she did.

"I know I didn't have to call but I couldn't be bothered typing out a text. Are you OK? Is there anything I can do for you?"

"I'm fine thanks Joe. I think I just needed a day of rest. Travis told me to rest and put my feet up, even though I told him I have the next four days off."

"Well, you tell Travis, that he's right and you have today off any way. Something came up and I've had a change of plans, so we're all having an extra paid day off today. I was just about to call you and tell you when I saw your messages."

"What's her name? Or do I even need to ask?" There's a silence, not really awkward but dead air, for a few seconds before she's says, "It's OK Joe, I won't tell anyone your secret. Not even James. Enjoy your weekend away with your *friend* and I'll see you back at the office on Tuesday."

"Thank you Jenny. You get plenty of rest, keep your feet up, and make sure Travis looks after you. If he doesn't, I'll kick his arse, okay?"

Jenny laughs, but replies, "Thanks Joe, you're a good man and an even better boss." And then she's gone.

I look up and Katy hasn't emerged from her room, so I decide to quickly make some breakfast and coffee. Our weekend starts now, and I plan to enjoy every damned second of it.

I move around Katy's kitchen, making some toast, finding some fruit and making some coffee. When I look for a tray, I don't find one. I thought every female on the planet had trays for taking food into their bedrooms, but then I remember, the other night when she bought in some dinner for us, all she carried was the plates, no tray then either. Instead, I find a bigger plate and transfer everything on it, including two mugs of coffee and slowly walk back into the bedroom.

"I come baring breakfast ..." I start, but then I almost trip over my own damned feet. Sitting up in her bed, leaning against her pillows, hair fanned out and a glow on her cheeks, is Katy. The only thing she's wearing is my fucking shirt. I didn't even notice that she'd come out of the bedroom to grab it, but it looks sexy as fuck on her. Why is that? Why do our shirts, business or casual, even t-shirts and hoodies, w*hy* do they always look so good on women? For the life of me, I've never understood it and I don't think I ever will.

"Isn't that perfect, because I am ravenous this morning." She says, with a cheeky, but satisfied grin.

"Me too." I murmur to myself.

"I'm sorry, what did you say Joe, I couldn't hear you?" she looks innocent, but she's not, she knows exactly what she's doing to me. She can see my dick getting hard in my boxer briefs.

"I just said, I'm starving too honey, but I'm also wondering when you managed to slip into the other room to grab my shirt?"

"I didn't grab your shirt from last night. You had on a t-shirt, remember?" she's right, I did too and my jeans. I wasn't wearing my work stuff when I got here.

"Then who's shirt *are* you wearing Kathryn?" I ask, I can feel the scowl taking over my face and I can hear the anger in my voice. She wouldn't dare wear another guys shirt when she's in bed with me, would she?

"It's your shirt Joe." She says with smile. "You left it here the last time you stayed over. You had a fresh one for the next day and you didn't think to grab this one." I look at her and I see her falter. "OK, so maybe I stole it and hid it under my pillow, so you'd forget it. I slept in it the last few nights so that I could smell you and feel like you were still here with me, even when you weren't." She admits so quickly, that it could have been one big word.

"You stole my shirt and slept in it to feel closer to me when I wasn't here?" I ask, just to clear my brain.

"Yes, that's exactly what I did Joseph." She replies, tilting her chin up, daring me to be pissed at her. The simple truth is, I can't be mad at her. She knew she couldn't see me for a few days, so she slept in my shirt to be close to me. I've never had anyone miss me before, not like that anyway. I don't know what to say.

Chapter Nineteen

KATY

I thought it would be sexy to be sitting here in the shirt Joe left here last week, when he came back in from calling Jenny and making us breakfast. That is, until he stops dead in the doorway. I'm about to apologise, when I recognise barely restrained want on his face. Maybe the fact that I have very few buttons done up is what has him so stunned?

"Joe?" I ask, "Do you want some help?" I go to move off the bed, but he speaks before I move too far.

"No!" I've never heard him yell before. "Don't move a fucking muscle Katy." He says in a whispered growl. It's like nothing I've ever heard before and I don't know whether to be turned on or run.

"Okay." I say and I hate the nervousness I hear in my voice. I was so sure about sitting here in his shirt and now. Now I'm not so sure it was a good idea.

"Katy, honey, you need to give me a minute, I swear if you move, this plate will be on the floor and that shirt. Well, the shirt will be ripped to shreds."

"Oh." It's all I can say in response to his admission. The shirt worked.

"Yeah. Oh." He grounds out. "I made you breakfast, and I intend on eating it. Before I eat you. Again."

Holy shit. I don't move, not a muscle and I can see the muscle in his jaw clenching. He's trying to control his body and even though we're talking about Joseph French here, not even he can demand his body to shut off. Not immediately anyway. I have a throw blanket at the end of the bed and I'm thinking about pulling it up to cover myself, I hear Joe take a deep breath, and before I can move he's standing beside me handing me the plate.

He coughs and says, "Can you hold this please, honey?"

I take the plate and watch him walk around the foot of the bed, settle himself on the bed and hold out his hand for me to hand him back the plate. Without a word spoken, that's exactly what I do, and then I wait. I can hear a bird singing outside, someone whistling as they walk passed the house, a horn honking and even someone laughing in the distance. With all of that, there's no sound in my bedroom other than Joe moving things from the large platter onto smaller plates that I didn't even see when he handed it to me.

"Here's your breakfast honey." He says, handing me a plate, loaded with toast, and fresh fruit. I place it in my lap as he hands over a mug of coffee as well. I take a sip of the coffee and groan. He makes great coffee.

"Fuck Katy are you *trying* to kill me this morning?" He asks, sounding pained and closing his eyes, I assume it's so he can't look at me.

"Ummmm no." I reply, my coffee in one hand, a piece of toast in the other. "I don't want you to die Joseph, you can however make me coffee any time you like. It tastes amazing."

We sit there eating in silence. I watch him from where I'm sitting without actually moving my head and I can see the concentration on his face. When our plates are empty a few minutes later, he takes mine and places it on the platter with his. Then he takes my almost empty mug from my hand and places it next his on the bedside table.

"I love seeing you sitting here in my shirt, but I can't wait to have you out of it Kathryn." The man doesn't say much, but holy shit when he talks like that ... wow! I feel my whole body flare to life and the need to press my thighs together to get some kind of relief from how much I want him is, un-freak-ing-believable.

The look on Joe's face in this moment, is intense. He is full of need, desire and I feel like it might bubble right out of him. It's almost scary, the look that he's sending my way, and everything in me is drawn to him. I want to soothe him in any way that I can.

I get up on my knees and slowly unbutton the shirt. When Joe moves like he's going to help me, I shake my head no. "Take off your boxers Joe." He doesn't move right away, and I say, "Now Joseph." I want to take control and make *him* lose some of the control he holds on to so tightly.

He doesn't hesitate, he drags his boxers down his legs and kicks them off the side of the bed, never losing eye contact with me. Watching me massage my boobs, his shirt hanging loosely on my shoulders. I *had* planned to take it completely off, but seeing Joe's reaction to me in it, I'm going to keep it on for as long as I can.

"Lay back, Joseph." I demand and much to my surprise, he complies without hesitating. There's a twinkle in his eyes and the corner of his mouth is twitching, like he wants to smile but doesn't want to give me a reason to stop. We both know, that if he wanted to, he could have our roles reversed a heartbeat.

Instead, he does what I ask, placing his hands behind his head and lying back on the pillows. If anyone was to see him, they would think he was extremely relaxed, but I can see the muscles all over his delectable body twitching, waiting for me to touch him. To have my way with him.

I move so that I'm almost touching his side, then I run a fingernail down his chest to his stomach, over his abs, to follow his 'happy trail' to his hips. That's where I stop. His cock is hard, twitching, waiting for me to touch it, but I don't. Instead I say, "Roll over."

Joe raises an eyebrow at me in question, "Roll over on to your stomach Joseph." Both eyebrows raise and the corners of his mouth twitch. For a second, I think he's going to tell me no, but then he rolls over and I am rewarded with the view of his back muscles and the most delectable gluteus maximus I've ever had the pleasure of looking at.

I take another minute to just drink in the sight of him and then I move. I straddle his thighs and watch as the muscles in his butt flex. I know I can't be too heavy for him, "Everything OK there Joe?" He doesn't answer in words, he just grunts at me. "If you're sure?" I ask again, I'm rewarded with another grunt and flexing butt cheeks. I can't resist those butt cheeks any longer and run my hands over them, squeezing and massaging them.

"Ahhhh what are you doing Katy?" Joe moans.

"Umm massaging your butt?" I say, with a smile on my face.

He moves his head on the pillow so that he can see me and says, "I can feel you laughing Katy and no man likes having his derriere laughed at woman. Least of all by *his* woman when they're both naked."

"I'm not naked." I say and see fire light in his eyes.

He doesn't speak, but he's still lying there, head resting on his hands, watching me while I run my hands all over his back, ribs, shoulders and upper arms. I tell myself I'm giving him a massage, but the truth is, I just want to touch him. Everywhere.

I've been moving around his body, touching him everywhere except his butt, but I can't resist anymore. I shuffle myself down his legs to rest behind his knees and start to rub his thighs, stopping just before I reach the crease where his legs meets his butt. I see his muscles flex and relax every time I move closer and then move away. He's still watching me, but his eyes are hooded. When I finally start needing his cheeks, he lets out a loud groan of pleasure. Hips start moving, grinding his cock into the mattress, his eyes are shut, and his mouth is slightly open. He looks like he's in a state of utter bliss. I stop suddenly and jump off his body.

"Roll over Joe." I tell him. His eyes fly open and I can see the unbridled lust in his eyes as he stares at me in confusion. "I said, roll over Joe." I demand this time. Fire flares in his eyes again, but he does what I ask him and within seconds he's lying on his back, staring me down. Daring me to keep pushing him. What he doesn't understand is, I *want* to see how long it takes before his resolve breaks. How long will he let me hold the reigns before he throws me down and takes them back? "Hands behind your head Joe." I tell him. I can see it written all over his face, he wants to take over and bend me over his knee to teach me a lesson but he's also enjoying this more than he ever thought he could.

I straddle his upper thighs, not touching his balls or cock. I want him wanting me so damned much that he can't help himself. Instead of touching *him,* I touch myself. I run my hands up my thighs, touch my hip bones, run them across my stomach under my boobs and then side of my boobs, pushing them together. Watching Joe's face the whole time. I haven't touched anywhere he really wants me to or him and he's wound so tight, he's vibrating. Yet he still doesn't make a move to change the situation. His hands are gripping the opposite wrist so tight, his knuckles are white. I can see the sweat beading on his forehead and feel his legs shaking underneath me.

I move my hands over my boobs, massaging them for a few seconds and then I pinch both nipples, making me moan.

"Jesus Katy are you trying to torture me or yourself?" he grinds out between his teeth. I swear if he clenches them much tighter he's going to crack a few before this is over.

I don't answer him, I'm too lost in the feel of my own hands on my body. I close my eyes, but I feel Joe move beneath me and my eyes shoot open and stare at him. He's started to move like he's going to sit up and I shake my head at him. I stop moving my hands, until he lies back down, hands behind his head, then I start moving my hands again. "Behave Joseph, or I'll stop." His eyes darken but he doesn't make a move. To reward him I lean down and take his nipple between my teeth and lightly nibble on it.

"Fuck." He groans, and I move across to his other nipple. Fair is fair after all and Joe's hips push up towards mine, looking for relief anywhere he can get it. I rest my hands on his hips and kiss down his torso, keeping eye contact with him the whole time. When I reach his cock, I don't touch him, just let my breath lightly flow over him, making his cock twitch and bounce on his stomach. I stick my tongue out, but don't touch him and his breath hitches. His chest is pushed out with the breath he's holding in anticipation of my next move. When I run my tongue over the tip of his cock, he hisses out the breath he's been holding in. I dip the tip of my tongue into the slit of his cock to taste his pre cum and he bites his bottom lip, like he's holding back because he doesn't want to break the spell. Without breaking eye contact, I run my tongue from the tip of his cock, down to his base and back up again, but I hesitate at the tip, raising an eyebrow at him in question. Does he want me suck on his cock? I'm pretty sure I know the answer, what guy could say no?

"Yes Katy. Please honey, you're killing me."

He's begging me for relief, not just with his words but it's all over his face. I suck his cock in all the way down to the base and drag my lips back up to the tip again, and Joe growls out, his eyes close in relief. I run my mouth up and down his cock a few times, until Joe is unable to string words together, all he can manage is grunts and groans of pleasure.

I take his cock in my mouth and back up to the tip again one more time, as I pull a condom from the chest pocket of his shirt that I put there earlier. Dragging my fist up and down his cock a few times to keep him blissed out, I roll the condom over his cock and then move fast. I move up his body, lean on his chest and lower myself over him, until he's buried in my pussy.

His eyes spring open and his gaze is intense, but I don't move my hips. Instead I enjoy the feeling of his cock being inside me and begin to massage my boobs again, pulling at my nipples every so often. Joe lies there watching my every move. When I give him the slightest of nods, he sits up, wraps his hands around my boobs and sucks a nipple into his mouth, making me moan. Loudly. My hips start moving, I can't be still any longer. I rise and fall, rise and fall, riding his cock and bringing myself to the brink of pleasure.

"I'm almost there Joe. Almost. There." I whisper, as I bite along his jaw.

"Fuck Katy. Me too. Come for me honey." I reach a hand between us and find my clit. When my finger touches it, I feel the zing all over my body.

"Ohhh Joe!!" I yell out. I let go and I feel Joe's hips pounding up into me and then he's roaring out my name.

"Katyyyyyy!!" He falls back onto the bed, taking me with him and I lie there, relaxed on his chest. My body rising and falling with every heavy breath he takes.

I can't move. I can barely breath. When Joe's breathing is under control he lifts me up and gently places me on the bed. He gets up and takes care of the condom, then he's back. Lying next to me and pulling me into his body.

"We'll pack and leave right after we have a nap." He murmurs into the top of my hair. My eyes are already closed, and I smile, because I couldn't move anything else if I tried. I fall asleep to the rhythm of Joe's breathing, pretty damned happy with myself.

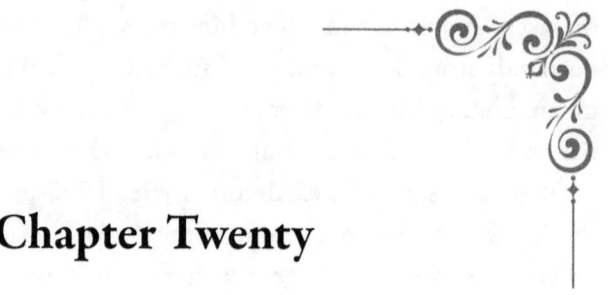

Chapter Twenty

JOE

I wake up after the best sex I've ever had, the only woman who has a chance of stealing my heart, lying across me. Using me as her pillow and I couldn't be happier. Which sends me into a blind panic, making my entire body go into high alert and it almost jumps off the bed. In the process, I wake Katy up and she looks at me with a happy, blissed out smile, drowsy still from being woken up.

"Morning Joe." She says, as she stretches her body like a lazy cat. Then she giggles and says, "Shit we already did the morning didn't we?"

"Yeah, we did." I reply and move to collect all the dishes.

A small hand lands on my arm, "Are you OK Joe?"

I look back at her beautiful face and my heart melts. I don't know why I suddenly felt so panicked, this woman can have any part of me she wants. "Of course Katy. I just want to clean up the mess in the kitchen. Why don't you go have a shower and pack some clothes for our weekend away?" I lean over and kiss her lightly on the lips, then I leave the room with the dishes without another word. I don't even look back to see if Katy's moving.

I get to the kitchen and start cleaning up the little bit of mess I created when I cooked breakfast. Washing, drying and putting away all the dishes. I turn to wipe down the bench behind me and see Katy standing there. She showered like I suggested, her hair still a little damp, and she's dressed in clean clothes.

"You didn't have to clean up my kitchen Joe." She says with a slight smile. "But thank you for doing it. Even if it was only to escape me and get out of the bedroom." She winks and walks closer to me. "Why don't you go have a shower Joe? Then we can talk."

"Do I have some clothes here that I can change into? I don't feel like wearing a suit." I ask.

"Yeah, of course you do. Just look in the wardrobe, I put some in there for you."

"Thanks." I kiss her on the forehead and head back to the bedroom, grab out some clothes, then go shower. I let the hot water flow over my body, the steam filling my lungs.

Not knowing how long I've spent in the shower I wash my hair and body and shut off the water. Stepping out, I dry myself and wrap the towel around my hips. I walk into the bedroom, not really taking any notice of my surroundings, off in my own thoughts. When I reach the bed, I see Katy sitting there, waiting for me.

"Hi beautiful, have you packed some clothes yet?" I ask, after giving her a kiss.

"No. I want to talk to you first. I need to make sure this is what you want Joe. I know you asked me to join you, but you seem to be regretting that decision this morning." She says and before I can answer she continues, quietly. "Was I too much earlier Joe?"

"No. God no Katy." I can't let her think she's done anything wrong. "That was the sexiest thing I've ever seen honey. I was so turned on by you today. I've never had any woman take control like that before. You wiped me out." I grin at her.

"Are you sure Joe?" I've never seen her unsure of herself before.

"Of course. I want to get moving so that we can spend as much time as possible away this weekend."

"Did you book an extra day?" she asks, and I'm confused,

"We're not staying in a hotel Katy, we're staying at my house, I don't need to book time in it." That's when I realise that I'd forgotten to mention that detail. "Sorry honey, didn't I mention it was my property?"

"No, Joseph, you didn't." She says with a shake of her head. "It makes sense now that I think about it. You never did mention a booking or time restrictions."

"No check in or check out limits for us honey." I say, while getting myself dressed. Katy's eyes are following my every move. "Does that mean you're going to throw some clothes in to a bag so we can get out of here?"

She smiles a big, bright smile, then starts moving around the room. I've never known any person to pack clothes that quickly. Within ten minutes, we're walking out the door to my car and heading to my house so that I can pack a few last minute things into my bag.

We're at my place for less than five minutes, before we're walking back out the door and getting back into my car. The lure of being away from prying eyes and having Katy to myself for four days straight is so appealing, I can't put it in to words.

The drive takes almost 2 hours and when we get into the small coastal town, we stop at the small supermarket to stock up on food and other supplies.

"Joe, we haven't see you around town for a while, and you never bring anyone with you."

"Hi Dawn, how are you?" I ask the older lady at the checkout, who just so happens to be the owner. "This is Katy, my good friend. Katy, this is Dawn, she owns this dinky little store and keeps all my favourites in stock for when I get into town." I feel Katy's body stiffen beside me when I call her my *friend,* but I have no clue what I should call her. She relaxes though as she talks to Dawn.

"It's nice to meet you Dawn, but I should warn you, keeping Joe's favourites in stock won't do you any good. He'll either come back or he won't. Not to mention, he's fussy about his food."

Dawn throws her head back and laughs. "I like this girl, she's just what you need Joe." Before either of us can reply, she's bagged our stuff, and I've paid for everything, then we're walking back out the door.

The rest of the drive to the house is quiet. Neither of us speaks, both of us lost in our own thoughts, and it's a little awkward. I pull up out the front of the house without thinking about where I am. I push the button on the remote I keep in my car, and the garage door starts to open.

Beside me, Katy lets out a gasp and it's the first noise she's made since leaving Dawn's store. I look at Katy and her mouth is hanging open and her eyes are wide. "Ohh Joe, it's beautiful. So you and yet just stunning."

"I think I'll take that as a compliment Katy." I grumble as I park the car in the garage.

"It was meant as a compliment Joe." Katy says as we both get out of the car and meet at the back to collect our things. "I'm not sure what I was expecting, but it wasn't this."

As I let us into the house from the garage and turn off the alarm, I can't help but wonder exactly what it was she was expecting to find.

"Wow, you've even got it alarmed." Katy says behind me.

"I'm not here very often, so yes I have a security system. I know I can trust the locals, but who knows who will pass through town and realise the house isn't occupied for most of the year?" I didn't think there was anything wrong with protecting my property.

"I didn't mean anything by it Joe, honestly." She doesn't say anything else because we've stepped in the house itself. It's nothing like my house she's been in so many times in the city. It's almost softer in a way.

"Let me give you the grand tour." I say. Taking her hand in mine I lead us into the kitchen and leave the shopping bags on the bench. "Kitchen." I say with a nod, before moving on to the bathroom and bedroom on the lower floor. Then I lead her up the stairs to the main bedroom and the adjoining bathroom. "This is my room. Our room for the weekend." I put my bag down on the floor at the foot of the bed and take Katy's from her hand and place it next to mine.

"This is your room?" she asks me, but I know what she really wants to know.

"Yes. No one else has ever stayed here Katy. James comes up with me, sometimes my mum, but they stay downstairs. For obvious reasons, because no matter what people said at school, James and I have never had sex. He's not my type and I'm not his, not in a million years."

She laughs, loudly. "I have a confession to make Joe and I really hope you can forgive me. This may not be the best place for me to make this kind of confession but here goes." She takes a breath, but I can still hear the laughter in her voice. "It was me. I started those rumours."

"What?" Is she kidding me? Why? Why would she do that?

"I did it because you always gave Kami so much grief and she liked James so much. I just wanted you to feel one miniscule amount of what she felt. In retrospect, it's one of the funniest things I've ever done, because I know without a doubt, you guys aren't gay." Once the last word is out of her mouth, she loses her shit in a fit of laughter.

I just stand there, watching her laugh and I struggle not to laugh myself. She's right, I did deserve it, but the only people who gave either of us any grief about it knew we were in fact, not gay.

"Oh Joe. Are you mad at me?" Katy asks, having controlled her hysterical laughter. I'm still thinking about how I can use this to my advantage when she reaches up and caresses my cheek. "I don't want to do anything to upset you Joe. That was a long time ago and like you said, no one actually *believed* the rumour."

"You're right, *most* people didn't believe it, but it did make for some pretty uncomfortable conversations over the years when kids who thought we had been outted, came out to us and then hit on us."

"Ohhh they didn't hit on you guys, did they?" Her eyes widen, and she looks so surprised I want to be offended but I can't. Instead, I let out a loud laugh.

She takes a swing and hits me in the shoulder which makes me laugh even harder. "You can be such an arsehole sometimes Joseph French, and just when I was starting to feel bad for starting the rumour to begin with."

She turns to walk away, but I reach out and pull her close to me. "I heard a lot worse things said about me Katy. Even worse about James, thanks to his father's reputation, so this one rumour was nothing in comparison honey."

"So you forgive me?"

"There's nothing to forgive."

"I know. I did it because you were being an arsehole and I don't regret it, not for a second." She pulls away from me and turns to walk away, I reach out and smack her cute butt, making her jump a little as a small squeal escapes her lips. "Come on, we've got food that needs to be put away before I can go exploring."

Then she's gone and I'm left standing in my room that I never share with anyone wondering what the hell I'm doing. Kathryn fucking Ellis is here, in the space I share with no one and she's already taking over.

After we put all the food away, Katy asks me to take her for a walk and show her the yard before it gets too dark. I'm proud of all the work we've done out here. Well mostly James has done, but it's all my design, what I wanted built out here. I started out helping him but when I constantly damaged either myself or what we were working on, he begged me to stop and let him get a couple of the guys in to help him out. I wanted to help build it with my own blood, sweat and tears, but even I know when to call it quits and leave it to an expert.

We walk around and then sit out on the back porch watching the sun set, then we go in to make ourselves something to eat. We settle in to eat while watching a movie that I can't recall. Katy leans her body into mine and I can feel her body relaxing, I look down at her face. Her eyes are closed, and her breathing is starting to even out. I turn off the TV, manoeuvre us around so that I can pick her up and carry her up the stairs to bed. When I gently put her down on the bed and start to undress her, she wakes up. She's warm, supple and compliant.

"Make love to me Joe." She says quietly and when I look into her eyes I know I can't say no to her.

I slowly undress myself and lower my body to hers. Her legs wrap around my hips and her hands reach up behind my head, her fingers twisting into my hair. I reach to take a condom from the bedside drawer when Katy whispers in my ear, "I need you Joe." Her words fuel my desire and make me move faster. I've got the condom on in record time and when I run a finger through her pussy lips, I can feel how ready for me she is. When I push my cock into her body, we both sigh. I move slowly, kissing all over her face, neck and chest, then back up to kiss every part of her face.

"Joe, baby, I'm so close. I need you. Please." I know she wants me to go faster but I can't. I need it to be gentle and slow tonight, so instead of picking up my pace, I reach between us and push on her clit. Rolling my finger over and over her until her breathing becomes erratic and then, without warning, she breathes out my name. I feel her clenching around my cock it's all I need to come myself.

I've never felt a connection like that before. Never felt so complete and overwhelmed. I wanted to enjoy every moment of bringing Katy pleasure.

I get rid of the condom and throw it in the bin next to my bed, pull up the covers and pull Katy into my arms. I kiss behind her ear and murmur, "Go to sleep honey." That's all it takes for her body to relax and her breathing to even out again. She lets out a low snort and sighs, making me chuckle but the noise disturbs Katy, making her wiggle her butt which is right up against my cock.

Willing the dirty bastard to go to sleep, I close my eyes and just enjoy having my woman sleeping in my arms. All night and then getting to spend the next few nights, just like this.

Chapter Twenty-one

KATY

I wake up wrapped in Joe's arms. It's the best sleep I've had in a long time and I feel happy. I know he freaked out a little at my place yesterday, but I don't want to worry about anything other than enjoying being us and seeing what we could really be like this weekend.

I make a move to get out of bed, but Joe won't let me go. "Just a few more minutes until I'm awake honey, ok?"

"Ok Joe." I say and settle back into his arms.

After a few minutes, Joe reaches down and smacks my butt, then he pulls away from me and says, "Go on, go to the bathroom, I'll go make some breakfast."

"I'm making breakfast this morning, how about you go to the bathroom and meet me in the kitchen?" I say, giving him a smacking kiss on the lips and moving to put on clothes.

He shrugs his shoulders, "If you insist Katy."

"I do, off you go." I shoo him away. I'm distracted by the sight of him walking away, watching his back and butt muscles work to move him. When he disappears into the bathroom, I shake my head and move my own body down the stairs to the other bathroom.

Moving into the kitchen, I look in the fridge and pull out everything I need and get cooking. Then I grab everything else from the pantry. I've got music playing on my phone and I'm in the zone. I don't even hear Joe come down the stairs. I only know he's there when I turn around to find him leaning against the wall with a smile spread across his face.

"What are you smiling about Joseph?" I ask, a smile of my own on my face.

"I'm just enjoying the vision in my kitchen, honey." He stalks over to me but doesn't touch me. "Do you know how much I enjoy having you in my space Kathryn?"

"No." I manage to squeak out. I clear my throat and say, "Why don't you tell me how much you enjoy me being in your space Joseph?"

"Too much." He growls. "So, what is this masterpiece you seem to be whipping up this morning?" His sudden change of subject and attitude almost gives me whiplash.

"Masterpiece." I scoff, I don't cook much but I can and do cook breakfast when I have the time and I make time for it on weekends and holidays. "It's nothing extravagant Joe, just bacon, poached eggs on toast with some hollandaise sauce."

"Not a masterpiece huh? Sounds like it to me." I smile up at him, I know he's just saying that. It's more than common knowledge that Joseph French is a food snob of the highest order.

"Sit down Joseph and eat your breakfast," I say with a roll of my eyes. He's trying to be all smooth and charming. It works on me without him putting in the extra effort, but he doesn't need to know that.

"Aren't you joining me?" He ask.

"Just give me a second and I'll be right there." I've placed both of our plates on the table and I bring two coffees to the table, he still hasn't started eating yet. "Why aren't you eating Joe? It'll get cold."

"I wanted to wait for you." He says simply and it's just his way. Easy, simple words, and always just enough to get his thoughts across. It's one of the things I liked most about him.

"Well, let's eat then Joseph." I say and start enjoying my breakfast, after a few minutes I realise he isn't eating. "Is something wrong Joe?"

"Not at all, Katy. Not. At. All." Well OK then.

"You're making me uncomfortable Joe. Stop looking at me and eat the breakfast I made for you." I lay my knife and fork down on the table.

"What are you doing Katy?" he asks. Can he really be so stupid?

"I'm not eating until you do. You're making me feel weird. You're just sitting there, watching me eat. It's damn weird Joe."

He shakes his head, "I'm sorry. It's just so nice to be sitting with someone who actually enjoys eating. So many people, women more so, think it's not polite to eat a bloody meal. I'm always more offended that they don't eat the food someone made the effort to make, than congratulating them for being polite."

"Well then, don't just sit there staring at me. Eat what I've cooked for *you*, before it's ruined please."

He picks up his cutlery and starts eating, so I picked mine back up and continue eating. He moans quietly a second later and I look up to see his eyes closed, and a look of absolute pleasure spreading across his face. I remember seeing that very look last night as he came. With that thought, comes the memories and my fork stops moving in mid-air and I swallow deeply. Joe opens his eyes and I quickly fill my mouth with food, stopping me from saying anything too stupid. For now anyway.

"This is delicious Katy." He smiles at me, not his sexy smirk or his amused smile, no this one is more subtle. "No-one has cooked breakfast for me in a very long time honey."

"Surely someone from your past has made you breakfast the next morning Joseph?" I don't say it to torment him, I'm just saying, surely *someone* has made the man a meal before that he hasn't had to pay for?

"No Kathryn. Coffee? Yes. But not a breakfast, cooked or not." I want to ask more but I don't think I want the answers.

"Well I'm more than happy to cook you the few things that I know how to Joe." I smile at him, hoping he sees it as the invitation it was meant to be. Nothing more is said until we finish our plates, with Joe scrapping his clean. "What have you got planned for us today?" I ask.

"I thought I could take you around town. Show you the sights as it were?" I nod my agreement.

"I would love that."

"But first thing's first Miss Ellis." He says, the sexy smirk tilting up the corner of his mouth. "We need to get you out of my shirt and into something that you can wear in public."

"Do you mean I can't wear your shirt in public Joe?" I take that as a dare myself. I'd forgotten that was all I had on and my underwear of course. I stand to clean up the dishes and Joe takes them from me.

"Go have a shower gorgeous, I'll clean up." He says, kissing me lightly. I move closer to deepen the kiss and he says, "We won't leave the house if you do that honey."

"I wouldn't complain about that for a second Joseph."

"Get moving woman." He smacks me lightly on the butt and gets me moving with a squeal and laughter.

While I'm in the bathroom I can hear Joe moving around downstairs. I obviously have no clue what he's doing down there and honestly, I don't really care. I wrap a towel around my body and walk back into the bedroom we're sharing. I notice that Joe's unpacked his clothes and they're all hanging in the closet. I should have known he was the kind of guy who always unpacks his stuff. He's just so ... particular about everything. I'm more of a, 'live out of my suitcase while I'm away' kind of girl.

I see the shirt I just took off sitting on the bed where I left it, and then I get an idea. He said I couldn't wear it out in public, but if I know Joseph French, that's not the only business shirt he bought on a weekend trip out of the city. I look in the cupboard and laugh. Of course he bought more than enough to dress a small office. A plan forms in my mind and I can't help the laugh that escapes me.

I get dressed, put my hair up in a ponytail and head back down the stairs to find Joe talking on the phone, staring out the window with a scowl on his face.

"No *Harry*, I won't be visiting you or Mum this weekend." He closes his eyes and lets out a deep sigh. "No I can't. Harry, I'm not even in town, I'm out at the ... " his eyes widen before he says sharply, "No! No you're not coming out here. We've been over this Harry, I don't want you here. This is *my* house not yours and the fact is, I have guests this weekend and I don't have space for you."

He hasn't seen me yet and I don't want him to think I'm spying on his conversation, so I walk up to him and gently put my hand on his shoulder. He starts, surprised but doesn't turn towards me or acknowledge I'm there for a few breaths. Then he looks at me and mouths, 'sorry'. I shrug my shoulders in reply. If he has to talk to his father, then so be it. I raise an eyebrow at him and nod my head to let him know I'll wait out on the back deck for him.

I turn to leave, and he reaches out and holds my hand. When I look back at him, he shakes his head no, so I stay with him.

"Harry, I have to go. No, you can't come out to the house this weekend. I already told you, I have guests and there's no room." He sighs, closes his eyes but pulls me in closer to his body, so I wrap my arm around his waist. "You're right Harry, I *don't* want you here, only it has nothing to do with you being my father and everything to do with you. Goodbye Harry." I can hear Harry French cursing up a storm as Joe hangs up the phone.

"Now there's a side of Harry people in town don't get to hear. I knew he was a piece of work Joe, but I didn't know he spoke to you like that." I reach up and gently touch his jaw, bringing his eyes to meet mine and ask, "Is he always like that Joe?" He nods yes. "Has he always been like that to you? Even when we were kids?" He nods again.

He rests his forehead on mine and closes his eyes. "Right up until I was almost a teenager, he was perfectly fine. We were the picture of a happy family and then something changed, and he started getting really nasty."

"Do you know what changed?" I ask, wanting to know but not really wanting to push him too hard. He doesn't share anything about his past or family life with anyone. I think the only one knows anything about it is James, and that makes sense because they supported each other.

"I overheard my parents fighting, quite a few times over the same thing, but I'm not exactly sure if what I heard is accurate."

"Do you need some help trying to work out if it's true or, as you say, accurate?"

"No." he says a little too quickly, but I can't make him share his thoughts or feelings with me, and I still don't want to push him either. "No, I don't want to think about Harry French this weekend. He's just being his usual bastard self thinking he can do whatever the hell he wants." He leans down and kisses the tip of my nose. "Are you ready to get out of here, and see what the town has to offer, Miss Ellis?"

"Why yes I am, Mr French." I say, giving him a smacking kiss on the lips, turning around with his hand still in mine grabbing my bag and walking towards the door.

Suddenly, I'm pulled to a stop just as I reach for the door handle. "What is it Joe?" I ask as I turn slightly to look back at him.

"Is that my shirt you're wearing Katy?" he says, his voice is deep, but I can't tell if he's impressed or not.

"Yes, yes it is Joe. You told me I couldn't wear it out in public, but I'm pretty sure I'm proving you wrong right now." Opening the door, I walk out the door, his hand dropping away. Do I add an extra swing to my hips as I walk away? You better believe I do. Do I think he's enjoying the view? You better believe it. I put on a pair of simple dark wash blue jeans and topped them off with one Joe's white shirts. I tied his shirt at my waist, buttons undone with a pale blue lacy camisole underneath, showing just enough boob to tease anyone. I lean against the car, boobs pushed up slightly and ask, "So, you coming Joe?"

He coughs, and I'm pretty sure I hear him mumble, 'She's trying to fucking kill me'. Instead of answering me, he walks over to the car, unlocks it and gets in, leaning over to push my door open. I step back as the door opens and then slide myself into the seat, buckling myself in, but Joe still hasn't started the car.

I'm about to ask him if everything is ok when he nods to himself, mutters something and starts the car. "How about we start with a coffee at the café and I'll show you around town. Then I can drive you to one of my favourite spots to sit and have lunch?" He looks over at me, a devastatingly handsome smile on his face. A smile that reminds me why I like him so much and what other people see isn't what he is.

Chapter Twenty-two

JOE

When I realise that the shirt Katy's wearing is mine I stop in my damn tracks. I've never thought of myself as the possessive type but seeing her in one of *my* shirts causes all kinds of reactions in my body, one of which is a distinct tightening in my chest, not quite pain, but definitely a longing for more. It also causes my cock to harden pretty damn fast, especially when she gives me sass about it and puts an extra swing in those sexy hips of hers as she walks to the car, almost making lose my hard-earned control right there on my front step.

Who would have thought that jeans and a man's business shirt could bring out the most basic needs in a man? Not me. I shake my head to clear it and walk over to my car. When I get in, I reach over and open her door for her from inside. I know *should* have been a gentleman and gone around and opened it for her, but I couldn't be that close to her without giving in to my base instincts.

Instead of pulling her into my lap and making us both come like I want to, I take her hand and thread our fingers together. I bring her hand up to my lips, drop a kiss on the back of it and then rest them on the console between us.

I pull up in front of the café, but I don't make a move to get out of the car.

"Are we going in Joe?" Katy asks me. I nod, get out of the car and walk around to her side of the car just as she's closing the door. I reach out and thread our fingers together again, an overwhelming need to touch her, buzzes through me. The feeling that if I don't hold on tight now, she'll be gone. Forever.

We're seated at a table and ordered before I can look at her. "Is everything OK Joe?" Katy asks, in a quiet voice and I hate that I've made her doubt herself, or us.

I reach over and take her hand in mine again, the need to touch her is too great not to and say, "Everything is perfect. You're here and we can relax. Just be together."

"That's the plan Joe." She says with a smile. "I can see why you like it here. It's a beautiful town, so quiet. Almost too tranquil, when you come from the city."

"It's not like we live in the heart of the city Katy." I laugh and she joins me, making the tension disappear and an easiness settle in its place.

We have coffee and cake, sitting there at the table just talking. Laughing and getting to know each other again. Once we're done eating, we order takeaway coffee's and I take Katy for a walk around town. It doesn't take long, but it's long enough and we're free. Free to walk together, free to hold hands, to stop for a kiss, without worrying about who might see us. I know we're both thinking it, but I don't want to jinx it.

We stop by the bakery, get a few things for lunch and head back to my car. Katy keeps asking me where we're going but I don't tell her, I want it to be a surprise. It's not like she knows the area anyway but what she doesn't understand is that this is the place James and I used to come to escape. To escape everything as soon as we were old enough to drive.

We pull up in the makeshift parking area that hasn't changed in all the years I've been coming here. There never seems to be more than a handful of cars here either and you never run into their occupants, it's like an unwritten rule up here, leave everyone else alone.

Reaching for the bag of goodies and then Katy, I lock the car and walk to the spot that has become my refuge. "Pull up a piece of semi-clean rock honey and I'll feed you."

"It would be my pleasure handsome." Katy doesn't hesitate to sit down in the dirt and it's one of the many reasons I love her. Yeah, I know. There's nothing else to call what I feel for Kathryn Ellis. I hand her a cold drink and the sandwich she chose, then I sit myself down next to her and we eat. Sitting in the tranquil beauty and drinking it in. "Thank you for bringing me here

Joe, it's beautiful." Katy says quietly, as if speaking any louder would destroy the tranquillity.

"James and I came here all the time as soon as we could drive ourselves. We found it by accident one day, driving away from the troubles that hung around our necks like weights at home." I laugh at the memory of how we landed here. "We ran out of fuel and the car just died, right out the front of Dawn's store. We were swearing and cursing like sailors and she came outside, told us to mind our manners and then called her husband to come help us out." I laugh and shake my head again, memories flooding my brain. "Neither James or I had ever had an adult take us to task and then look after us before. Her husband, ironically his name was Joe but never call him Joseph, filled up the tank and then drove the car to their house. They made us stay the night, because we weren't driving home at night and the rest, as they say, is history. James and I came back to town every chance we had. Dawn feeding us and making sure we were safe, Joe making sure we had a male influence that wasn't an alcoholic or dickhead. He taught us both how to look after our cars, he took James under his wing and showed him the basics of carpentry. Dawn saw that I knew how to work with numbers and helped me get my footing there. We owe, I owe them everything." I haven't looked at Katy while I've spoken, too lost in my memories.

"What happened to Joe?" she asks, quietly.

"He died a few years ago." I close my eyes, that memory still stings. "We kept putting off coming up here, you know, life work, stuff just got in the way. Then one day, Jen, Dawn's neighbour called to tell me that Joe was in the hospital. James and I raced up here, but we were maybe an hour too late. When we got here, Joe was already gone, and Dawn was on her own. He was chopping up the wood that we were supposed to have done weeks ago. The stress gave him a heart attack and he was gone." I swallow down my guilt. "I try to come up as often as I can but, like Dawn said yesterday, it's been a while. I can't remember the last time James made it up here."

"So, you built a house up here to be closer to Dawn?"

"Yeah. I designed it, well mostly. I *told* James what I wanted, he drew up some designs and I shuffled things around until I got what I wanted, then we built it."

"You guys built it? Together?" Katy asks and I should be annoyed at her shock that I built anything but I'm not.

"Well, OK James and a few guys from his crew built it and I was their goffer. James won't let me touch tools, powered or not." I say with a shrug of my shoulders. "Tools and building, they're not one of my many talents honey."

"I can't believe James would even let you on a work site at all, to be honest handsome." Katy laughs, it's a beautiful sound and I laugh with her. She's not wrong, some people are made to work with their hands, I'm not one of them. Give me a spreadsheet and some numbers to crunch and I'm in my element.

"He let me on site so far as I could help others do things, I wasn't allowed to touch the tools. Not even a fucking hammer." I say with laugh. "But yes, we built it, with James' own two hands."

Katy's laughter rings out through the quiet of the lake and bush that surrounds us. "I'm glad you have each other Joe."

"Me too Katy, me too." I'm not sure where we would have ended up if we hadn't of had each other.

I kiss her gently on the forehead, she tilts her head back and kisses my lips just as gently. Just like always, within seconds kisses with this woman turn hot and needy.

When I pull away she moans and reaches for me, but I'm already up on my feet, rubbish in hand and pulling her to her feet. I want her, but I won't be taking her out here where anyone can stumble on us. I'm not a horny teenager anymore. "I need you too Katy, but not here."

We make it back to the car, and my house in record time. I dump the bags on the kitchen bench, not once letting go of her hand and then led her to the bedroom. *Our* bedroom, where I strip out of my clothes as she reclines back on the bed, watching me. Then it's her turn. I peel off her clothes and she's fucking stunning.

I run my hands up her thighs, skimming up her ribs, straight up to her glorious breasts and I palm them, massaging them like it's the last time I'll get close enough to. I lean down and run my tongue over her nipples, one at a time, until they start to stiffen.

"Joe." Her voice is raspy and full of need. Her hands are buried in my hair, pulling and tugging, driving me insane. "I need you Joe. I need you inside me."

I grab a condom, roll it down my hard cock and line myself up with her pussy. With her hands kneading her breasts, my hands holding her legs up to my chest and our eyes locked, I enter her pussy. We both sigh and Katy closes her eyes. "Watch me Katy." Her eye snap open and I start moving. My hips pump back and forth at a steady pace, building the pleasure but not to the point of orgasm just yet. I want to prolong the pleasure, enjoy loving the gorgeous woman in my bed.

"Ohhh Joe." Katy moans, pinching her nipples and pushing her hips up to meet mine, never once breaking eye contact. It's the hottest, most intimate sex I've ever had.

Katy bites down on the corner of her lip, one sure sign she's getting close.

"Faster Joe. Please." I can hear the begging in her voice and every instinct tells me to give her what she wants. My hips move faster without any conscious thought, I just want to give her what she needs.

I grip her thighs tighter, positive she's going to have marks there in the morning, but I couldn't care less about that right now. I can feel her body start to shake, the tremors working their way through her body and I can't hold back any longer. I draw my cock out of her pussy and then slam back into her, over and over again until she's screaming my name and her pussy clenches around my cock. My body takes over and I'm all about my own release. Within seconds of Katy's, "Ohhh fuckkkkk Joe!" I'm done. I let go of her legs and they land softly on the bed.

I take care of the condom, and when I get back I lift Katy off the bed, pull back the covers and gently lay her back down. I lay down beside her, pulling the covers over us as I do, covering us up. Then I pull her into my body, I want her as close to me as I can get.

This is how I want to fall asleep every night. This beautiful woman by my side, knowing she'll be here every morning maybe we can make a life together.

WHEN I WAKE UP THE next morning, the bed next to me is warm, but empty. I can hear Katy's voice and I can't work out where she is. Then I start to laugh, I stretch my sated body and get out of bed. When I reach the bathroom, I lean up against the doorframe and watch. Katy's in the shower, my shower, shampoo bottle in hand and she's singing. Not for the first time, she brings a smile to my face while she's singing.

"Shit." She squeals. "How long have you been standing there Joseph?" She almost drops the bottle, juggling it so it doesn't hit the floor. "You almost gave me a heart attack."

I don't answer her, instead I walk over to the shower, open the door and step in.

"What do you think you're doing Joe?" she squeaks. We've had sex I don't know how many times and still she gets all shy and nervous around me.

"Saving water honey." I reply and soap up my hands. Without saying another word, I run my soaped up hands up and down her arms, back and stomach. She doesn't move, so I soap up again and squat down and wash from her ankles up to her thighs. I've missed all the good bits, for now at least. I stand up and Katy's eyes are half closed, "You OK there Katy?"

Her eyes snap open and she says, "Of course I am. I can wash myself Joseph, I've been doing it for years without your help and I'll do it for years to come, without your help."

She moves to snatch the soap out of my hands, but I move faster. "Not today you're not." Before she can respond my hands slide over her breasts, massaging, kneading and of course, cleaning every last inch. I watch as the soap bubbles travel down her stomach, my hand follows them, and I find her clit, erect and waiting for my attention. I run my finger slowly over her, lean over and whisper in her ear, "Still wanna shower by yourself honey?" Then I bite her ear and slide two fingers into her pussy, the only sound I get is a growl as her hips push into my hand.

I kiss and nibble along her jaw, and down her throat to her collarbone. A shudder runs down her spine and I feel her pussy clench around my fingers. "How you going there honey? Enjoying your shower yet?" I ask, my voice low in her ear.

"Arghhhh Joe."

"Yes Katy? What can I do for you honey?" I ask.

"Joe. I'm so." She takes a deep, shuddering breath. "Joe I'm so close, please don't stop."

"I promise I won't stop until you come all over my hand, Katy." The dirty talk takes her over the edge and her nails dig into my shoulders as she comes. All over my hand. I bring my hand up to my lips, and wait until she opens her eyes, then I suck them into my mouth and lick them clean.

"Holy shit Joe." I couldn't agree more, holy shit is perfect.

"Think you're all clean now Katy?"

She laughs and says, "You're the dirty one Joseph." Swatting me on the shoulder.

"I don't hear you complaining honey." I say with a smirk, I smack her butt and push out the door. "Now get out of here so I can get cleaned up and we can have breakfast."

"How come I don't get to make you dirty?" She asks with a pout that I almost give in to.

"I'm dirty enough already and I have other plans for you today, so move that gorgeous butt and get dressed, before I have my wicked way with you again and we never get out of here."

I can see her weighing up her choices, then I growl, making her jump and she wraps a towel around her delectable body, and she's gone. I shower fast, dry faster and walk back into the bedroom with a towel wrapped around my waist. I quickly get myself dressed and make my way down to the kitchen. I find Katy leaning against the bench, doing something on her phone and I say, "Come on, I'm taking you out for breakfast." I take her hand in mine, pick up my keys and we're gone.

I drive to a café in the next town for breakfast. We've been light-hearted and joking around all morning, it's nice to be able to relax. I excuse myself to go to the bathroom and when I wander back into the dining room, I look at Katy. She's beautiful, sitting at our table, enjoying the sunshine streaming through the window. She's watching something outside and when I get closer I can see she's got a smile on her face, but that smile hasn't made it to her eyes, they're almost sad. I look outside and see a mother with a couple of kids laughing and running around. I clear my throat and speak as I reach our table, "Everything OK Katy?" I ask quietly, as I sit down.

She looks over at me and her face has transformed, she's smiling brightly, too brightly perhaps and when she speaks, she sounds almost too happy. "Yes, of course it is. It's a gorgeous area Joe, I'm so glad we came."

"I'm glad you came too." I say, with a smirk, hoping to get her to laugh. We've left the café and are walking around the centre of town, and she laughs quietly.

"I can't take you anywhere Joseph." I squeeze her hand, already held tightly in mine.

"You can take me anywhere you want," I lean in and whisper in her ear and I feel the shudder work through her body.

"Jesus Joe, you can't say that ... " she starts to say but I smother her words with a kiss. A kiss that was supposed to be sweet and tender, but I can't help deepening it when she responds so passionately to me, opening her mouth for more and gripping my side with her free hand.

She pulls away suddenly when a kid shrieks somewhere in the distance and rests her head in the crook of my neck. The mother and her child walk passed us, smiling at Katy the woman says something along the lines of, 'enjoy your alone time while you can'. She smiles back at the woman, but I feel Katy stiffen in my arms.

Katy doesn't say a word as we walk back to the car. The short drive back to the house is quiet, the music playing on the radio the only noise. I reach over and take her hand in mine again, holding on tight. I pull into the garage, the door closing behind us and move to get out of the car, Katy doesn't move right away, but before I can speak she's suddenly out of the car and in the house. Pacing in front of the TV and chewing on a fingernail. I start to ask her what's wrong, but she speaks before I can.

"I need to know something Joe and I want an honest answer." She stops pacing for a second to look at me, and I nod.

"I will always be honest with you Katy." I say.

She nods to herself and then starts up with the pacing again. I throw my keys down on the table, but I make no other movements.

"Do you want a family Joe?" she asks, but before I can answer she speaks again. "You know, the wife, the kids, the dog and the white picket fence? The whole picture perfect thing?"

"Do I want a family?" I ask, and she nods, still pacing and making me really fucking nervous. "Before we got together, I hadn't really thought about it to be honest Katy. My parents aren't exactly a great model of family life, but yes, I've always wanted kids of my own. A family to call mine. To create a family and make it everything I ever wanted." I take a couple of steps closer to Katy, I need her to stop with the pacing long enough so that we can talk. "If you're asking do I want all those things with you, then the answer is yes."

"I can't give you that Joe." She says, a sob wracks her body as she takes a step away from me, but I don't let her go too far.

"What do you mean Katy? What can't you give to me?"

"All of it. Any of it. I can't give that happy family to you Joe."

I reach out to bring her into my arms, to hold her but she steps out of my reach. "I didn't mean now Katy. I didn't even mean any time soon. We have things to sort out first and."

She doesn't let me finish, "No Joe. You don't understand. I can't have kids. I can't give you the family you want." The tears are streaming down her cheeks now and I have no idea what the hell she's talking about.

"What do you mean, Katy?" I ask, but before she can answer or I can ask any more questions, there's a loud noise at the front door, some cursing and then the door flies open.

"What the *fuck* are you doing here Harry? I told you I had company." I ask, as my father stumbles loudly into the room. "And since when do you have a key to my home?"

"This isn't your *home,* this is your escape." He looks up from the mess he created and finally see's Katy standing next to me. "When you said you had people here, I figured you meant James. You never bring anyone else up here. Not even me."

He's right, I don't. "So how do you have a key then?" I know I didn't give him one.

"I've had it for years. Been coming here when you're not here since you built the thing." He looks at Katy and says, "I'm sorry, did I interrupt something? Looks like you're breaking more hearts hey son?" I've never wanted to punch the old man more in my life.

"No Mr French, that would be my job today." She gives him a weak smile, then looks at me. "I'm just going to go pack my stuff." I reach out for her, but she dodges my hand and heads up the stairs. I don't want her to pack, I don't want my father here and I *want* to talk about this.

"It's alright son, whatever she did it's better to find out now and learn your lesson. Women are liars, they lie to get what they want and then they leave. I thought I taught you better than to get attached to one." Harry sniggers.

"You know what Harry? I don't care what you think. What I want is for you to hand over that key and trust me, the locks will be getting changed this week, so even if you don't hand it over, you won't be getting back inside without an invitation."

"You arrogant little son of a bitch ... " He starts, but I don't let him finish. I know he's about to go off on one of his many rants about how ungrateful and selfish I am, but I'm over him and his shit.

"Get out Harry. I'm going up stairs to talk to Katy, I want you gone by the time I get back. You're not welcome here." I don't give him a chance to answer, I turn my back on him and head up the stairs. I can hear him cursing and calling me a few choice names, but the only things in my mind is getting to Katy.

When I reach the bedroom, she's already packed and holding her phone, which she puts in her pocket when she sees me. "I don't understand Katy. What the hell just happened? Please don't let my father ruin our weekend, I want to talk about this."

"This isn't about Harry, Joe, it's about us. We want different things. Look, I've come to terms with the fact that I can't have kids. Well that it's a real possibility that being a mother will never happen for me, but I can't ask you to accept never having kids Joe."

"You're not asking me Katy, I'm telling you. Yes I want a family, including kids, with you but that doesn't mean we have to make those choices now does it? No matter the reasons for you not being able to have kids."

"I have endometriosis Joe. It doesn't mean it's impossible for me to have kids, but it does mean it's highly unlikely and I can't ask you to give up having kids of your own."

"You're not asking me to do anything Katy. I just want to be with *you*, it's all I've ever wanted."

"No Joseph. I've had the best time this weekend, but now I just want to go home. Please." She looks at me and I can see the resignation in her eyes. "I can get Kami to come and get me, but I'd really rather not."

No, of course she doesn't want to call Kami, because then she might have to tell her she's with me. It's almost like this is her excuse to run. To leave me behind and never have to tell Kami anything. "Fine. We'll head home Kathryn, but this is *not* over. Not by a long shot."

Without another word she grabs her bag and heads downstairs and I'm left standing there wondering what the fuck just happened and how I can get my father out of my life once and for all.

Within twenty minutes I'm packed, the house is locked up tight again and we're in the car driving home. Katy hasn't said another word to me. I don't even know if Harry was still here when she got downstairs, but he was gone when I went back down, and the key was on the kitchen bench.

That's one thing dealt with, now I just have to get Katy to talk to me. The whole trip back, I'm planning in my head what to say but keep stopping myself. I want to say the right thing, I just don't know what that is. When I pull up outside her house, we've barely spoken more than a dozen words to each other.

I get out of the car, hand her bag over, but I don't let go of the handle as I say, "We need to talk about this Katy."

She nods and says, "Give me a couple days please Joe? I need some time."

"Time for what Katy? To talk yourself even further out of this relationship?"

"There is no relationship Joe." She says, looking at the ground.

"Look me in the eyes and tell me that Katy." Her head flies up and her eyes meet mine. They're cold and hard.

"There is no relationship Joe. You must have realised that when I couldn't bring myself to tell Kami about us?" Her voice is harsh and while I know she's being nasty to make it easier to walk away, it still cuts like a knife. I let go of her bag in shock, and she takes the opportunity to turn on her heel and walk away. There's nothing else I can do but watch. Watch her walk away from me, from us and let herself into her house and lock the door, with me outside.

What the fuck just happened?

Chapter Twenty-three

KATY

The drive home from Joe's house in the country is quiet. I can see he's trying to work out what to say to me, but I don't want to talk, so I close my eyes and pretend to be asleep. I let him take my hand in his because I want to feel his touch for as long as I can before I walk away.

My body tenses the closer to home we get, but he doesn't let go of my hand. When he pulls up outside my house, I pull my hand from his and get out of the car without looking back or saying anything. I can't.

When I finally look at him, he looks like I've taken away his favourite thing in the world, my heart breaks, but I steal myself, hardening my heart. I knew getting involved with Joe, with anyone, was a bad idea and still I let myself fall in love with him. Yeah I know, I'm stupid.

It almost breaks me when he asks me to look him in the eye and tell him we don't have a relationship. It's the hardest thing I've ever done but when it's done, I turn and walk away. Letting myself into the house, I lock the door behind me, even though I know he won't follow me. He's not the kind of guy that will beg me to change my mind. He'll give me the time I asked for and by then, I'll have steeled my heart and be able to walk away. For good.

I drop my bag, not caring where it ends up and slide down the door to the floor. The tears started rolling down my cheeks as soon as I turned my back to Joe and now they're making the front of my shirt wet. Shit, making his shirt wet.

I'm not sure how long I sit there, crying my eyes out over the only decision I could make, but I get to my feet and tell myself to get over it. I've made my choice and now I have to live with it. I can't give Joe what he wants, what he needs, and while he doesn't understand that right now because he's hurting, he'll understand in the long run.

I've had a long time, a decade or more, to come to terms with the fact that children of my own probably won't be on the cards for me. I know that there are other ways of making a family that don't include having our own and maybe I should have discussed those options with Joe, but I saw the excitement in his eyes at just the thought of having kids of his own.

Instead of wallowing in the sadness in my heart at my decision, I spend the rest of the weekend cleaning my house. I want to be wrapped up in Joes arms, instead I clean and watch soppy movies. Eating and drinking my feelings, like the healthy human being I am.

Work is harder than I thought it would be on Tuesday, I was looking forward to the distraction of being busy but all everyone can talk about is their amazing long weekends. Joy notices my mood and keeps most of the other guys away from me, leaving me to sit in my little corner of the office, getting my work done.

At the end of the day, only Joy and myself are left. Everyone else, including Mr Wilks, have left for the day.

"Katy." I look up to see Joy sitting in the edge of my desk, "Are you OK, hun?"

I'm looking at her, I see her lips move and I hear her voice. I even understand her question, but I don't know how to answer. Is everything OK? Am I OK? I don't feel OK. "I will be Joy, thanks for asking." I say, when I realise that she's still waiting for me to answer.

Before she can ask me any more questions, my phone starts ringing. "Sorry Joy, it's my Dad, I have to take this." I say.

"OK Katy. Call me if you need anything, please?" she says.

I nod and say, "Thanks, I will."

"Hi Dad." I say answering my phone.

"Hey honey, how was your weekend?" he asks. He had a suspicion I was going away with Joe and I really hate having to tell him it didn't work out.

So, instead of going into any details, I just say, "Good, Dad. What about yours?"

He's quiet for a few beats, and then says, "Why don't you come out to the house and have dinner with us? We haven't seen you in ages."

"You saw me just a couple of weeks ago Dad, and it's not like we haven't spoken since then, in one form or another." I laugh, but it sounds empty, even to me.

"Indulge your old man would you sweetheart? It feels like forever since you've come out to the house and joined us for dinner. I know your Mum won't mind and I promise to have something chocolatey for dessert, just for you."

I laugh quietly. "Thanks Dad. I'm just leaving work now, so I'll be there soon."

"We'll see you soon then sweetheart. I love you." he says.

"I love you too, Dad." I reply, choking back a sob as I hang up. I love my parents and I agreed to dinner because my Dad invited me and let's face it, I don't have anything else to do, but telling my Dad about Joe, isn't going to be easy.

I lock up, walk the short distance back to my house, get in the car and head to my parents' house. I'm both looking forward to dinner and dreading it. I know my Dad is going to want to know what happened and my Mum isn't going to know anything was going on at all.

I pull up in their driveway, turn off the car and sit there for a minute. I've had the drive to think about what I'm going to say to my Dad, yet I still need to take a few deep breathes before I get out of the car and walk to the front door. Before I can reach for the handle, it swings open and there he stands. My Dad, my rock. He takes one step outside and waits for me with his arms open wide, waiting to hold me. The one man I can love, without thinking about it. I launch myself into his arms and hug him tight.

"Ohh sweetheart, whatever it is, we can work it out. You're the strongest woman I know, and I believe in you." His words just bring the tears closer to the surface. As I control my emotions and my breathing, my Dad turns us around and pulls me into his side, closing the door behind us, before I even realise he's done it. Then he walks us to the lounge room and pulls me down onto the couch. Never letting me go. Even now as an adult, there's no place like my father's arms, I always feel safe and loved. Cared about. "You don't have to tell me anything sweetheart, but I'm going to guess it has something to do with Joseph?" he asks. He said I didn't have to explain what happened, but I know he wants to know.

I nod my head, trying to collect my thoughts and my will to actually speak about him out loud. "Yeah it does. We broke up." I say and I feel my Dad stiffen beside me. "Don't Dad, this isn't his fault, it's all mine."

"If he did anything to hurt you Katy sweetheart, so help me I'll ..." I don't let him finish, I don't want him blaming Joe for anything.

"Stop Dad. He didn't do anything except admit that he wants a family. The whole perfect picture of a couple of sweet kids that look like him, a dog and the white picket fence. I can't give that to him Dad, you know I can't, so I walked away."

"Do you love him Katy?" he asks me softly. My Dad's question surprises me, and I pull back to look at his face. "You do don't you Katy?"

I nod my head, "Yeah I do." I admit for the first time out loud.

"Then why are you walking away Katy? You know there's more than one way to have a family. Especially these days and Joseph strikes me as the kind of man who just wants to be with you. Sure he'd love a family with you, but I doubt he would care how that happens. I saw the way he looks at you Katy. He loves you too."

This time, I shake my head, "No Dad, I can't ask him to sacrifice what he wants for me."

"Did you even give him the option, or did you run away Kathryn?" My Dad rarely uses my full name, he knows how much I hate it. "You didn't, did you? You made the choice for the both of you." He closes his eyes and shakes his head, "I'm disappointed Kathryn, I never would have called you selfish before now."

I pull out of his arms, "I'm being selfish for walking away and giving him a chance to have everything he wants? Really?" I ask, I can't believe what I'm hearing.

Just then, my Mum walks in and tells us that dinner is ready. She couldn't have better timing. Dinner is awkward and a little strained. While it's usually because I can't find anything to talk about with my Mum that doesn't cause a disagreement, this time it's because my Dad is annoyed at me.

"Is everything ok with you two?" Mum asks, looking between myself and Dad.

My Dad smiles at my Mum and says, "Everything is just fine my dear." But he doesn't look at me while he says it.

"If you say so dear." My Mum huffs then turns her attention to me. "So, how was your weekend away with Joseph at his cottage?"

"It's not exactly a cottage Mother." I say, before I can think of covering my surprise that she knows about the house or that I was there recently.

"So, you did visit there with him this weekend?" she asks, a smile twitching the corner of her mouth.

"Yes, I did Mother." I say. I really don't want to have this conversation again. Dad may be disappointed in me, but my mother will be devasted that I lost such a perfect potential husband. "We left because Harry turned up and Joe wasn't very happy."

"So I heard. It's about time Joe stood up to that man and told him what's what. How dare he think he can let himself into his son's home without permission or knowledge on Joseph's behalf. You know, I keep telling Felicity she could do so much better. I don't know why she doesn't just divorce the man and move on." My mother tuts and shakes her head. Like everything is as easy as snapping her fingers to fix.

"Sometimes things aren't that easy mother." I say quietly.

"You're right of course Kathryn, but sometimes, things really are that simple and easy." She's speaking softly and looking at me like she understands how I'm feeling, which is unusual because we rarely agree on much of anything. "Sometimes it's as simple as loving the other person enough to make things work. Sometimes it's enough for them to love you, not for what you can give them, but for what you can have together."

"I'm sure you're right." I know the smile I give her is tight, but I don't think I'm strong enough to have this conversation tonight.

"Harry hasn't done anything for Felicity or Joseph in years and he doesn't deserve their loyalty." There she is, the gruff woman that I love.

"You're right mother and I think Joe might have finally had enough of Harry this weekend."

"Good. Who wants dessert? Dad requested something with chocolate, I'm going to guess that's because his oldest daughter was joining us?" she smiles at me.

I smile back, knowing that's the exact reason he asked for a chocolate dessert. Now, I bet he's wishing he hadn't ask me to dinner and definitely hadn't requested my favourite dessert. Yes, I mean anything chocolate, with very few exceptions. "What are we having?"

"Your Dad got you some chocolate cheesecake. He said something about you needing your favourites tonight." She smiles at and continues, "Your Dad always looks after you."

I glance at my dad and say, "Yes, he does."

When dessert is done and my Mum has packed up some leftovers for me, because apparently I can't cook for myself. I can cook, I just rather not when I'm the only one eating.

My dad says goodbye and then wanders back into his study, without a backward glance.

"Is everything OK Kathryn? I've never seen you and your father so short with each other."

"Not even when I was being a rotten, rebellious teen?" I laugh, trying to lighten the mood and distract her.

"No, not even then. He always defended you, even when you were being a brat." She laughs, but I'm not sure there's any humour in it. "What's going on Kathryn? Does it have something to do with Joseph?" my mother asks, her voice more gentle than I've ever heard it.

I consider lying or just shrugging it off as just a difference of opinion, but the look on her face makes me confess. "Yes, it's about Joe. I broke up with him." I answer quietly. "Before you ask, yes that does mean we were together for a while and yes, Dad knew. Well, he didn't know for sure, but he worked it out."

"Well, your Dad has always known you pretty well." She says with a sad smile. "Why did you break up with him Kathryn?"

Here's the thing, telling my dad was hard but explaining to Anna the reasons why I can't stay with Joe, it makes me feel almost childish. "He wants a family, and I can't give him that, so I walked away. It was the hardest thing I've ever done, and Dad doesn't agree with my decision."

"You love him don't you? Joe I mean." She asks, and I can't speak, so I just nod my head. "Do you think you did the right thing Kathryn? For you and Joseph?" Again, all I can manage is nodding my head. "Did you discuss the reasons with him Kathryn or did you just walk away? Look darling, I'm not disagreeing with your choices, you have to live with them in the long run, but it's Joseph's choice as well. Isn't it?"

Once again, my only reply is a nod of my head. I can't speak because I know I'll break down and cry. If there's one person you don't show weakness in front of, its Anna Ellis.

"If you need anything Kathryn, even just to talk about it, I'm always here. I hope you know that?" She says, and I can see in her eyes that she really means it.

That makes me even more emotional. "Thanks Mum." I choke out, tears pooling in the corner of my eyes. When she hugs me good night, I almost lose it there and then. It's very rare in my adult life, even my childhood to be honest, that Anna has shown any kind of emotional support, or physical for that matter.

When we break apart, she reaches up and pats my cheek, saying, "I love you Kathryn, and I want to see you happy. I hope you know that?"

I can't answer, once again I'm just nodding like an idiot, then I turn and walk to my car.

The tears start rolling down my face as I start my car, and I look up to see my dad looking out the window, watching me drive away. It hurts that he's disappointed in me, but I still believe I'm doing the right thing and even the sad look on his face can't change my mind.

Chapter Twenty-four

JOE

The hardest thing I've ever had to do in my life is watch Katy walk away from me.

I could tell by the way her body tensed and her shoulders shook, that she was crying as she walked away from me. I watched until she was behind the closed door and then I stood there for a few more minutes. I wanted to stand there until I knew she was OK. I wanted to go inside that house, hold her close and tell her that it would be OK. We could work it out.

I take a step towards her house but instead of moving closer, I force myself to walk away. She asked me to give her a couple of days and I made a promise that I would give them to her, but does that mean I have to like it? I don't fucking think so. This is not how I pictured this weekend ending.

Did I think we'd talk about our future? Well sure, at some point, not necessarily this weekend, but eventually. Do I regret telling her what I wanted for our future? Not for a second. I do wish I understood what she means when she says she can't give me what I want.

I realise I'm still standing on the path outside her house, so I get in my car and I drive. When I stop the car, I look up and realise I've driven to James' house, and there's a car parked just behind his in the driveway. I know that car. I could easily blame myself or Harry for what happened this morning, and I do, but in my head, it all begins and ends with that one person.

Kami fucking Parker.

She's been the bane of my existence since her and her bitch mother walked back into town like they owned the place. She's had her eyes on my best friend since we were kids and I won't let her hurt him. I won't let history repeat itself, not if I can help it. James has to go out of town in just over

161

a week for a job, and I'm determined to use that time to make him see what she's really like.

I leave without talking to James, and when I get home it's quiet and empty. I've gotten used to having Katy here, either that or I'm at her house. I miss having someone else in my space, sharing the day's events and a meal. I miss Katy. How am I supposed to give her space? I'm barely surviving the first few hours and she wants a few days? How the hell did I get to the point where I can't function properly without being able to contact her?

I send a message to James, instead of Katy, to remind him he's got a job out of town soon and get a return message telling me to mind my own business. How's that for a thank you? One day he'll be happy I helped him out.

I spend the rest of what was supposed to be my weekend away with Katy, putting a few things in to into place.

I give Katy a few days, just like she asked and then I send her a text message to let her know I'm thinking about her, that I'm not walking away and that sooner, rather than later, we are going to sit down and talk this shit through. I don't get an answer and even though I wasn't really expecting one, it still pisses me off. I know how deeply being polite is ingrained into her and the fact that she can't bring herself to reply, even just a short something, cuts me.

At this point, I'd take a text telling me to fuck off and leave her alone, rather than the silence I'm getting. Day after day of nothing. Not even one message to let me know she's ok.

I should take the hint and walk away I guess, but I just can't. I want to give her the space and time she thinks she needs to sort out whatever it is she's needs to sort out, but it's killing me.

While I'm waiting for Katy to talk to me, I know I'm not a pleasant man to be around. Jenny is telling me to go to hell, which never happens. While I could put it down to being in her last few weeks of pregnancy and hormones, I know I really can't. Nadine is running in the opposite direction if she sees me coming before I can speak to her and that girl is not afraid to speak her mind, its why I hired her in the first place. According to Jenny, I can be pretty intimidating, and I needed someone with a backbone while she's on leave with the baby. I don't see myself that way, I just like things the way I like them. I know I'm being a grumpy arsehole at the moment, but I don't think

I'm being too unreasonable in wanting things done right though. We've all still got a bloody job to do and it needs to be done right.

So that I'm not terrorising my staff unnecessarily while thinking about Katy, I lock myself in my office and just get shit done. I don't want to talk to anyone, I don't want to deal with clients. I only deal with the ones that insist on talking to me, but by the end of our meetings, they're wishing they'd stayed away.

I have one such meeting any minute and I can't find the files I need. Instead of going out to see Jenny and asking her like a normal man running a business, I shout, "Jenny, where are the damn files for the Wallis meeting? Why aren't they here on my desk like usual?"

The outer office is quiet, and I don't receive an immediate answer, instead I look up to see a heavily pregnant woman slowly walk into my office and lower herself in the chair opposite me with a huge sigh. I don't know whether the sigh is because she's off her feet, or because she has to talk to me.

"How are you doing Jenny?" I ask, feeling like a complete arsehole because I shouldn't be taking my frustrations about Katy out on her. For one, she's pregnant and her husband, Travis, will kill me if anything happens to her or the baby. Secondly, she's the best assistant I could ask for and I want her to come back. No, I need her to come back when she's ready after the baby arrives.

"Funny you should ask that Joseph, because I was going to ask you the same thing." I can't remember the last time Jenny called me Joseph. Either inside or outside of the office.

"What do you mean? How would I know how you're feeling Jenny?" I ask, with a grin.

"Don't be smart with me Joseph." She glares at me and I have to say, I'm starting to feel sorry for her kid and he isn't even here yet. She's really been working on her mum look and voice. "Now we all know you're a grumpy bastard at the best of times, but these past few days have been terrible, even for you. You're going to tell me what's going on because Nadine and I don't have to put with your grumpy arse."

I sigh, not knowing where to start because no one actually knew I was seeing Katy. Just like she wanted it and I can't help but feel like she wanted it that way so she wouldn't have to explain why we'd broken up. Like she'd always planned for us to end.

"You can deny it all you like, but we all know you were seeing someone, and I think I can take an educated guess as to who the lucky lady was. What did you do to screw things up Joseph?"

"Why do people assume that I'm the one who did something wrong?" I ask, my voice a bit harsher than I intended.

"Because you're you and you're a man." She says, like it's the most natural thing in the world and I should just understand.

"What the hell is that supposed to mean?" Now, I know my voice was too harsh and loud, because she graces me with another harsh 'mum' look.

"Joseph French, you and I both know you're a grumpy bastard at the best of times, but the past few months, you've been different. Easier to work with." I open my mouth to speak, but Jenny just keeps on talking. "Now, don't get me wrong, you're a really great boss. Who, generally speaking, is pretty easy to work with, but when you get in a mood, we all know to leave you in peace. But these past few days bossman, you're rough even for you and I can't leave this office in this kind of disarray." She looks at me, waves her hand and says, "So come on, spill."

We sit there staring at each other for what feels like an eternity. Jenny's really getting into her upcoming role as a mother, because I crack under the pressure. Maybe it's just that I want someone other than myself to know what happened. Maybe I just want another person's opinion on what the fuck happened. An opinion from a woman might be helpful too.

"We broke up." I say, simply.

"Well I know that captain obvious. Why did you break up? What happened?" she asks.

"I don't know." I say honestly, my voice almost a whisper.

Jenny leans forward slightly, "What do you mean you don't know? You have to know why you guys broke things off, Joe."

"I really don't Jenny, I'm confused. Honestly." I rest my head in my hands.

"Joe, look at me." Jenny says. "What happened the last time you saw her? What did you say?"

"We spent the weekend at my place in the country, where we could just relax and be ourselves. It was great. No it was fucking perfect. We were even talking about telling everyone we're together, talking about our future together and then she went all quiet. When we got back to the house, she was telling me it was over because she couldn't give me what I wanted. I don't know what the hell changed. Then Harry barged in, Katy packed up her stuff and asked me to bring her home, a day earlier than we'd planned."

By the time I'm finished talking, I'm pacing my office while Jenny watches me from her chair. I can feel her eyes on me, but I don't care. My hands are in my hair, pulling at it in frustration.

"Hey, Joe, you need to calm the hell down. I can see why Katy wanted to keep things quiet for a while to see where you guys were headed. I don't think Kami is going to take the news too well. Her best friend in love with her worst nightmare?"

"I didn't say who it was." I start but Jenny talks over me.

"You did actually, but that's not the point. You've missed something Joe, why does Katy think she can't give you what you want? What were you guys talking about before Harry showed up?"

"We were talking about our future. We saw a mum with her kids running around the park, they were laughing together. The mum walked past us and told us to enjoy the peace while we could and then, Katy asked me if I wanted kids. I said yes, I wanted my own family, and I wanted it with her." I take a deep breath and continue. "I told her that I had always wanted a family, one that was mine and I wouldn't treat them like Harry has treated me. I wanted it even more now that we were together." My hands are back in my hair, pulling and twisting in frustration. "The next thing I knew she was quiet, and when we got back to the house she was crying and telling me that she couldn't give me what I wanted, and it was best if we just called it all off now. Before we got in too deep and full of regrets."

"Did she explain why she couldn't give you the family you wanted? Think Joe, what exactly did she say? Did she say it was because she doesn't want kids herself? Or where was there another reason?"

"I don't know. Things got a bit messed up because then Harry showed up and ... "

"Forget about Harry. Tell me exactly what Katy said Joe." She pleads with me and I make myself think and think hard.

"She said she couldn't have kids. Medically there was a reason."

"What reason Joe? Think god damn it." Jenny almost yells at me.

"She's got endometriosis. The doctors told her it would be near impossible for her to get pregnant." I say, relieved I remembered the reason. "But I don't care about that, I just want to be with her. I don't care how or if we have a family, I just want to be with her."

"Did you tell her that, Joe?" Jenny asks me quietly.

"Yeah. I did, and she still walked away Jenny. She told me that we didn't have a relationship and never will. She said that was why she hadn't told Kami yet, because she knew we wouldn't last." I can feel the emotions building inside my chest, it hurts. Physically, to say it all out loud.

"She's hurting too Joe. She thinks she's doing what's best for you both, but if what you're saying is true, about you just wanting to be with her. No matter what else happens, then you need to fight for her Joe."

"I've been trying Jenny. She won't answer my calls, or my texts and I don't want to just show up at her house, only for her to not answer the door or tell me to fuck off."

"Well, maybe you should give you both a little bit of time to calm down and then try again. Win her back Joe. You already won her over once, how hard could it be?" she asks, smiling at me, but I can see the tears in her eyes, and they tell me the truth.

"I don't know if I can keep doing that Jenny." I say, so quietly I'm not even sure she can hear me.

"You can and you damn well will, Joseph French. You fight for what you love, and you love Katy Ellis."

Shit, she's right. I'm completely in love with Katy and I can't give up on her. On us. I won't, but I will give her some space. We'll both have some space and get our heads sorted and then, then I'm going to win her back again.

"Thanks Jenny. You're right."

"You're welcome and I know." She winks at me.

I help her to stand up and then pull her in for a hug. "Fight for her Joe." She whispers in my ear.

I've got a fight on my hands, but it's one I'm determined to win. Kami Parker be damned.

Chapter Twenty-five

KATY

I'm sitting at my desk later in the week trying to concentrate on getting some work done, but I'm seriously fried after a hard week. Emotionally hard, anyway. When my phone starts vibrating across my desk. I look at the screen and see that it's Kami calling. I answer the phone, we make our way through the normal pleasantries and then she asks me to have dinner with her. A request that I readily agree to, because Kami is a brilliant cook and I've missed my best friend. I finish up work early for the first time in ages, I've got a date with my best friend, and I'm not giving it up for anything.

I buy some good wine and take myself to Kami's, determined to enjoy myself, because even though I won't tell her his name, I know I can talk to her about what happened with Joe.

When Kami asks me about the guy I was seeing. She can tell it's over and here I was thinking it didn't show on my face anymore. I answer her the only way I can, with the truth. He didn't do anything wrong and neither did I, there were just details we couldn't work out and we decided to stay friends. If only that were the case and Joe wasn't messaging me a million times a day, asking when we could get together and discuss everything.

I tell Kami I don't want to talk about him anymore and I want us to enjoy our night. So, I set the table as she dishes up roast chicken and vegetables. We laugh and talk, catching up. Then we sit on the couch with dessert and watch a movie that she lets me choose, but it doesn't hold my attention. I'm so tired because I haven't been sleeping, and I fall asleep before the movie is over.

When I wake up the next morning on Kami's couch, my head is on a pillow and a blanket is covering me, I see a message from Joe sitting on the screen of my phone. It's simple and heart breaking all at the same time; 'Babe,

I miss you'. It breaks my heart even more when my first thought is, I hope he sent it after Kami went to bed and she didn't see his name.

I stretch on the couch and get up to make some coffee for us, but Kami's already sitting at her kitchen table. I pour myself a coffee and sit down across from her.

"It doesn't seem like your guy is quite as sure about your break-up as you are Katy." She doesn't mention any names, so I don't ask if she saw one.

"He will be Kam, he just needs some time." I say.

"Stop pushing guys away just because you might not be able to have kids of your own. It doesn't mean you can't have a family you know it Katy and it doesn't mean you don't deserve a guy who loves you." She says, no judgement on her face, just the usual sadness when we have conversations like this.

"I can't give him what he wants Kam, it's that simple." I reply, looking into my coffee and suddenly feeling sick.

"Are you OK Katy?" Kami asks, her voice full of concern.

"Yeah, I'm just nauseous all of a sudden. Honestly, the thought of drinking this coffee makes me want to throw up. I must be coming down with something, I'm going to head home before I give whatever it is to you hun." We hug and kiss each other on the cheek, much to my annoyance because I really don't want to make Kami sick, but she insists she'll be fine. I grab my bag and head home. When I get inside I strip out of my clothes and have a cool shower, which makes me feel slightly better. Then I sink into my bed and fall into a fitful sleep. Dreams of Joe and babies and children with his serious demeanour and beautiful, soul searching eyes. I wake up in a pool of tears on my pillow and a broken heart.

I wipe my cheeks and sit up, resting my back on the pillows and reaching for my phone to see what time it is. I slept half the day away and my stomach growls to remind me I haven't eaten since dinner last night at Kami's. I drag my body out of bed and wander into the kitchen, where I'd planned on getting some food, but the need for an ice cold water is overwhelming so I pour myself a drink. It's gone in seconds and then I pour another. With my thirst quenched, I open the fridge and then the pantry to decide what to eat. Nothing in there looks appealing, but fried chicken sure does. So, I pull up a food ordering app on my phone, place my order and then make a couple of pieces of toast to tide me over. What? I'm hungry and the delivery is going take a while. When I've finished my toast, I check the delivery time on the app and decide I have enough time for a quick shower.

I'm sitting on my couch, refreshed and feeling so much better than I did earlier today, waiting for the chicken to be delivered. I've messaged Kami to let her know that I'm feeling better, that I must have just needed a decent sleep, but she hasn't answered me yet.

There's a knock at the door just as I'm putting my phone down and it startles me so much, I almost drop the damn thing on the table in my rush to get to my food. Only when I open the door, it isn't the food delivery that I expected. In front of me is a guy with a flower arrangement in his hands.

"Miss Ellis?" He asks, and I nod my reply. "These are for you."

"Who are they from?" I ask, as I take them from him.

"I don't know, I just deliver them Miss Ellis." He says with a shrug of his shoulders and then he's gone.

I'm still standing there like an idiot with the door open and the flowers in my hands when Ben appears in front of me. "Hi Katy, I've got your dinner for you." He says a little too happily.

"Umm hi Ben, I thought you delivered for the Chinese Restaurant?" I ask, confused.

"Oh I do, but I deliver for a few places in town. I have to earn money somehow and one delivery job just isn't enough you know?" He states, completely serious.

"Oh yeah of course." I reply, like I have any clue what the hell he's talking about. "Thanks Ben."

"No worries Katy, it's my job." He replies and I nod, agreeing. He turns to leave, then turns back and asks me, "Are you and Kami Parker still friends Katy?"

I'm startled into the present and say, "Of course, why do you ask?"

"Well, you used to order meals together and lately you've ordered them separately, that's all. I guess things change."

"We've just both been a bit busy Ben." I think, it's a little creepy that he's taken so much notice of what we do.

"They're pretty flowers Katy, you should take them inside and give them water. "Enjoy your dinner." He says then turns and leaves.

I close the door and walk into the kitchen, that's when I notice the little white envelope hidden among the flowers and pull it out. The card inside almost breaks my heart all over again.

'I'll be here when you're ready to talk Kathryn, always Joe xx'. A sob escapes from my lips before I can stop it. I take my dinner to the couch and turn on a soppy chick flick, leaving everything else in the kitchen.

My phone dings telling me I've got a message and I almost dread looking at the damn thing, but I pick it up anyway. When I see Kami's name on the screen, I sigh with relief. She's just realised she's in love with James. Funny thing is, I know I'm in love with Joe too, only we can't have our happily ever after. Kami and James can though, and they've been in love with each other since we were kids.

I send back a message telling her to be careful, even though I know she already has his heart too, and then I tell her I love her. When I get a message saying she loves me too, I feel the tightness in my chest lessen slightly. I've got Kami and my sister, that's all I need.

I settle in and finish my movie, just as the credits start rolling I get another message and I smile, thinking it's Kami with another revelation that the rest of us already know. Instead, I see the one name on my screen that I don't want to.

Joseph French. I know what you're thinking, if I really don't want to hear from him anymore, I should block and delete his number, but I can't bring myself to cut myself off completely. He messages me a few times a day. Sometimes just to say hi and ask how I am, other times to tell me he misses me. I don't answer any of them, but it hurts every time I see his name.

Joe: *Katy please talk to me.*

Joe: *Katy, I've fallen in …*

I don't read the rest of that one, I delete it before I can see how it ends, because it's already over. The flowers sit there on the bench, mocking me but I can't throw them away, but I haven't put them in water yet though either. Instead I throw my rubbish away and head to bed. Exhausted even though I did nothing today. Mentally, I'm done in.

Joe's scent is still on the spare pillow, I hold it tight for a few seconds and then throw it on the floor, as far away from me as possible. Tomorrow, it's going in the bin.

I think I'll find peace in my dreams, but the last thing I'm thinking about as I fall asleep is Joe and that's who I dream about. I dream he's happy, smiling, playing with his daughter, and laughing. He's looking at me and I feel the same happiness, until I get the full picture of his happy family, and it doesn't include me. Someone else has made him happy. I wake up to a tear dampened pillow again, and I'm miserable.

I roll over on to my back and sigh. I wish I could just move forward. Leave him behind me and let go, but it's just not that easy. Somewhere along the way, I fell in love with Joseph French and now I'm struggling to let him go.

I make a move to sit up and my stomach lurches at the movement. I bring my hand up to my mouth, even though I know if I throw up, my hand isn't going to do too much to stop it.

I bolt from my bed to the bathroom, thanking my lucky stars that it's connected to my bedroom, and kneel in front the toilet. It feels like I'm going to lose my dinner and everything else I've eaten in the last month, but instead, all I do is dry retch for about 5 minutes.

I flush the toilet, even though nothing happened, rinse my mouth at the basin and splash water over my face. When I look up into the mirror I see a pale face looking back at me. At least I *look* exactly how I feel. Awful.

I shake my head in amazement when my stomach rumbles. How the hell can I be hungry when I was just heaving over the toilet bowl?

On shaky legs, I walk into the kitchen and stand there, wondering what to have to eat. The sudden urge to have some cereal with cold milk hits me, and I grab a bowl and fill it. I sit down at the bench, not bothering to walk to the table, and even though I start out slowly, wary of upsetting my stomach again, the cereal is gone quickly, and I want more. Once my second bowl of cereal is finished, I head for the shower. I'm already feeling better than I did when I woke up.

I'm feeling so good, I take myself to the supermarket to stock up on groceries. I start to feel a little light-headed, so I grab a bottle of water and some chocolate. When I get the register to pay for everything, including the water and the now finished chocolate.

I get home, unload my shopping, pack away all the cold stuff and then stand there looking at the rest. Screw it, that can all wait, I'm exhausted all of a sudden. I grab a snack and a drink, then sit down on the couch to watch a movie. The problem is, I don't see most of the movie, because I fall asleep on my couch.

When I come to, the credits are rolling and my stomach grumbles. Again. So I haul myself up off the couch and make my way to the kitchen. I sigh when I see the mess I've left for myself, but I force myself clean. Then, I make myself something to eat. I normally don't cook when it's just me, but I just bought all this food and I don't really want to wait for a delivery.

I sit at the bench in the kitchen to eat my dinner and check my phone. I check everything online and see that I've got a couple of messages. Kami messaged me to check in on me, so I reply telling her that yeah I'm still a little under the weather and tired, but honestly fine. I think I just have a cold or something. Kami's reply comes through quickly, telling me to rest, keep up my fluids, and to call her if I need *anything*.

When I wake up the next morning, mentally ready to head into work, my body revolts. The minute I move, my stomach churns and I race for the bathroom again. Once I'm done dry retching once again, and splash some water on my face, I call Mr Wilks and let him know I won't be in. The only question he asks is if I need anything, he knows I'm sick if I'm not coming in. When I tell him I've got a virus of some kind, he tells me to take as much time off as I need to get better.

"In fact, don't come in for a few days Katy, just let me know when you'll be back in."

"Thanks Mr Wilks, I appreciate that, but if it lasts another day I'm going to the doctor." I say.

"Keep your germs to yourself and get better soon Katy." Mr Wilks says, then he hangs up.

I look at my phone and laugh. He didn't mean that the way it sounded, and I know it. His way with words is astounding, in his absentminded way. He says the right things, just in a jumbled up fashion.

My stomach grumbles, and again I'm amazed at how I can feel hungry when not so long ago I was bent over the toilet. I walk into the kitchen, grab myself some food and a glass of juice, then sit down at the table, checking emails.

When I'm done I decide to grab a bottle of water and lie on the couch to watch another movie. I fall asleep again and only wake up to see the credits rolling. My stomach wants food again, so I grab something to eat. I have a shower to freshen up and lie down on my bed for a minute. You better believe it, I fall asleep again and wake up fucking hungry.

For the next couple of days, this is my routine, so I end up taking myself to the doctors. He tells me he thinks it's a virus that's going around, all my symptoms match, but he'll take some blood and run some tests anyway, just to make sure it's nothing else. Then he tells me the only thing to do is what I *have* been doing.

Sleep, rest, water and food.

So, I call Mr Wilks and tell him I'll be off for the rest of the week, but I'll work from home when I can.

That's how I spend the rest of my week. Sleeping, eating, dry retching, and working in between. Two days after I see the doctor, he calls to let me know that what I've got is a virus, best as he can tell anyway. The blood tests came back negative for a whole range of things, including pregnancy.

I don't hear him after he says *negative for pregnancy*. It never even occurred to me that he would test for that. I guess all the symptoms were there and being female it's just one of those tests they do automatically. I never even contemplated a negative result, but it makes my reality hit home and my resolve to stay away from Joe is set in stone now.

I thank the doctor for calling to let me know and put my phone down. I stare at the TV not really seeing whatever movie is on now, it's a bunch of movements in front of my face.

I'm not pregnant.

I should be relieved, but I'm not and that makes me feel stupid.

To distract myself and my depressing thoughts, I check my messages, Kami has kept checking in on me this week. When I'm done answering her, leaving out the non-pregnant part, I swipe through and answer any of the others I need to and delete the ones I don't. Then I come across a couple from Joe and I don't know whether I want to read them or not, but being the glutton for punishment that I am, I open them.

Joe: *I'm heading out town for a day, maybe two this week.*

Joe: *Just in case you're trying to reach me for anything.*

Joe: *The reception out where I'm going is shitty at best.*

Joe: *When I get back, we're talking. No excuses.*

I sigh and put the phone on the table. I can't deal with him right now. I drag my butt up off the chair, put my dishes in the sink and walk to my room. Plugging in my phone so it can charge. I strip down, leaving only my knickers and tank top on and crawl into bed. I swear, the minute my head hits the pillow, I'm asleep.

But my dreams are more like nightmares again.

Chapter Twenty-six

JOE

I'd like to say that running my own business and getting in James' is helping to keep Katy out of my thoughts every day, but it isn't. She's always there and I keep sending her messages to let her know I'm thinking about her, that I miss her, and I want to talk to her. I know it seems creepy, maybe even stalkerish, but I want her to know that I miss her and I'm thinking about her.

At the office, Jenny told me she cancelled all my meetings for a few days because, and I quote, 'no one should have to deal with your pissy attitude right now'. I should have been angrier about it, but I couldn't bring myself to be, she's right. I don't want to have to deal with clients right now anyway.

So, instead of taking my frustration out on Jenny or Nadine, I simply give them a nod of my head and shut myself in my office.

It's not even mid-morning one day when I decide I don't want to be there anymore and make the decision to go see James at his worksite.

I message Katy telling her I'm going out of town. That where I'm going has patchy mobile reception at best, and I may be uncontactable, if she decides she wants to talk. I receive silence, again. Even after I tell her we *will* be talking when I get back.

Does that make me an arsehole, demanding that we talk? I don't know but I really don't give a shit either. I need to talk to her and tell her that I don't care about having kids, I only care about *her*.

When I get out to James' worksite, I'm already in a bad mood and even though he told me he didn't need me out there, he looks relieved when he sees me. Then he explains why. That he busted his phone and needs a new one, but he can't leave the site. I see it as the perfect opportunity to rid him of the curse that is the Parker women.

I go into what James calls 'town' and look for a place to get him a new phone. His phone is smashed beyond repair and he won't be able to use it again. The salesperson in store is beside himself to help, I can't imagine they get too many people wanting a new phone and a whole new set up too often. His whole face lights up when I pay him cash for his services, he doesn't ask any questions, just gives me everything I need to put my plan into action.

When I get back to the worksite, I tell James I got him a new phone, I see the relief wash over his face, and I wonder if I'm doing the right thing. Then I remember, I need to save him from himself, so I ask if he wants me to set it up for him. I tell him I've got some work of my own to do and if I can use his makeshift office for the afternoon, I can help us both out. When he tells me to go ahead, I'm almost giddy, because now I can put everything into place. I walk into the office and set to work. I've already told James his phone is beyond fucked, now I can start up his new phone and instead of adding all the contacts from his laptop, I delete a few. I can't just delete Kami's that'll look suspicious, so I either tell him he lost all contacts, or I delete enough that it makes sense.

I decide I can't delete them all, because that would mean he'd be losing business contacts and I just can't do that to him. So, instead I go through all of his contacts list on the laptop and take out all the old numbers and then a few personal ones. Number one on the list to go, Kami Parker.

Before I remove her number, I make the decision to send her a final message, from a number that she doesn't know, but she will. I smile, knowing that I've got everything in place now for the end of the 'relationship'.

Unknown number: *Getting out of town and putting some distance between us, will make breaking it off a little easier.*

I jump when James comes into the office a little while later. I brush it off as concentrating on work and he easily accepts it. I feel guilty abusing his trust, but I just can't see any other way to do this, he isn't listening to me when I tell him that Kami will break his heart.

I hadn't realised that I'd been in the office for so long, until he tells me it's time to go home for the day. I decide it's too late to drive home and we head out for dinner. I'm surprised when he takes me to a place that looks more like a storefront than a place to sit and eat but when we walk inside, the smell is divine.

I listen to James piss and moan about how much he doesn't want this new contract, when just a few short weeks ago he was busting his balls to get it and now he wishes he'd never taken it because it's out of town. The new guy that he's dealing with isn't making the situation any easier, but he's being an idiot. This contract could mean bigger things for his business and not so long ago, he was more than happy to be building that business.

I'm more than happy to be helping do it too, and not just because it helps my business. I might do a lot of his paperwork, mainly because he hates it, but it is his business, and I've enjoyed watching it grow. Despite his family and the reputation his father has earned in this town, the quality of his work and the hard work he's put into it has paid off. I don't want a pretty face to take that all away from him.

After dinner, we head back to the motel and go to our separate rooms. James is expecting a video call from Kami. One that I know he isn't going to receive, and I need to get some sleep so I can drive home in the morning.

I meet James in the motel restaurant for breakfast the next morning. He looks like hell. Like he didn't get any sleep at all.

"You look like shit James." I say, trying to make a joke about it. "What did you do, sleep on the floor last night? You know the floors not clean, right?"

"Actually, I slept on the couch most of the night and it wasn't comfortable at all." He says, stretching his neck from side to side.

"Why the hell would you do that? You'd never fit on there." I ask, honestly shocked that he would even try.

"Because dickwad, I was waiting for Kami to call me. We were supposed to do a video chat, but she never called, and I couldn't call her, because her number was one of the ones we lost yesterday. I don't why I lost her contact details but kept most of my work ones." He shakes his head, obviously confused. "I don't understand why some numbers are gone, and others aren't. I thought it would either wipe the whole lot or keep the whole lot. I'll never understand."

He looks so dejected, I start to wonder if I've done the right thing. "What about your laptop, didn't it still have all her contact details in it?" I ask, already knowing the answer, but I have to ask him.

"No. For some reason her number was wiped in there too." He looks me in the eye and asks, "Did you do something with my computer yesterday?"

"Well, yeah but all I did was plug in your phone to get all the contacts off it. It must have had a fit and deleted some of your contacts in there too." I shrug my shoulder. "I don't understand everything about computers and phones you know." Just most of them and I know that it's one of James' weaknesses.

"No, but you know more than I do Joe. Could you have a look at my laptop and see if you can retrieve the files or whatever you do please?" I make to answer him, to tell him no I want to head back, but he looks at me, his eyes filled with misery and I can't fucking say no. "I know you're heading back home this morning, but could you please just do a quick check?"

I find myself nodding my agreement. I can't speak, if I speak I might spill the truth and I can't do that without hurting him. So, I grab his laptop and sit at the table where we're having breakfast and pretend to have a look around his files. I know I won't find them, because I deleted them. There is no trace to be found, I didn't want him finding them in the recycle bin by accident, so I removed every trace that I could think of. I know James all too well, and even though he doesn't know one end of a laptop from another, somehow he's the kind of guy who would find what he's looking for with plain, simple dumb luck.

Half an hour later, James has put breakfast and coffee in front of me and I've got the sad task of telling him, "Sorry man, I just couldn't find the files. I tried everything I know, they're just not there anymore."

"Now see, this is why I don't trust technology Joe. I know you laugh at me because I haven't quite come easily into all this new technology but if I still had a contacts book, this wouldn't have happened." He says glumly.

"No, you're right, because no one ever dropped a book in water, accidently set it on fire or lost pages." I say, trying to lighten the mood. I don't succeed and the next words out of his mouth absolutely stun me.

"If I write my new number on a piece of paper, and a short note, will you pass it on to Kami for me please?" His trust almost guts me.

"I'll try to, but you know there's not a lot of trust between Kami and myself. I'm not sure she'll believe anything I have to say to her."

"You have to make her understand Joe. For me." He pleads.

"Yeah, OK." What the hell else was I supposed to say? No way man, as if she would believe I'm coming from a sincere place, I'm not.

"Thanks man, I owe you." He slaps me on the shoulder and stands up, a smile on his face for the first time this morning. "I knew I could trust you to help me out." Anyone would think he could sense that I was up to no good. "Well, I have to get over to the jobsite, and you have to get back home. I guess I'll see you when I get home in a few days."

"Make sure you let me know when you get home and we'll catch up for sure." I smile, but it doesn't feel sincere. James doesn't notice, he just claps me on the shoulder again, and walks out to his truck.

"Are you coming Joe, or are you staying for another coffee? I'm sorry, but I need to get moving." James says, standing at the driver's side door to his truck.

"I think I might grab another coffee and then head out. I'll see you when you get back to town." He smiles and nods, jumps in his truck and waves before he backs out and heads to the jobsite.

I wait until his truck disappears, then I jump in my car and head in the opposite direction towards home. There's only one thing on my mind the entire drive home.

Getting to Kami and giving her this note from James.

As I pull into town, I look at the clock and realise it's almost closing time. I stop at the café and grab a coffee. Then I sit and wait for Ms Parker to be on her own. I know how creepy that sounds, but I don't feel like having a public confrontation with her, or that guy she's got working for her. I see the guy leave and then twenty minutes later Kami walks out the front door and locks up.

I get out my car and quickly walk over to her. When I reach her I cough to get her attention.

Without looking around she says, "I'm sorry but we're closed for the day, come back tomorrow and I'll help you anyway I can."

"I'm not here for a book Kami." I say, trying my hardest not to show how much she annoys me.

"So why are you here then Joe? We both know you don't want to be." She says, with a smile plastered across her face that doesn't reach her eyes. She doesn't want me to be here anymore than I want to be *here*.

I clear my suddenly dry throat and say, "I'm here because James asked me to come by and let you know that he broke his phone yesterday. I was there checking up on how things were going, so I went into town to grab him a new one. Unfortunately, he's lost some of the contacts because he had them saved wrong." I can't look her in the eye, I feel like she'll see the truth if I do. "Anyway, he wanted me to give you his new number, so you can call him, and he can save your number again, so here it is."

"Thank you Joe." She says quietly, trying to look me in the eyes.

She starts walking away, until I speak again, "He's also going to be away for longer than he originally planned. Things aren't going too well on this one."

"I know, he told me that the new project manager was being a pain in the butt. He also told me that he might be there longer than he originally thought." She turns to look back at me. "You're not telling me anything I didn't already know Joe. We have spoken since he's been gone you know." She says in a snarky voice.

"I just want you to understand." I say looking at my feet, then pulling my eyes to hers, I continue. "He's worked really hard to get where he is Kami. He's pulled himself up out of the mess that his father made of the family name and made a business and a life for himself. He was dragged down and made to feel less than, all because his father was a drunk and couldn't keep it in his pants. He has respect now, a business that is successful and even if people still associate him with Kevin Harvey, they can see that he's nothing like the guy who let everyone down."

"I know that Joe. I know how hard it is to get a business started and to keep it running." She takes a deep breath and takes a step closer to me. "I don't know why you hate me so much Joe, I have no idea what you have against me, but I don't care anymore either. I know how hard James has worked to get out from under his father's reputation. You think that I'm going to somehow ruin him and his business, I can see it written all over your face, but I have no intention of doing that. Ever."

"I never said it was your intention Kami, I just think that." She doesn't let me finish.

"No Joe don't finish that sentence. We could break each other's hearts Joe, but that's still none of your business. You're telling me not to ruin him, but maybe you should think about being a good friend and supporting him in his decisions?" With that, she's gone, and I'm left standing on the footpath, wondering if she's right and I should just be happy for them.

Then I remember what I've already set into motion. I wonder how long it will take her to realise that the text message she received yesterday is James' new number?

I hope that the cryptic words I sent make her start to wonder and second guess her relationship with James.

Chapter Twenty-seven

Kami checks on me every day but in the end I have to ban her from coming over. She's got enough to worry about with her business and, well James. Even if he is working out of town for a while. Not to mention, I don't want her to get sick. I'm sure James will be home soon and the last thing he wants is to find his girlfriend that he hasn't seen for a few weeks, sick.

Anyway, I've made use of my time off from work wisely. I've caught up on tv shows and movies that I miss because I'm normally too busy to watch them. You know, normally I'm always at working.

I've also been working from home a bit, much to Mr Wilks horror. I don't think he realises that I can't give him a virus through the internet yet. Much to my amusement, he told Joy to tell me to cut it out or we'd get a virus at work. That gives me a chuckle every time I hit send on an email or job.

By the end of the weekend, I'm rested, relaxed and while I still feel a little off colour, I feel a *lot* better than I did at the start of the week.

Over the weekend I hear from Kami a lot and make her promise to stay away from me and my germs, but when I realise I haven't heard from her since then, I start to worry. By Thursday I call the bookstore to see what's going on, only for Ed to tell me that Kami's not at the store. When I ask where the hell is she, his reply stuns me. He says he doesn't know *where* she is or *when* she'll be back, just that she went home because she couldn't concentrate on anything. All Ed knew was that she left after James called and she refused to talk to him. She even refused to reply to his emails and then said she wouldn't be talking to him again. Ever, if she could help it.

"What the hell happened Ed?" I ask, completely confused.

"I'm not really sure Katy. One minute I was talking to James on the phone and he was his normal self. When I walked into her office to say he was on the phone for her, she shook her head and said, 'no tell him I'm not here'. When I said he already knew she was there, she said she wouldn't talk to him, so I could tell him whatever I wanted." He took a deep breath and continued, "The next thing I know, as I'm asking what the hell, she's packing her bag and telling me she's working from home today and I can get Mel in for anything I need help with."

"Ok, so when was that?" I ask.

"A couple of days ago. She called me later that day to ask me if I would run the shop for a while with Mel, or I could just close it up for a few days." He says, his voice full of concern and disbelief.

"She said *what*?" I screech down the phone to the poor guy. "She left you in charge of the bookstore for how long?" I ask.

"Thanks for your vote of confidence there Katy." Ed says, sounding hurt.

"I'm sorry Ed, I didn't mean it like that. I meant I'm surprised that she's leaving the bookshop at all for an extended period of time. Not to mention, she hasn't told either us of where the hell she's gone. Or explained what the hell happened." I explain.

"Well, if it's any consolation, James doesn't seem to know what the fuck happened either. He says everything was fine, great the last time they spoke, but he smashed his phone and lost a few numbers. Unfortunately, Kami's was one of them."

"That doesn't sound like something Kami couldn't laugh off and forgive him for though Ed. Come on, we're talking about Kami Parker here. She doesn't say a bad word about anyone, and yet she's gotten all twisted up over a broken phone? I don't get it." I say, totally bewildered.

Ed and I say goodbye, because there's nothing else to say. He promises to call me if he hears from Kami, and I do the same.

I put my phone down on the table and sigh. What the hell went down that Kami took herself, out of town without telling Ed or myself exactly where? I can't believe that she would walk away from the bookstore so easily, there *has* to be a logical reason for it.

I keep calling and messaging Kami, but she doesn't answer me.

The calls keep going right through to the answering service she uses, it doesn't even ring.

The next morning, I wake up to my phone ringing and I jump to answer it, ignoring the dizziness that my fast movements create because even though I'm feeling a hell of a lot better than I have been, moving too quickly makes me dizzy. I'm hoping to see Kami's name on the screen, instead it's a number I don't know.

"Hello? Katy speaking." I answer, because who knows, it could be a work thing.

"Oh, thank fuck you answered Katy. Have you heard from Kami? Do you know where she is? Is she ok? What the fuck has happened Katy? Tell me where she is, please? I need to talk to her, and she won't answer her phone."

"Well hello to you too James." I say, when he finally takes a breath. He sounds panicked. If he hasn't spoken to Kami, then something serious is going on. "What's going on James?"

"I don't know. She won't answer my calls Katy. She won't talk to me, in any format." He says, in frustration, and I can just imagine him rubbing his hand over his face.

"When was the last time you spoke to her James?" I ask, trying to work out a timeline between the last *he* heard from her, and the last time *I* heard from her.

"Earlier in the week. I dropped my phone and shattered the fucking screen. I couldn't get a damn thing on it to work, but I didn't have the time to leave the site during the day to get a new one. Then Joe showed up in what happens to have been genius timing, he went and got me a new one." He says in a rush.

"OK, so you got a new phone. What happened then? Didn't you call her with your new phone?" I ask.

"No, I lost a few numbers when the guy in the shop changed everything around, and we had a video chat date set up for that night, so I didn't call her to tell her."

"So, you had your video chat and you told her you had a new phone and needed her number again, right? So, what are you panicking for and why did she leave town without telling anyone?" I ask.

"No. We never did have the video chat. I waited up for her to call, because for some reason, her contact details were missing from the laptop too. I sat up all night on the couch in the hotel room and my laptop never rang.

When I woke up later, the laptop was flat. I've been trying to get a hold of her ever since, and she's not answering." He says, sounding completely shattered. "I even called the shop and I could hear Ed talking to her, but she refused to talk to me. I even emailed her, and she didn't answer."

"Did you try calling her again?" I ask, even though I already know the answer if he did try, because I assume he got the same dead end that I did.

"I got Joe to go past the bookstore on his way home to tell her I had a new number, and hand over a note to her." He says. Then he asks me quietly, "Do you think he gave it to her? He wouldn't not give it to her would he?"

"I don't know James, but I want to think that he wouldn't do anything to purposefully hurt you like that." I reply, just as quietly.

"I know you know him better than most people Katy." He says and then pauses, before saying, "You know Kami better than most too. Do you think she would take a note off him, even if he said it was from me?"

"I really don't have an answer for you James. You need to ask Joe if he handed over the note, I can't answer that one for you." I sigh. "As for Kami, I thought I knew her, but she's not answering me either. Nor did she tell Ed where she was going. Just said she needed to get out of town for a while and that if he couldn't open the shop for whatever reason, she was ok with that."

"She told him to close the shop?" he asks, sounding as shocked as I felt when Ed told me that little bit of information.

"Yeah." I say quietly. There's about 30 seconds of silence between us before I say, "There's something we're missing here James, and I'm not sure we can get any answers until Kami shows her face again."

"I think you're right Katy, and I can't come home until this stupid job is finished." I can hear the frustration in his voice.

"You get your job finished and I'll let you know if I hear from her." He growls in my ear and I sigh. "Until Kami decides to come home or contact one us, there's nothing else we can do."

"Thanks Katy." He says.

"I wish I had some answers for both of us James." He mumbles another thanks and I hear him sigh as he hangs up.

I look at my phone, wondering what the hell happened to make Kami run like this. I can't believe she would leave town, and not tell me. I understand that that's exactly what she's done, but it's so un-Kami like, it's alarming.

I change James' contact details in my phone while it's in my hand and I'm thinking about it, then throw the thing down on to the bed.

Rolling over on to my back, and throwing my arm over my eyes, I can't help wondering what's going on. I have a weird feeling in the pit of my stomach. One that has nothing to do with the nausea that I'd already been feeling. A really heavy, black feeling in the very pit of my stomach.

There's a reason she ran.

I'm hoping against hope that Joe isn't behind that reason. If he is, I think I'll kill him.

Chapter Twenty-eight

L ater that night James sends me a text asking me if I gave Kami the note. Me: *yeah I passed on the new number but dude she didn't really look very happy.*

Not even a minute later, his reply comes through, and we continue to send a few more back and forth.

James: *what do you mean she wasn't happy?*

Me: *as in she didn't seem to believe me, but she took the paper*

Me: *hasn't she called yet? She said she would*

I ask him, checking to see if my plans are falling into place.

James: *nah she probably got busy at the shop*

Me: *she was closing up and going home when I gave it to her, sorry dude.*

It takes a few minutes for him to answer after that one.

James: *did you get her number off her?*

Me: *no .... but, do you really think she'd give it to me dude?*

James: *no ... thanks anyway.*

I go to bed that night and sleep easy knowing everything is set in motion. It may not be exactly as planned, but I didn't really have an exact plan when I started this, I just wanted Kami away from James.

A few days after my messages with James, I wake up and see that Katy's finally messaged me back. While I'm eager to see what has made her reach out to me, I'm also slightly nervous. When I *read* the message, I'm disappointed, because she doesn't want to talk about us.

Katy: *Kami's left town and you're the last person to speak to her. Did she tell you where she was going?*

Me: *How do you know I'm last one who saw her?*

Katy: *James told me. What did you talk about?*

Me: *So you'll talk to James but not me?*

I wait for a few minutes for an answer, but I don't get one, so I tell her the truth.

Me: *I gave her a note from James with his new number on it. That's it.*

Katy: *So she didn't mention she would be leaving town?*

Me: *No. She just said thank you for the note and left.*

Me: *She didn't tell you she was going out of town?*

Katy: *She didn't tell anyone. Just told Ed if he was busy not to open the bookstore.*

Katy: *It's not like her. I'm worried.*

The guilt for what I've done starts sinking in. I never thought about the repercussions if Katy finds out what I've done.

Me: *I can come over if you want? I don't want you to stress and worry alone.*

I don't think I've done anything to help my chances with Katy. The link between them didn't occur to me, I've kept Kami and Katy separated in my mind because I don't want to think about their relationship affecting mine with Katy. I never thought that Kami would run out of town though. James isn't here, so it's not like she needed to disappear. I figured they'd have a blowout and end things. My thoughts never went any further than them not being in a relationship anymore. Saving James from Kami and hopefully having the bonus of Kami not stepping in on my relationship with Katy.

While Katy takes her time answering me, I sit here waiting. Does her hesitation mean she's thinking about it, that she wants me to come over, or is she trying to work out how to tell me thanks, but no thanks?

My phone makes a noise and I jump, hoping that she'll invite me over.

Katy: *Thanks for the offer but I'm ok. Just wanted to see if you happened to know where she took off to.*

With just one message, my hopes are dashed. Again. I thought if she could bring herself to message me about Kami, then maybe she was lifting her self-imposed contact ban on me. Guess I should have known better. There's Miss Parker, barging into my life and making trouble for me. Somehow she's always there to make me look like an arsehole.

I'm still lying in bed angry about the whole situation, when my phone starts ringing. Thinking that Katy changed her mind I grab my phone quickly, but when I look at the screen, it's not Katy's name displayed there.

"James. What's up man?" I ask, hopefully not sounding as pissed off as I feel.

"She's not answering me. She's not calling me back. Are you sure you gave her that note? Did you explain that I lost her number? Did she understand what you meant, Joe?"

"James. Calm down man." I say, sitting up. "I gave her your note, explained about the phone and the number."

"If you explained and she understood then why won't she talk to me? I've called the shop every day, I've emailed her, but she doesn't answer. Ed told me she's gone away for a few days. She left the shop in his hands, to open or not to open, Joe, that's not Kami." James says in a rush of words. He's panicking because she's gone without telling anyone where she was going. Did I think that's how she'd react? No. I thought she would break up with him and walk away.

"I'm sorry James. Katy messaged me earlier to ask if I knew where Kami had gone. She didn't mention anything about leaving town when I saw her."

"She won't talk to me Joe." James says with a huge sigh. He sounds unhappier than I thought he would. I thought he would be ok, well not ok with it, but he's never gotten this wound up over any other woman that has chosen to end things between them. "I know she was there the first time I called, but when Ed went to pass the phone over to her, she refused to even talk to me. She told him to tell me she wasn't there, but I *heard* her Joe." He says, miserably. "She was there, and she refused to talk to me. I just don't understand why."

"Maybe she just needed some time away James? Time to think about things. You guys have moved pretty quickly you know." I say, feeling like a fucking arsehole the whole time. They moved slower than Katy and I did.

"I was ready to tell her I love her Joe. When I came home, I was going to tell her how much she means to me. I wanted to make us happen."

"I'm sure she'll talk to you when she gets back into town James." I say.

"Yeah sure. See you when I get back in a few days man." He says.

"What do you mean a few days, I thought you had at least another week out there?" I ask, because he told me he had at least that when I was out there, thanks to the changes this guy keeps making.

"Yeah, we did, but now Kami isn't answering me, and I need to talk to her. Face to face, to work this shit out. Considering I'm not sleeping anyway, I figured I'd just smash out the last minute stuff here after the guys leave for the day." He says, "I told Simon that if he couldn't sign off on changes and make a decision, the guys and I were out of here."

"James, it's your job, your reputation on the line here man." I say, my voice not hiding my frustration. "You can't let what's happening with Kami take your focus away from your work. You know, the business you've built."

"Shut up Joe. You've got no idea what you're talking about. Do I want to get home so I can sort out this stuff with Kami? Hell fucking yes I do, but the fact is, Simon's been jerking my chain from the beginning and I'm over it now. My patience has gone. No job is worth this kind of stress man. My guys aren't happy either and that's not on."

"James, you've worked so." He doesn't let me finish.

"Don't Joe. You've already lectured me on how much effort I've put into *my* business. I know, I was there remember? I don't want to hear it again. I'm busting my balls here to get the job complete to everyone's satisfaction. Then, I'm coming home to talk to Kami. I'll see you in a couple of days."

Before I can respond, he's gone. Katy's gone and Kami's left town, but I'm sitting here feeling like a complete dick. I'm mad at myself, at Kami, at James and at Katy.

I can't help but think that perhaps if Katy had felt like she could tell her best friend about us, then none of this would be happening.

Why couldn't Katy tell Kami about us? I don't know whether she's embarrassed, ashamed or if she thinks Kami just won't accept us. They've been friends forever, surely if Katy tells her how we feel about each other, she can to live with it?

OK, so if I wasn't such an arsehole to Kami when were kids, she might be a bit more receptive to me being in a relationship with her best friend. We're adults now though, we've grown up, surely that counts for something, doesn't it? It's not like I've given Kami a hard time in recent years.

So I didn't want James working at her shop, that wasn't giving the woman a hard time, that was me protecting my brother from heartache, and just like that I understand why Katy found it so difficult to tell Kami about us.

Yet, while I can understand her reasoning, I can't help but wonder what else is going on here. It can't just be the family that I said I wanted. I mean there is more than one way to have a family these days and I would rather have Katy in my life, by my fucking side every day, than not have her at all. I don't care about kids, I know I said I wanted them, but that doesn't mean I can't deal with whatever Katy's health throws at us.

I feel like this was all set in motion way before now. If Kami's mother could have just, I can't even finish the thought. It hits me like a ten tonne truck. I did this. No-one else. I have to stop blaming Helen and Harry, Kami as well. Now that I've had time to sit back and really think it all through. I'm the one who's wrong!

I did this.

I need to talk to Katy. I need to explain to her what I've done. I need to explain why I've hated Kami all these years and why I didn't want her with James.

I need to talk to James. To explain and apologise.

I need to talk to Kami and explain what happened. Why I took it all out on her. I need to tell her what I suspect has been the truth all these years and ask her to trust me. I need her to do something for me, but for her to agree, she needs to believe me and trust me.

I decide I'll start with Katy. She's here, in town and sort of talking to me again. When I send her a message about getting together to talk, I don't get an answer. So, I call her, and it goes straight through to message bank.

I keep trying to get Katy to talk to me. I message and call her, and I know that I'm verging on being that crazy stalker guy, but the only thing I can think about is talking to her. Clearing the air and getting everything out in the open.

By the time Friday rolls around, Jenny's had enough of me and my attitude. She tells me without mixing any words that I need to go home and get my shit together over the weekend. If I can't get my shit together and work things out with Katy over the weekend, then she's going on maternity leave early and taking Nadine with her, because and I quote, 'I'm not leaving that young girl here on her own to deal with you grumpy old man.'

Old man? She's only a year younger than me, maybe two, if that.

Instead of arguing with her, I take my sorry arse home. I feel for her kids, because that woman is going to be a fierce mother, and they won't be getting away with kind of Tom foolery if she has anything to say about it.

I message Katy again without any luck. Then I message James to see when he thinks he'll make back to town, but I don't get an answer off him either.

I fall asleep on my couch, staring at the TV, but not seeing a damn thing. When I wake up the next morning, I know what I need to do.

I move off the couch and walk into my bathroom, when I look in the mirror I don't recognise the man staring back at me. No wonder Jenny told me to get out of the office until Monday. If I was Nadine, I'd be scared of me right now too.

Chapter Twenty-nine

<u>KATY</u>

Joe: *I can come over if you want? I don't want you to stress and worry alone.*

It takes me way longer than it should to answer him. I want to say yes. I want him to come and comfort me. I don't want to be alone and worried about my best friend, but I don't want to give him false hope. This thing between us is over.

So, eventually I send him back a message.

Me: *Thanks for the offer but I'm ok. Just wanted to see if you happened to know where she took off to.*

When he doesn't respond, I know I have no right to be annoyed with him. I'm sure I've hurt him by saying, thanks but no thanks and yet, I still wanted him to message me and insist that he come over. I feel like, and again I know it's wrong on all kinds of levels, that if he *really* cared about me, he would *want* to be here. I've pushed him away for so long now, that I think I fear that he might actually be giving up on me. On us.

Holy crap I'm a rotten human being. I can't have it both ways and I realise as I finish that thought that's exactly what I want. I'm torn in two. I want him, with every part of my being and yet, I want him to want *me*, but I need him to walk away.

I wonder if this is the last straw. Asking him about Kami, the one person that he can't stand, and then refusing his offer of comfort. I can't stomach the thought of losing him completely. The sick, perverted side of me is taking comfort in the texts and missed calls. At least he's still thinking about me, but then again it's only been a few weeks, I would hope he hasn't moved on just yet. Despite what people might think of Joseph French, he's not that kind of guy.

I think a clean break would be the best for both of us. I nod, agreeing with myself and hoping no one else can see the conversation I'm having while I'm alone on my couch. With that resolved, I tell myself it's a good thing he didn't answer me and an ever better thing that he didn't appear on my doorstep without an invitation like I was half expecting him to when he didn't answer.

I don't know whether to feel relieved I don't have to deal with an appearance from him or be completely devasted that I think I've finally made him give up. I crawl into bed and cuddle up to the shirt I found in my room that Joe left here, it still smells like him and his aftershave. I fall asleep torturing myself with what if's and dream of what could have been.

Over the next few days, all I do is go to work and come home again. I'm exhausted. I eat, I work, and I sleep. I don't hear from Kami, James or Joe. I don't even get a call from Ed to checking in to see if I've heard from his boss. To be honest, I don't want to talk to any of them, I don't seem to have the energy for anything these days.

Just as I'm drifting off to sleep late Friday night, my phone vibrates across my bedside table, indicating I either have a message or a call. It doesn't vibrate long enough for a call, so I'm guessing it's a message. I reach over to grab it, trying to stay covered and comfy in bed.

With all the anticipation building in me as to who it might be, I'm almost disappointed when I see my sister's name on the screen.

Olivia: *hey just checking in sis, haven't heard from you in a while.*

Huh, I say out loud. Who does she think she's kidding? It's not like we message or call each other every day, or even once a week for that matter. She's busy, I'm busy. Sure we check in every now and then, but she's kidding herself if she thinks I don't know she's fishing for gossip because she's spoken to one of our parents.

Olivia: *ok, so we don't check in often, but we* do *check in every now then and I want to know how you are.*

Olivia: *Mum told me you broke up with Joe and dad's not happy with you. Are you ok?*

Me: *Thanks for checking in Liv but I'm fine. I'm more worried about Kami right now than myself. I'll get over Joe, I have to.*

Olivia: *What happened? He was* so *into you Katy, and you really liked him too. It's the first time I've ever seen you get defensive and embarrassed by any guy.*

That's because he's not just any guy, but I can't say that, because there's no way I'm having this conversation with my little sister right now. One day maybe. Way, way in the future, but not right now. I'm not ready for that discussion.

Me: *Sometimes it just doesn't work. It can't work for whatever reason and that's just what happened with Joe.*

It's the basic truth and that's all she's getting out of me. For now anyway. When I feel the vibration of another message come through from the phone sitting on the pillow beside me, I debate whether I really want to read or answer any more of my sisters questions.

Against my better judgement, I reach for my phone and realise that it's actually a call and not a message like I thought. I'm instantly irritated though when I see Kami's name on the screen. She's finally unearthed from wherever she's been hiding away and decided to call me back.

"And where the *fuck* have you been bitchface?" I say when I answer it. No greeting, no how are you, just right to the point.

"Hi to you too Katybear." She answers, using the childhood nickname she has for me. At a guess she's hoping to calm me down so she can talk to me.

"Don't you dare fucking Katybear me! Do you know how worried I've been about you? What the fuck Kami? You can't leave town without telling anyone, but you *especially* don't leave town without telling *me*!" I yell at her.

"Please don't yell at me Katy. I told Ed I was leaving town, but I'm sorry I didn't let you know I was OK. Can we meet up tomorrow and I'll tell you everything?" There's a minute of silence that I guess she's hoping I'll fill, but I'm not going to make this easy for her. I was so fucking worried about her. "Please?" She says in a soft pleading voice, because really there's nothing loud about this woman, that's my job.

"OK. I'll meet you at the shop when I'm done at work. I assume you're going into the shop tomorrow?" She won't be able to stay away now that she's back in town.

"Yes, I am. I'm meeting Ed there in the morning." She replies.

"Of course you are. I'll meet you there then." Without another word, I hang up. I can't wait to hear what her excuse is for running away and not telling anyone where she was.

In frustration, I silence my phone and toss it back on the bedside table. I don't want to hear from anyone else tonight. After what feels like forever, I fall into a fitful sleep and wake up the next day feeling almost as tired as I was when I went to bed. Not the best way to start the day when you know there's going to be an uneasy talk with your best friend.

Not the best way to start any day really, but I would rather have started today in particular with a little more brain power than I am.

Either way, I have to get my shit together, because I have to go to work in an hour to meet with Mr Wilks. I drag myself out of bed and in the shower. The sooner I have my meeting with Mr Wilks, the sooner I can have my meeting with one Kami Parker.

When I walk in the door at work, my boss greets me immediately, "Good morning Katy, thank you for coming in this morning."

"Good morning Mr Wilks. Am I early?" I ask, confused. "I thought this was a staff meeting."

"You're right on time Katy, and it *is* a staff meeting of sorts. We're not waiting for anyone else though, it's just us." I'm surprised to learn that only the two of us are involved today. "I just wanted to check in with you and see how you're feeling now."

"Oh," I say, now I'm a little worried about my job. "I'm feeling much better now thank you Mr Wilks. I was back in the office this past week and my work hasn't suffered. I kept up to date from home even while I was sick." I say, feeling like I'm selling myself in a job interview.

"Oh I know Katy, your work hasn't suffered at all. I just wanted to have a conversation in private with you. You know, without all the ears around and gossiping that happens around here from time to time."

I nod, not really knowing how to answer him or what the hell to expect. I can't remember too many one on one meetings I've had with Mr Wilks since I started working for him. Well, not like this anyway, plenty where we're discussing work or I'm taking notes, for sure, but not a personal chat though.

"Oh Katy, I didn't call you in because I was worried about your performance here at work, no not at all. I'm actually really impressed with the amount of work you got done from home. I'm even thinking of making that an option around here for a very select few." He shakes his head, I'm not sure whether he's clearing it or, shit I don't know what. "I'm sorry if I gave you the impression your job was on the line Katy, that wasn't my intention."

I let out a sigh, and a breathe I was unaware I was holding. "I have to admit you had me a little worried Mr Wilks. I mean, I know I had some time off, but I kept working and I had a certificate from my doctor."

"I know Katy, and I'm sorry to worry you." he mutters something to himself and then talks to me again. "Are you sure you're ok Katy? Do you need to sit down?"

"Thanks for your concern Mr Wilks, but I'm feeling pretty good today, almost back to normal actually." I smile at him, hoping that I'm reassuring him.

"Well, I just wanted you to know that I'm here for you and that your job is safe, no matter what, and that we can work around any issues you need to. Like working from home for example, because you certainly proved that's a viable option." He nods and smiles at me. It feels like he's trying to reassure me about my job and something else, but I can't put my finger on it at all.

"Thank you Mr Wilks, I'll be sure to keep all that in mind if I decide to make any changes in the near future." He nods, a smile spreading across his face as he pats me on the shoulder, walking us towards the door to the office.

"Good, good. I think we should keep this conversation between the two of us for now, the rest of the office can wait until you're ready to tell them yourself, ok?"

"OK, sure." I smile and agree with my boss. I've never been so confused before, normally my boss is a very intelligent and capable man, but he's really weird today. Maybe I should call his wife and make sure everything is ok? Would that be going too far? I don't know, I'll think about it later, because we're at the door. "Until I'm ready to tell them what, Mr Wilks? It's a virus, I don't really need to change where I work or my hours, but like I said, if I do need to make some changes, you'll be the first to know.

"OK. Are you sure there isn't some other reason you'll need to have flexible working hours? Like maybe a baby or will your young man be able to help you out? Does he have flexible hours too?" Oh. OH! Now I get what he means. Damn he looks so excited by the idea too, I hate to burst his bubble, but I have to set him straight.

"There is no baby Mr Wilks. I promise you, I've got a virus but it's mostly out of my system now. A baby isn't really in my future for a few reasons, but no Mr Wilks, I'm not pregnant." I say with a smile that I hope makes him feel a little better.

"Oh. I'm sorry Katy. Mrs Wilks and I were talking and well, she said that's how she felt when she was pregnant with our kids, and we just assumed." He sighs. "I'm really sorry for the mix-up Katy. I never meant to upset you."

I reach my hand out and rest it on top of his, hopefully reassuring him. "It's OK Mr Wilks, you didn't know and you're right, they are symptoms of morning sickness, just not the cause of my symptoms."

"OK, well you go and enjoy the rest of your weekend with that young man of yours. I'll go home and tell Mrs Wilks she got things a little muddled up and see what else she has planned for us this weekend. See you Monday morning Katy." He says, waving at me from the door, watching me get in my car and pull away.

Well. That was a strange conversation with my boss. One I never really expected to have either, I'm glad he's willing to give me flexible hours though, that's got to be a bonus!

The drive to the café is an easy one and when I look at the clock in my car, I realise I'm early for my catch up with Kami. So I decide I'm going to the bookshop, and I'll grab her before she can escape and disappear on me again.

I pull up behind the bookshop, and park next to Kami's car. At least I know she's here or will return to get her car. I sit in my car for a few minutes, gathering my thoughts and trying to control my anger. 'She's your best friend Katy, she didn't hurt you on purpose and your emotions are running wild the last couple of weeks. You need to be calm when you're talking to Kami.' This is the pep talk I give myself before I finally get out of the car.

I take a deep breath, calm myself and get out before locking my car. As I step away from my car I think I hear my name called, but I don't turn around, I must be hearing things.

Then my body stiffens, because I hear it again, louder, but I don't, I can't turn around, because I know that voice and I don't want to talk to him. Especially here, now.

"Katy. Honey, can we talk, please?" He asks, and I can't help but hear the pleading and desperation in his voice.

"Don't Joe." I say, my own voice is strained and pleading as well.

"Don't what honey? I'm not allowed to talk to you, to talk things through?" He asks me.

"Don't call me honey. You don't get to call me that anymore, Joseph." I say, my voice harsh and edgy. I still haven't turned around to look at him, I can't. If I do, I know, without a shadow of a doubt, I will give in to his pleading eyes and gorgeous face. Why? I miss him. Plain and simple. I fell in love with this man, and if he asks me to talk, I know he'll talk me around. That he'll make me believe him when he says I'm what he wants. That kids don't matter that much to him, as long as he has me, but I know in my heart, he'll change his mind later and he'll regret us. Me. I just can't live with seeing that on his face, however long it is down the track.

Chapter Thirty

<u>JOE</u>

Instead of dwelling on the last week, I get in the shower and clean myself up. As I dry myself and get dressed, I'm weighing up my options. Do I message or call Katy again today, taking the risk that she won't answer, again. Or, do I just go by her house, work, the café, or just walk around town for a while?

Without realising what I'm doing, I get in my car and find myself parking at the café that I know she meets Kami at for lunches during the week, then I get out and start walking around town. I check out the shops on Main Street that I haven't had a chance to look in for a while. When I get close to Kami's bookstore, I hesitate. I know Katy's worried about her best friend, but does that mean she'd go to the shop to talk to Ed or see if Kami's there? I decide to not look in there just yet, I don't want to see Kami, and walk to the café to get a coffee instead. From the café I can just see the rear entrance to Kami's shop, and while I'm waiting for my coffee, I see Katy's car drive passed and park behind the store. I take a few steps to the door until the barista calls my name. I smile, say thanks and take my coffee, but the minute I'm out the door, the paper cup ends up in the rubbish, I don't even take a sip out of it.

When I get within a few metres of the cars, I see Katy getting out of her car and my heart stops beating for a second and my step falters. She's more breathtaking than I remember, and I know, without a doubt, that I love her, and I need to win her back.

"Katy." I yell, but she doesn't hear me. My voice doesn't carry, because it's more a whisper of her name on my lips. I reach the rear of her car as she raises her bag to her shoulder, her back to me, so she hasn't seen me yet. "Katy." My voice finally works like I want it to and is more normal.

I know she heard me, because I see her hesitate and her whole body stiffen, but she doesn't turn around to look at me.

"Katy. Honey, can we talk, please?" I ask, and I can't help the pleading and desperation in my voice, and I hate it.

"Don't Joe." She says, the strain evident in her own voice.

"Don't what honey? I'm not allowed to talk to you? To talk things through?" I ask.

"Don't call me honey. You don't get to call me that anymore, Joseph." She says, her voice harsh and she still hasn't turned around to look at me.

"OK Kathryn." Two can play that game. If that's how she wants to play it. "Do I get to have my say then? Am I allowed to have some answers to my questions, and have you listen to how I feel about our relationship? Or do *you* get to make all the decisions about how I feel, and what I want?" I ask, the anger I feel coming through in my voice. "Or are you the only one who gets to make decisions like walking away? Even if that's not what I want." I guess I *do* get to have my say after all.

"Joe." She says quietly, so quietly, I almost miss it. "You don't know that. You don't understand the implications of being with me, it's all fireworks, happiness and understanding right now. What happens when you realise that you don't get your happily ever after? What happens when you decide to leave me after however many years, but you've left it too long and then you're too old to start again and have kids? What happens to me, when a few years down the track, you decide that I'm not enough and you *do* want a family and I can't give them to you? You get to walk away then and start fresh, get that family that you desire." She finally turns to look at me, tears are streaking her face. "I'd rather deal with that heartache and loss now Joe. We can both get over it in time, but in a few years, when we've invested more time, and emotion." She shrugs, "What happens then Joe?"

"I don't care Katy. There are different ways of making a family honey, we don't *need* to have kids of our own to be a family." She stands in front me, her hands holding tightly to the strap of her handbag, shaking her head. "Look at what James and I have, we're a family because we made one. We're not blood, but that doesn't matter." I need to make her understand, to see what I see.

"Joe, that's not the same thing and you know it. You guys are like brothers, you chose to be that way because you needed each other. That's different to not being able to have kids of your own flesh and blood Joe."

She starts to walk away but I reach out for her hand, she pulls away and turns to me, her face full of anger.

"What are you doing here, anyway? If Kami sees you she's going to work it out you idiot and then I'll lose my best friend." Katy says.

"I saw you drive passed, and I took a guess as to where you were going. She rarely uses this door, she won't see or hear us Katy. I needed to see you, I've had a shit few days. I did something Katy, something stupid. I screwed up."

"Joe, I don't have time for this shit. Kami called me last night, she wants to have lunch and talk. Seeing that she left town for a few days without notice, I really want to talk to her to find out what the hell is going on, because the last time I spoke to her she was happy, so happy and I was freaking stoked for her. I know you're not happy about them being together Joe, but I am. He's good for her, they work together, and I won't have you ruining it for them."

"I miss you Katy. I miss you so fucking much, and I can accept them together, now. I just, I can't accept you not being in my arms. I love you more than—"

"No, Joe." Katy sighs. "Joe, I can't do this, it broke my heart to walk away from you, from us, but you can't get over whatever you have against Kami and I won't lose my best friend."

"I can Katy, that's what I'm trying to tell you. I made a mistake, so many mistakes. James is miserable because she won't call him back, and it's all my fault. I can't keep blaming Kami for things that aren't her fault, I know that now."

"Oh Joe, what the hell did you do?"

Suddenly another voice joins the conversation and I know beyond shadow of a doubt, I'm fucked now. "Yeah Joe, what did you do to ruin my life this time? Hmmmmmm?"

Shit. I know it's Kami's business and I shouldn't be surprised for even a second that she's here, or that she heard us talking, but I am. Plain and simple. The minute I hear her voice and see her face, my defences are up again.

I'm always in defence mode around this woman, and none of them understand why.

"Fucking hell Kami, how long have you been standing behind the fucking door listening?" Katy yells at her, just as surprised by her sudden appearance as I am. I watch as Katy goes into defence mode too, but not for the same reasons I do. I know she feels completely cornered now. She's wondering how much of what was just said Kami heard and how much she has to explain.

They're yelling at each other and I'm not listening, I'm trying to work out how the hell I'm going to get Katy away from here so that I can talk to her without Kami around. If Kami's here, then that means she home, obviously, which means it's going to be damn hard to get Katy to leave with me. She wants answers from Kami, and she has no desire to talk to me.

Next thing I know, Kami takes a step towards me with every word she spits out, "What. The. Fuck. Did. You. Do. To. Fuck. With. Me. This. Time?"

"You're all going to hate me once you know." I say in barely a whisper, but I know they both hear me, and Katy can see my whole body shaking.

"Don't worry Joe, I already do so you're not losing anything with me." Kami says.

"That's where you're wrong, I am losing everything because of you." I growl out, pointing at her. Suddenly I feel nothing but rage again for this woman, even though I know the only person I'm angry at is Harry. Fucking Harry French. Let's not forget Helen Parker and her role in this sordid little fucking tale. I see red when I think of those two and everything they've put both of our families through. I can't believe that Kami can be so blasé about it, so forgiving of her mother and her transgressions.

Katy's hand rests lightly on my arm at first, then her grip gets steadily tighter, as I realise I'm stepping towards Kami. I look up into Katy's eyes, and I can see her pleading with me. *Make it stop. End this Joe, you told me you could let it go and you were ok with Kami being my best friend'.*

There's so much pain and hurt in her eyes, it's killing me to look in them, so I don't. I square up to Kami and decide now is the time.

I start to tell them what I did. It wasn't James, it was me that sent that message and all hell breaks loose.

Chapter Thirty-one

"Fucking hell Kami, how long have you been standing behind the fucking door listening?" I yell at her, surprised by her sudden appearance.

"It's _my_ fucking door _Katy_, in case you forgot?" Kami never curses, and I can't help the shock on my face when she does. Now I know she's pissed off with me.

"I'm sorry Kami, you're right. If we wanted to have a private conversation, it shouldn't have been here." I say, sending Joe a filthy look.

"Don't let me stand in the way of you two getting all cosy in my parking lot, not at all." I go to speak but Kami holds up her hands to stop me. "I heard enough to understand a few things Katy, and one of them is that this man has never grown up and still likes to play with my emotions and interfere in my life. You've played with me for the last fucking time Joe French, I've had enough of your mind games to last me a lifetime and I'm not playing anymore." She takes one step towards him with every word she speaks, "What. The. Fuck. Did. You. Do. To. Fuck. With. Me. This. Time?"

"Now Kami, calm down and let him speak, I've never seen you like this before." I stop mid-sentence when she turns her glare my way.

"You want _me_ to give _him_ a chance to speak and explain himself, after all these years of torture, _you_ want _me_ to take it easy on _him_. Thanks for your loyalty Katy, I really appreciate it."

"That's not what I meant Kami and you know it. I meant let him explain himself before you go ripping his head off. You look like you could kill him, hun." I say, my voice filled with annoyance.

"Depending on what he says next, I could." She snarls in response.

"You're all going to hate me once you know." He barely whispers, I only hear it because I'm so close to him. I can see his whole body shaking.

"Don't worry Joe, I already do so you're not losing anything with me." Kami says.

"That's where you're wrong, I am losing everything because of you." He growls out, pointing at Kami, his sudden change in mood shocks me.

"No, you're losing things because of your actions, not mine. What. Did. You. Do. Joe?" Kami asks, venom and demand in her voice.

"It wasn't James." He starts, but I have no idea what he's talking about. "That text you got from the unknown number that ended up being James' new number. He didn't send it, I did. He didn't lose any contacts when I got him the new phone. I deleted a few, including yours, so that he couldn't call you. He needed to concentrate on the job he was on, it was a big deal for his company and his plans to expand."

"YOU DID *WHAT*, Joseph?"

We all look up to see James' truck parked right next to Kami's car. I don't know when he arrived, but we all know he's here now!

I don't think I've ever seen anyone as angry as James is right now and the fact that his anger is directed at Joe is completely unnerving.

What the hell are these two talking about? What fucking text message did Joe send to Kami and what the hell did it say?

I feel like I'm the only one who has no fucking clue what the hell is going on.

"Why would you do that Joe?" Kami asks, confusion and sadness in her voice.

I hear Kami ask Joe why. Why did he do it, but I don't hear his answer. All I can hear are words, mumbled by distant voices. Honestly, I'm not sure what answer he can give that will make any of this ok.

There are no excuses for his behaviour.

He did this.

Joe and James seem to have an entire conversation without saying a word, just angry looks and daggers shooting from their eyes. They both seem as angry as each other, just for different reasons. James' reasons I understand, Joe's on the other hand. I don't know.

As much as I know that they're mad at each other, my attention is on Kami. I'm watching my best friend to see how she's dealing with Joe's confession. She's as shocked at James' appearance as we are, which means she didn't know he was back in town. I reach out for her hand, to offer her some comfort but she jumps at my touch and pulls away from me without even looking my way. The physical rejection stings, but the emotional rejection hurts even more.

As I drop my arm to my side, wondering how the hell I can fix the damage to our lifelong friendship, a few words sift through. Snippets of what Joe is saying, his excuses, hit me.

"I sent James a text about the woman I was seeing." I don't let him finish that thought.

"Are you saying you did this because of *me*? Because of *us*, Joe?" I ask him quietly, disgust lacing my voice. I can't believe he's blaming me for his decisions.

"What?" James asks. Kami breaks in, not giving Joe or myself the chance to speak.

"Oh yeah, didn't you know James? At least I'm not the only one who wasn't bought in on the secret." Suddenly, she turns to me, anger and disappointment coming off her in waves. "Hell Katy, you know he's always hated me, and as far as I can tell, it's been for no reason. I understand that you can't help who you fall for, trust me on this one, but really? Did you think I didn't love *you* enough to at least *try* to get over it? You didn't trust me, you didn't even give me a chance." She shakes her head, I've never heard her speak like that before to anyone, but especially not me.

I want to take her pain away, but she won't even look at me. Knowing that I caused her pain, makes it worse. I try to speak to her again, but she turns away from me and then all hell breaks loose.

One minute Joe is standing almost by my side, the next he's on the ground, cradling his face in blood covered hands.

I hear talking and shuffling but all of my attention is on Joe. I kneel down to check on him and he groans as I pull his hands away to get a better look. I gasp and swear under my breathe, "Holy fuck."

"You best get him to the hospital Katy, I think his nose is broken." Kami says, after she's already shoved James in her car, after wrapping up his hand.

"Thanks Kami, I will. I'll call you later to check in with you." I reply with hesitation.

"Just text me what's wrong with him, I don't really want to talk to you right now." Kami replies tersely.

"Umm yeah sure, I can do that. Can you let me know how James' hand is, please?" I asks, softly. "We'll both want to know how he is." She grunts in reply and starts to get in her car, when all of a sudden, the back door to the shop is flung open again.

"What the hell is happening out here? Are you OK Kami? We could hear yelling in the shop." Ed yells out all in one breath, and then he surveys everyone in the parking lot.

"Everything's just fine Ed. My best friend was seeing the one guy who hates me. That guy hates me so much that he sent fake text messages to me, hoping to break James and I up and then James hit him. Now, they both need a doctor. One needs stitches, and the other needs a nose reset." Kami takes a breath.

"Are you OK Kami? Can I do anything?" Ed asks, the poor guy looks completely confused.

"Just look after the shop, please? I'll let you know what happened soon, OK? Thanks Ed." Ed nods, and Kami gets in her car and takes off.

"Did you need any help getting this idiot into your car Katy?" Ed asks me, but I don't think he's angry with either of us, just thinks we're both stupid.

"Thanks for the offer Ed, but we should be ok. It's his face that's busted, not his arms or legs." I say, full of sarcasm and very little sympathy.

"If you're sure Katy?" He asks, sounding a little unsure of my capabilities.

"Look Ed, I appreciate the offer, but you can go back into the bookstore and keep that open, just like you have for the past week." I say, as I help Joe to his feet.

"There's no need to be a bitch about it Katy. I was just making sure you're ok, because even though Kami's obviously pissed off with you right now, you're still her best friend." He says with some irritation in his own voice.

"You're right and I'm sorry. It's just that shit hit the fan around here and honestly, I don't even know what the hell is going on." I sigh, because I really have no clue about a message, or anything else the other three were talking about. The only thing I know is, Joe got James a new phone because James busted his, the rest is a mystery. "Look, I have to get Joe to the hospital to see how bad his nose is. I suspect it's broken. Can you just look after the shop and whatever else Kami needs. Please."

"Sure Katy." He nods and walks back into the bookshop, closing the door with a thump behind him that makes me jump.

"Come on you big idiot. Let's go get your face looked at and repaired. Then you and me? We're talking mister and not just about us either."

"If you had just spoken to me when I asked you to Katy," Joe starts, but I don't let him continue.

"Oh no you don't. You don't get to blame this shit fight you've gotten yourself into on me Joseph French." I growl at him, shaking my head as he falls into the passenger seat of my car. I grab some tissues from the glove box and shove them into his hand. "Here, clean yourself up a bit and then grab some more tissues so you don't bleed all over my damned car."

I walk around the front of my car to the driver's side door, before I get in I take a few seconds to take a deep breath and clear my head. This is a cluster-fuck of all proportions and I don't know how to make it right.

First up though is getting Joseph fixed up. Then, oh boy, then he gets to have that talk he's been wanting for a few weeks. Idiot.

Chapter Thirty-two

JOE

I hear Kami question me about why I did it all, but instead of answering here, I turn to James and say, "You know why James." I stumble out.

"No, I don't know why Joe. I know you've hated Kami for as long we've known each other, but you've never explained why. You're about to though." James grinds out.

"I'd rather not have that conversation out here James." I say, trying to pull myself back together. I've never, in all the years I've known James and all the things we've seen together, seen him so full of rage and hatred. Even when he's been dealing with his father.

"I don't really care what you want Joe, not today." His voice becoming a deep growl. "*What* did you do? Tell me NOW, Joseph."

"Stop fucking calling me Joseph and I'll think about it." I growl back at him. I clear my throat to gather my thoughts, then I speak again. "I was worried about you and your business James, I want to make that very clear from the beginning." Still no-one makes any movements or noise. I've got a captive audience whether I want it or not, and I really don't want to do this here. "Look, I didn't set out to do this, I just …. I took advantage of a situation I guess."

"What did you do Joe? What was so bad that Kami didn't want to talk to me anymore, to not even listen to an explanation? Not that I had one because I *still* don't even know what I'm supposed to have fucking done!" James asks, his voice deceptively quiet and dangerously so.

"I, well I ummm – I deleted all her details from your phone." I mumble. Standing here in front of them and explaining what I've done, I feel like a fucking hateful bastard. I could justify it at the time, but looking them in the face now, I see that what I did was fucked up and wrong.

"Okayyyy. That means I couldn't contact her, but Kami knew I was in a dodgy area, that wouldn't have made her so mad that she'd never want to see me again. There has to be more, what else did you do Joe?" James says, still not seeing the whole picture.

"I also deleted her from the files on your laptop." I say.

"Again, that meant that I couldn't contact Kami, nothing about that relates to *her* contacting *me*. That is unless you didn't give her my new number like I fucking asked you to. You *did* give her the new number when you got back into town, didn't you Joseph?" James asks, getting agitated again.

"Oh yeah, he gave me your number James. How long had you had that one for?" Kami confirms that I did what I was asked to do, but then she put another nail in my coffin by telling James he could have just broken it off with her *before* he left town.

"James didn't have his new phone or number when you got that text Kami." I have to speak up before James does, because I know he has no damned clue what she's talking about.

"I sent a total of maybe four texts the afternoon I got it and they were all to the arsehole standing over there." He points at me, but he's looking at Kami, begging her to believe him.

"Kami." I hear Katy say quietly.

"No Katy. Just no." she says just as quietly as she turns to walk to her car. "Not right now, I just can't."

"Okay." I can hear the pain in Katy's voice and it almost kills me.

Kami turns back towards me and says, "As for you Joe, I don't care why you did it, I only care that you did. You've been doing this kind of shit to me since we were kids, humiliating me, embarrassing me, harassing me and just plain hating me. This is some new level to stoop to even for you, I can understand wanting to protect a friend, but this. This is something I have no words for."

Then she continues walking away from us to her car. I can see all the pain I've caused right here in front of me and I hate it. Everyone I love is hurting and it's all my fault.

"Your mother and my father, they were a couple when they were younger." I say to Kami's back, causing her to stop in her tracks.

"What on earth does that have to do with us? How does that explain how you've treated me all these years? Whatever happened between them, was exactly that, between them." Kami says, as she turns to look at me with a completely astonished look on her face.

"He was in love with her and then she left town. When she came back, she had a husband and you." I close my eyes and take a deep breathe before I can think about continuing.

"But that would mean he would have already married your mother and had you by then as well. So why was he so bent out of shape?" Kami asks, confusion written all over her face, and I completely understand because I feel it too.

"My mother was his second choice, yours was his first." I see the realisation hit both Kami's and James' faces, but I can still see the anger there too. "He got on with his life when she left because she told him she would never give him what he wanted. A family. They would never get married and never have children." I say with a resigned sigh. Sounds just like the conversation I had with Katy a few weeks ago.

"Oh Joe." I hear Katy gasp, but I don't look her way, I can't. Instead, I continue with my explanation.

"When Helen came back to town with all that she'd said she wouldn't give him, he turned bitter. My mother suffered, and so did I. I wasn't *you*. He became the nastiest bastard I've ever met and made my life fucking miserable."

"How is that *my* fault Joe? Or yours for that matter?" Kami says and makes a move to leave again, until James speaks, that makes her stop in her tracks.

I don't want to look up and see the accusations written all over his face, but I know I need to face up to my mistakes. I need to do this. For my relationship with Katy and my friendship with James.

"So, let me get this straight. You've made Kami's life a living hell all because your father couldn't deal with being dumped?" James asks, his voice full of disbelief.

I nod my head in answer, but I don't get the chance to voice anything, because James is on a roll.

"You've hurt Kami emotionally and sometimes physically, for years and kept me from asking her out, all because your father had his feelings hurt?" It sounds so stupid when he says it like that. "Even since we got together however many months ago, you've been planting seeds of doubt in my head. Then you delete her details from my contacts, while I'm away knowing that I can't get away to come home and see her. Knowing full well that I wanted that contract and more like it, because I'm the fucking idiot that never thought to keep secrets." He says, his voice low and menacing. "*Then*," he pushes on, "you send her a message that you know she's going to misconstrue to mean that I don't want to be with her." He looks at me, I can see him thinking and I know where he's going next. The day I went to see him and bought him a new phone. "No wonder you were caught off guard that day in my office, you were setting up this little revenge plot. Revenge on behalf of the father that treated you like you didn't exist, instead of being loyal to the friend that has had your back for close to twenty years. You can't break the heart of the woman I love without breaking mine too Joe. I told you how I felt, and you still went through with it all."

"I'm sorry James. I didn't really think you were that invested and by the time I did realise, I couldn't stop it. It just had a life of its own and." I don't get the chance to finish before I feel the bones in my nose crunch and I land on the ground, flat on my arse.

The girls are yelling and there's mumbled talking all around me. I can't understand a fucking thing though, because my face and nose are throbbing so badly, my ears are ringing, and my eyes are watering.

By the time I can gather any of my senses, Katy's helping me to my feet, I watch Kami's rear lights disappear into the distance and Ed's looking at me like I killed his puppy.

"Come on Joe, you have to help me get you into my car." Katy says and I can't tell how she's feeling by the tone of her voice. Then again, I can't tell if the sky is up or down right now. "Here," Katy says, shoving some tissues into my hands. "Clean yourself up a bit and then grab some more tissues so you don't bleed all over my damned car."

I do as I'm told and watch her walk around the front of her car to her door. When she gets there, she doesn't get in the car straight away, she stops and takes a few deep breaths. I'm not sure but I think she's also talking to herself.

"Katy." I mumble out from behind the tissues I've got plastered to my face.

"No Joe." She shakes her head and starts the car, but before the car moves she looks at me and says, "Not right now ok Joe? Let's just get you to the hospital and get your nose fixed. We can talk after that."

"Ok." I reply, I start to nod my head, but it rattles my brain too much, so I stop. "I just want to say, I'm sorry baby. I never meant for any of this to happen."

"What? You mean you didn't intend on getting your nose broken when you decided to take matters into your own hands and break up your best friend and the woman he loves?" she asks, sarcasm dripping from every word.

"No. That's not what I set out to do, funnily enough." I sigh.

"Funny that!" she snorts and starts the drive to the hospital. "Imagine Joe, for just one second, if that had been Kami's reaction to *us* being together. Now think about how *you* would be feeling right about now." She says quietly as we go over a bump in the road that not only takes my breathe away, but also my ability to answer her.

I let my head fall back against the headrest and close my eyes. Suddenly I feel exhausted beyond belief. I press the tissues I wadded up earlier tight up against my nose and sigh deeply. My nose and eyes are swollen, and no doubt starting to bruise. The throbbing ache at my temples gives me an idea as what kind of a headache I can look forward to.

I've lost everything, all for loyalty to a man who has never done anything except treat me like a burden. James was right, my loyalty should have been with him. With the man who has stood by me through thick and thin. The man that has always had *my* back, instead I've repaid him with deceit and disrespect.

I've lost Katy. I am under *no* illusions that she's here, taking me to the hospital because she's a good and decent human being. One who wouldn't leave an animal, let alone a pathetic human being like me, wounded on the side of the road. One of the many reasons I love her. Guess I'm going to have to find a way to stop doing that, or I might turn into a grumpy old bastard.

The thought makes me laugh and I cough to cover it but that just causes me to groan in pain.

Great, no best friend, no girlfriend and I'm turning into my old man. What a perverted twist of fate, turning into the one thing I hate the most because I screwed it all up over loyalty to a man who hates me.

"What's so funny Joe? I wouldn't think you had too much to laugh at today." I don't open my eyes to look at her, I can't stand to see the look of sympathy or her anger.

"Nothing beautiful, absolutely nothing. You're right, I have absolutely nothing at all to smile or laugh about today and even if I did, it hurts too damned much to try." She doesn't need to know that my pain is emotional as much as physical.

"We'll be at the hospital in less than a minute Joe. Then we'll get the pain fixed up." If only she understood that there are no doctors, nurses, bandages or plasters that can heal my heart. So, instead of explaining, I stay quiet as she pulls into a parking space right out front of emergency.

Katy offers to help me walk into the hospital. "It's my face that's broken, not my legs Katy." I remind her.

"Fine, have it your own grumpy way, I was just trying to help." She says in exasperation. "Maybe I should leave your sorry arse here all on its own to deal with this mess?"

"I'm sorry Katy, I just meant that I'm ok to walk." I say, regretting my attitude right away. "I'm in pain and feeling a little on edge. Defensive you might even say."

"Alright, let's just get you sorted then shall we?" she says with half a smile. It's more than I've gotten off her in weeks, so I'll take it.

Chapter Thirty-three

At the hospital Joe's quiet. I don't know if it's because he's in pain, doesn't know what to say or is just plain ignoring me. We've been sitting next to each other in the waiting room in complete silence. I had to swap out the tissues in the car for him because they filled up with blood. The triage nurse gave us some packing to hold under his nose, and told us the wait wouldn't be too long, as long as an emergency didn't come through. I hope that there isn't an emergency, not because I don't want anyone hurt, but because I'm not sure how much blood this packing can take.

An hour and two more wads of packing later, I watch yet another nurse walk in the doorway to the waiting room. "Joseph French?" she says, looking around the almost empty room.

Joe goes to stand up but almost falls back down again before the nurse and I grab an arm each.

"Whoa, I'm feeling a little light-headed." Joe mumbles behind his wad of packing.

"Well a possible broken nose, combined with the blood loss will do that Mr French." The nurse says. "Sit back down before you fall down, and I'll go find you a wheelchair."

"I don't need a wheelchair, it's a broken nose, not a broken leg." Joe says as he attempts to stand up again, only to land down on the plastic chair. "Okay, I guess I'll use that wheelchair."

"Men can be so damned stubborn." The nurse says to me and I smile at her, agreeing.

The nurse comes back with a wheelchair and Joe drops his arse into it, holding his face in his hands. I guess he's trying to protect it from the bumpy ride, who knows? At this point, I don't really care, the smells of the hospital are getting to me and making me feel nauseous. I haven't felt this bad for a couple of weeks now, I thought I was getting over this damned bug.

The nurse looks my way and asks, "Are you OK?" her voice is full of concern that she didn't really show for Joe, which I have to admit, I find amusing.

"Yeah I'm good. It's just the smells, they're getting to me and making me feel a little unwell. I don't know how you can stand them every day." I say, she looks at me and nods in understanding. She must get told that a million times every shift.

She pulls the wheelchair into a room, I can't call it a cubicle, it has a door. The nurse must see the look on my face because she explains, "We need the room so that we can close the door once the doctor starts resetting his nose." I nod, like I'm understanding, but in all honestly I have no fucking clue why they'd need that kind of privacy. "Yeah the noise can be pretty horrific and he's going to be in some pain." I nod again, and after helping Joe up onto the bed, she wheels the chair back out and disappears.

"Katy." Joe says on with a moan, so I move closer so I can hear what he has to say. I'm here because he's hurt and I wasn't leaving him broken and bloody in the car park behind the book shop, but that doesn't mean I'm here to comfort him. "Katy, honey, I'm sorry."

"Joe, this isn't the time nor the place for this talk." I can't even see his face properly, his eyes are almost swollen shut.

"I know, but I need to say something honey." He mumbles behind the tissues and wading packed over his face.

"Can you stop, please Joe?"

"Talking?" I see one eye looking at me in question.

"That and calling me honey." I ask him, even though I feel like a bitch doing it seeing he's in a hospital bed. "We broke up, remember?"

"No. *You* walked away from me. *That's* what I remember Kathryn." He doesn't get to finish his thought because the doctor bursts into the room, with the nurse who wheeled him in, hot on his heels.

"Good afternoon Mr French, I'm Doctor Andrews. I hear you ran into someone's fist and came off second best, is this correct?" Doctor Andrew's finally looks up and his eyes lock with mine for a few seconds until the nurse coughs.

"Yeah there was a bit of a disagreement." Joe says, as Doctor Andrews pulls all the gauze away from his face and I snort at the understatement of the year. Everyone in the room looks my way again and I feel my cheeks heat with embarrassment. "And a fist connected with my nose, yes." Joe finishes.

"Right. Well we could get you to have an x-ray, if you want to be really sure, but I'm looking at your nose and I'm pretty confident in saying its broken. Like I said though, we can send you for an x-ray if you like, but I think it's a waste of time." Joe looks at me and I finally see the extent of the damage done to his face. Both of his eyes are starting to bruise, there are patches of blood all over the lower half of his face and his nose. Holy fucking shit, his nose is actually crooked. I feel the tears well in my own eyes and I have to look away.

"Well, by that look, I'm guessing I don't need the x-ray doc, so how about we just go about fixing it so I can get out of here?" Doctor Andrews nods and looks at the nurse.

"OK Mr French. I'll get Annie here to get you some pain meds, while I sort everything else out to get your nose put back and set." With that he turns to the nurse and they start talking.

When they leave to get whatever they need, the room is left silent. The tension between us so thick you could cut it with a knife. A blunt butter one at that. I'm trying to think of something to say, something we can talk about that isn't James and Kami, his broken nose or our past.

The door opens and the nurse walks back in, relieving the need for either of us to say anything. "There's a chair just behind you. You can pull it forward so you can sit down and be a little more comfortable."

"Thank you." I say, dropping Joe's hand and moving the chair closer to the side of the bed. "Ahh nurse Annie, how long will it take?"

"Setting Mr French's nose?" I nod in answer. "Not long. We just have to wait for the painkillers to kick in first, but they shouldn't take long. No more than a few minutes. We'll know as soon as they hit."

"Oh OK, thank you."

"It's Annie." She says.

"Hmmm?" I sort of ask, distracted.

"You don't need to call me *nurse* Annie. My name is Annie, I'm not a doctor, I don't need the reminder of my title every other second."

"Oh. Right OK. Thanks Annie." I say, with what I can only guess is an extremely weak smile.

"I heard that, *nurse* Annie." Doctor Andrews says, as he walks back in the room, giving Annie a look that says a million things, but I can't be bothered trying to decipher any of them.

"Are you sure you're OK? You look a little pale." Annie asks me, ignoring the doctor, but rolling her eyes when I look at her.

"Yes, I'm fine. I, ummm, don't like the smell of hospitals. I don't know how you can stand to be here all day long." I say, feeling like an idiot. Mainly because Joe's the patient not me and Annie seems to think I'm the one who needs to be taken care of, but also because now they're all looking at me and I realise it's their job to stay in a bloody hospital all day long. I'm sure they get used to the smell of it.

"It does take some getting used to, that's for sure." Annie says, smiling at me.

"Hey Katy. Kathryn, honey, where are you?" Joe says, but his words are a little slurred. His hand is reaching out for me and when I catch it, he holds on tight. "I won't let you go honey, no matter what you say. I love you."

Ahhh crap on a cracker, to use one of Kami's favourite sayings. I look over at Annie, who looks a little shocked to be honest, and ask, "He won't remember anything that's happened will he?"

"Probably not, but I find that people usually speak the truth when they're under the influence of strong painkillers like these." She says, sympathy written all over her face. "So, my advice is, let him down easy if you don't feel the same way."

I take Joe's hand in mine and he holds on tight. Doctor Andrews turns and looks at Joe. "I think he's ready." Annie nods at the doctor.

"Can I get you to stand a little further down the bed Katy?" Annie asks me. "I need to be up at his head so that I can help the doctor."

I try to let go of Joe's hand and move away, but he won't let go of me. "Joe I'm just moving down the bed a bit."

"Katy, honey, don't leave me. Please." If he could hear the pleading in his voice he would be mortified.

"Joe, I'm not leaving, I need to get out of the way so that Doctor Andrews and Annie can do their job." I explain as I pull my hand from his and move around Annie.

"Jeff Andrews has a thing for you, you know? I saw that look in his eyes. If I didn't need his help, I think I might knock him out."

Holy shit could this get any more embarrassing if it tried? "Joe, Doctor Andrews is fixing your nose and whether he has a thing for me or not doesn't matter, OK?" I can see him getting all worked up over his perceived notion of Jeff Andrews being anything except a bad decision.

"It matters to me Katy." Joe grumbles, his eyes closing as Annie touches his nose and he uses his hand to push her away. "I'm trying to talk here." He says.

"And I'm trying to fix your nose Mr French. You can talk to Katy later, I promise."

"She'll still be here when you're done?" he asks.

Annie looks at me and I nod my head, "Yes Mr French, Katy will still be here when I'm done."

"Call me Joe, Mr French is my arsehole father."

"Sure Joe. Let's get this nose fixed alright?"

"Sure but I can't feel anything wrong with my nose Annie." Joe says, his words a slurred mumble.

"That was the plan Joe." Annie chuckles slightly then turns to me and says, "This is going to sound horrible, but we need to do it OK? Not to mention, there's going to be a fair bit of blood."

I take a deep breath and swallow my nerves, this is Joe's pain, not mine. "Sure, thanks for the warning."

"You're not going to like this Katy." Jeff's deep voice says from the other side of the bed. "Maybe you should wait outside? We'll call you back in when it's done."

"No, I want her to stay." Joe says, trying to sit up.

"It's OK Joe, I'm right here and I'm not going anywhere." I say, placing my hand on his leg so that he knows I'm still here. I feel him relax immediately and I'm almost positive I hear Jeff mumble something about him being a selfish bastard.

"Alright, here goes." Jeff says. Then the room is filled with the sound of bones crunching and moving around, Joe moans, blood starts flowing out his nose and down onto the protective sheet Annie placed on his chest. That's the last thing I remember, as the noise and the smell gets to me and I pass out.

When I wake up, Annie and Jeff are looking slightly worried about me and I've got a killer headache. "What happened?" I ask.

"You fainted." Jeff says as I reach my hand up to touch my forehead. "You hit your head on the gurney as you went down. You've got a nasty gash on your forehead that I'd rather you didn't touch right now. Annie will get you cleaned up so that I can have a look."

"What about Joe? Did you get his nose fixed up?" I ask, worried that I stopped them from doing what we came here for, and to stop them fussing around with me.

"Yes, he's reset and ready to go after we clean him up a bit." Jeff says, as Annie starts cleaning up the cut on my face.

"There you go Doctor Andrews, all ready for you." Annie says and steps away.

"Thanks Annie." He says as he walks past her, and she gives him a slight nod. "Annie just made the area around the wound numb and I'm going to put a couple of stitches in to close it up, OK?" he asks me, and I nod my reply. "You won't have to come back in and get them out, they should dissolve on their own in a couple of days. Now, I'm just going to ask you a few questions and I need you to answer them properly, OK?"

"Sure."

"What is your name?" he asks.

"Kathryn Ellis, but you already know that." I say, frustrated.

"How old are you Katy?"

"Well that's just rude, I know your mother taught you better than to ask a lady her age." I say with a huff, because I *know* Mrs Andrews wouldn't approve.

"You're right, she'd be horrified I asked but I have to. What day is it?" he asks.

"It's Saturday." I answer.

"What's your mother's name?"

"Again you already know. Anna Ellis, father is Frank Ellis and my sisters name is Olivia. Are you happy now? I've got all my faculties Jeff. I remember who you are *Doctor Andrews* and I remember the lovely Annie here too. I also know that I'm here because Joe needs his nose fixed, we're not here for me."

"Annie said you've been feeling unwell, is that true?" Jeff asks me, I look over at Annie and she's concentrating on cleaning up Joe's face, and not looking my way.

"Yes. I've had a virus." I answer.

"For how long Katy?"

"A few weeks, *Jeff*. I've already seen a doctor and he said I just need to wait for it to leave my body. You know the usual suggestion, keep fluids up, eat when I can and rest." I say with a shrug.

"OK, I want to keep an eye on you as well seeing as you hit your head. We'll leave you both in here and check in on you in ten minutes or so."

"That's not necessary Jeff, it was just the blood, sound of crunching bones and the smell of the hospital, they all combined, and I went down."

"Katy, I need to make sure you don't have a concussion. So yes, it is necessary for me to check on you as a *doctor* and I take that pretty seriously."

I look over to Joe who is sleeping on the bed, his nose in a splint and the bruises under his eyes looking all kinds of nasty. I laugh quietly, aren't we a funny pair? Him with his nose in a splint and me with a waterproof patch on my forehead. When we walk out of here, people are going to think we did this to each other. That thought cracks me up and I can't control my laughter, until I have the thought that sobers me up instantly.

I want to share the funny situation with Kami, and I can't. Instead I send her a message.

Me: *How's James' hand?*

Kami: *He split open a couple of knuckles. They've been sewn up now.*

Me: *Wow he really put some effort in to that punch hey?*

It takes a while for the next message to come through, I'm just happy she actually read and answered the first one.

Kami: *He deserved it. Is his nose broken?*

Me: *He did. Yes it is.*

Then my phone is silent, and Annie comes in with her implements of torture, I hate needles. I mean I'm not going to faint again, but I hate the fuck-

ers. So, instead of watching Annie, I think about the fact that Kami actually answered me and asked how Joe was. I know she's mad and she has every
right to be, I am to, but I also know she can't stay mad at me for long. She
never has been able to in the past, I'm hoping she can't now too.

"All done Katy."

"Thanks Annie." I smile at her.

Just as Annie finishes cleaning up Joe starts to wake up. I didn't think
we'd been here stuffing around with my head for that long, but Annie doesn't
seem surprised.

"Joe don't try to sit up too fast or you're going to feel dizzy. Just take it
slow." Annie says as she reaches over to help him sit up.

"Katy."

"I'm right here Joe." I sat next to the bed and take his hand in mine.

"I thought you left with the doctor." Joe says, obviously still confused.

"No I stayed right here. How are you feeling?"

"I'm OK. My face hurts, but I guess that's what happens when you run
into an angry fist." He tries to laugh, but he groans, as pain spreads across his
face. "Fuck."

"You're going to need to rest for the next few days, Joe. You're also going
to need someone to stay with you just to make sure nothing goes wrong."

"I don't have anyone who can stay." Joe says, and I speak over him. "I'll
stay with him." I don't know who is more shocked by my words. Joe or myself.

"Are you sure Katy?" Joe asks me, looking at me properly for the first time
since he sat up. I don't get the chance to answer him, because he's asking me
more questions. "What the hell happened? What did you do to your head?
I didn't see anything back at the book shop. Did you get caught up in the
middle of him hitting me? I'll kill him." I see the anger building on Joe's face,
even Annie takes half a step back from him.

"OK first thing first. Yes I'm sure I'll stay with you and no James didn't
hit me. Neither did you, in case you were wondering. I passed out when they
manipulated your nose back into place and hit my head on the base of the
gurney."

"You just need to wait here for another half an hour so that we know
everything is OK, then we can get you out of here OK?" Annie says.

Joe and I nod at Annie and she leaves the room, taking away any reason to talk. I sit down in the chair next to Joe's bed, and while the silence is nice, because my head is aching, it also makes me a little nervous. We've both rested our heads back and closed our eyes and without realising it, I've fallen asleep until Annie comes back in just over an hour later.

"Sorry it took so long guys, we had a small emergency come in."

"That's fine Annie."

"So does that mean we can get out of here now? I'm feeling fine. Well, as good as I'm going to get for a few days anyway, and I'm sure you could use the bed for someone who needs it more than me." Joe says as he gets off the bed. He wobbles on his feet for a second but then finds his balance.

"Wait and I'll go get a wheelchair for you." Annie starts, but Joe waves her away.

"I'm good thanks Annie, I'll walk out. If you need me to sign something, I will but I just want to go home if that's all the same to you?"

"You need to keep the splint on for a couple of weeks. If there's any swelling or bleeding, you need to come back and see us. That's most important over the next couple of days, which is why you need to have someone stay with you. If nothing unusual happens, you can go see your doctor to get the splint off, rather than come back here and wait for ages." Annie hands Joe some papers for him to sign and then we're walking back out to my car in silence.

The silence in the car as we start driving is deafening. I turn up the music on the radio and tap my fingers on the steering wheel. I like silence as much as the next person, but this one feels very uncomfortable.

"I'm just going to go by my place and grab a few things. Unless you'd rather go straight to your place and I can grab some things later?" I say loud enough for him to hear over the music.

"Just take me home please Katy." He says.

"OK sure. I'll come back out a little later then and grab some clothes and stuff. I'll have to come out to get us some dinner anyway." I nod, mostly to myself because I'm thinking out loud.

"No. I mean just take me home, I'll be fine on my own. You don't need to babysit me."

"You need someone to stay with you Joe, you heard Annie." I say.

"No I don't. I'll be fine Kathryn, I'll call my mum and she can come and check on me. She'll have fun fussing over me." he says, without looking at me, but I can see his reflection in the window.

"Well, sure you should call Felicity and let her know before someone else does, but that doesn't mean I'm not staying with you for the next few days Joseph." Stubborn man.

He suddenly turns away from the window to look at me and I see the anger all over his face, but it's the hurt in his eyes that really hits me. "You and I both know that the last place you want to be right now, is in my home. Anywhere I am for that matter, so why don't we save each other a load of trouble and admit it? I told the nurse what she needed to hear so she could let me out of there, but I don't want to burden you with my sorry arse, so you're free." He says and then looks back out the window again.

Instead of going straight to his place, I go to mine. I park in the driveway, look over at Joe and say, "You've got a choice. You can sit here in the car and wait for me, I won't be very long, or you can come inside and wait for me. Either way, I'm grabbing a few things so that I can come and stay with you for a few days. I don't care what you think, I want to be there to look after you."

He looks at me when I speak, but when I'm done, he turns back to the window. Guess he's staying in the car then. I take the keys, not only so that I can unlock the front door, but also so he can't drive my car away and escape. I walk into my bedroom, grab an overnight bag and throw some clean underwear, something to sleep in and a couple of changes of clothes into it. Then I walk into the bathroom and grab the necessities. Within five minutes I'm walking back out the front door, locking it behind me and getting back into the car. Joe hasn't moved since I left him, and he doesn't say a word to me before I start the car and drive to his house.

Before I've even turned the engine off, Joe's out of the car and walking to his front door. It's then that I realise he had to get into town somehow. "Where did you leave your car Joe?"

"In town Kathryn." Is the only answer he gives me.

"That's helpful Joseph. Where about in town did you leave it, Joseph?" I ask, trying not to be too fucking snarky but he's pushing my limits.

"I'll pick it up tomorrow." He says, walking inside and throwing his keys on the kitchen bench, and walking straight to the fridge.

"I don't think you're supposed to drink beer with the medication they gave you Joe." I say quietly.

"What do you care Kathryn? You're not my mother and you're not my girlfriend, you've made that painfully obvious." The hurt I feel is like being stabbed in the heart. I know he's hurting, in more than one way, but ouch!

"Fuck you Joe. You know I care about you, and you can try your best to push me away, but you're stuck with me for at least the next few days. Like it or not." He doesn't get the chance to respond because my phone rings. I don't recognise the number, but I answer it anyway. "Hello, Kathryn speaking."

"Well, isn't that a bit formal for two people who've known each other forever Katy?" Jeff's voice rumbles through the phone.

"I guess it would be if I recognised the number, but I didn't, therefore I played it safe, and was polite. What can I help you with? Now isn't really a good time."

"I was calling to follow up on how you and Joe are feeling. Joe was my patient today and as it turns out, so were you."

"That's why you're calling?" I ask, not convinced with his motives. "Well, Joe's fine considering how much pain he must be in and I'm not even feeling dizzy. So I'd say we're good." I'm shorter with him than I should be, but I'm not in the mood for his 'concern'.

"Well, that and I wanted to ask you something." When I don't say anything, he continues. "Are you and Joe, *together*?"

I look over Joe leaning against the kitchen bench and as much as I want to tell Jeff that I'm a free agent, I know I'm not. "Yes."

"That's your answer? Yes." He takes a deep breathe. "After everything he's done to Kami, you choose *him*? How does she feel about that?" He asks, and it's a valid question and I know the answer, I choose not to give it to him though.

"That's my answer Doctor Andrews. Is there something else I can do for you?"

"No, I guess you answered all my questions. Just remember, if you feel dizziness or there's any vomiting, head straight back in to see us OK?"

"I will. Thank you Doctor Andrews." I say and hang up the call.

Chapter Thirty-four

JOE

"I will. Thank you Doctor Andrews." I hear Katy say into her phone. Doctor Jeff Andrews. I knew he'd gone to medical school, but I didn't realise he was working back in town. I can't help wondering if Katy knew he was back.

I wander back into the kitchen while I wait for her to finish talking to him, I grab a drink and wait for her to come join me. Katy's voice behind me makes me jump. "Guess we're going to have to get you some straws huh?" I didn't hear her come into the room. "Sorry, didn't mean to startle you." She says in a small voice, one I'm not used to hearing from her.

"You didn't, I'm not used to having other people in my home, that's all, and I forgot you were here." I reply, sounding like an arsehole even to me.

"Well, get used to it, because I'm here for a few more days yet." She says with a huff, opening the fridge and getting herself a bottle of water. It's on the tip of my tongue to tell her to make herself at home, but the truth is, she's the only other human being that's ever spent any significant time here other than James. "I'm sure you've had other *people* here before me Joe, and you'll have other *people* here after I'm gone again too."

I know what she's hinting at, and I don't discourage her assumptions, but neither do I agree with her either. My mother, James and Katy. That's the long list of people that 'hang out' in my home. No-one else has been here.

"Like I said, you don't have to stay Kathryn, I can get my mother to come look in on me." I'm pretty sure I could even convince Jenny to make sure I survive the next few days, if I had to.

"I'm staying." Katy replies firmly. Stubborn as always, even when she's not feeling well herself.

"If you're sick, then it's probably not a good idea for you to be here anyway."

"It's only a virus Joe, so there's no danger to your health. Mostly. Having your mother here will annoy you, Jenny is about ready to have her baby and you're not asking Nadine to come here either. That leaves me or James. Guess you're stuck with me." She answers, raising an eyebrow at me, challenging me to argue with her. I can't be bothered arguing, I'm too tired.

"Fine." I say, giving in to the inevitable. I'll let her have this win. "A couple of days to make sure there's no complications. Then you're going home." I see the hurt flit over her face, her mouth dipping down into a slight frown.

"Glad you finally agree with me. Now you need to." I don't let her finish, she might be staying here, but she doesn't get to tell me what to do.

"I'm going to lie down. Those drugs that Doctor Fantastic gave me are making me tired." I say.

"You mean the painkillers that Doctor Andrews gave you are working?" she asks with a smirk.

"I mean, he wanted me asleep and he got his wish. Does he know you're here, looking after me? I bet that wasn't part of his plan." I say, angrier than I have any right to be.

"He doesn't know I'm here, but then it's none of his business where I am. Annie said you needed someone to stay with you. Here I am." She says, arms spread wide, showing me exactly where she is.

"You're a free agent now, as I'm sure he's aware, by the look on his face when he recognised you, he'll be calling again soon." What am I doing? I went to find her to ask her to give us another chance, now I'm pushing her into the arms of another man. A man that can no doubt give her everything she wants, and she gets to keep her best friend as well.

"Geezus Joe, just take the painkillers and go lie down would you?" She shoves two pills that I didn't even see her get out, into my hand and my bottle of water in the other.

"I don't need any more." It's her turn to not let me finish my thought.

"No? You'd rather have the pain catch up with you and *then* take the pills? Jeff said you need to keep on top of the pain for the next few days."

"Well if *Jeff* said so, I guess I'd better take them." I say, swallowing the pills and stomping off to my bedroom.

She doesn't follow me, and I can't decide if that makes me happy or more miserable. We've shared this bed before, in fact, Katy's the only one I've shared this bed with.

I lay my exhausted body down and my eyes are closed before my head even hits the pillow.

I KNOW I'M ASLEEP AND this is all a dream, even as Katy turns around and notices me. She raises her hand to wave and as she starts to speak, my eyes roam her body. She looks so happy and then I see it, her round belly. She's pregnant and I can't help the smile that spreads across my face.

"Joe, I'm so glad you could make it." Dream Katy says and I'm wondering why the hell I wouldn't make it anywhere she is, especially if she's pregnant. Then I see him. Doctor Jeff Andrews, reaches his arm around her middle, gently caressing her stomach and reaching out his out hand to shake mine.

"Joe, we're so glad you're here, it wouldn't be the same without you." he says, a huge grin spreading across his face like he knows he won the prize. I guess he did, because that's when the rest of the scene comes into view. The beautiful house, white picket fence, the bounding Labrador and the backyard teeming with kids and other adults celebrating. Celebrating what I have no clue, but I feel like it doesn't even matter.

I start recognising faces in the crowd. My mum laughing and smiling with a group of other women, looks up at me and smiles a sad, knowing smile, but then goes back to chatting away.

James is here, and I start to walk towards him until he turns to look at me, rage still on his face, and Kami by his side, both of them have a child in their arms. James' face warning me to stay away.

My father is here too. He looks remarkably happy for a man who hates crowds and people in general. Then I realise why he's so happy, no-one wants me here, but he's welcome.

All of a sudden, I'm out on the footpath, looking in from the outside. Watching everyone I love moving on with their lives without me. The sky starts to darken and the storm clouds gathering, leaving me standing out in the cold rain, watching.

I wake up shivering and I realise I didn't get under the covers, didn't even have the energy. Staring up at the ceiling I know I have to accept that everyone will move on and I will have to pay the price for the mistakes I've made.

"Joe." I hear Katy's voice, it's soft. "Are you awake?" I don't move and I don't answer her, I'm not sure what to say. "Joe." She says my name again, so softly I barely hear it, but I know she's standing next to my bed before she puts her hand on my arm. Still, I don't move.

"Yeah, I'm awake. What do you need?" My voice is still rough from sleep, and no doubt rough because of the emotions lingering from my dreams.

"I came in to see if you were awake. You were mumbling in your sleep earlier, and I didn't want to wake you. You need to rest so that you can recover quicker, but I made us some dinner if you feel up to eating?" she asks.

Geezus, she made *us* dinner. "What time is it?" I ask, trying to distract myself from whatever it is that I'm feeling.

"It's late, close to 8 o'clock." That makes me turn to look at her.

"You ate already, didn't you?"

"No I was waiting for you to wake up."

"Why? You should have eaten without me Katy."

"Well, truth be told, I had a snack, or two, while waiting but I wanted to eat dinner with you when you were ready. No-one wants to eat alone Joe."

Her admission gets me moving. I swing my legs over the side of the bed and go to stand up, but I moved too quickly, and my head can't keep up, sending me back to sitting on the edge of the bed.

"Take it easy Joe, your balance is going to be off for a few days. You're going to end up with more injuries if you push yourself too hard." She scolds me.

"I'm fine. I just moved a little fast, that's all." I reply defensively.

"Come on, let me help you out to the table and I'll dish up our dinner."

I let her take my arm and lead me to the table. Not because I need the help, but because I want her touch. I need to feel her, even if it's just for a few minutes. I sit at the table and watch her move around my kitchen. She knows where everything is and doesn't have to search for anything. It's not the first time she's cooked in this kitchen, but it's the first time I've gotten to watch her. If she can feel my eyes on her, she doesn't show it. The task of getting dinner served up her only purpose right now.

I tried to help but she pushed me back down into the chair and told me to stay where I am. So instead I watch, without complaint, constantly reminding myself not to get used to her being here.

Dinner is on the table and I'm waiting for Katy to come sit down.

"Start eating Joe, I'll be there in a minute." She says.

"I'll wait for you." I say. I mean I can wait, I'm not that hungry to be honest but I know she wants me to eat, so I will. I'm also just enjoying sitting here watching her. Even if it does sound really creepy.

She sighs but walks over and sits in the chair opposite me. "Happy now? I'm here, we can eat."

"Thank you for making dinner Katy."

"You're welcome Joe, now eat it before it gets cold." She scolds me, and I laugh.

"Well, maybe you shouldn't have taken so long to sit your gorgeous self down to join me then." I realise what I've said when I hear her sudden intake of breath, but I can't take it back now. I *won't* take it back, ever.

"Yes, well I'm sorry but like I said, I've been snacking since we got home because I got hungry and didn't want to wake you."

"You don't have to eat with me then Katy, I was waiting for you to join me because I thought that's what you were doing."

"Let's eat." She says, smiling and picking up her knife and fork.

"Are you OK Katy? I ask. She nods her head. "You're not feeling dizzy or ready to chuck are you? I heard Doctor Fantastic tell you to watch out for concussion and on top of being sick already."

"It's just a virus. And I don't have a concussion. I didn't fall asleep and I'm getting a bit tired now because it's late OK? My body is healing still too." She answers.

"Are you sure? Is that what Andrews was calling you about earlier?" I want to know what he wanted, and I can only hope it was purely professional.

"Yes, and he was checking on you as well. We both ended up being his patients today." She smirks.

"So, he didn't call you to ask you out on a date?" I ask, not looking at her, concentrating on the meal in front of me.

She stops eating, and says, "No. No he didn't ask me out on a date and he's not likely to. Even if he did I wouldn't go."

"Why not?" I ask, knowing what I want the answer to be.

She hesitates and then says, "Because I don't want to go on a date with him."

"But you guys were together at one time, weren't you?" I ask, already knowing the answer, thanks to my mother keeping me up to date with all the happenings in the Ellis family.

"Yes, we did date for a while. Quite a while actually, thanks to both of our mothers, but we both decided in the end, that we weren't right for each other. We were in different stages of our lives. He was heading into his second year of residency and well I wasn't ready for that kind of commitment."

"What kind of commitment was that Katy?"

"The settling down, moving in together kind Joseph." She says, looking me right in the eyes. "Either way, that was a very long time ago. Ancient history."

"It didn't look like it was ancient history when he recognised you in the hospital earlier today." I know I'm pushing, but I can't help myself.

"Probably because he wasn't expecting to see me there."

"With me you mean. He must have recognised my name."

"Well, to be fair, no he probably wasn't expecting to see me with you, but I also doubt he was expecting to run into me at all, no matter who I was with. I wasn't expecting to run into him, that's for sure."

"So, you didn't know he was back in town?" And working in the local hospital that you took me to for treatment, I say in my head, not wanting to ask her out loud.

"No, I had no clue he was back." She says.

"Your mother didn't keep you informed of his whereabouts then?" I ask, pushing again.

"Again the answer is no Joe. After we broke up, she was telling me what he was up to, but after a while I told her I didn't need, nor want to know. He was a friend, a *good friend*, but I didn't need my mother keeping me in the loop." She says, shaking her head. "There are plenty of ways to do that on social media if I had the inclination, and for the record, I haven't checked on him at all. Hadn't thought about him in years until today actually."

"Right." I can't help the bite in that one word.

"Yes, right." She says, just as sharply.

Silence fills up the space around us, the only noise is our cutlery scrapping against the plates, and every now and then, our glasses getting put back on the table after a drink. I notice she's still drinking water, so I say, "I have wine in the fridge, you could have had some of that if you want."

"No, I'm good with water, but thank you." Then we're back to the silence again as we finish eating.

I place my cutlery on the plate and Katy gets up and starts fussing around clearing everything away.

"Katy, come sit back down for a second could you please?" I ask.

"Just let me get this cleaned up and then I'll get your pain killers." She seems nervous, but I don't know why, it's not her that's about to spill her guts and explain everything I've ever done wrong. She's always given me the same level of shit back that I've dished out, not once flinching away from me. Not even when her best friend was on the receiving end of my shitty attitude. Especially then.

"Katy, please? I want to explain a few things."

"You don't have to explain anything tonight Joe, we've got a few days together, remember? You must be in a fair bit of pain right now. Let yourself heal a little bit, then we can talk."

"No." I say simply.

"What do you mean, no?" She asks, confused.

"I mean, no. Stop moving around and staying away from me." I sigh when she doesn't make a move to sit back down at the table. "Please Katy. I understand we have a few days, but I need to explain a few things. Things I've been wanting to explain to you for weeks. Weeks that you wouldn't talk to me. Not by text, not when I called, or when I came to your house. You owe it to me to at least listen."

Slowly she puts our plates down on the bench, but she grabs my pain medication and another bottle of water. "You need to take these though."

"OK, but after I've had my say, because these make me fall asleep." I need to get this off my chest while I can.

"OK, but you're taking them soon." I nod my agreement.

"I'm not sure where to start." I say. Now that she's agreed to listen, and so much has happened, I don't know where to start.

"At the beginning. That's generally where you start Joe. The stuff that you've done recently, the stuff you admitted to today, that can wait. I want to know *why* you did it, not *what* you did."

"It starts with Harry and Helen."

"So I figured. So they were together when they were teenagers, is that right?" I nod my head in agreement.

"Madly in love if you ask Harry." I say.

"I take it Helen wasn't as 'madly in love' as Harry was?"

"I'm not sure how she felt, I've never spoken to the woman. I keep my distance, because I don't know what I might say to her. "

"OK, but I'm still struggling to understand what that all has to do with Kami and why you've hated her all these years."

"I don't." I was about to deny hating her best friend, but the dirty look she cuts my way, stops me. "I can say now that I never hated Kami, I hated everything she represented and what her existence did to *my* life."

"I don't understand Joe." She says, confused.

"I overheard my parents fighting years ago, well fighting is a bit of a stretch. My father was explaining how my mother was his second choice and how miserable and disappointed he was with how his life turned out. I remember him saying look at the beautiful daughter he could have had. Kami Parker was so much better, so much more than his son could ever be, and he had to watch from afar." I take a deep breath, it feels good to finally get this out in the open, but it's also painful, laying myself bare. Even to Katy. "Harry knew I was standing there, and he still said that he wished that Kami was his and I wasn't. He knew that I was his flesh and blood but still he wanted me gone so that he could have Kami instead. That was the day he started treating me like I was nothing, that I meant nothing to him, and it was all her fault. I wasn't Kami and he made sure I knew it. Every. Single. Day."

"Oh Joe. I can't imagine how overhearing that conversation and knowing he said it so that you would hear it, must have made you feel, but that's still not Kami's fault. I can see how as a child you would hate her, but that doesn't explain why, as an adult, you continued to hold onto that grudge." She holds up her hand to stop me from speaking. "No Joe. Surely as an adult you can see what you did was wrong?"

"I do now, yes. I see how I let my father's behaviour rule my own. I can see that by allowing my hatred of him power everything that I did and didn't do, has made me lose everything." I sigh and rub a hand over my face, then wince in pain when I reach my nose and forehead. Shit I forgot about my broken nose for a minute, how the hell does that happen? "My dislike of Kami has ruled the way I've treated her and for that I am sorry. I got so used to treating Kami with contempt and finding ways to make her life a misery, that it's become a way of life. When I realised she and James were together, and how serious he was about her, I didn't want history to repeat itself. Call me all kinds of crazy and fucked up, but I put her in the same box as her mother. I figured that eventually she'd hurt him, and I wanted to save him from that pain before he got in too deep. Only, I didn't realise how deep either of them were already in, before my latest bout of stupidity exploded in my face."

I need a minute to gather my thoughts and have a small drink of water. I'd rather be drinking something stronger like whiskey or bourbon, or anything alcoholic right now, but I'm guessing that's not such a good idea with the painkiller Andrews gave me, and I don't think Katy would let me anyway.

"OK, I don't need you to explain what you did when we were kids, I was there, I lived it with her. What did you do a week ago that sent Kami out of town and made James hit you so hard, he broke your nose and split his hand open? Because I get the feeling that I'm the only one who has no clue what happened today behind Kami's shop. All I *do* know is that all hell broke loose."

"Fair question." I say and Katy nods and waves her hand for me to continue. "Well, we broke up. You walked away thinking you could make decisions for both of us and I was mad. I wanted you to talk to me, so that I could tell you how I felt, what I wanted. Instead of you assuming everything and then telling me you couldn't give me what you think I want."

"Alright, we can talk about that later, I promise, but what does that have to do with whatever happened a week ago?"

"When you didn't want to talk to me, I decided I wanted to get out of town for a while. A few hours, a few days, I didn't care, I just needed to get away. Then I spoke to James on the phone, and I knew he was struggling with the job he was on. The guy he was dealing with was being a pain and I knew his heart wasn't really in the job anymore. I assumed his feelings were directly related to leaving Kami while he was out of town and I saw red. I was angry that he was letting her dictate his life, his job. He's worked hard to get his business off the ground, to get out from under his father's bad name and really make it work. He's wanted to expand, move out of this town and into the next, even the next and hopefully get bigger jobs. Contracts that will put his company, his name on the map. Then he went out of town on his first large contract, and all he could think about was not being with Kami. I didn't see that he had fallen in love with her, that they were both already in so deep. All I saw was my best friend, my brother who'd always had my back, losing what he'd worked so hard for."

"So, what exactly did you do? I mean whatever it was, sent Kami racing out of town and James running back home to work it out when he couldn't reach her." Katy asks.

"When I got out to where James was working, he was so happy to see me. He'd smashed his phone and needed a replacement and he asked me to go get one for him."

"Seems reasonable to me, I don't understand what set you off? He's running a business, he needs his phone."

"Well, that's just it, he wasn't worried about clients, suppliers or his staff being able to contact him, all he was worried about was the fact that he had a video chat with Kami later that night and she wouldn't know why he wasn't answering." I sigh, not really wanting to tell Katy what I did after that, but I know I have to be honest and tell her everything if I have any chance of her forgiving me. "I did what he asked. I went into town and got him a new phone, but I also got a new SIM card which meant he didn't have any contacts on the new phone. I told him he'd managed to damage that as well, then I offered to set the new phone up for him by transferring the contacts off his laptop to his phone."

"You deleted her contact details, therefore he couldn't let her know he had a new number and the one she tried to call, was it still connected? Did it just ring out, or did it just not ring at all?" I nod my head in answer. "But that doesn't explain why she took off out of town like a bat out of hell without telling anyone, including me, where she was going. There has to be something else."

"Well, that's the thing. When I got his phone put together I sent her a message from it. An edited version of one that I'd sent him about us, and I knew she would misinterpret it."

"What did it say Joe?"

"It said something along the lines of, 'it will be good to get out of town, let the memories fade. It will make it easier that way.' Or something like that anyway, I'm not sure exactly." I say, looking anywhere except at Katy. I know I did the wrong thing. "When I left James the next morning, after he hadn't heard from Kami the night before, he asked me to go see Kami and give her a note that he'd written for her. It was a note with his new number and telling her what had happened to his phone."

"OK, but why did she take off?" I can see the second she realises what happened. "She realised that the message you sent came from James' new number and thought he'd sent it and it meant that she was nothing to him. She was hurt and had to get out of town."

"That's exactly what happened, yes." There's nothing else I can say. "I've felt guilty ever since, but I didn't want to explain it to James until he got home. I did try to talk to you about it, but you wouldn't answer my calls." Before she can say anything, I put my hand up to stop her. "I'm not blaming you, I'm just saying I wanted to explain but I couldn't. I knew how worried you were about Kami when she took off. I didn't think she'd just up and leave, especially without telling you, and I didn't think James would break a leg to get home to work out why she wasn't talking to him either. Like I said, I didn't realise they were already in so deep with each other."

"Would it have made a difference if you had known?" She asks.

"Probably not." I answer honestly. "I did what I thought was the right thing, I did it to protect James from himself and Kami."

"Oh Joe. You idiot." She's not wrong, I am an idiot.

"I blamed her for losing you. You might have walked away because you thought you couldn't give me what I wanted, but it also meant you didn't have to tell your best friend you were dating the boy that made her life misery in school." I take a deep breath, "I blamed her for James not concentrating on the business he's worked so hard to make a success. I blamed her for me losing *my* best friend, but most of all, I blamed her for Harry being a shitty father."

"Joe, Harry's a dick because that's just who he is. He chose to blame a kid, two kids actually, for his own unhappiness, when in fact that was his choice and Helen's."

"I know, but it was easy to blame someone else." I sigh. "I'm not sure I deserve to ask for forgiveness for my fucked up behaviour."

"James will forgive you, it will just take some time"

"And you? Can you forgive me? What about us?" I have to ask, even though I can see the answer written all over her face, I need to hear her say it.

"We'll talk about us tomorrow Joe. Right now we both need to get some sleep." She hands me the painkillers and water, watching me to make sure I take them. I know I've got ten minutes at most before I start feeling sleepy. I'm a light weight when it comes to these things, because I never take them.

"Let's go to bed then before I fall down. You can't carry me to bed."

"I'm not sleeping in your bed Joe, you have a spare room, I'll stay in there. I already put my stuff in there while you were sleeping."

Well that answers that. "Goodnight Katy." I walk to my bedroom turning off the lights along the way and she walks in the opposite direction to *her* room. I don't watch her walk away, I want her in my bed, in my arms but it seems that I've lost that as well.

"Goodnight Joe. Call out of you need anything."

"Sure. Sleep well Kathryn." I won't call her for help, not even if I fall flat on my broken face and can't get up.

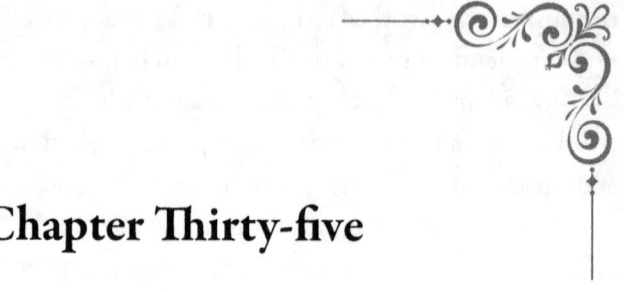

Chapter Thirty-five

KATY

Joe's confession was something else.

The reason I walked away from Joseph was *because* I saw the longing on his face when we saw that mother with her child at the park that day. I could see everything he wanted written all over his face, he wanted the chance to be a better Father than Harry. He needs to have that, and I can't give it to him. It broke my heart to walk away, because I'm in love with him. I was even ready to tell Kami all about us and suffer the consequences.

Who am I kidding? I'm *still* in love with him.

As I lay in bed thinking, wishing for things to be different, I wonder if I'll ever get to sleep, there are so many things running around in my head. I'm also keeping an ear open just in case Joe needs me for anything. Not *that* kind of anything, although I'm not sure if I'd have the willpower to tell him no if he came to me.

I wake with a start, sweat covering my body after yet another nightmare about babies and Joe. I can see a sliver of sun breaking through the curtains, so I get up and have a shower, then slowly get dressed. I have to go out and get something sorted for breakfast, I gather every bit of strength I can muster because I'm still fighting this stupid virus and walk out to the kitchen. Joe isn't up yet so I can take my time getting breakfast together.

I switch on the coffee, then I look in the fridge to see what I can make for us, the man has a fridge *full* of deliciously edible food. I decide to make us up a batch of pancakes, they're quick, easy and tasty.

I close the fridge, milk and eggs in hand when Joe speaks, scaring the crap out of me.

"You know you don't have to cook every meal for us, Katy. I don't normally eat a full breakfast anyway." He says with a shrug, then grabs two coffee mugs and starts pouring the steaming liquid into them.

I love the smell of coffee, especially first thing in the morning. It helps kick my brain into waking up every day.

"You need more than just coffee this morning Joe. You're on pretty strong painkillers and if you don't eat, you're going to start feeling nauseous."

"You're right Katy, but I don't want you cooking and running around after me. It feels wrong." He says, and I'm not sure whether that's sweet or insulting. I go with insulting because I'm hanging on by a string right now and I'm grumpy.

"Well Joseph, if I didn't want to 'cook or run around after you', I wouldn't have told Annie that you had someone to look after you when you got home last night and for the next few days. Sit down, shut up and let me look after you." I growl out and point towards the table. "Sit down Joseph. Please."

"OK." That's it. Just one word and he gives in. There isn't an argument, or snide remark, he just does what I tell ask to. Weird, very weird. I let it go for now, because I want to make something to eat. He's not the only one who needs something in his stomach.

There is silence, no talking or music, while I mix up the pancake batter and start cooking. I can feel him watching me, but I just move around his kitchen doing what I need to do and making sure he doesn't move from his chair. He made a move to help me with something a little while ago, I shot him a look that I hoped said, 'sit your gorgeous arse down and behave', and I'm going to assume I succeeded, because he sat said gorgeous arse back down in his chair and held up his hands in surrender. I know his kitchen, and I know how to cook, I don't need his help. I shake my head at the stubborn man and start setting the table.

With the plates, cutlery and the assortment of pancake toppings I found in his pantry are all set out on the table, I finish cooking the pancakes and place them between us, then sit down. I needed to keep busy in the quiet, because it was making me nervous. I don't know what he saw when he was silently watching me but having his eyes on me really puts me on edge.

"Breakfast is served." I say a little too brightly. Something I'm not exactly renowned for being, especially early in the morning. Which reminds me, I still don't know what time it is. "What time is it Joe? I haven't looked at a clock yet this morning." I ask him with a smile.

"You mean to tell me you got up, had a shower and started to make breakfast without even looking at the time?" Joe asks me with a smirk, I just nod in reply. Can't speak, eating pancakes, seriously! "Who does that?" He asks obviously suspicious and mildly amused.

"Me that's who. I was awake and the sun was shining. So, I figured it was time to get up and moving. Mainly because I didn't want *you* to get up first thinking you needed to look after *me*."

"Me? I wouldn't do that!" Joe says, with a sexy smirk on his lips. Lips I want to kiss so badly that I can't help staring at them. That is until Joe coughs, bringing my eyes back to meet his that are now some incredible shades of black, blue, purple with a slight tinge of green around them. "If you keep looking at me like that Kathryn, things that you've pulled the pin on *are* going to happen, and by the look on your face, you'd enjoy them."

I fill my mouth with another forkful of pancakes to stop me from saying something I shouldn't. Something like *'kiss me Joe or fuck me Joe'*, because that wouldn't be good. No it would be *great,* but I don't want to give him the wrong idea.

I stand up suddenly to start cleaning away the dishes, but I move too quickly, and it makes my head spin. Between this ridiculous illness and the wound on my head, I'm a damned mess.

"Katy honey, are you OK?" Joe asks, his voice full of concern, as he reaches forward to steady me.

I lean into him a little and say, "Yeah. I moved a bit too quickly and was just a little dizzy there for a second there."

"Sit down for a minute then Katy, the dishes can wait." He says.

I don't sit down at the table, instead I say to him, "I'm just going to the bathroom for a minute." Without waiting for a reply from him, I walk away. When I get to the bathroom, I close the door and lean against it for a second, getting my balance back. I take a few deep breaths, then walk over to the sink and splash my face with some cold water. After a few seconds of leaning on the edge of the sink, letting the water drip off my face, I rub it dry with a towel.

When I walk back into the bedroom, I find Joe sitting on the edge of the bed, waiting for me. "Damn it Joe, was it too much to ask for you to give me some privacy?"

"I guess it was, yes. I didn't come busting into the bathroom Katy, so personally I think I was quite restrained." He says, his eyebrows and mouth drawn down into a frown.

"Geezus Joe, you can't do this." I say, suddenly exhausted.

"Do what Katy? Be concerned about your health and wellbeing, especially after you hit your head? I'm such an arsehole for caring I guess." He says.

"That's not what I said, Joe and you know it." I say in frustration. This man just makes my brain hurt some days.

"Then what did you mean Katy? I don't understand why you're so angry with me. I don't get where I went wrong this time, or for that matter while we were away either. When did I give you the impression that you weren't enough for me? That I was asking for things you couldn't give me?"

"Look I'm annoyed because you still can't give me my space and as stupid and irrational as it sounds, even to me, you pissed me off in my dream last night and I'm still annoyed."

He reaches his hand out to hold mine, I don't fight him, because I don't have it left in me anymore. "What did I do in your dream honey?"

"I really wish you'd stop calling me honey." I say, in exasperation, it makes me feel things I shouldn't. He doesn't give in though, he just sits there looking at me, waiting. Bruised eyes, a small cut on his swollen lip, and the bright white splint on his nose. How is it even with all that he can still look so attractive to me? "You really want to know?" I ask, although I'm pretty sure I know the answer. He nods slightly, not breaking eye contact. "Fine! You got everything you want, and it wasn't with me. Feel better now?" I move to turn away from him, pulling my hand from his and put some distance between us.

"If I wasn't with you then I didn't get everything I wanted Katy. Haven't you worked that out yet? Geezus Katy." He says, the irritation in his voice is unmistakable. "Look at me." He demands.

"No." Is all I say, I don't want him to see the tears that are rolling down my cheeks.

"Fine. I'll say it anyway then." He takes a deep breath and even though I didn't hear him move, I can feel him standing behind me, not touching me, but right there. "I want *you*, Kathryn Ellis. No-one else." I go to speak but he won't let me. "No. Let me finish, you've had your say and then you walked away. Now you get to let me speak. You *think* you know what I want, but you never even took the time to *ask me*. You're right about one thing, I do want a family. I want the white picket fence and the kids and the dog, but I want them with you. If we can't have that, then I'm OK with that too. You want to know why?" I nod yes, because I don't think I can find any words to speak. "Because I love you Katy. I am in love with you and I want only you. No-one else, ever again. I want forever with you, and whether that includes kids, biological or adopted, I don't fucking care." He turns me around to look at him, holds my face in his hands, and wipes the tears from my cheeks.

"Oh Joe." I don't know what to say, more tears are pouring down my face.

"Don't cry honey. I just need you to understand, I know I'm no Prince Charming after everything I've done, but that doesn't change how I feel about *you*. I'll do everything I can to prove to you that all that's in the past. I'm going to work hard to prove to you and to Kami and James, that I'm not that idiot anymore. I'm a man you can trust, because I just want to be with you and for us to be happy. However that ends up looking."

I'm left standing there, my face resting in the palms of the man that I adore, stunned silent. It's a rare occurrence, Kami can attest to that fact. She'd love to be here to witness it, well maybe not so much right now.

"Katy. Say something, please honey?" Joe says, his voice full of tension.

Chapter Thirty-six

"Oh Joe. I don't know what to say." She says, closing her eyes. I walk back over and sit on the bed, my head is starting to ache, and I need to sit down.

Well it wasn't quite the response I was hoping for. A declaration of her love for me would have been nice. Maybe it's too soon, especially after everything she's just learnt about how I treated the man I considered family.

"Katy, look at me honey." I ask. When she lifts her eyes to mine, I ask her, "Do you love me Katy?" I swear I stop breathing, and time stands still while I wait for her answer. If she says no, I can accept that and walk away, it will hurt like hell, but I can do it. If she says yes though, after everything I've done, I'll be the luckiest man on the planet.

"Oh Joseph French. You are the most annoying, frustrating, ridiculous and I have to say, most stupid man I have ever met. Of all the stupid things you've done in recent times." I'm still holding my breath, I don't know which way this speech of hers is going to go. "Do I love you? You mean, do I love you enough to tell my best friend you're it for me? Do I love you enough to forgive all of your stupid behaviour towards my best friend?"

She walks over and stands between my legs, grabs my face in her hands and looks me in the eyes. I swallow hard and say, "Yes. All of that."

"You want to know if I love you enough to forgive you and move forward? Together." She asks me, her eyes sparkling. She's teasing me, but I still don't know what her answer will be, not for certain.

"Katy, honey, you're killing me." I say, not giving a shit how desperate I sound. I am desperate, I need to know how she feels.

"Joe, I fell in love with you that first night at your friends restaurant. I hated you when you left me high and dry later that night, but I loved you."

She kisses the corner of my mouth. "I loved you more when you came back." She kisses the other corner of my mouth. "I loved you so much when we went and stayed at your house in the country that when I saw the desire in your eyes when you saw that little girl with her mum, I walked away. I believed I was doing the best thing for both of us, but it broke my heart Joe, because I already loved you so deeply that the thought of you moving on and having children with someone else almost broke me."

"But I'm not having a child with anyone else, honey." I say.

"That's true, but you have to understand, that may not happen with me either and I'm so damned sorry about it Joe."

I pull her in close to me and say, "Why are you sorry? Because we may not get what you picture as a perfect family or life? That life is what we make of it together and you don't get to be sorry for making me the happiest man alive because you're mine."

"Really?" Katy asks, her voice so timid and unsure. I've never seen her like this before. This woman that I love has all the fire and confidence in the world. Did I do this to her, or is it a by-product of this condition of hers? Does she really think that the right man, the one who loves her like she's his world, would care about having children with her? What kind of arseholes has she been dating before now?

"You. Are. My. Everything." I close my eyes and control my emotions as much as I can, before I say, "Katy, I can't tell you how happy you've made me. The only things that would make me happier is for you to tell me you feel the same. That you love me, and we belong together. Forever. I don't need you to commit, to marry me right now, or even move in with me right now. But I need you to know, all those things, they *will* happen. And I won't regret you, or us no matter what happens."

"Oh Joe." The tears are flowing down her cheeks, and for a heartbeat I think she's going to tell me I'm dreaming, that's not how this ends. Instead I hear the sweetest, words I've ever heard in my life. "I love you Joe French. With my heart and soul, I love you."

I don't let her finish what she's saying. Don't get me wrong, I want to hear all those words, each and every one of them, multiple times, but right now I just need to hold her.

I stand up from the bed, scoop her up in my arms, wrap her legs around my hips, and spin us both around. I shouldn't have, because with my nose broken and strapped up, my balance is all kinds of fucked up, but I don't care.

"Joe what are you doing? Put me down!" Katy squeaks out as she holds on a little tighter to my shoulders. I laugh and then suddenly I can't stand up anymore and I fall backwards on to the bed, bringing Katy down with me. "Oh my god Joe, are you OK?" Katy asks, concern making her voice a higher pitch than usual.

"Oh Kathryn Ellis, you have no idea how much more than OK I am right now." I say laughing, even though it hurts like hell. "Pack up your things honey." I tell her, untangling our bodies.

"Oh, OK then." She says, scrambling off me to shove all her things back into the bag.

"Is that everything you bought over?" I ask.

"Yes." Her voice is quiet and unsure again, but it won't be for long.

"Good." I take her hand in mine and take her bag off her with the other, leading her out of the bedroom she stayed in last night and into my bedroom. *Our* bedroom whenever she's here and I'm hoping that becomes every damned night eventually. I toss her bag onto the bed, drop her hand from mine and start to unpack her things. When I'm done, I start making room in my drawers and cupboard for the small amount of things she has with her. Katy stands where I left her just watching me. When I've cleared the space I start filling them with her things. Neither of us have said a word, and I'm sure I'm not putting them where she would want them, but that's not the point, she can change whatever she wants later. "Stay in my room, in *our* room with me from now on? I hated knowing you were in the house last night and not being able to hold you."

"Yes." She says on a breathe. "I want to stay in here with you. It hurt me too, knowing you were so close and yet, it felt like you were so far away. I just wanted to come in here and crawl into bed next you."

"I wish you had honey. Think of how much better we both would have slept." I say.

"You didn't need any help to sleep, those tablets do a good job of knocking you out." She laughs. She's not wrong. "Talking of these tablets, you need to take some more."

"No Katy, they make me sleepy and I want to enjoy having you here with me." I'm not above begging her. "If I promise to relax and behave, can we forego them for a while and just sit down on the couch together?"

"OK, sure just let me clean up the kitchen. Also, you have to promise me if the pain starts to become too much, you'll tell me. There are pain relievers there that aren't as strong and won't put you to sleep."

"Promise, but you can leave the kitchen until later. It's not like we won't be eating again today." I say, and I assume she agrees with me when she takes me by the hand and leads me to the couch. We sit down and she reaches over for the remote. "What do you feel like watching?"

I grin and tell her exactly what I want to watch, she rolls her eyes and starts searching for it so we can stream it. As the opening credits start on my favourite actions flick, Katy leans over and says quietly in my ear, "You know this doesn't mean everything is OK right? We're OK but we need to talk some more, and you need to talk to Kami. You need to explain things to her."

"I don't think she's going to be too receptive about talking to me, but I'll try."

"You underestimate my best friend Joe. She loves me and when I tell her I love you, she's going to try her hardest to forgive you, but you have to give her a reason to. You have to explain everything to her, and don't leave anything out. Lying by omission is still lying Joe."

"I'll have to trust you on that one Katy, if I was Kami, I don't think I'd ever want to talk to me again. As for James, I don't think it's going to be anywhere near that easy to fix what I've broken, and I don't mean my nose either. That will be healed in a couple of weeks, I don't think James will be any kind of close to wanting to talk to me by then."

"I think you underestimate your friendship too. I've seen you two guys together for years, and I don't believe he'll hold a grudge forever. I don't think he's going to make it easy for you though. It's definitely going to be harder to win James over than it will be Kami. You just have to give him some time, all the time he needs and then maybe a little bit more." Katy says, solemnly but honestly.

"It should be hard for them to forgive me. I don't think I could forgive someone too easily if they tried to keep us apart. I think I'd want to kill them actually. I don't deserve their easy forgiveness and if they gave it, I would always be wondering if they really did forgive me, or if they felt it was the easier thing to do." I say.

"Well, I know Kami will come around eventually. She just needs a little bit of time." I don't know if I believe her, then she reaches her hand out to rest on my thigh. "Trust me Joe, I know Kami Parker, and she can't hold a grudge. She won't forgive you easily, you'll earn it, but she will forgive you."

"I hope you're right Katy, because I know how much your friendship with Kami means to you. That itself should have made me stop all this bullshit before it went too far, but I was in too deep already. I know there are no excuses for what I've done, but I was coming to confess it all to you and then to James when he came home. I didn't know either of them were back in town already."

"Well, you've got two weeks of physical healing, I suggest you use that time to think about what you can say to Kami and James, to help them understand what the mess in your head was thinking."

She's right, I know she is but I'm not feeling too confident about getting either Kami or James to talk to me too soon. Even if they did, I have no clue what I could say to them at the moment to fix things between us. I definitely need to talk to Kami though, and I can only hope that she'll listen to everything I've got to say.

I've certainly got some fun times ahead of me.

Chapter Thirty-seven

J oe and I spend every day of the next couple of weeks together either at his house or mine while he heals, just talking things through, and while I can now understand what he was thinking and why he did what he did, I can't agree with his behaviour. As a kid he saw his actions as harmless and it was his way of dealing with Harry's shitty behaviour, but it sure as hell doesn't excuse his behaviour as an adult. As a grown man he should be to able understand that his previous behaviour was that of a kid being an arsehole but no, he had to take it further and try to wreck our best friend's relationship.

Every one of his actions towards Kami made her life a living hell for way too many years. I know how much pain and hurt she endured, because I've witnessed it firsthand.

He feels terrible and understands that he was wrong. Now, but his previous attitude baffles me, because that's not the man I know. He's worked hard to distance himself from Harry and his bad attitude towards the world and built a reputation and a business he can be proud of. He wants to make up for everything, but James still won't talk to him and Kami is polite. That's about all she is right now. Polite.

When I take Joe back to the hospital for his check up and we don't get seen by Doctor Andrews, but another doctor in a clinic at the hospital. I can't say I'm unhappy about the situation. The doctor removes the splint, asks Joe a few questions and then gives him the all clear. No sports or overtly physical activities for the next few weeks so that he doesn't get another hit to the face, but other than that, he's all set.

I see the glint in his eyes and the mischief written all over his face. The doctor reads him well too, because he chuckles, then coughs to cover it up and tells us we can leave.

Joe jumps off the bed, takes my hand in his, thanks the doctor and then we're on our way to the car.

"Joe slow down. What's the hurry? Where's the fire?" I ask him, laughing and trying to pull my hand from his. I stop walking, which forces him stop as well. "Joe. What the hell is going on?"

He steps back, crowding me with his body, his hands on my hips and pulling me in close. "Katy, we've spent months apart and then, when I finally get you back and we spend almost every day together while my face heals, I still can't have you like I want you." he pulls me impossibly closer, his hot breath ghosting across my ear and whispers, "I want you Katy. Every which way I can take you."

"Oh." Is all I manage to say. What else does a woman say to that?

"Yeah, oh. Can I have your keys please?" He asks, holding his hand out waiting for them as I pull them out of my jeans pocket. "Thank you. Now can we get out of here please?"

I nod to answer him, because I still can't find any words. He takes my hand in his again, and we're moving towards my car at an unbelievably quick pace. He unlocks the car just as we reach it and is in the driver's seat before I can even get my door open.

"Your place is closer than mine. Is that OK with you?"

"Ahh yes." I say, mentally cataloguing how clean the house is.

"I don't care how clean it is Katy, I only need one room honey." He winks at me, his dirty smirk spreading across his lips. He pulls my car into the garage, and it's barely turned off with the handbrake on before he's got me out of the car and in the house. The door from the garage into the house slams shut and I'm pinned between it and the hard body of the man I want more than anything else right now.

"Katy." He murmurs against my throat, causing shivers to race through my body. Could he get any sexier? No, not when he needs me so much that I can hear it in his voice. No-one has ever made me feel like this. This wanted, needed and cherished. "I need you Katy. Tell me you need me too honey."

"Oh Joe." I can't speak. My hands are roaming his body, they can't stay. I need to feel every part of him all at the same time. It's been a while since we've been physical, wanting to give us both time to heal, physically but emotionally as well. I didn't want to rush into the physical without feeling like we had made everything right between us as well. "I need you."

"Tell me Katy." I can feel his voice rumbling through his chest pressed tightly against mine, and his breath on the skin where my neck meets my collarbone, sending more shivers down my spine.

"You. Me. Bed. Now. Joe." I say, my voice a husky whisper that I barely recognise. Without a word, Joe picks me up and I wrap my legs around his hips, as he walks us to the bedroom.

Joe pulls his lips from my skin a whimper escapes my lips at the loss of his touch. He forces my body off his and I reach out for him as I feel my body falling. I land on my bed with a squeal of shock and Joe smirks down at me, his chest bare as he works on the button and zip on his jeans. I don't know when he had the time to get half naked but I'm not complaining, not at all. I sit up, running my hands over as much of his exposed skin as I can reach. I need the feel of his heated skin, otherwise I'd need to pinch myself to make sure this isn't a dream.

"Damn this better not be a dream honey, I need you so much it would kill me to wake up from seeing you spread out in front of me, but I can't have you." His voice is a deep rumble, full of need.

I don't know how he knew what I was thinking, maybe I said it out loud, I don't know. I realise I don't care, as he takes my top off, "Your turn." He says, then gently pushes me back on to the bed to make fast work of making my jeans and shoes disappear, leaving me lying there in just my underwear on display for him.

"I've missed you Katy." He says, his eyes roaming over my body. I should feel self-conscious, and previously I would have attempted to cover myself up, but with Joe I don't feel that need. I know he likes what he sees, and he can't wait to devour me. It's written all over his face for one. For two, his eyes are dark with desire as well, nothing to mistake there.

"Me too Joe." He's standing beside the bed, thumbs hooked into the band of his dark grey boxer briefs, as if frozen in time. "Take them off Joe." I say, looking down at his boxers. "I want to see your cock."

He groans, "Only if you take yours off too." I don't hesitate, my underwear is gone, flung who knows where in the bedroom. I manage not to take my eyes off him while I do it and I'm rewarded with the pleasure of watching him remove his own. For a few seconds we're both just staring, drinking each other in for the first in weeks. Without warning, he's on his knees, pulling my legs over his shoulders, hands under my butt cheeks and dragging my pussy to his face. "I've been wanting to taste you again since the last time I had your taste on my tongue, but you are pure temptation spread out for me right now and I'm not waiting a second longer. Finally I can have you." And he doesn't wait.

"Joe." My voice is a whisper and I'm not even sure he can hear me, but I'm damned sure he can feel my hands in his hair, scraping his scalp with every pulse of pleasure travelling through my body. His flattens his tongue and drags it through the lips of my pussy, licking me up and down, causing me to lose my ability to speak words. I push my hips up to his face that I'm pulling down to my body. He growls and slides a finger inside my pussy, finding that spot that makes me lose all reality and control.

"That's it honey, come on my tongue." His hot breath against my pussy and the vibration of his voice takes me over the edge and my hoarse voice breaks as I cry out his name.

My whole body turns to jelly and my breathing is laboured. I feel his hands underneath me at my hips and he's pushing me up the bed, giving me more space to recover my sense. He kisses his way up my body until he reaches my lips, then he kisses me like it will be the last one he ever gets from me, it's so deep and full of passion. I pull back, "Joe, babe, I need to breath." I say, laughing.

"Ahh breathing's over-rated Katy." He says and dives back in for another kiss. I pull away slightly.

"I'm not into necrophilia thanks Joseph." I say, laughing, mainly because he stops, pulls back from my lips to look in my eyes.

"That's a little too kinky even for me Kathryn." Then he kisses the breath from my lungs again. I'm not sure, but I think he did it so I couldn't respond to his kinky remark.

I wrap my legs around his hips, my arms around his shoulders, and while his guard is down, I try to flip us over. My unsuccessful attempt makes him laugh. "If you wanted to be on top, you only had to ask honey, and I would have obliged." He says in my ear and then flips us over, chuckling the whole time. How can he even muster the brain power to use words like 'obliged' right? How his brain isn't scrambled enough if he can still speak like that! "What's with that cheeky grin Kathryn?" He draws out my name and its sexy as fuck, but I don't let him distract me.

I slide my body down his and slip between his legs, my palms sliding down his chest to his abs, which tense under my touch. "Kathryn." He growls and reaches out for my hands intent on pulling me back up his body. "I thought you needed my cock in your pussy?" He asks, knowing that his dirty talk will hit me right where he wants it to, but I won't let him change my plans. He needs to be as blissed out as I am.

"Katy-" He starts again, but he doesn't get the chance to finish his thought, because I wrap my hand around his cock, running it up and down his shaft, then I run my tongue through the slit at top. He lets out a loud groan, his hands gripping on to the sheet tightly and his eyes rolling back into his head. I smile against the tip of his cock, he raises his head to look at me about to speak but I take the head into my mouth and suck, making him lose all ability to speak for a few seconds. Drawing his cock further into my mouth, I moan knowing that he'll enjoy the vibration on his cock. With one hand resting at the base of his cock, I gently grab his balls in the other and play with them as I draw my mouth up and down his cock, I close my eyes, listening to his noises of pleasure. Knowing that I'm making him feel like that makes me wet again. I look up his body and see his mouth is hanging open, his eyes shut, and he's relaxed, enjoying my mouth on him.

I close my eyes again enjoying the sensation of making Joe feel good. Suddenly he moves and my front is plastered to his front. "Stop! I'm going to come!" He says.

"What the hell Joe, isn't that the *point*?"

"As much as I enjoy having your lips wrapped around my cock, I want to be buried deep inside your pussy when I come." He declares, his voice so deep I don't recognise it and he's looking me in the eyes like he can see deep into my soul.

"Oh." It's the only thing I can think of saying.

"Yeah. Oh." He rasps out. He reaches for his jeans on the floor, tipping us both over a bit when he moves.

"There's some in the drawer Joe, just grab them." He looks at me like I've said the wrong thing, then I realise what he must be thinking. "They've been in there since we were together the last time Joe." He opens the drawer and pulls out the sealed, unopened box of condoms that were waiting for him. He rips the packaging from the box and drags out an entire strip of them, then throws the packet back in the drawer and closes it. "Bit cocky there aren't you Mr French?"

"*Very* cocky Miss Ellis." He says, then he reaches up behind my neck and cradles my head in his hand, bringing my mouth to his, he kisses me gently. "I love you Katy and I couldn't imagine my life without you."

"I need you Joe." I say, his words making me a puddle of emotions. "Now and forever." I lean in and whisper in his ear, as I slide his cock into my pussy.

"Fuck Katy, you feel so good." He groans, closing his eyes, his hands gripping my hips tightly. Then his eyes fly open, "Are you sure honey?"

"Yes Joe. You've got less chance of getting me pregnant than you do being hit by a bus." I shrug a shoulder, "It wouldn't be the worst thing in the world to have your baby though." Before he can say anything, I move, rolling my hips slightly, making him groan. He drops the condom strip to the floor before gripping onto my hips tightly again.

Then, we're both lost to the pleasure. He sits up and kisses the breath out of me again and somehow twists his body to suck one nipple into his mouth, then the other and it's my turn to let out a groan of pleasure, my hands buried in his hair. He falls back down to the bed taking me down with him, his hands squeezing my butt cheeks, running up and my butt crack and back.

I push on his broad chest to sit back up, needing more. Needing him deeper as I ride his cock. His hands massaging my boobs and squeezing my nipples, I can feel my orgasm building. "Come for me honey." He grinds out between clenched teeth. "Come on my cock."

"Joe."

"You feel so good honey."

"Joe." His name falling from my lips.

"Come for me Katy." He says again, his teeth grinding together even harder.

"I'm going to. Oh Joe."

"That's it honey, come on my cock." In the back of my mind, I'm sure I hear a noise somewhere in the background, but I'm so caught up in Joe and our pleasure that I don't take any notice.

I'm riding out my orgasm as I ride Joe to his and Joe roars my name as he comes. Joe's holding me up in the sitting position with his hands gripping my boobs when I freeze in fear.

"Katy, darling are you OK?" I swear I hear my mother's voice ask, but she can't be here, now, can she?

I look towards the door just as my mother enters my room. I close my eyes, hoping it's just a bad dream, but when I open them again a second later, she's still standing there. I'm still sitting on Joe's cock, and he's still shuddering through the last convulsions of his own orgasm.

"Oh, hello Joseph." She's says, like she's found us watching a movie, snuggled up on the couch.

"Mrs Ellis." Joe says in a very strained voice.

"Anna. Please. I think we're beyond formalities now don't you think Joseph?" She asks him, as she looks me dead in the eyes. "Sorry darling, I didn't realise you had company. I'll see you kids downstairs shall I? I hope I didn't interrupt the *ending*."

"Ahh sure." I say, because what else can I say really?

As she turns to leave, I hear her mumble loudly to herself, "I'm glad I didn't send your father over now and I'm betting he'll be glad too for that matter!" Then she's gone.

I still haven't moved, I think I'm frozen in place entirely by my mortification. My mother just walked in on me riding my boyfriend, my boobs in his hands and him growling out my name in pleasure.

I rest my face in my hands, shaking my head and say, "No, no, no," repeatedly. "This can't be happening. That didn't just happen, did it?" I ask through my hands.

Underneath me I can feel Joe's body jerking in laughter. "Honey, it's OK. I'm sure your Mum is fine."

"Stop laughing Joe, it's not funny. Not even close." I slap his chest and my hand rests there, feeling the heat from his body and his heartbeat. How can I be getting worked up again when my mother just caught us in bed together. "It's mortifying Joe."

His body stops shaking and he forcefully removes my hands from my face. "What's mortifying? Being found with me?" He asks, and I can see the hurt in his eyes.

"No! I didn't mean that, I meant being caught at all. I know I'm a grown woman, but I really didn't need the trauma of being caught by mother sitting blissfully happy on your fucking cock."

"We're adults Katy and I'm pretty sure she didn't assume you were a virgin, honey." He slaps me on the butt and bucks me off his body. "Come on, let's not keep her waiting down there for too long, never know what she might find next." He says, laughing, as he pulls on his jeans.

"You can't go commando with my mother here Joseph!" I say.

"Honey, she just saw more of me than I ever intended her to in my lifetime. I think her not knowing that I don't have my boxers on isn't going to make too much difference." He's still laughing. I'm so glad he can find the funny in this situation.

"Did she say she was going to send my *father* over to check in on me?" I stutter out, as I recall what she muttered to herself as she left the room.

"Yup. She did." He says, not looking at me as he does up his jeans and pulls on his shirt. I can *feel* the smirk on his face from my place still on the bed.

"I am *so* glad she didn't, *that* would have been *so* much worse." I groan and throw myself down onto the bed, burying my face into the pillow.

I feel the side of the bed sink beside me, then Joe's rubbing his hand gently up and down my back. "Come on Katy, we're all adults here. Let's not keep your mum waiting any longer. I'll go downstairs and give you a few minutes to get dressed, but you better be down in a few minutes OK? I'm not dealing with this on my own."

I move my head to the side and look at up him, "Yeah OK. Give me a couple of minutes to clean up and get dressed, and I'll be down." He nods and moves off the bed and out of the room. It takes me a few more seconds to move but then I think about what they could be talking about down there and I move faster than I thought possible.

What I find when I get downstairs is my mother and Joe sitting at my kitchen bench, drinking coffee, eating some donuts that she bought over, laughing and chatting away like nothing out of the ordinary just happened.

"Hello darling. I made you a coffee and Joseph might have left you a donut or two, if you're lucky." She says, smiling at the man in question. "You must have worn him out Kathryn." She says, winking at Joe. I knew it was a bad idea to leave these two together alone for any length of time.

"Thank you Mother." I say, trying sound grateful and not annoyed.

"I'm a hungry man, what can I say?" He winks back at her. Holy crap, these two are trouble, but I've never seen my mother this happy before.

"Did you come over for a reason?" I hold up my hand, asking her to let me finish. "I only ask, because I don't think you've ever turned up here unannounced or used your key before."

"I just came by to check in on you. It's been a couple of weeks since you called, and Dad was worried about you."

"He could have called me you know." I say, knowing he's still annoyed at me with the way I ended things with Joe.

"I'm guessing that even though he wouldn't have wanted to walk in on what I did just now, it would have made him happy anyway." She says, a grin spreading across her face and her eyes twinkling. "Anyway, I can see that you're in good hands, so I'll leave you kids to it." She gives Joe a tight hug and says goodbye.

"Walk me to the door Kathryn?" She asks, as she loops her arm through mine.

"Sure." I say, looking back at Joe who's smiling like a lunatic.

"I'm going up to have a shower, see you soon Anna." He calls out.

"I'll see you Sunday for dinner Joseph. If you join us I know Kathryn will be there too." She smiles at him over her shoulder.

"You've got a deal Anna." He laughs and takes the stairs two at a time up to my bedroom. I can't help but watch him as he goes.

"You've got a good man there Katy." Anna says, in almost a whisper. "Don't let him go this time."

"We're still working a few things out, but I have no intention of losing him this time. He's my forever." I smile, and I imagine that it looks as goofy as it feels, because my mother wraps me in her arms and it's the tightest I ever remember her holding me.

"Good. You keep rocking his world like you did just now, and he won't ever leave you." She says quietly in my ear.

"Wow. Just, wow Mum." I say, shocked that those words came out of my very straight laced mother.

"You know, your Dad and I were young once too you know, and we don't do too badly now either with you kids out of the house." I don't let her finish that sentence, it's more than I've ever wanted to know about my parents.

"That's more than I've ever wanted to know, thanks Mum." I say, cringing.

"I love you Katy, and I'm happy to see you so very happy and content. It's all I've ever wanted for you." She leans in and gives me a light kiss on the cheek.

I reach out and pull her into a hug. "Thanks mum, I love you too." When we part I can see the tears sitting on the edge of her eyes, but she doesn't let them spill.

She coughs and says, "See you *both* on Sunday for dinner Kathryn." And then she's gone, it's not until the door closes that I notice she's left her key to my house on the entrance table.

I feel arms wrap around me from behind, "Everything OK Katy?" Joe asks, quietly, because his mouth is right against my ear.

"Yeah." I say. "For the first time in a long time Joe, I think things are close to perfect. We still have some work to do with our best friends, but I think we're going to be OK." I sigh and then say, "No, not OK, we're going to be great."

He spins me around in his arms and kisses me until I can't think anymore. When he releases me, I'm still a little stunned and he playfully smacks me on the butt to get me moving. "Go have a shower so we can get shit done honey."

I don't care what 'shit' needs to be done, I just want to get it done with him.

Epilogue
4 months later

<u>KATY</u>

The past few months have been interesting if nothing else. Kami and I are talking about everything and anything again. It was tense and uncomfortable for a while, but in the end our lifelong friendship and need to have each other around won out.

I've explained why I felt like I couldn't tell her that I was dating and then had fallen in love with Joe. It was hard to talk about for a while and I know it hurt her, but we've slowly regained our friendship, and I'm so glad it didn't get lost among the lies and manipulations.

James and Joe's friendship hasn't been that easy to rebuild, no matter how hard we try. We've tricked them into having dinner, but it was so awkward, we stopped. Joe doesn't want to say anything to piss James off and James, well he just doesn't seem to know what to say to Joe anymore. Their easy friendship isn't so easy anymore. It's more like a truce to keep us girls happy.

When Kami moved in with James, I asked Joe if he would come and help. In the hope that they would manage to have a conversation while moving heavy furniture between the houses, but no such luck. Joe was annoyed with me for manipulating him again, because he thought James knew he was helping. James didn't want any help from Joe and told both Kami and myself to stop meddling in things that didn't concern us. They still worked together to get the furniture moved because James needed the extra set of muscles, but neither of them were very happy about it.

Kami and James sorted everything out between them pretty quickly once they realised what Joe had done. I mean their only real issues were a lack of communication and a jerk who made them doubt their relationship. When I tell Kami as much she asks, "Do you truly love him Katy?"

Kami and I have never been anything but honest with each other, and so my answer is pretty simple. "Yeah Kami, I do. I know he's done some shitty things, some really terrible things to you, and to James, and while I can see the damage he's caused, I also see the lost little boy behind it all. I see the man that just wants to love and be loved. I know he's been an idiot and caused you pain. I know he's really hurt James, but we'd already spent a lot of time together before all this came to light and I got to know a different Joe. He regrets what he did, and not only because it means that he lost his best friend but also because he knows it hurt you and in turn me. "I sigh and say, "I also know he wants the chance to make it better. To be a better person to you both."

"I'm not sure what he can do Katy." She sighs as well. "James just can't understand. He keeps telling me this isn't the Joe he knows, that Joe always tried to be everything that Harry isn't. He's so hurt that he did this to *him*, to us. Katy I want to give him a chance. For you and for him, but he needs to really make some changes."

"He will Kami. We promise you that." I make the promise on behalf of both of us and she knows that means something to me.

I'm glad our friendship is back to where it was, because I get the feeling I'm going to need my best friend much more than she could ever imagine in the next few months.

A few weeks ago I went to the doctors at Joe's insistence because I started to feel unwell again. Just like I had months ago when I got that virus. Dizzy spells, sensitive to smells, and throwing up in the mornings.

The doctor called me with the results of my blood tests a few days later and to say I was shocked with the results is an understatement.

I was at Joe's house, and we were about to sit down for dinner when my phone rang. "Hello, Kathryn speaking." I say answering my phone, because I didn't recognise the number.

"Good evening Miss Ellis, it's Doctor Marcan I just got your blood test results and thought I'd call you right away with the good news."

"Good news? So it's not the same virus I had a few months ago then?" I ask, already feeling happy, especially when the doctor chuckles.

"No Miss Ellis." He says.

"Call me Katy, please." I say.

"Well no, it's not a virus as such, Katy, you're pregnant." I can hear the smile in his voice as I slide my butt into the nearest chair, thankful that there's one close by.

"Are you sure Doctor Marcan?" I can't help asking.

"Well, obviously nothing is 100% accurate until you have a baby in your arms Katy, but yes it's rare for a blood test to be wrong. Although, we'll get you in as soon as possible for an ultrasound, that way we can check how far along you are."

"How did this happen? I mean I know *how* it happened obviously, but I didn't think I could." I ask, surprised, happy and little worried about the man sitting across the table from holding my hand that isn't holding the phone, looking worried himself.

"Well, we know your condition makes it difficult to conceive but it wasn't an impossibility Katy. You know that as well as I do." He pauses, probably wondering why I'm not jumping for joy at this point. "Are you happy about this pregnancy Katy?"

"Yes." I take a shuddering breath to collect myself. "Yes, I am Doctor Marcan, I'm just in shock that's all."

"Congratulations Katy and we'll see you when you come in for that ultrasound ok?"

"Yes, yes of course I'll make the appointment in the next couple of days. Thank you again Doctor Marcan" I say and then hang up. I'm sitting there in shock, with my phone in my hand.

"Katy, are you OK?" Joe asks and I can't answer him. Am I OK? I really have no fucking clue. I never thought this would happen and for Joe to be the father of my unborn baby. It's insane. It's insane right?

He's holding my hand across the table one minute and the next, he's crouched in front of me, holding both of my hands in his. I manage to nod my head yes to answer his question. I'm not sure I could speak even if I tried.

"Katy, you've gone pale. Are you sure you're OK?" He sounds so worried and I know I have to answer him, I know I have to tell him, but how? Direct and to the point is probably best, that floats with our new open, honest terms of the relationship, but when I look at him I feel uneasy for some reason.

"I'm going to be sick." Without any further explanation I bolt to the bathroom and throw up. Once I'm done, I get up from the floor and rinse my mouth out. When I look up, the woman reflected back at me in the mirror seems like a different person.

Fuck, I'm pregnant. I'm going to be a mum.

I'm having Joe's baby. Holy shit.

There's a gentle knock on the door, and Joe says, "Honey can I come in?"

"Yes. No!" I shout as the door starts to open.

"OK." He says confused.

"I'll come out." I open the door the rest of the way and take his hand in mine then walk us both over to the bed and sit on the edge. "Joe."

"Honey, whatever it is, we'll deal with it together. I promise." He says.

"Joe." I take a deep breath, close my eyes and say, "Joe, I'm pregnant." When he doesn't say anything I look up to gauge his reaction, but I can't read him. He's gone still and looks shocked.

"Joe." I say quietly, the panic in my voice pretty obvious. "Say something. Please."

"You're pregnant?" He asks.

"Yes." I answer him quietly.

"We're having a baby?" He asks, his voice quiet but steady.

"I guess so, yes." I say quietly.

"But I thought you said, when? When did this happen?" He asks, and I'm not sure whether he's panicking or whether he's excited.

"Well, I'm not a hundred percent sure until after we have our first ultrasound and they do measurements and stuff, but I'm going to say our first weekend together a few weeks ago." I say.

"Our first time together was long before that Katy, if I remember correctly." He says with a smirk.

"I meant when we got back together. You know, when Mother walked in and caught us at the end of the act?" Joe cracks up. He's rolling around on the bed holding his stomach, tears rolling down his face. "What's so funny you dork? I just told you I'm having your child and you're *laughing*!

Suddenly he stops laughing and he's sitting upright again before I can blink.

He gently holds my face in his hands and kisses my lips softly, before speaking. "We're making a family together Katy, there's nothing funny about that honey. I want to spend the rest of my life with you, kids or no kids, but as it turns out, it will be *with* kids, or at least one kid anyway."

"I love you Joe and I can't wait to have our baby." I'm grinning like a lunatic I'm sure.

"I'm going to be a father!" He says, shock in his voice like he just realised what me being pregnant means. "I'm going to be a dad." He stands up, taking me with him. Then he sweeps me off my feet and spins me around. Then just as suddenly as he had me off the ground, he puts my feet on the floor and says, "Oh shit Katy I'm so sorry I shouldn't have done that. You've got to tell me when I do something stupid OK? I don't want to hurt you or our baby."

"Joe, I'm not fragile and the baby isn't either. You know women have been having babies for hundreds of years, yeah?" I ask, laughing at his sudden change in behaviour.

"I know but they weren't *my* woman and they weren't carrying *my* child. It's my job to protect you, both of you, for the rest of your lives, and that's what I plan on doing, honey."

I grab his face in my hands and I squeeze gently, laughing at this crazy, protective adorable man, but then I get serious. "I know I said we're not fragile, but I don't want to tell anyone just yet." He goes to speak, protest would be my guess, but I have what I think is a valid reason. "Not because I'm not happy about it, and not because I don't want to shout it from the rooftops, but *because* this isn't a normal pregnancy. I could still lose this baby Joe, thanks to my body being defective."

"Won't happen honey. My swimmers are too strong and stubborn for that to happen and we're not giving up." I can't help but laugh at his macho positivity. "But, I understand why you don't want to say anything to anyone. How about we go to this ultrasound and see what they say and go from there?" Practical Joseph French at your service ladies and gentlemen.

"Sounds like the perfect plan Joe. I love you." I don't get to say anything else because his mouth comes down on mine once again, silencing anything else that I might want to say.

JOE

THE LAST FEW MONTHS have been a real rollercoaster. Between my broken nose and friendship, Katy taking me back, Katy repairing her friendship with Kami, it's been a rollercoaster.

Then we found out Katy's pregnant!

I'm going to be a father. A *dad*. With Katy, the love of my life. I can't wait and it's hard to not share the news with the world, but it's even harder knowing that the first person I wanted to tell wouldn't want me to tell him.

Katy and Kami have been trying their best to help me fix things with James, but I'm not sure it's something that is ever going to happen. It sure won't be a quick and easy fix. The girls have patched things up and while it's still a little awkward when I'm around, it's getting better.

After an 'accidental' meeting at a restaurant that we all knew was a set-up, helping to move Kami in with James, and then dinner at Katy's, I told her to just stop.

One good thing came out of dinner that night at Katy's though. I talked one on one with Kami. I'd been trying to grab the opportunity for months but hadn't managed it, until that night.

Helping clear the dishes, I follow Kami into the kitchen.

"Thanks Joe but you didn't have to help me." She says with a smile that doesn't quite reach her eyes. She still doesn't trust me. I can't say I blame her after all these years.

"I wanted to," I reply, with what I hope is a genuine smile. "I do have an ulterior motive though."

"Oh, and what might that be Joseph?" She asks, not hiding her suspiciousness or nervousness.

"Look, I'm not trying to be mean OK? I'm not backing you into a corner of Katy's kitchen to give you a hard time. Honestly, that's over, I'm done with all that bullshit." She doesn't say a thing. "You've made James really happy, I can see that now that I look at the two of you properly."

"You mean without prejudice or preconceived ideas?" She asks.

"Yeah, all of those things Kami." I take a deep swallow and rub the back of my neck with my hand, feeling nervous and waiting for James to come looking for her. I don't want to say what I have to with him or Katy around. "I want to tell you something and then ask you a favour. I understand if you don't believe what I say and tell me to fuck off, but I need some answers to my questions."

"OK, you've confused me now Joe. What do you need to know?"

"It's about our parents. Your mum and Harry."

"Not this again Joe? Really? OK so they were high school sweethearts, they've let it go, can't we?" Then she starts to walk away but I can't let her, not now.

"That's just it Kami, I don't think either of them let it go and Helen coming back into town, with a kid in tow kind of opened old wounds."

"OK, so Harry's a miserable, horrible bastard, I get it Joe. I really don't understand-" I don't give her a chance to finish or walk away from me.

"Have you thought about how close we are in age? Have you ever done the maths, Kami?" I ask her, watching her face wrinkle with the thought.

"No, I tried not to think about you at all Joe." She shakes her head. "Both of our parents moved on fast once my mother left town, so what?" She shrugs her shoulders, and then I see the idea I've planted take hold of her. "You're not suggesting?"

"Yes I am. I think we might be siblings Kami."

"Oh. Crap on a cracker Joe! Do you know what that means for everyone? Our parents, all of them? Us?" Her eyes are wide in shock and horror. "Is that what was behind all of your behaviour towards me? You treated someone you *thought* was a sister with utter contempt?" I hear the disgust in her voice, and while I know I have no right to be angry, that doesn't stop me from wanting to defend myself.

"I overhead Harry tell my mum that he *knew* you were his and that I was second to you. He knew I was standing there Kami, he did it on purpose. To hurt me and I blamed you. Unfairly, obviously but I was a kid who didn't know better." I don't want her to speak, so I keep going. "He said he spoke to Helen and she didn't say you were his, but she didn't say you weren't either."

"No denial, no admission? Sounds like something she'd do." I feel bad for Kami, she looks so damned sad. "So, what do you want me to do with this information? Confront my mother?"

"No. I don't want Helen or Harry involved, I'd rather keep it between us. You, me, Katy and James. Eventually." I answer her.

"I don't understand, what do you mean, eventually?"

"I want to do a DNA test, if you'll agree to one Kami. I want to know if we are related. Actually, I need to know."

"Why? So that you can justify your bad behaviour? Or to try and get me to forgive you faster because we're blood related? Blood isn't everything Joe, you of all people should understand that." She whisper yelled at me, not wanting to alert the other two to what's going on.

"No. Nothing like that at all Kami. I want to know if I have a sister. You're right, I know that blood doesn't mean shit, but I want it to." I say, but I'm not prepared for what she asks in return to agreeing to do the test.

"Fine Joe, I'll do the test, but only if you tell me one thing. If you don't give me an honest answer and I find out later that you lied to me here in Katy's kitchen, I will tell James you attacked me in here tonight." I feel sick, because no matter what she asks me now I know I will be nothing but brutally honest with her, because James will leave me a broken mess if he thinks I touched Kami.

I nod my head, "What do you want to know?" I *thought* she wanted an honest answer about something I'd said or done in the past, but her question actually knocks me for six.

"How far along is Katy's pregnancy?" She doesn't disguise her pain at not being told.

"How did you know?" I ask.

"She's my *best friend* Joe. How can you think that I *wouldn't* notice?" She asks me. I'm not sure how to answer her.

"Look, we haven't told anyone Kami, not even our parents. Katy and I made the decision to keep it to ourselves for a while. Partly so that we could have that time for us, but also because we wanted to make sure we were past the danger period, not that that really runs out for Katy. As you would know." Her face softens and she gives me a small nod. "Once we get to the halfway mark, we're going to start telling people. I'm pretty sure you'll be one of the first people to know. Personally, I wanted to tell James the minute we found out, but I also don't want James to be my friend again because he feels like he has to be."

Much to my surprise, Kami hugs me, it takes me a few seconds, but I gently hug her back. "I'll do the DNA test Joe, just let me know what you need."

"I have the kit at home, maybe we can get together to do it? That way you see me, and I see you doing it, nothing is hidden." She nods her agreement.

"Have you told Katy what you suspect?"

"No. This whole thing between the four of us is still so awkward, I don't want to add to it, and now I don't want to stress her out unnecessarily." We hear a chair scrape on the floor, knowing that it's probably James looking for his girl, because we've been in here for a while, we step apart.

She starts to walk away but turns slightly to look over her shoulder at me and says, "For the record Joe, I forgive you, I may never be able to forget everything you've done, but I do forgive you. We all need to move on, and this is the only way that we can. James will forgive you too, he wants too, he can't right now, but he will. Just give him some time."

"Thank you Kami."

With that she's gone, and I'm left alone in the kitchen wondering if I'll have a sister *and* a baby in the next few months.

⁂

2 months later

KATY

KAMI AND JOE HAVE MET up a couple of times since that dinner at my house and every time I ask either one of them what the hell is going on, I get the same response from both of them. "Can you trust me? Just for a few weeks, please?"

I'm not saying there's something going on between them that James and I need to worry about, not at all but *something* is going on. I'm just not sure what.

Joe has been to every doctor's appointment and scan with me. We're now at the point where if we don't start telling people, they're going to think I'm eating too much food. I can't disguise my rounded stomach with loose clothing for much longer.

When I received the text from Kami inviting us to dinner at their house, I have to admit I was shocked. I didn't think James would agree to having us there, well Joe. That text is one of the few I get off Kami in the week leading up to the dinner. Which is highly unusual, and Joe is acting like he's walking on live electrical wires all week. I know that he and James are tentatively talking, mainly about business but still, they're talking.

I managed to pin Joe down and have a conversation about telling our families, including Kami and James about the baby. That's if Kami hasn't guessed already and is too upset to ask me. Joe is skittish and edgy all week and I don't know if it's because we're going to tell them about the baby and he's worried what Kami's reaction will be or whether it's because of whatever him and Kami have going on.

When we get to the afternoon before dinner at Kami and James', I've had about as much as I can take of Joe being distracted and vague with me. We stayed at his place last night because it's closer to Kami's and I wanted to sleep in. Not needing to rush around to get ready sounds like heaven to me until Joe gets a large official looking envelope delivered and his behaviour starts becoming even more erratic and weird.

"Joseph French." I say, standing in the doorway to his office watching him pace back and forth in front of his desk, looking at the offending envelope like it might kill him. When he hears my voice, he stops dead in his tracks, but doesn't turn to look at me. "What the hell is going on? You're a nervous wreck over that envelope and I want to know why. Right now Joe."

"Kathryn." He starts to speak, and I can hear his hesitation in just that one word, my name.

"No *Joseph*, tell me what the fuck is going on *right now*." He spins around and storms towards me, stopping a step or two short of slamming into me.

"Or what Kathryn? What are you going to do if I don't tell you *right now* what's going on? What if I made a promise not to tell anyone until there were answers? Do I break that promise? Are you going to leave me?"

I close the distance between us and hold his face gently in my hands, "Joe how can you think that? Unless it's something you've done that I can't forgive you for, you're stuck with me baby. I'm not going anywhere."

"What if I've hurt Kami again? Not on purpose, but maybe I have and I'm an idiot." He tries to turn away from me, but I don't let him.

"What's going on Joe? Please tell me baby, I hate seeing you torn up like this." I close my eyes, when I reopen them he looks scared. "Come on Joe, it can't be all that bad after everything that's happened." I laugh quietly, trying to break the tension in the room.

"I asked Kami to do a DNA test with me." He says and I have no clue what to say that.

"What? Why?" I ask him, confused. "Why would you need Kami to do a DNA test Joe? I don't understand."

"Helen and Harry – " I don't let him finish.

"Not this shit again Joe. Why can't you let their relationship go? They were kids, it was so long ago, and nothing came of it, they both moved on." I don't let him finish what he's saying. His obsession with Helen and Harry's relationship is getting beyond ridiculous, it was years, decades ago.

"It's not that Katy, I don't care that they were together. I couldn't give a shit about their old relationship. Except for the fact that I'm pretty damned sure that so called relationship created a child, one that Helen won't admit to, but Harry would love to announce to the world.

"What do you mean Joseph? You're talking gibberish." He stands there looking at me for a minute, waiting for something to click. Looking in his eyes, I see when he knows I've put it all together. "Do you mean, Kami is the product of Helen and Harry's high school relationship? But, you're so close together in age, that can't be right. Can it?" I'm confused, I don't think it works timewise.

"Katy, I've done the maths so many times I couldn't count them anymore." He says with a sigh.

"Oh Joe. Is that what's in the envelope, the results?" I ask, needing to know the answer.

"Yeah." He says, resting his forehead on mine. "I'm not opening them until I'm in the same room as Kami. I don't want her to doubt the results for one second, whether they're positive or negative."

"Are you going to take them tonight and get your answers?" I ask him quietly. "Does Kami know you've got them?"

He nods his head, "Well, we were hoping they would get here earlier than today but here we are. I just messaged Kami and told her I had them.

"Does James know what you suspect? Does he know you guys had a DNA test done?" I need to know if I'm the only one left out of the loop.

"No. Kami didn't tell him either. I think she's telling him now so that it's not too much of a shock when we open the results." He closes his eyes, pulls me in close to him, and says quietly in my ear, "I wanted to have the evidence in black and white in front of me before I told you. I didn't want you to stress over it, especially since you found out you were pregnant."

"Oh Joe. You don't need to protect or shield me from these things. I want to know what's happening to you babe. You shouldn't have had to carry this on your own."

"I didn't. I had Kami and I must admit, it felt nice."

"Well then, let's get this show on the road. I'm betting Kami wants to know those results as much as you do."

"Aren't you a little curious yourself? Don't you want some more details before we head over there?" he asks.

"Yes, to all of the above, I'm also annoyed that the two of you thought you had to keep this shit to yourselves and you dealt with it alone. Before you tell me *again* that you had each other, that's not how this works Joe, we have each other. You and me. I mean I'm glad you and Kami have bonded over it, but it still stings a little that you never once told me what you suspected all these years. After everything we went through and all that talking we did after James broke your nose, I thought it was all out in the open." I turn to go put on some shoes so we can leave, but I look over my shoulder and say, "I think James is going to feel the same way. Betrayed."

He doesn't get the chance to reply because his phone chimes with a message as I walk out the door. He follows not far behind me, watching me slip some shoes on. "That was Kami." I don't look up from what I'm doing, I just nod. "She wants us to go around now, if that's not too soon?" He says it so quietly, and I know he's nervous and I hurt him with what I said.

"Joe," I say looking up at him. "I'm putting my shoes on so we can go. I get that you're nervous, and I'm going to be by your side the entire time babe, I'll support you no matter what, but you have to know that keeping a secret like this from me after everything, it hurts."

"I know and I'm sorry. I just didn't want to say anything if it was nothing. If we're related not then this is just another bullshit move on my part, isn't it?"

I shake my head, "No." and I truly believe that. "This one is putting an end to all the bullshit finally Joe. Once the results are in, promise me we can leave it all behind us?"

"That's a promise I can keep honey." He walks over to me as I get to my feet, holding my hands in the final movements. Trust me this standing up from sitting caper is starting to become a challenge. Another reason we have to start telling everyone I'm pregnant. "I love you Katy Ellis."

"I love you too Joe French, but that's not a get out of jail free card you know?" hoping to lessen the punch, I kiss him.

He rests his forehead on mine, sighs deeply and says, "I know honey." He drops a light kiss on my forehead, drapes an arm around my shoulders and says, "Let's go get this done honey."

JOE

THE DRIVE OVER TO KAMI and James' house is pretty quiet, the only noise is coming from the radio in the car. Luckily it isn't a long drive to get there. It feels excruciatingly long today though.

No, today it feels like we're driving cross country and I'm going to my own execution. I know that's not what's going to happen, but I can't help but feel that James is going to want to deck me once he knows what's been going on. I've kept it from him all these years, and while I understand why Katy's annoyed with me, I think James has much more reason to be angry.

I pull into the driveway that was the entrance to my second home for years and I don't turn off the car. I can't. I don't know what waits for me inside. From the test, Kami or James. I wonder if she's had enough time to explain what's going on to him? I feel a hand rest on mine, but I don't turn to look at Katy, I can't. Instead I'm staring at the front door of my best mates house, one that I know as well as I know my own and I wonder if I've done the right thing.

"You're right to want answers to your questions Joe, and you did the right thing by asking Kami for her permission to the test."

That makes me look at her. "What do you mean? How could I have done the DNA test without her permission? I would never have done this without a sample that she didn't handed over herself with the permission to test it." I say, surprised that what I'm saying is true and that Katy would think I would do it any other way. "Do you really think that I would?"

"Joe."

"I know what I've done in the past Katy, but that's exactly where it all is. I'm not that person anymore. I would never do anything to hurt you, Kami or James. Not on purpose."

"That's not what I mean Joe. I meant that you've done the right thing, and even though James might be hurt, like I am, that you guys decided to keep it quiet, I don't think he's going to be angry." She explains, but I still have my doubts that she trusts what I said.

"OK." I say, turning the car off and reaching for the envelope. "Let's get this over with. I can't deal with not knowing anymore and I want everything out in the open from today."

"Does that mean we're telling them about the baby today too?" She asks, and I'm not sure what that emotion is in her voice, so I turn to look at her.

"Yes Katy. Everything. Including the fact that we're looking for a house, together, in this very area. No more secrets, I'm done with them." I kiss her and reach for her hand with my empty one. When she takes my hand and squeezes it tightly, I know I'm doing the right thing.

Katy knocks on the front door and a minute later it swings open, Kami standing there smiling nervously. "Come on in guys."

We walk in and I notice James sitting at the kitchen bench looking, shocked and a little pissed off.

"By the look on your face I'm guessing Kami told you about our suspicions?" I ask as I walk passed him and when I look at him he nods his head once.

"Do you know too Katy?" He asks her, looking right passed me.

"I found out just before we left to come here." Katy replies. "But I don't know the results, he hasn't opened the envelope yet."

"Why didn't you tell us sooner? Why wait until now to tell us?" James asks, looking between Kami and me.

"We didn't tell either of you or anyone else for that matter, any earlier because we didn't want anyone freaking out." Kami answers him quietly, holding his hand in hers. "There was no point in making everyone anxious about the results. This way, the four of us can read the results together and deal with whatever the outcome is."

"I still wish you had told me Kami, you didn't need to go through it alone." He tells her quietly, but I can hear the anger in his voice.

"She wasn't alone James," I say, "but I understand what you mean, and I would be annoyed with Katy if the situations were reversed. We decided there wasn't any point getting everyone worked up over it if it was nothing."

"I wouldn't call it nothing, Joe." James says, his anger directed solely towards me.

"Look he's right, you're right we're all right OK?" Katy says, with frustration in her voice, as she tries to remain Switzerland. "Can we just get the big reveal done and deal with it, please?"

I offer the envelope to Kami, but she shakes her head no. "You open it Joe, I don't think I can." She says, wringing her hands nervously.

James pulls Kami tight into his side and Kami pulls Katy into hers, pulling her away from me slightly, but she still manages to keep one hand on my arm as I open the stark white envelope. I hesitate, I'm not sure I want the answer now I have the chance to find out. I look up at the three faces eagerly waiting to find out, so I pull out the report and start to read it.

I hear James' sudden intake of breathe and I know he's read the answer on my face. I clear my throat and I drag my eyes over to meet Kami's. "Well, what does it say?" She asks me, her voice quiet but firm.

"The test is," I take a deep breath and swallow before I continue. "The test is positive."

"Positive? What does that mean?" I hear Kami ask, in a voice that that can only be described as a squeak.

"The probability of shared paternity is 98.5%. Meaning, we share a father, Kami. You're not a Parker, you're a French."

A few seconds later, James has scooped Kami up and carried her to the couch, to sit with her in his lap. She hasn't said anything and then suddenly she says, "That cocksucking arsehole, Joe French is my fucking BROTHER?"

I laugh, loudly, breaking the silent shock in the room.

"Did I say that out loud?" She asks James and then she looks at me when he nods a yes. I can see the arsehole's shoulders shaking with laughter. "Oh Joe, I'm sorry, I thought that was just in my head."

"No need to apologise Kami. I am a cocksucking arsehole." I say, laughing.

"You're right sweetheart, he *is* a cocksucker, he always has been." He looks over the back of the couch at me, then suddenly he's laughing uncontrollably.

I let the results of the DNA test fall to the kitchen bench, and then start laughing again myself. Kami looks between the two of us and shakes her head but she's laughing pretty hard too.

"You guys are fucking crazy." Katy says loudly over all the laughter. "You just found out your siblings and you're laughing like maniacs about Joe being a cocksucker." She shakes her head like she just can't understand us at all. "I think the baby we're going to have in a few months begs to differ your assessment of Joe's sexual preferences."

Everyone in the room freezes and Katy slams her hands over her mouth, realising that she just let the cat out the bag. Or the baby news out of the shadows anyway.

"Really Katy? You're going to have a baby?" Kami asks, giving me a side glance. This woman is good at what she does I have to admit.

Katy nods, tears threatening to spill from her eyes. I reach out and pull her in close to me. "Really. Her endometriosis was no match for my swimmers Kami Parker." I say, still laughing. Kami is up on her feet and throwing herself at Katy before I finish speaking. James follows her from behind the couch and I feel my whole body tense. I have no idea what to expect and it hurts a lot to know that I don't know him anymore.

"Congratulations man." He walks over and reaches his hand out to shake mine. Automatically I reach my hand out to meet his, when he clasps my hand he pulls me in to a hug and pats me on the back. "Honestly man, I'm so happy for you guys." He says, a wide smile spreading across his face. "I know it's something you've always wanted Joe." He says when his mouth is close to my ear and the girls can't hear him.

He releases me from his grasp and then pulls Katy into a huge bear hug. "I'm so happy for you darling girl. I know how much you've struggled with the thought of never being a mum, but look at you, you're glowing." He kisses her lightly in the cheek. "You know, if this guy ever does anything to hurt you or this kid of yours, you just let me know and I'll kick his arse for the fun of it." We all laugh, but I think we understand that he's not entirely joking.

Kami drags Katy into the kitchen to finish getting dinner ready and to get all the pregnancy and baby updates, leaving James and I alone.

I cough, uncomfortable without the girls in the same room as a buffer. I want to apologise to him, but I don't know where to start. "Look, James." I start just as he says, "Joe."

"Let me, please?" I ask, he nods and waves his hand for me to continue. "I'm sorry James. I could say I don't know what I was thinking or doing, but I knew, I just thought I was doing it for all the right reasons. I've had a lot of time to think in the last few months and I know I was blaming everyone else, Harry mostly, for my own shitty behaviour. I take full responsibility for everything I did and understand that you can't trust me anymore and while I hate that we can't be what we once were, I can't accept that we can't rebuild our friendship." I take a deep breath, I didn't realise that I was holding it until I stopped speaking.

James stands there, unmoving and not speaking. There's no expression on his face and its unnerving. I'm used to being able to read him like an open book. He speaks suddenly making me jump a little.

"I'm taking a page out of Kami's book and I'm going to forgive you Joseph. I don't think I can ever forget what you did to us, but I think we all have to put it behind us so that we can move forward." Then he smiles, and it spreads across his face. He slaps me on the back, "I've got a baby girl to protect or baby boy to corrupt. I can't walk away from baby French now can I? But I make you a promise right here and now Joe, you hurt Katy or that child and it's me you'll have to answer to. You understand?"

"I plan on keeping that woman, that child and any other that comes into our world safer and happier than either one of us ever imagined possible James."

He slaps me on the back, hard and says, "Good, then we won't have a damned problem will we?"

"No, we won't." I smile in reply.

Kami and James have already set the table, so we grab drinks for everyone, then help the girls bring in the food. We sit down and start dishing ourselves out what we want. The silence comfortable, and for the first time in what feels like forever, I feel like I'm where I'm supposed to be.

"So, is there any other news anyone wants to get off their chest now that we're all sitting down together in a pleasant manner." James' question breaks the silence, and I see him, and Kami share a look between them. I don't ask them about it instead I speak up.

Taking Katy's hand in mine I say, "We're looking for a house to buy together." I look at Katy and she nods her encouragement. "We're going to sell both our houses and move a little further out of town."

"Where are you looking?" Kami asks, but when I look at James, it's like he already knows, and he smiles.

"We were hoping you'd be ok with us looking out this way?" Katy says, a little hesitantly and I hate that she's unsure about how her best friend will feel about her moving closer to her.

"Really? Close to us?" Katy nods her head. James and I watch them both as they converse without words for a few minutes. Then Kami squeals. "OH MY GOD! You're moving closer to us? When? Can we help with anything?" She looks at Katy, "You know you can't lift anything, right?"

"Kami. I'm pregnant, not broken." She laughs holding her friend close.

Kami pulls out of their embrace and stomps over to me, poking me in the chest with her tiny finger and I can't help the laugh that escapes me. James shakes his head at me, "Oh no dude don't laugh at her. She can be mean when she wants to be." That just makes me laugh harder, until the jabbing in my ribs becomes serious.

"You're not going to let her lift anything, are you Joseph?" She asks me, and I know she's annoyed but she's so darn cute while she is.

I hold back my laughter and say, "No Kami, I won't let her lift a gorgeous finger. James and I can do it all and maybe some removalists. How's that?" I ask, trying to placate her. It obviously works, because she nods and turns all of her attention back on Katy.

"When. When do you move?"

"When we sell our houses and find the house we think fits us as a family." Katy answers her, "Hopefully before the baby arrives."

"You're moving my niece or nephew closer to me and I can't wait. I'll help you look if you want?" Then Kami stops and looks like she might actually have a panic attack. James moves in behind her to hold her and starts to ask if she's OK, but he doesn't get a word out before Kami squeals again. "OH

MY GOD! This baby won't be my adopted niece or nephew because of our friendship, this baby will really be related to me. *You're having my brothers baby!*"

The girls squeal and hug each other, bouncing up and down in excitement. I have no idea what to do, so I just smile at their happiness. Tonight is going better than I could have ever imagined. The girls move away and start talking all things babies, that's when James chooses to ask me something that I don't want to think about, but I already have the answer to.

"What are you going to tell Helen and Harry?" He asks, and the girls stop talking and look our way, waiting for me to answer.

"Nothing. Kami and I spoke about it already and we agreed not to tell them." I sigh. "The truth is, I didn't do this or ask Kami to do this, with the intention of confronting either Helen or Harry. I didn't even do it for Kami honestly, I wanted to know the truth. Not so that I could justify of my behaviour, but because I wanted to know if I have a sister. Nothing changes, it's just something I needed to know." I shrug my shoulders and look down at my feet. I can feel all three sets of eyes on me and it's making me very uncomfortable.

"Well, I guess you being a giant jerk to Kami all these years proves what a DNA test just confirmed. You're her little brother." James says, laughing and the girls join in. "Too soon? Oh well too bad." James laughs harder when I don't respond to him.

"James, stop it." Kami chastises him. "Leave him be, can't we just spend this one night, just the four of us and be happy?" He nods and reaches out to pull her into his arms.

"We actually have some news of our own. I'm going to be needing a best man in around twelve months' time, and the jobs yours, if you want it Joseph?"

"Are you kidding me? Of course I want the job you idiot." I say, this time it's my turn to smack him on the back.

"You've got time to make me like you again, and this baby will certainly work in your favour. Not to mention, I'm marrying your sister, you have to like me." It hits him at the same it hits me. "We're going to brothers in laws. How weird is that?" This causes another round of uncontrollable laughter.

I stop laughing and sit back in my chair and watch the three people who mean the most to me enjoy spending time together. Not so long ago, I thought this would never happen and even though we still have a long way to go, things are looking better.

James stops laughing and looks at me, when he smiles at me, I smile back. I'm happy to have my friend back, no matter how much harder I have to work to make him trust me again.

Dinner goes along without an argument. The girls talk everything babies, moving house and weddings. Us guys manage to put in a few comments here and there, but mostly we just agree with the girls.

WHEN OUR BABY SON IS six months old, he's the ring bearer at his Aunty Kami and Uncle James' wedding. Anna, Katy's mum carries him down the aisle and then carries him to the altar when the rings are called for. Katy and I would have done the job, but we were already in the wedding. Neither Kami or I were comfortable with Helen doing the honours, so she asked Anna and she agreed readily. Anything to spend more time spoiling her only grandchild. She's also babysitting for us tonight so that we can enjoy the party.

Katy and I moved into a house half a block away from the newlyweds about a month before Jackson arrived. It's rare that we don't see one another at least once a day. I'm so grateful that my son will grow up knowing his aunty and uncle. I wasn't sure it would be the case when Katy first told me she was pregnant.

Things aren't like they were before, they're better. I've earned their trust and I'm a changed man. Harry doesn't come near me anymore after telling me that Katy was nothing but a whore, trapping me with a kid, hoping to get my money. Nothing could be further from the truth.

We still haven't told Helen or Harry what we know, but I don't think it matters. Kami and I know, and that's all that matters.

As I sit back in my chair, my attention is caught by the laughter of my son as his uncle tickles him until he can't breath and then passes him to his mum. My beautiful Kathryn. The love of my life. We've talked about getting married, but it just isn't a big deal to either of us. We're a family now, we don't need to be married to prove it. I laugh watching Katy spin around the dance floor, Jackson squealing with delight.

She must feel me watching because she looks my way and smiles. A happy, content smile and weaves her way to where I'm sitting. "Mum wants to take Jackson home, so I thought I'd bring him over to say goodnight."

I take my son from his mums arms and squeeze him tight. This boy will never feel unloved a single day of his life. I leave big sloppy kisses all over his chubby face and then hand my giggling boy to his Grandma. "Thanks for getting him all excited Joe." Anna says, but I can see the sparkle in her eyes. She takes any and every opportunity to spend time with him and we both know it.

"You're welcome Anna, I hope you and Poppy enjoy your evening with my adorable spawn." She laughs and says goodnight to Katy. Leaving us behind to enjoy the night.

Before can I can say a thing, Katy kisses my cheek and whispers in my ear, "Later tonight handsome you're all mine, but right now, I'm going to party with my sister in law." Then she's gone.

I hear someone sit in the chair next to me and I don't look their way because I know exactly who it is. "Best day ever Joe. When are you going to make an honest woman out of Kathryn?"

"Any time she asks me James, but she doesn't want to be married right now, and I'm happy to live our life the way it is." I look over at him and smirk. "I mean I'm glad you got hitched to the old ball and chain. My sister deserves a good guy, but Katy, she doesn't need or want the ring and ceremony."

"But you're going to buy her a ring, aren't you Joseph?" James asks me.

"You bet I am, but we don't have to follow it up with a wedding."

He smiles. "Good times Joe, good times."

"Life is definitely good right now my friend." I say, glad that I can call him that again.

"Perfect Joe." He says, his smile wider than his face.

THE END

Also by Chelle Pimblott

Built for Love
Built to Last
Built for Trouble

Drake Wines
Vineyard
Sandy Cove - A Drake Wines Novella
Winery
Lori's Memories - A Drake Wines Novella
Brewery
Sara's Forever

Sneaky Love
Sneaky
Sneaking Around
No More Sneaking Around

Standalone
Barefoot & Dumped!

www.ingramcontent.com/pod-product-compliance
Lightning Source LLC
Chambersburg PA
CBHW071458110726
47908CB00003B/654